Ab

Bronwyn Scott is the author of over fifty books. Her 2018 novella, *Dancing with the Duke's Heir* was a *RITA®* finalist. She loves history and is always looking forward to the next story. She also enjoys talking with other writers and readers about books they like and the writing process. Readers can visit her at her Facebook page at Bronwynwrites and at her blog at bronwynswriting.blogspot.com

Regency Rebels

Regency Rebels:

The Reckless Rakes

BRONWYN SCOTT

MILLS & BOON

First Published in Great Britain 2023
By Mills & Boon, an imprint of HarperCollins*Publishers* Ltd,
1 London Bridge Street, London, SE1 9GF

www.harpercollins.co.uk

HarperCollins*Publishers*
Macken House, 39/40 Mayor Street Upper,
Dublin 1, D01 C9W8, Ireland

ISBN: 978-0-263-31983-5

MIX
Paper | Supporting
responsible forestry
FSC
www.fsc.org
FSC™ C007454

This book is produced from independently certified FSC™ paper to ensure responsible forest management.

For more information visit: www.harpercollins.co.uk/green

Printed and Bound in the UK using 100% Renewable Electricity at CPI Group (UK) Ltd, Croydon, CR0 4YY

RAKE MOST LIKELY
TO REBEL

For Monsieur Rouse, high school French teacher
extraordinaire:
Votre ardeur pour la langue insuffle mon fil. Merci.
(*Je regrette,* I have not conjugated 'to inspire' for some
time. I hope the form is correct on *insuffle*!)

And for Ro and Brony –we will see the City of Light
(La Ville Lumière) togeher soon.

Chapter One

Dover docks—March 1835

There were no pleasures left in London. One could only hope Paris would do better. Haviland North turned up the collar of his greatcoat against the damp of the early March morning and paced the Dover docks, anxious to be away with the tide.

All of his hopes were pinned on France now and its famed *salle d'armes*. If springtime in Paris should fail to stimulate his stagnant blood, the rest of Europe awaited to take its turn. He could spend summer among the mighty peaks of the Alps, testing his strength on their crags, autumn among the arts and graces of Florence, winter in Venice feasting on the sensuality of Carnevale and another spring, if he could manage it. This time in Naples, basking in the heat of southern Italy with its endless supply of the ancient. If those destinations did not succeed, there was always Greece and the alluring, mysterious Turkey.

The exotic litany of places rolled through his mind, a mantra of hopefulness and perhaps a mantra of fantasy. His father had promised him six months, not a year or two. It would all have to be managed very carefully. In truth, Haviland preferred it not come to that simply because of what the need for such lengths indicated about his current state—that at the age of twenty-eight and with everything to live for: the title, the vast fortune that went with it, the estates, the horses, the luxuries other men spent their lives acquiring—he was dead inside after all.

He'd had to fight hard for this Grand Tour, abbreviated as it might be. His well-meaning father had relented at last, perhaps understanding the need for his grown son to spread his wings beyond London and see something of the world before settling down. Haviland had won six months of freedom. But it had come at a great cost: afterwards, he would return home and marry, completing the plans that had been laid by two families three generations ago.

He could hear his father's voice, see him behind his massive desk in the estate office as he delivered his verdict.

'Six months is all we can spare. You're different than your friends. They don't have your expectations. Even Archer is a second son and when it comes down to it, his duties are different than yours. They can be gone for years. We can't possibly spare you that long. The Everlys are eager to see the marriage done, and why delay? You're twenty-eight and Christina is twenty-one. She's been out for three Seasons, which is very respectable at this point, but to make her wait any longer will arouse unnecessary suspicions where there are none.'

His marriage, like everything else in his life to date, had been arranged for him. Everything had been accomplished *for* him. He simply had to show up. He often thought it was the very idea that there was nothing to turn his hand to, nothing that required his effort that had spawned this dark yawning gap in him. He'd struggled for nothing, been denied nothing, not even good looks. He'd managed to snare the lion's share of the family's handsome genetics along with the fortune. Perhaps that was why fencing appealed to him so intensely—it was something he could work at, something he could personally excel at on his own merits.

Excel he had. Haviland touched his booted toe to the long, slim case lying at his feet to assure himself it was still there, the one piece of luggage he hadn't allowed to be stowed out of his sight: his rapiers, specially made for him from the fit of the grips to the weight of the thin blades. There wasn't a gentleman in London who could touch him in the art of the foil and still it wasn't enough. There was more to know and he hungered for the excellence that would come with new knowledge. He would go to Paris and study. With luck, he'd move on to the Italian masters in Florence. He knew six months wouldn't see him to Italy. It wasn't near enough time. He would need a miracle, but anything could happen if he could just be off.

Haviland took out his gold pocket watch, a gift

from his grandfather upon completing Oxford several years ago, and flipped it open to check the time: quarter past five. His companions should have been here by now, which meant they'd show up any moment. None of them were extraordinarily concerned with punctuality but all of them were as eager as he for this journey, for reasons of their own. He closed the watch, his thumb running over his grandfather's carefully chosen, although not highly original inscription: *tempus fugit.* He'd wasted enough time already. This journey was a chance for the clock to start again, however briefly, for his life to start again.

Haviland's gaze strained in the lifting gloom, trying to make out the arrival of his companions. Who would come first? Perhaps Archer Crawford, his oldest friend. They'd suffered Eton together and then Oxford before moving on to the Season, exhausting the joys of London year after year after endless year until the pleasure had become *de rigueur.* Only loyalty to his mother had kept Archer in London this long. Now that anchor was gone and Archer was as anxious as he to be off.

Then again, the first to arrive might be Nolan Gray, depending on whether or not he'd had a good night at the rough tables of Dover. Nolan had ended more than one night with a tersely offered invitation to duel. His extraordinary skill at cards left many gentlemen lighter in the pockets. Over their years on the town, Nolan had developed the ability to defend his talent and his honour from the business end of a pistol at twenty paces.

Whoever arrived first, it wouldn't be Brennan Carr. He would most definitely be last and he most definitely hadn't spent his last night in England sleeping. If he knew Brennan, the night had been spent in the arms of a willing woman. Haviland chuckled to himself at the thought. Brennan could always make him laugh. Brennan had made London survivable long after it had lost its appeal.

Hooves and wheels clattered on the docks, a coach emerging from the lifting fog. Two men jumped out, coats swirling about them. One of them barked an order in a deep commanding baritone that carried in the morning air. Haviland smiled, recognising the voice. Nolan and Archer had come together and it looked as if Archer had brought a horse. Or the horse had followed Archer, which wouldn't surprise Haviland at all. Archer was always collecting stray horses the way some people collected cats or dogs. In the gloom, Haviland could see Archer tying the beast to the back of the carriage. He heard Nolan's voice carry across the pier.

'I win!' Nolan shouted as they approached. 'Haviland is already here *and* he has his case.' Nolan clasped him on the shoulder affectionately. 'Good morning, Old Man. Is everything loaded? I told Archer you'd be here overseeing.'

Haviland laughed. 'You know me too well. I saw the two coaches go on an hour ago and they loaded our trunks last night.' They'd decided the best way to make haste to Paris and then to destinations beyond would be to supply their own private coaches for travel. They'd have to buy or rent horses in Calais, but Calais was prepared for such purchases. Travellers who could afford it crossed the Channel with their own carriages. Those who couldn't afford to were reliant on public transport or whatever vehicles were for sale. Haviland had been more worried about finding two coaches for sale at prices that didn't border on extortion when they arrived.

'You trusted them with your trunks, which, may I emphasise, contain *all* your necessary belongings for the duration, but not with one small fencing case?' Archer pointed to the case at his feet.

'I told you that, too.' Nolan crowed. 'But, no, you insisted he'd have sent it ahead.' Nolan tapped his temple with his forefinger. 'I know these things. I'm a student of human nature.'

'Too bad you couldn't study that at Oxford.' Archer goaded him. 'You might have got better marks.'

But Nolan merely laughed. He and Archer had been sparring for years. They had each other's measure. 'What can I say? It's true. You two were the scholars, not me and Brennan.' He looked around. 'Is Brennan here yet?'

'No.' Haviland couldn't resist the ribbing. 'Did you expect him to be? Scholar of human nature that you are?'

Nolan gave Haviland a playful shove. 'A scholar of human nature, yes, a psychic, no.' He grinned. 'So who is she? We've only been in Dover a night. It's not the barmaid from the inn. She went off with another fellow.'

Haviland shrugged as the captain of their packet approached. 'Milord, you'll want to get on board. We'll be leaving in twenty minutes or so.'

'Thank you.' Haviland gave the man a short nod. 'We're waiting for the last member of our travelling party.'

He didn't expect the captain to be sympathetic and the man wasn't. 'The tide does not wait, milord. You've been lucky. We can leave at once. Some folks sit in the inns for weeks, waiting for the right wind and weather.'

'Understood,' Haviland answered, casting a final look at the docks as if he could make Brennan materialise. The captain spoke the truth. He'd heard all nature of accounts from others who'd made the Channel crossing about the risk of having to wait, their travel plans at the mercy of the elements.

'I should have stayed with him.' Haviland said as the captain moved off. He blamed himself. One of the things that made his friendship with Brennan work was balance. Brennan made him laugh and, in return, he kept Brennan focused and out of trouble. But last night he'd been worried about the luggage and the arrangements and he'd left Brennan to fend for himself. Admittedly, he thought there'd be very little damage Brennan could do knowing there was an early departure. Apparently, he'd been wrong.

The trio headed towards the gangplank to board. 'I'll wager five pounds Brennan misses the boat.' Nolan announced. 'Archer, are you in? If I'm wrong, you can win back your losses.'

Once on board, they leaned against the rail, all three of them scanning the docks for a last-minute sign of Brennan. Haviland checked his pocket watch, the minutes racing by. It wouldn't be the same without Brennan. Perhaps Bren could catch a later boat and meet them in Paris? Brennan knew the route they'd planned. Did he have enough money? Probably not. Brennan never had enough funds.

Beside him, Nolan started at the sound of chains rolling up. 'They're pulling the anchor. He's not going to make it.' Nolan blew out a breath and leaned on his arms. 'Dammit, I didn't want to win that bet.' The three of them exchanged glances, their disappointment silently evident. Their trip was off to an ominous start.

The boat began to nudge slowly away from its moorings as commotion broke out on the docks. A horse pulling a heavy dray full of crates reared in its traces, followed by a loud, vituperative spray of cursing. A barrel fell. More cursing. Something, *someone*, was on the move. Haviland squinted. There was something else running too. Was that a horse? He hadn't time to consider it, all of his concentration was fixed on the figure sprinting towards them, two more figures some paces behind giving serious chase. Bare headed, shirt-tails flying, and coatless, the figure came racing.

'It's him! It's Brennan!' Haviland shouted. He waved and called out, 'Come on!' He didn't like the looks of the men behind. As they closed, Haviland could see a pistol flash in one of the pursuers' hands.

He definitely didn't like the looks of them now. Haviland cast a glance at the gradually widening gap between the boat and the dock. It would be impossible, even dangerous from where they stood, to hazard a leap. The gap was too wide, but at the rear, where the boat was still near the dock, it might be possible. It would be a hell of a jump, but Brennan would have his speed to carry him.

Haviland gestured wildly to the rear of the boat, shouting instructions through cupped hands as he raced towards the stern. 'The back, Brennan, head for the back!'

Nolan and Archer were behind him. Archer shouted something that sounded like, 'The horse, Brennan, get on the horse!' The horse Haviland had spied had now passed the men in pursuit and had pulled up alongside Brennan, matching his stride to Brennan's as if to encourage him to get on. This was madness! But facing two men with guns didn't seem like much of an alternative. Brennan's pursuers were too close now, the boat moving too fast for Haviland's tastes. The horse would stand a better chance of making the leap. Haviland added his voice to Archer's. 'Bren, the horse, now!' he urged.

Haviland watched Brennan swing up on the fast-moving bay, and watched the pier end.

They leapt.

They landed.

The horse went down on his knees.

Brennan rocketed towards Haviland, taking him to the deck as a pistol report sounded from the docks, a bullet whistling overhead. 'Dammit!' In the excitement over the horse, he'd forgotten about the gun and nearly gotten himself shot. What a fine start to the trip that would have been. Instinctively, Haviland wanted to rise and see where it had come from. He grunted at Brennan's weight on top of him, but Brennan wouldn't let him up.

'Stay down!' Only when the boat had moved a safe way from the docks and Brennan deemed it safe to rise did he let him up.

'Good lord, Bren, what have you got yourself into now?' Haviland rose and dusted off his trousers. Beyond Brennan's shoulder he could see the men on the docks shaking impotent fists their direction. Whatever it was, it had been worth shooting someone over.

Brennan stopped in the midst of tucking in his shirt tails and quirked an auburn eyebrow at him in mock chagrin. 'Is that any way to greet the friend who just saved your life?'

Haviland answered with a raised dark brow of his own. '*My* life, is it? I rather thought it was yours.' He stepped forward and pulled Brennan into an embrace, pounding him on the back affectionately. 'I thought you were going to miss the boat, you stupid fool.' Sometimes Brennan worried him. He took too many risks, treated his life too cavalierly as if he doubted his own worth.

Greetings exchanged, the horse being looked after in a makeshift stall by Archer who had some explaining of his own to do, the threesome took up their places at the rail. 'So,' Nolan drawled, tossing a sidelong glance Brennan's direction. 'The real question isn't where you've been, but was she worth it?'

Brennan threw back his head and laughed up to the sky as if he hadn't a care in the world, as if he hadn't been dangling over the side of a boat minutes ago with an angry man shooting at him. 'Always.'

Haviland smiled into the distance, a little spark starting to ignite deep inside of him. It was a good sign. He wasn't dead yet, wasn't entirely numb yet. England faded from sight. It would be a while before they'd see those shores again but in the meanwhile, it was going to be one hell of a trip.

Chapter Two

*One month later—the viewing room of the
Leodegrance salle d'armes*

Mon Dieu! The Englishman was exquisite. Alyssandra Leodegrance's breath caught behind her peepholes as he executed an aggressive flèche against his opponent in the main training salon. Every movement spoke of lethal grace, his foil a natural extension of his arm as he effortlessly deflected Monsieur Anjou's sophisticated series of ripostes.

Alyssandra pressed her eyes more firmly to the peepholes of the *salle d'armes*'s private viewing chamber, hardly daring to believe what she saw: Monsieur Anjou, the *salle's* most senior instructor, was labouring now with all his skill to launch a counter-offensive and yet still the Englishman would not be thwarted.

'He has forced Monsieur Anjou into *redoublement*!' She could hear the excitement in her own hushed voice as she tore her eyes away long enough to toss a smile at her brother, Antoine, seated beside her in his wheeled chair, his own gaze as raptly engaged as hers.

Antoine gave a wry grin at her smug tone. 'You're enjoying it too, aren't you?'

Alyssandra shrugged her shoulders, feigning indifference, although they both knew better. There was the courtesy of professional respect between her and the senior instructor, but not much else. She put her eyes back to the holes, not wanting to miss a moment more. *Redoublement* was probably the last position Julian Anjou had expected to take up.

It had been ages since she'd seen Julian beaten and it did her heart good to see the arrogant master humbled. He hadn't been humbled since the time she'd beaten him. That had been two years ago and he would not admit to it. He preferred to call it a draw done at his expense to save *her* pride. Not that he wasn't an excellent fencer. Julian Anjou's arrogance was well deserved, but having earned it didn't make him any more tolerable.

The Englishman initiated an elegant *balestra* followed by a lunge, a traditional but fearless combination, his efforts confident and deliberate. He knew precisely what he was doing and what he hoped to accomplish. The sparring match had become a chess game. 'Checkmate,' she whispered under her breath as they circled one another again—Julian pressed to the extreme to keep the tight frame he was known for, the Englishman athletic and unwinded even after the long bout. A crowd of students and junior instructors had gathered at the edges of the floor.

He must dance like a dream, all that grace contained in those broad shoulders and long legs. The errant thought caught her off guard. After years of assessing men from a purely athletic standpoint as fencers, she seldom spared a thought for the more sensual applications of the male physique. Apparently, she was sparing a thought for it now. A shiver, wicked and delicious, shot down her spine as the Englishman moved in a tight circle around Anjou just out of reach of the man's foil. It was easy to imagine the confident press of his hand at a woman's back, of that hand guiding her skilfully through the crowded floor of a waltz. What woman wouldn't want to be led out on to the floor by such a partner, his body pressed ever so slightly to hers, their bodies attuned to the subtle pressures and nuances of the other?

She had to stop. Now she was being fanciful. It had been three years since she'd had a serious suitor or even been interested in one, nor was there any time for one at the moment with the tournament looming. She gave herself a mental scold. The *salle* and Antoine were her life now. Until that changed, there was no room for romantic games. A sharp movement from the floor refocused her attention. She'd been so engrossed in her little tangent of a fantasy she nearly missed it—the moment when the Englishman's blade slipped past Julian's guard and his buttoned tip pierced the master in the chest.

Julian swept him a bow, acknowledging the defeat, but his face was hard when he took off the mask and retreated to his corner to wipe the sweat from his brow. The Englishman did the same, pulling off the mask and tossing it aside, revealing a face a woman could study for hours and still not discover the whole of it; there was the strong, sharp length of his nose dominating the centre, the dark brows and long, defined cheekbones that likely did incredible things to his face when he smiled. Right now, he was not smiling and they lent him a slightly rugged air. And his mouth, with that thin aristocratic bow on top, and sensual, fuller lip on the bottom, was positively wicked. Suffice it to say, that mouth alone could keep a girl imagining all sorts of wicked things all night.

'He was perfect today,' Alyssandra remarked. She and Antoine moved back from the holes to talk, to plan. The Englishman would want to know if there was another master above Anjou with whom he could continue his studies.

Her brother's eyes held hers in all seriousness for a moment. 'Not intimidated, are we?'

She huffed at the idea, marking it as ridiculous with a shrug of her shoulders. 'Appreciating him is not the same as being intimidated by him.' Intimidated? Hardly. Excited? Definitely. Her body fired at the knowledge of it.

No, she wasn't intimidated. Men in general did not intimidate her. She'd faced men who'd believed they were the best, men like Julian. She revelled in the thrill of matching blades, of wearing them down and striking when their arm was weak and their pride

too strong. She sensed, however, that the Englishman would be different. A true challenge, but one
she would overcome, she was confident of that. She'd
been watching and learning. She was ready and now
so was he.

The Englishman had been coming to the *salle
d'armes* for three weeks. At first, she'd watched him
because he'd been new and new was always intriguing. He had started with informal matches against
the gentlemen who came purely to exercise. Having
dispatched them, he'd moved on to those who came
to study the art more seriously until there was no one
left to face, no one left to coach him except Julian. It
had been a testament to his skill and to his wealth that
Julian had consented to take him on. Julian took on
only a few select pupils with the skills and finances
worthy of instruction from a great master. Now, Julian had been beaten. The Englishman had earned
the privilege to face her; she, who was even more
exclusive than Julian, not because of the money, but
because of the secret. None of her clients ever knew
they faced a woman. The mask gave her anonymity,
her skill preserved it. No one would ever believe a
woman could possess such a talent.

Alyssandra reached for her mask, her sword arm
already feeling the grip of her hilt in her hand. 'Shall
I go out now?'

Antoine shook his head. 'No, sit and watch with me.
Your Englishman is not quite perfect, no matter what
you believe.' He gave a crooked half smile and nodded
towards the peepholes. 'They're about to start again.'

She and Antoine pressed their eyes to the holes once more. She watched and waited patiently for Antoine to make his point. They had done this countless times since his accident had rendered him incapable of fencing. She was his legs now and he was her mentor. One of the benefits of being a twin was being able to read her brother's mind after a fashion. He could read fencers, but she could read him. She knew what he was thinking quite often before he spoke. Like now. They weren't even looking at each other and yet she sensed he saw something in the Englishman's parry.

'There!' Antoine exclaimed in hush tones although there was no threat of being overheard. The room was soundproofed. 'Do you see it?'

She did see something, but what? 'No,' she had to admit. She was astute at assessing her opponents, but her brother was a master at detecting the subtle movements of a fencer. It was what had made him so good.

'Right there, he drops his shoulder,' Antoine said. 'Watch closely, he'll do it again.'

This time she did catch it, but only someone of Antoine's skill would have noticed without instruction. Julian certainly hadn't or he would have taken the opportunity to drive his button into the Englishman's briefly unprotected shoulder.

'When he recovers from a parry, he drops the shoulder. It's when he's most vulnerable.' Antoine winked at her. 'We'll help him fix that, of course, but only *after* you've established yourself with him.'

'Bien sûr.' Alyssandra laughed with him. It was an

effective strategy for gaining a student's respect to beat him a couple times before showing him why he'd lost. It proved the instructor knew what he or she was doing in theory as well as practice. But she sobered at the solemn look on her brother's face. 'What?'

'You *can* beat him, right?' he asked, worry creasing his brow. 'If you can't…' He didn't finish the sentence. They both knew the reputation of the salon was at stake, as it was any time Alyssandra faced an opponent, masquerading as Antoine Leodegrance, the famed Parisian swordsman.

She smiled to alleviate his concern. 'I will beat him. All will be well, as it always is. You have taught me perfectly,' she assured him. She understood his concern. He wanted her to be safe, but he was also frustrated with his own impotence to provide for them without relying on the masquerade. It had been three years since Antoine's accident, three years since they'd instigated this ruse in order to keep the successful *salle d'armes* running. No one would willingly study fencing under a woman's guidance.

Their *'petite déception'* had worked splendidly up until now. There was no reason to think it would not continue to work. Only one other knew of it and that was Julian, who had as much to lose as they if the secret was exposed. Of course, they had not thought to keep the ruse in place for so long. They'd hoped Antoine would recover the use of his limbs and return to his rightful place as the *salle*'s master at arms. It was only a matter of time, the physicians had said confidently at the beginning.

After three years, though, she had to wonder how much more time could be allowed to pass before they had to admit Antoine's recovery was an improbability? And if he didn't recover? What did that mean for the two of them? Antoine was all the family she had, but they could not sustain the masquerade for ever, for many reasons, not the least being her hopes for a family of her own. The longer she kept up the ruse, the longer she put off her chances to make a worthy match. It might be too late already. Etienne DeFarge had married another last spring, unwilling to wait any longer. Any hopes she'd entertained in that direction were gone now.

But those were thoughts for another time, for a far-off future if it ever came. They had no bearing on tomorrow or the next day. What *did* matter was the Englishman. Alyssandra turned back to the peephole, intent now on her quarry, all dark thoughts of the future thrust aside along with more seductive visions of a dancing Englishman complete with long legs, broad shoulders and a *very* kissable mouth. *Tomorrow*, she thought silently, *you, sir, shall meet your match.*

Chapter Three

'*En garde!*' Julian Anjou called out, stepping back from the two fencers in the private *salle*. Haviland assumed the position and faced his opponent, the masked and silent Antoine Leodegrance. Leodegrance had bowed to him respectfully, but other than that, all communication had taken place through Anjou acting as an intermediary. Masked and silent, Leodegrance had an almost surreal presence.

By pre-determined agreement, Leodegrance made the first '*attaque*'. Haviland understood this encounter was more an exercise than a bout. There would be no score kept. Leodegrance would want to see the variety and depth of his skills first-hand. And, frankly, Haviland wanted to see Leodegrance's. It wasn't everyone who had the privilege of viewing the selective Parisian's skill up close.

Parry and thrust, *balestra* and lunge, *battement* and *liement*. Haviland met the drills with ease, his eyes making a study of the great Leodegrance. The man had slim, graceful movements, elegance personified in even the smallest of motions. His parry from the *sixte* position was flawlessly delivered, his blade up, his wrist supinated. It was the subtlety of these motions that gave the man his edge, the litheness of his movements. Haviland dodged, barely avoiding the tip of Leodegrance's foil.

By Jove, the man was quick on his feet! With the slightest of efforts, the merest flick of his wrist, Leodegrance had nearly pricked him. There was a certain style to the flick of his wrist that was patently his own and Haviland made quick note of it. It seemed to give him an extra ounce of flexibility in wielding the foil—something easier to note without the Italian preference for a basket over the hilt. With the French blade, one's grip was exposed on the handle. Leodegrance was using that to envious advantage.

Gradually, the nature of their exercise began to change. The space between them became charged with a competitive electricity. Something combative leapt and sparked between them, a lethal chemistry, more akin to sensual attraction. Leodegrance's manoeuvres became a seductive dance, stealthy and mesmerising; his strikes came more quickly until Haviland was fully engaged.

The exercise had transformed into an *assaut*. Haviland grinned beneath his mask, enjoying the thrill of competition. They circled, each one stalking the other, arms and foils held out in full extension to define their space and to protect it. Leodegrance's frame looked as fresh as when they'd begun, his arm appeared strong. Haviland wondered if it was a bluff. His own arm was starting to ache and yet he dared not waver. Surely, Leodegrance, as slenderly built as he was, was physically affected by the duration of this match.

Haviland wished he could see beneath the full-face mask. Was Leodegrance sweating? He could feel his own sweat trickling down his back, down his face. Leodegrance made a *flèche* at lightning speed, requiring him to put up a riposte and he did so, proud of the speed of his own reflexes. Haviland parried and moved to launch his own attack. That was when Leodegrance's foil found his shoulder. He felt the hard press of the wooden button before he saw it, so fast did the strike come. He stared at it in full surprise for a moment before remembering his etiquette.

He bowed as Anjou had bowed before him yesterday in acknowledgement of a fair match and in acknowledgement of the other man's superiority. It did not gall him to be beaten—*this time*—it did gall him, however, that he hadn't seen it coming. The final attack had been most unorthodox, coming as it did on the heels of Leodegrance's deflected offensive. Haviland had parried the attack. It had been his turn to initiate one of his own, only Leodegrance had not waited. Haviland saw in hindsight what Leodegrance had done—he'd turned the move into a feint, a move designed to distract his opponent both in body and mind, while the real blow was delivered—a most effective *fausse attaque.*

Leodegrance accepted his bow and offered a slight

one in return. Haviland reached up to remove his mask, thinking Leodegrance would do the same. The man did not. Instead, he strode over to Anjou and conducted a conversation in low, hurried French, looked his direction one more time, raised his foil in salute and departed the room with a farewell as unorthodox as his final attack had been.

'*Bien, monsieur, bien.* You've done well. Master Leodegrance is very pleased.' Julian Anjou came to him, all smiles. It was the most pleasant Haviland had seen the instructor look. 'He has asked you to come back Thursday for another lesson. Also, there is a small competition in a matter of weeks. Master Leodegrance would be honoured to have you entered.'

'He could not tell me himself?' Haviland interjected sharply. This was by far the oddest lesson he'd ever had. 'Are we to never speak? Does he ever remove his mask?'

'Of course not!' Anjou sounded shocked, as if he'd uttered blasphemy. Anjou lowered his voice, tinged with a hint of French condescension. 'It is because of the accident, *monsieur*. You are an outsider, so perhaps you do not know. The scars are too hideous, too distracting for opponents. He wears the mask out of deference for *you*, *monsieur*, for all of his pupils.' He gave a thin smile. 'We are French, perhaps we are vain, but we put much stock in our beauty. Beauty is life to a Frenchman. We would not willingly inflict ugliness on anyone.' Anjou inclined his head in a dismissive gesture. '*Jusqu'à demain, monsieur.*'

Haviland watched him depart with a shake of his

head. That was the trouble with Frenchmen. They never quite answered your questions even when they did.

'We're going to have trouble with that one.'

Alyssandra looked up in time to see Julian slip inside the private viewing room to join her and Antoine. 'He's no trouble. I can manage him. I proved it today.' She pulled her hair free of the pins that kept it tucked up and in place when she was Antoine Leodegrance and let it fall free about her shoulders. That felt better. She stretched her arms, relieving the tension that had built up in them during the match. She had handled the Englishman, but it had taken much of her strength and skill to do so.

'Not that kind of trouble.' Julian fixed her with a stare before moving his gaze and his conversation to Antoine. 'Our Monsieur North has been asking questions. "When can he meet you?" "Why don't you take off the mask?" "Why won't you speak to him?"'

'But you handled it all beautifully.' Antoine gestured towards the peepholes where he'd watched the entire lesson. 'I saw it. He understood.'

'But he does not accept it,' Julian answered sharply. 'He's been asking questions around the clubroom when the men gather after their exercise and in the main *salle*. He talks to everyone and everyone talks to him.'

'Let them talk, there's nothing anyone can tell him.' Antoine remained unconcerned.

Alyssandra walked up behind Antoine's chair to

stand with her brother. It was a gesture she knew aggravated Julian, a non-verbal reminder that she and her brother were united on all things. 'We've seen his sort before. He's just another Englishman on the first leg of his Grand Tour. He's just passing through like so many of them.'

Julian gave her a shrug of concession. 'In that regard, you're right and perhaps we can use that to our advantage. Those Englishmen are all looking for the same thing on their tours; a little cultural experience and a lot of sex.' Julian paused thoughtfully for a moment. 'You should arrange for him to meet one of your more sophisticated friends. Perhaps Madame D'Aramitz?'

'Are you suggesting we spy on him?' Alyssandra rebelled at the idea of Helene D'Aramitz enjoying North's charms and reporting back all the details.

Julian's eyes were twin orbs of calculation. 'Yes, I am suggesting exactly that.' He flashed her a cold smile. 'I can keep an eye on him when he's here at the *salle*, but it will be up to you to use your connections and to keep an eye on him in society.' He gave Antoine a respectful nod. 'If you'll excuse me, I have a lesson to prepare for.'

'I don't think North is a threat,' Alyssandra said after Julian left.

'Maybe, maybe not.' Antoine blew out a breath. 'I hate being tied to this chair. It should be me out there fencing him. We shouldn't even have to worry about an inquisitive Englishman, but because of me, we do.'

What could she say? Her brother could no more

change the facts of his existence than command his legs to walk. 'We'll manage. Julian makes too much of it.'

'I think Julian is right. He does bear watching so he's not given the chance to become trouble. But, I don't think Helene D'Aramitz is the answer. She's a terrible gossip and far too perceptive. Then we'll have her asking questions, too. She'll want to know why we're so interested in what North does.' Antoine's face became thoughtful. 'If anyone is going to watch him in society, it should be you. It will eliminate the risk of exposing ourselves unnecessarily to outside parties. Will you do it?'

Her stomach somersaulted at the prospect of engaging the handsome Englishman on two fronts: as the masked, mysterious Leodegrance, and in person as herself. Part of her—the very feminine part of her that responded to him as a handsome man— revelled in being able to meet him on her own merits. But the other part of her understood the enormous risk she ran. *'La petite déception'* had just become a *grande* one. She must don two identities in order to preserve one. The feminine part of her could not afford to be distracted from the professional goal of protecting the *salle* and Antoine. She would start tonight. She had a fairly good of idea of where North and his friends would be. Anyone of note was attending Madame Aguillard's Italian musicale.

Alyssandra squeezed her brother's hand. 'Yes, of course, I will do it,' she said as if there'd ever been a choice.

Chapter Four

The match lingered on his mind that evening, distracting Haviland from Madame Aguillard's elegantly appointed entertainment. The musicale was unable to hold his attention for long no matter how lovely the Italian soprano, or how talented the pianist who accompanied her or even how often the hostess herself trailed her beautifully manicured fingers down his arm in provocative suggestion. No matter the enticement, his mind drifted back to the faceless, silent Leodegrance. Even without words, without a visage, the man had a charisma that had drawn Haviland. The force of that presence was disturbing to say nothing of the circumstances in which it had been felt. Fencing with Leodegrance had been like fencing a phantom. He'd never faced an opponent shrouded quite literally in such mystery. He couldn't quite get over it, or past it.

'Stop brooding,' Nolan scolded *sotto voce* as they moved through the crowd at the intermission. 'It's

bad form, and our hostess is bound to notice. You're
still thinking about the match.'

'No, I'm not,' Haviland said defensively.

Nolan chuckled. 'Yes, you are. You're a terrible
liar. It's a good thing you don't aspire to cards. It's
probably some fetish of Leodegrance's. He's French,
after all.' Nolan shrugged as if to indicate being
French explained away any unexplainable eccen-
tricities.

He clapped Haviland on the back. 'As for me, I'm
off to the card tables in the other room. I, for one,
won't risk disappointing my hostess. There's an inspector playing who is apparently unbeatable.' The
French were mad for gambling, and Nolan had immediately become popular among the card set. After
almost a month in Paris, Haviland still found it odd
how the ability to gamble for large sums of money
acted as a superior calling card in French society.

'I hear there's a certain pretty French widow playing tonight too.' Archer joined them, catching the last
part of the conversation as he handed off the flutes of
champagne he'd retrieved from the refreshment table.

Nolan smiled broadly. 'Madame Helene is a talented card player. I fancy she recognises those same
skills in myself.'

'Well, probably not those particular skills, but
certainly others if rumour is to be believed.' Archer
laughed.

'What rumour would that be?' Nolan raised his
eyebrow in mock chagrin.

'The "rumour" from our dear butler that you

haven't been home before breakfast for the last week,' Archer supplied.

Really? Haviland hadn't noticed. He watched Archer and Nolan spar in friendly fashion and felt detached from their banter. He should be glad everyone was finding Paris so hospitable. Archer had found a horsey set of young men eager to share their knowledge of the Continental breeds. Nolan had been easily assimilated into the aristocratic gambling circles and Brennan, well—he had been easily assimilated into several French beds as far as Haviland knew. But what he ought to feel and what he did feel were different.

What he felt was lonely, left out. He'd spent his waking hours at the *salle d'armes*. He was away as much as the others and he missed most of their days. They were together in the evenings in some form, two or three of them usually, although seldom all four. Even tonight, three of them were here at Madame Aguillard's, but Brennan was absent.

Perhaps it was better this way, establishing this sense of distance. Haviland sipped his champagne. At some point, the others would continue on the tour without him unless by some magic he wrested another six months from his father.

Nolan departed for the card tables, and Archer picked up the threads of their conversation from earlier that afternoon when he'd returned home from the *salle*. 'I've been giving your match some consideration,' he began thoughtfully as if that discussion had not been broken by hours of intermission. 'How do you know it was Leodegrance if he wouldn't remove his mask?'

That thought had crossed Haviland's mind, too, but he'd quickly discarded it. 'The man was too good to be anyone else. His talent spoke for him, which might be what he intended all along with his secrecy.' The effort seemed unnecessarily dramatic, but perhaps Leodegrance was a dramatic sort of man and there were the scars to consider as well.

'Then it's settled. You have your explanation and you can enjoy the evening.' Archer shot him a sideways glance etched with challenge and took a large swallow of his champagne.

'What is that supposed to mean?' Haviland said crossly.

'That you don't really believe your own explanation about talent speaking for itself. You think something is afoot. Admit it.'

'That's ridiculous. There *was* an accident a few years ago. We even heard about it in London. It's entirely plausible he's become a bit reclusive as a result. It's not as if Anjou's explanations about the scars don't make sense,' Haviland argued. Perhaps Nolan was right. He just needed to stop brooding. When Archer pressed him to see a conspiracy, he simply couldn't come up with a motive for such efforts. Perhaps that was what Archer intended all along; to make him see the foolishness of his notions. A silent look of comprehension passed between them.

Archer smiled in confirmation. Haviland had read him aright. Archer clapped him on the shoulder. 'Put it to bed, old friend, and have some fun. You need a distraction. Perhaps I could get our hostess to introduce you to one. There's several pretty ones here tonight.'

The crowd around them ebbed, affording Haviland a glimpse across the room. Archer shifted to the right to deposit his empty glass on a passing tray and there she was—a distraction to end all distractions. She must have come late. He would have noticed her earlier otherwise. She was the sort of woman who could command a man's attention without doing a thing. She was proving it right now, simply standing against a wall and stealing his breath along with any ability to formulate coherent thought.

'Archer, don't move. I think I've found my distraction.' She was a stunning brunette in an evening gown of crinkled taffeta the shade of gentian blue. The gown was plain by French standards, unadorned with ruffles or embroidered hems, yet the plainness lent itself to an understated elegance, as did the exquisite tailoring. For all its lack of affectations, this was not a poor woman's gown and no one would mistake the wearer for a peasant.

'I take it it's not a masked man?' Archer raised an interested eyebrow, but remained obediently frozen.

'Hardly.' Haviland inclined his head in the smallest of gestures for Archer to follow his gaze. 'Turn your head slowly and remember I saw her first.' He did see her, the woman beyond the dress. When he looked at her, he saw the confidence of her carriage, the delicate beauty of her very bone structure that declared her a woman of high birth. There was strength, too, in that delicacy. This was no retiring wallflower and yet she was alone.

Archer smirked. 'What are you thinking?'

Haviland gave him a wry grin that spoke volumes. 'I'm thinking I'm looking at Plan B.' One last *affaire*, one last opportunity to drink from passion's cup before settling into his marriage. He might not have chosen Christina Everly, but neither had she chosen him. He would not shame her with infidelities after they wed, regardless of the circumstances surrounding their union. Until then, however, a gentleman need feel no such restraint, especially if travelling abroad.

The woman in question looked their direction, catching his stare, the slight raise of his eyebrow. She answered his silent enquiry with the flick of her wrist, her fan opening in a sophisticated gesture that covered just the bottom of her face. Haviland's gaze dropped to her hands. She held the fan in her left, and Haviland smiled at the discreet sign to approach. Negotiations complete. Beside him, Archer let out a low whistle of appreciation. 'Now, that's a woman to cross a room for.'

'I doubt men stop there,' Haviland said under his breath. They'd cross mountains, even oceans for her. She was the sort of woman who could wreck a lesser man, one given to baser instincts and spontaneity. Thank goodness he wasn't such a man. 'Here, hold this for me.' Haviland handed his flute to Archer.

'Why? Do you think you'll be back for it?'

Haviland chuckled. 'With luck, no', and then he crossed the room.

* * *

Alyssandra felt a little tremor of anxious anticipation skate down her spine, so strong was her awareness of him. His eyes were on her, piercing and intense, demanding she meet his gaze as he approached, demanding she be aware of him. But it was too late to back out of this exquisite deception. This was what she'd wanted, what she'd orchestrated her evening around in the hopes of it happening.

She'd not known with certainty that he'd be here, but she'd known it was highly possible. The odds had favoured her. Madame Aguillard's soirée in the seventh *arondissement* was a coveted invitation and the Englishman and his friends had become coveted guests in certain circles. Men with money and connections could not be kept secret for long, and North was positively delicious on both accounts. He had looks and was heir to a title and a fortune, both English, which made him more impressive than his Continental counterparts. French nobles and Italian *contes* were thick on the ground and notoriously light in the pockets. In short, Haviland was the stuff of mothers' dreams. Even French *mamans*.

Who wouldn't jump, nay, who wouldn't *leap* at the chance to marry their daughters to such prestige and such security? There were those who would leap for much less than an offer of marriage. Alyssandra reminded herself she wasn't here for purely selfish reasons. It was what her brother *needed*. Her presence here tonight was professional. She had to remain objective just as if she were facing him from behind a fencing mask. There was no room behind the mask for carnal thoughts and there was no room for them now, although that didn't seem to be stopping them from trying to intrude.

She'd heard the women talking behind their fans all night. *'With a body like that, he cannot help but be extraordinary in bed,'* one woman had remarked. Another had commented, *'I just want to look at him, preferably naked.'* Alyssandra could understand the sentiment. He was gorgeously made, lean hipped and broad shouldered. She had studied that physique from behind peepholes for weeks now in anonymity. She had seen that body up close today during their exercise and it had been positively scintillating. It was in part responsible for the more feminine side of her wanting to risk the encounter tonight. She wanted to test the electricity between them. Would it happen again or was the spark between them limited to the fencing floor?

Around her, women whispered, watching his approach with interest and perhaps hope, from behind their fans. His stride was purposeful, confident, his gaze locked on her, making his destination clear to those who hoped otherwise. Alyssandra raised her chin just a fraction, enjoying a moment of defiant victory. The Englishman was coming for *her*.

Alyssandra lowered her fan and met his gaze with equal strength. She let the rush of excitement over meeting him as herself fill her, let him take her hand and bend over it with eyes that never left hers. He would never look at her incarnation of Antoine Leodegrance the way he was looking at *her*, all banked fire and desire in those blue eyes. His lips brushed her gloved knuckles. Even that briefest of touches sent a jolt of awareness up her arm. The connection she'd sensed today at the *salle* was still there.

'*Mademoiselle, enchanté.* I must apologise for my boldness. I could not wait for a proper introduction. May I present myself? I am Viscount Amersham.'

She'd known all of his names, of course. It was on his application at the club although he preferred to go by his given name there. Therein lay her advantage. He was meeting a stranger. But she was not. She knew him, whereas, there was nothing to connect her to Antoine save her name, and that would be revealed when and if she chose.

She let a little smile play across her lips, her eyes flirting coolly, her body trying to ignore the hot spark that passed between them upon contact. 'I know who you are.' She gestured to the groups gathered around them with her closed fan. 'Everyone knows. You've become quite the celebrity.' She rose and retrieved her hand, breaking the electric connection. 'Your reputation precedes you.'

'What reputation would that be?' He arched a dark brow.

She gave a laugh and spread her fan again, enjoying having the upper hand for the moment. 'Are you fishing for a compliment, *monsieur le vicomte*? I don't think vanity becomes you. I think you know very well what sort of reputation.'

'*Touché.*' He grinned, showing even white teeth

in that kissable mouth of his. It was every bit as delectable up close as it was from the distance of the viewing room or from behind a mask. His blue eyes danced, his gaze taking in all she had to offer. She was acutely alert to the skim of his eyes roaming over the slender length of her neck, how they'd dropped discreetly to the low sweep of her *décolletage*. His attraction to her was not in doubt.

Electric awareness crackled between them, broken only by their hostess signalling the end of the intermission—a critical moment that would define the direction of the evening and perhaps even their association. Allowing him to go back to his seat would suggest at worst she did not return his level of interest or, at the very least, she had not been serious when she'd summoned him. She must act quickly. She had done the summoning; the next move was hers. She had to be one to establish the purpose of having called him to her.

Alyssandra placed a hand on his arm, braving the physical pull of him. Men had crossed rooms for her before. Tonight, she had even encouraged such a response, knowing how well she looked in the gentian blue and the careful upsweep of her hair, both of which showed the silhouette of her body and the profile of her face to advantage. Would it be enough? 'Some of the others will go to the card rooms instead of returning to their seats. Perhaps you might enjoy a tour of the gardens? I have been here before, if you're interested.' He was a sophisticated man. He would hear the *entendre* in her words and the invitation, just as he was aware she would see the silent interest he communicated with his eyes.

'I have heard much about the beauty of the French gardens. I would be delighted to see one in person if you could be spared?'

Alyssandra smiled. 'It would be my pleasure.'

He allowed her to step slightly ahead of him, his hand at the small of her back to guide her through the crowd finding their seats, his hand confident of its reception, as if it belonged there. She could hear his voice, low and familiar at her ear. 'It will be mine as well, I am certain of it.' She recognised, too, what this was; the touch, the words, the very closeness of him. His body was advertising its skills in his touch, in his bid for familiarity. These were the opening moves to a seduction and it would be up to her just how far they would go. Suffice it to say, it was much harder to be professionally objective just now.

Chapter Five

There was nothing wrong per se with the garden. It was inherently respectable with its paper lanterns and exotic-shaped shrubs. The incipient lure to wickedness was Alyssandra's construction entirely. She knew very well they'd not come out here to be respectable, or even to see the topiaries, although the famed shrubs did make a good ruse for the reality: They'd come outside to test the waters of their attraction in the way sophisticated men and women do who are not necessarily looking for attachment but something more fleeting: momentary pleasure, momentary escape.

While she understood the allure escape held for her, she was hard pressed to imagine the allure of escape for a man like Haviland North, whose life was already perfect. And yet what did she know of him? He was here after all, wasn't he? In Paris, hundreds of miles and a body of water way from home. The Tour itself was an escape of sorts and those on it escapees.

It often stood to contrary reason that the more perfect something looked on the outside, the more rotten it was on the inside. What imperfections might the handsome viscount have, hidden away behind those blue eyes? It did make a girl wonder what he might be running from, and there was nothing sexier than a man shrouded in intrigue.

It was part of her mission to peel away those perfect outer layers and get to those imperfections beneath. Of course, she wouldn't peel all those layers tonight. That took time and trust. Tonight was about establishing the latter. 'Do you see the shrub shaped as a dog?' She pointed to the shape near a fountain. 'It was modelled after Madame Aguillard's favourite hunting hound. The fountain itself is made from marble imported from Italy.'

'Very impressive.' North said, walking beside her, his hand always at her back, offering a physical reminder of his presence.

'Very expensive, if you ask me,' Alyssandra shot back. It had always struck her as foolish to have imported the marble at extra cost when there were quarries nearby. It was darker now. There were fewer lanterns and even fewer guests in this remote corner of the garden. Her pulse began to leap. They'd reached their destination—somewhere private.

'It seems we have reached the perimeter of the garden.' North commented, his eyes full of mischief. 'What do you suppose we do now?'

Alyssandra wet her lips and turned towards him so they were no longer side by side, but face to face. 'I've talked far too long. You could tell me about yourself. What brings you to Paris?' She stepped closer, drawing a long line down the white linen of his chest with her fan. She'd genuinely like to know. She'd spent the past three weeks making up stories in her mind about what he was doing in France.

But she'd not come out to the garden to acquire a thorough history of Viscount Amersham. That would come in time, as those layers came off. Tonight was about making first impressions, ones that would eventually lead to...more. Even so, she rather doubted her brother had expected 'more' to involve stealing away to the dark corners of Madame Aguillard's garden with somewhat illicit intentions. Julian, on the other hand, had envisioned exactly such manoeuvres when he'd suggested Madame D'Aramitz.

'I *could* tell you my life story,' he drawled, his eyes darkening to a deep sapphire. 'Or perhaps we might do something more interesting.' Those sapphire eyes dropped to her mouth, signalling his definition of 'interesting' and her breath caught. *Something more interesting, please.*

It was hard to say who kissed whom. *His* head had angled towards her in initiation, but *she* had stepped into him, welcoming the advance of his mouth on hers, the meeting of their bodies; gentian-blue skirts pressed black-clad thighs, corseted breasts met the muscled firmness of his chest beneath white linen.

Her mouth opened for him, letting his tongue tangle with hers in a sensual duel. She met his boldness with boldness of her own, tasting the fruity sweetness of champagne where it lingered on his tongue. Life pulsed through her as she nipped his lip, and he growled low in his throat, his arm pressing her to the hard contours of him. She moved against his hips, challenging him, knowing full well this bordered on madness. Desire was rising between them, hot and heady.

'You are bold for an Englishman.' She sucked at his earlobe until she elicited another growl of arousal.

'Is that a problem?' he whispered hoarsely against her throat, his lips nuzzling the column of her neck, his hands moving over her rib cage, warm and sure. A hand closed decadently over a breast, a thumb offering a circling caress over the fabric of her nipple. It was both a siren song and a swan's song. This had to end.

'It is if I have to go and I do.' She summoned the shreds of her resolve. If she didn't pull away, she'd end up half-naked in the garden, her dress around her waist and his hands on her breasts. The only layers that would end up being peeled would be hers and that would hardly bring him back for more.

Alyssandra stepped away, smoothing her skirts, taking a formal tone designed to cool anyone's growing ardour. 'It has been a most enjoyable evening, *monsieur le vicomte.*'

'Perhaps you might call me Haviland,' he offered abruptly as if the use of his title offended him. She thought she understood. After such an intimacy he wanted to be a man, not a title. It was not so different from the reason she was reluctant to give him her own name.

'*Bon nuit*, then, Haviland.' She dropped a little curtsy in a flirty farewell. Maybe she would escape this encounter unexposed after all.

She turned to go. His hand closed on her arm. 'Not so fast, my lady of mystery.' His voice held a tone of authority beneath the seduction. 'While we've had some pleasure tonight, one pleasure yet eludes me. Might I have *your* name?'

She did not mistake it for a request that could be denied or flirted away. How would Haviland North, Viscount Amersham, a man used to power and obedience, feel about her name now? Would he be angry? Would he feel betrayed or used? She dropped her eyes, assuming a demure, penitent posture. 'May I tell you a secret?'

'Absolutely. I love secrets.' His voice was a sensual whisper close to her ear, but she did not miss the firmness in it. His tolerance had limits.

'I must beg your forgiveness. I fear I have had you at a disadvantage.' She looked up beneath her lashes, gauging his reaction.

'Ah, so it's absolution you're seeking.' His eyes narrowed in assessment.

'Not absolution, sanctuary. If I tell you, you must promise not to be angry.' She let her eyes dance, building the mystery so that he would promise her anything to hear her secret.

He leaned close, a smile on his lips. She could smell the clean scent of linen and sandalwood soap on him, 'Sanctuary it is, then. Tell me your secret.' Good, curiosity had got the better of him. She hoped bad judgement hadn't got the better of her.

She locked eyes with him and let her secret fall into the night between them just before she fled. 'My name is Alyssandra Leodegrance.'

Curses tumbled through Haviland's mind. He'd spent four glasses of brandy and three hours sitting in the dark and he still could not get past it. He'd been kissing Alyssandra Leodegrance, his fencing instructor's…his instructor's *what*?

This was where things got fuzzy and it wasn't entirely the brandy to blame. What exactly *was* her relationship to Leodegrance? Was she his sister? His cousin? His wife? The latter wouldn't surprise Haviland, although it would repulse him. Frenchmen were forever throwing their wives at guests. It was considered rude not to ogle one's hostess as a means, he supposed, of congratulating the husband on such a splendid catch. If he had thought for one moment she was another man's wife, *any man's* wife, let alone Leodegrance's, he would not have kissed her no matter how lovely she'd been.

'You came home early.' Archer stood in the doorway of the sitting room, his form barely outlined by the lamp left burning in the entry.

'Maybe *you* came home late.' It was nearly three in the morning, after all. Haviland drained the last of his brandy.

'May I join you?' Archer gestured towards the decanter on the table, ignoring the cross response. He poured a glass and took the chair opposite him. 'I suppose this means the meeting with our lovely stranger didn't go well?'

Typically, Haviland enjoyed Archer's directness, but usually it was aimed at someone else. 'It went well enough, very well, actually.' Those particular memories were still warm. His mind was a riot of snippets, all of them full of her in bright, vivid colour: the mysterious spark that lit the depths of her chocolate-brown eyes; the long, black lashes that made her appear demure and seductive all at once. Those lashes had been quite engaging when she fluttered them, the perfect foils for her sophisticated conversation with its hidden messages, the blue of her gown, the lace and paint of that exquisite fan she'd employed so expertly, that sexy flick of her wrist...a flick practically identical to his instructor's.

Haviland had not fully appreciated that flick at the time. In hindsight, it was easy to say he should have recognised the resemblance right then. Antoine Leodegrance's wrist movement was signature.

'Then what's the complaint?' Archer nodded towards the empty glass. 'By the look of the decanter that wasn't your first brandy of the night.'

'Her name. She's Alyssandra Leodegrance, only I don't know what that means precisely.' Not just in terms of her relationship to Leodegrance, but in terms of what had she been doing with *him*? Had she known who he was ahead of time? Had she deliberately put herself in his path in the hopes of engineering what only appeared to be a chance meeting between two strangers? The more he'd drunk, the more it seemed likely and the more his mind had unwound each piece of the conversation, each gesture. When he held such speculations up against the oddness of his previous encounter with Leodegrance, meeting Alyssandra tonight began to look more than coincidental.

'If Leodegrance is a recluse, perhaps he sent her to vet you on some level?' Archer mused out loud, his train of thought mirroring Haviland's more private ones.

Haviland looked into his empty glass, debating whether or not to pour himself another and decided against it. Four was quite enough, and he had no desire to wake up with a thick head if it wasn't too late for that already. 'That makes little sense at this point. For Leodegrance's purposes, I've already passed. I've beaten his senior instructor. Vetting me now seems like an effort made too late.'

'Or it makes perfect sense. Now that you've reached Leodegrance, it may be that he wants to be sure you're worthy.' Archer raised his brows over the rim of his glass. 'We should have Nolan vet *him*. Nolan is far better at these sorts of games.'

But he and Archer weren't too bad at it either. One could not come of age in the *ton* without a healthy amount of social intuition. The second explanation, that Leodegrance felt the need to protect himself, perhaps reassure himself that his latest pupil was indeed an appropriate candidate for the honour, seemed logical. Haviland had already proven his skill, but

Leodegrance would want more. He'd want to make certain Haviland's social credentials were what they were supposed to be and that his wealth was more substantial than mere rumour. Leodegrance would want to know he was a man who didn't just say he was rich, but was wealthy in truth. But that didn't explain most of what had happened with Alyssandra. Skilful conversation would have accomplished those goals. Frankly, there hadn't been that much conversation between them and what there had been had been pure flirtation. Fencing hadn't come up once.

'Ah, I see, she did more than vet,' Archer said softly when the silence stretched out between them. 'Did she fulfil your need for distraction, then?'

Good lord, yes. Just watching her had been a tantalising fantasy. Tasting her, touching her, had been a different elevated plane of sensuality altogether. That's where his pride came in. Had she'd been told to do those things or had they been part of the natural chemistry at work between them? Which all came back to the initial question: *Had she known him before he'd said his name?*

She had not told him her name until the end and she had done so penitently, knowing full well it would mean something to them both. And it had. She'd fled into the night, not waiting to hear his response, and he'd fled to the dark privacy of his rooms to mull that response over.

'I hope she isn't his wife,' Haviland said quietly. It would ruin everything. He'd have to leave the *salle*, have to forfeit instruction with Antoine just when he'd begun lessons with the master. He'd have to start over, one of his precious months of freedom now wasted. But most of all, he hoped she wasn't Leodegrance's wife because he wanted to see her again, wanted to kiss her again, wanted to feel what he'd felt this evening in the garden again. He wasn't sure he'd ever felt such initial, intense attraction before, hadn't ever felt such overwhelming fire course through him at a woman's touch. It was exquisite and quite obviously addictive.

'Because you are my friend, I hope so too,' Archer replied, rising from his chair. 'But be careful. A woman like that knows her way around a man. That makes her dangerous to a man like you who has so much to protect.'

A title, a family, a reputation, a fortune—Haviland knew all too well the things he had to protect. What he wouldn't give to forget all that for a while and simply be a man. He'd thought tonight, with her in the garden, perhaps such forgetfulness might be possible. But that was before he'd known her name. Now, his hopes hung in the balance of a kiss and its motives. Why had she done it? Why had she kissed him? For passion or for a plan?

Chapter Six

'You did *what*?' Antoine's disbelief radiated in all possible ways, in his tone, in the look on his face, even in the sloshing of his tea when he set it down too forcefully as her confession spilled out over breakfast.

'I kissed him,' Alyssandra repeated firmly, meeting her brother's eyes. She would not look away as if she was embarrassed by what she'd done. She was twenty-eight and well past the age of needing permission for her actions. If she could successfully masquerade as a fencing master, she was certainly capable of deciding who she was going to kiss. Her brother's attitude of indignation sat poorly with her this morning. She was not a child or even a naive girl out of her league with men like Haviland North. Alyssandra buttered a piece of bread with unnecessary fierceness. 'It was just a kiss, Antoine.' Had he forgotten she'd once been highly sought after before their fortunes had changed?

'Why? This is not what we'd talked about. You

were supposed to talk to him, not kiss him.' Antoine fought to keep his voice from rising. 'It's not just a kiss! Who knows what he'll be thinking now.'

'It hardly matters what he thinks. He'll only be here long enough for you to make some money on him and that's all that matters to you and Julian,' Alyssandra shot back uncharitably. How dare he ask her to play this double masquerade and then question her execution of it.

'Yes, plenty of money; money from lessons, money from the tournament when I wager on him. Money for the *salle* when people see the kind of fencer we can turn out. That money keeps you in this fine house, keeps you in gowns like the one you wore last night,' Antoine retorted sharply.

She supposed she deserved that. It was an unfair shot on her part. Money always made Antoine prickly. He was acutely aware of the limits of his ability to provide for them. There was always enough, but just enough. She bit her tongue against the temptation to remind him just how much of that money she helped earn. He would not appreciate it and she already had one black mark against her this morning.

'Since he truly is only here a short while there's really no harm in it, is there?' Alyssandra soothed. She sensed there was something else bothering him. She felt terrible. Guilt niggled at her for causing her brother angst. She wanted to believe there was no harm in last night's kiss, that she could indulge herself just a little. At times she felt that she had become a recluse, too, along with Antoine.

Before his accident, she used to go out to all nature of entertainments. She used to dance, ride in the parks and the woods outside town, shop with her friends—many of whom had long since married and had children. Now, she seldom went out at all. When she did it was only in the evenings after the work at the *salle* was done.

At first, she'd stayed in because she felt guilty about dancing and riding when Antoine, who'd loved those activities, could no longer do them. They'd been things the two of them had done together and it seemed disloyal to her twin to enjoy them without him. In the early days after his accident, there had been nursing to occupy her. Then, there simply hadn't been time. Antoine had needed her at the *salle* and at home. Any attempts at maintaining her old social life had eventually faded, replaced by other needs.

'We have to be careful,' Antoine said. 'A conversation is one thing, but a kiss might have him sniffing around even more than he would have otherwise and that's hardly solving the problem.'

Alyssandra knew too well how fragile their masquerade was, how lucky they were it had lasted this long and how little it would take to see it all undone. Everything was done covertly. They kept only the most loyal of staff. No one could see Antoine leaving the house or entering the *salle*, carried by his manservant. No one could come to the house. Antoine conducted all his business in writing or at the *salle* where he had Julian and her to act as his legs.

She understood maintaining the ruse was a great

sacrifice on Antoine's part, too. If he allowed everyone to know his injury was lingering, he could go about publicly in his chair, or with his manservant. He could attend musicales and plays, the opera, picnics even. But to do so would mean the end of the *salle* and the end of their income. Ironically, without income and means there would be no social invitations to such events. They would be nothing more than the impoverished children of a dead *vicomte*. It was not a bargain Antoine could afford to make. So in exchange for social security, Antoine had fashioned a secretive, reclusive life for himself—a life that consisted of his family home, the elegant Hôtel Leodegrance in the sixth *arondissement*, his father's *salle* and his sister's well-being; three things only after a life that had been full of so much more.

'I'm sorry.' Alyssandra bowed her head. She had been selfish last night. She should not have kissed Haviland North. She should have resisted the temptation to seize a little pleasure for herself when Antoine could seize none. All the choices he had made had been for her, for them. She should do the same. They were all each other had left. Perhaps that was what was worrying him this morning—a fear of losing her.

The very thought of having caused him such pain when he already had so much to bear made her chest tight. She'd not thought in those terms last night— indeed, she'd hardly thought at all in Haviland's arms. She rose and went to Antoine, kneeling at his side and taking his hands in hers, tears in her eyes. 'I will not leave you. I promise. You mustn't worry about that, never again.'

Antoine placed a hand on her head. 'I know it's hard and I know it's unfair to ask you to stay,' he said softly. 'Don't think I don't know what it costs you. You could be out dancing every night. What would become of me without you? I am afraid I'm too scared to find out, but perhaps I won't always be. Maybe some day I'll find the courage to let you go.'

She shook her head in denial. 'You must never worry. You are my brother—' Hurried footsteps interrupted her. The butler stepped into the room. She rose and smoothed her skirts. 'What is it, Renaud?'

The butler drew himself up, trying with great effort not to look disturbed. 'There is a gentleman downstairs. He is asking to see you. He has given me his card.' The butler handed it to her, hiding a very French sneer of disdain. 'He's English.'

Her initial reaction was one of relief. No one was asking to see Antoine. People had stopped asking to see Antoine years ago at home. The story about facial scars had worked well in keeping people away. But the sight of the name on the card put a knot in her stomach that curled right around her buttered toast. She passed the card silently to her brother. Antoine had been right. It hadn't been *just* a kiss. The kiss had become an invitation to seek her out and he had. Haviland North was here, in a home that hadn't seen a visitor in three years.

'You'd better go down.' Antoine handed the card back to her.

'Take him for a walk through the back garden or over to the Luxembourg Gardens. That will look civil enough.' What he meant was 'normal' enough and it would get North out of the house, away from any telltale sign of Antoine's incapacity.

Antoine glanced at Renaud. 'Did he say anything about the nature of his business?'

'No, he did not.'

But Alyssandra knew. She had no illusions as to why he had come. He was here to make her accountable for last night.

'You played me false last night.' Haviland announced the intent of his visit the moment she stepped into the drawing room. This was not a social call and he would not treat it as such by dressing it up as one, nor would he allow her to escape the reckoning he'd come for. It would be too easy to forget his agenda in those deep-brown eyes, too easy instead to remember those lips on his, the press of her body against his.

He'd come as early as he dared in hopes that morning light would mitigate his memories of the midnight garden and show them to be just that—fantasies exaggerated by the lateness of the hour and his desire for distraction. He'd also come early simply because he wanted the situation resolved. Resolution would determine his next course of action.

He might have come earlier if finding the house had been easier. No one at the *salle* had been eager to give up the address, directing him only to the sixth *arondissement*. No one, not even Julian Anjou, had refused him outright, of course. They'd said instead in the indirect way of the French, 'The master does not receive anyone.' Haviland had been forced to rely on general directions from merchants and shopkeepers who recognised his description of Alyssandra and eventually made his way.

Alyssandra gestured to a small cluster of furniture set before the wide mantel of the fireplace. 'Please, *monsieur le vicomte*, have a seat.' He grimaced as she returned to formality as she had at the last in the garden. 'Shall I call for tea or perhaps you'd prefer something more substantial? Have you eaten?' The formality and now this. It was a deft reprimand regarding the hour of his call.

Haviland shook his head. The last thing he wanted to do was sit and eat. He understood her strategy. If he was determined to not make this a social call, she was determined to do the opposite. A social call required a different set of rules, polite ones. He was intent on something a little more blunt, a little more direct.

She sat and arranged her skirts, the unhurried movements calling attention to the elegant slimness of her hands, the delicate bones of her wrists. Haviland could not help but follow her motions with his eyes. She was in no rush to answer his accusation and her sense of calmness rather took the wind out of his bold claim. He'd expected the passionate woman of last night to leap to her own defence and deny him. He'd expected her to engage him in a heated argument at his charges of duplicity. She did neither.

She arched a dark brow in cool enquiry as he sat.

'You are disappointed? Perhaps you thought to make some drama of this?'

'I do not appreciate being toyed with,' Haviland said tersely. 'You did not tell me who you were.'

She dropped her lashes and looked down at her hands as she had last night and, like last night, she was only playing at being penitent. 'I did not think it mattered so much at the time. We understood one another, I thought.'

Inside the drawing room perhaps they had understood one another. They had made eye contact, she'd given him tacit approval to approach, to flirt. At that point, a name had not been of issue. 'It mattered a great deal in the garden,' Haviland answered, his eyes resolutely fixed on her face, watching for some reaction, any reaction that might give her away, daring her to lift those deep-brown eyes to his. She was far too serene for his tastes. He wanted her agitated. She'd kept him up all night, damn it.

She did lift her gaze, a worldly half smile on her lips to match the hint of condescension in her eyes. 'Then I kissed you and apparently that changes everything for an Englishman. Are all of you so chivalrous? Tell me you've not come to propose marriage to atone for your *great* sin.'

'I am not in the habit of kissing women whom I do not know. That makes me particular, not chivalrous,' Haviland corrected. She was mocking him and he didn't care for it, although he recognised it was an offensive move of some sort, a protective strategy, something to put him on the defensive much like a reprise in fencing after an attack has failed. He recognised, too, that she would not be much help in supplying the answers he wanted without his asking directly. 'Are you his wife?'

She made him wait for it, studying him with her eyes, letting precious seconds pass before she uttered the words, 'No, I'm his sister.'

Haviland felt the tension inside him ease. One mystery solved, but another remained. He asked his second question, the one that mattered more in the larger sense. The first question had been for his private pride. 'You knew who I was last night the moment you heard my name. Why did you pretend otherwise?'

'You promised me sanctuary in exchange for my secret.' She stood and pierced him with narrow-eyed speculation. How had he lost the upper hand? She had played him and now, somehow, he was the one in violation.

'Is this how an Englishman keeps his word? By interrogating a lady?' Her retort was a powerful dismissal. Manners dictated that he should rise, too, but he knew where that would lead if he didn't change the direction of this conversation. It would lead to farewell and he had not yet got what he came for. Her manoeuvre had been skilfully done. She'd put his own leave-taking into motion, taking control of the interaction out of his domain.

Haviland rose. He was skilful, too. He wasn't going to be outflanked. He smiled charmingly. 'You are right, of course. My curiosity has got the better of my manners. I can do better if you would give me a chance. Would you do me the honour of accompanying me to the park? It's a lovely day, and I'd prefer not to walk alone. Or should I ask your brother?' He did not think she needed the approval. He'd added the request for formality's sake. He didn't want to risk angering the eccentric Leodegrance. It was also a goad. She wouldn't refuse a dare. She was old enough to make her own decisions as she'd exhibited last night. A woman who kissed like that didn't live under her brother's thumb.

'There's no need to ask him,' she said too quickly. 'I'll send for my hat and gloves.' He was not prepared for the odd look that crossed her face ever so briefly. Was that fear? Anxiety? She was hiding something, that much was clear. Perhaps it was nothing more than the fact that she hadn't told her brother she'd met him last night. And perhaps it was something more. Maybe Alyssandra Leodegrance was a woman with secrets.

Chapter Seven

In for a *sou*, in for a *livre*. Alyssandra drew a deep, steadying breath and slipped her arm through his with a confidence comprised mostly of bravado. She couldn't cry off now for at least two reasons. First, she'd promised her brother she'd keep Haviland close even if the two of them disagreed on the method. Second, Haviland had come back for more. Coming back had been the plan since the moment she'd put on the blue dress. She'd not flirted with him for the simple prize of a single night and a few stolen kisses. She'd played for bigger stakes and she'd got them in spades. The only surprise was how early he'd called. He'd wasted no time coming back for more.

That in itself was impressive. It was something of a feat for him to have made it this far. 'How *did* you find our home?' she asked as they made the short walk to the park. 'It's hardly common knowledge.' *For an outsider*, was the implied message. There were plenty of people who knew where they lived.

The *hôtel* had been in the Leodegrance family since the sixteen hundreds. But everyone who knew them knew Antoine did not receive visitors. It was difficult to imagine which of their acquaintances would have given up that information to an Englishman. His only connection to them would be through the *salle d'armes* and while his skill was respected, he was still an outsider. Surely, no one there would have told him.

'By trial and error mostly. Shopkeepers.' His eyes rested on her. 'I did not think it would prove to be such a secret.'

'My brother likes his privacy,' she answered shortly, making sure he heard the warning in that and the caution not to come again. Visitors were not welcome.

'And you? Do you like your privacy as well?' Haviland was probing now and not so subtly.

'When I want company, I go out.' Her retort was pointed, in the hopes of dissuading him from pursuing this line of question. It would be a good time to let the subject drop. They'd arrived at the wide gates of the Luxembourg Gardens, and there was a small crowd of people to navigate: nannies with children, children with kites and boats for sailing in the fountains. She was conscious of Haviland's hand moving to the small of her back to negotiate the knots of people at the entrance.

Even the smallest, most mundane touch from him sent a jolt through her. Some men just knew how to touch a woman. Haviland North was one of them. Etienne's touch had been comfortable, but nothing like this. If a simple touch from him could ignite such a reaction, it made one wonder what other more intimate touches could do.

'Like last night?' he said once they'd found their way clear of the people at the entrance. *Touches like last night?* Those had certainly been more intimate. It took her a moment to remember where they'd left the conversation. Then she realised with no small amount of disappointment he was not talking about touches, but about company.

'Did you come looking for me or for any company in general?' His tone was edged with ice. He'd misunderstood her answer. He was thinking she was a loose woman, looking for intimate male company whenever and wherever it pleased her. She wanted him to be warm and charming as he had been last evening, as he had been before he knew who she was and everything had turned into a fencing match of the verbal variety. Her identity had made him wary as she'd known it would.

'*You* approached me, as I recall. *You* crossed the room.' It would be entertaining to banter with him if so much wasn't at stake. He was clever *and* bold, not afraid to say the audacious. It made conversation an adventure, wondering what would come next, what her response would be. 'I hardly think it's fair to blame me.'

He shrugged, contemplating, his eyes on her mouth. 'If I had known who you were from the start, it might have changed the, ah, "direction" of the evening. There's no denying being who you are complicates things. I kissed the sister of my fencing instructor. Surely, you can understand the precarious position that puts me in.'

Kissed was a relative understatement and they both knew it. They'd acted precipitously. She'd been a stranger to him. They'd owed each other nothing but passion in those moments. Then she'd become someone and everything changed.

'And I kissed my brother's star pupil. Certainly, *you* can understand the position that puts me in.'

He gave a wry smile. 'No, I'm afraid I don't. What position is that, exactly?'

She met his smile with a coy one of her own. They were expert wits toying with one another the way expert fencers tested the skills of their opponents. How much to reveal? How much to conceal? 'The position of deciding whether or not I can trust you. There's so much to consider if we were to become, shall we say, entangled.' It was hard to play cool with his body so close to hers, his eyes lingering every so often on her mouth, just enough to remind her of what their mouths could do. She had to resist. She could flirt all she liked, but ultimately, resistance was in her best interest. She needed to keep him close, but not too close. Too much intimacy and he would start asking more questions.

'What is there to consider?' he drawled, playing his end of the game with audacious charm. He was overtly in pursuit, driving her towards a particular conclusion to this conversation by stripping away her objections.

But she knew the game. Alyssandra ticked off the considerations on her fingers. 'First, I must consider your motives. Are you using me to gain an entrée with my brother? If so, it won't work. I don't appreciate being made an intermediary pawn and my brother doesn't receive anyone. Second, I must ask myself what kind of liaison are you looking for? Based on what I've seen of your like-minded countrymen, I can only assume you're looking for a short-term sexual companion, an exotic adventure to write home about. That, too, is an unappealing motivation. I have no desire to become an Englishman's souvenir, a story that is trotted out in his clubs back home when he's sloshed with brandy and reminiscing.'

Her words were sharp as she laid down her terms. She'd meant them to be. She wanted him to understand she would not be used no matter how strong their attraction. But Haviland merely laughed and gave her a wide smile. 'I agree entirely. Neither option sounds even remotely appealing. Those are not things I would ever want for myself.' That wide smile almost disarmed her.

Almost. Agreement was a most effective strategy and while she hadn't expected it, she was ready for it. 'I suppose you want me to ask what do you want?' She tried for a bored tone, or at least one that suggested she'd travelled this path before when, in reality, she couldn't tear her gaze from his blue eyes and her pulse speeded up in anticipation of his answer. What could a man with a perfect life possible want that he didn't already have?

His voice dropped, low and private, and the size of her world shrank with it until nothing existed but him, her and the tree at her back. 'What if I said I was looking for something else—an escape? What if I could offer that same escape to you? Don't tell me you wouldn't be interested. I can see the tension in you. Your life is not a free one. I can see it.' Those blue eyes dropped to her mouth again. 'Why not escape, even if it's just for a little while, to find pleasure with a man who knows how to provide it?'

He *was* bold. 'Are you propositioning me?' She could be bold, too. The game was heating up. Too bad she could do nothing more than let the pot boil.

Haviland shook his head. 'No, nothing as base as that. I'm merely asking you to consider the possibilities, that's all.' He smiled and leaned towards her ear, his voice a whisper. '*I* have already considered the possibilities and found them positively delectable.'

She was going to swoon right there and she might have if she hadn't been so sure that was what he was after. It took all of her sangfroid to muster the words, 'Has a woman ever said no to you, Haviland North?'

He grinned. 'No, not that I recall.'

She leaned into him, letting her mouth hover as near to him as she dared without touching. 'Then this is your lucky day. I'm about to be your first.'

He chuckled, low and throaty, a sexy invitation to repeal her decision. He didn't take rejection like any man she'd ever known. 'Then I shall delight in helping you change your mind.'

'You flirt like you fence, all *balestra* and lunge.'

'It's an aggressive combination.' His response was sexy and sharp in its immediacy. His eyes hooded so she couldn't see them, his forehead pressed to hers. 'So you *did* know me before last night. So you *have* seen me fence.' His tone was flintily accusatory.

She bit her lip. 'I *did* say your reputation preceded you. It stands to reason that you're a phenomenal fencer if my brother is willing to take you on.'

'So you did.'

She swallowed. He was going to kiss her. And he might have if Madame Aguillard hadn't swept down upon them with her little coterie of friends.

'There you are, *monsieur le vicomte*! And how nice to see you, too, *mademoiselle*.' She nodded at Alyssandra. 'You're out twice in as many days,' she added cattily, her eyes drifting between the two of them, but it was clear who the centre of her attention was. 'My friends have been dying to meet you, Amersham.' She gushed in rapid French to Haviland.

'Je suis enchanté.' Haviland smiled, overlooking the familiarity, but it was a polite smile only, nothing at all like the wicked smiles he'd been giving her. Alyssandra took a petty satisfaction in knowing he preferred sparring with her over Madame Aguillard's company.

'I am giving a little dinner party tonight,' she said after introductions had been made. 'Perhaps you and your friends would like to come?' She stepped close to Haviland, affording him a view of her bosom if he so chose to look. Alyssandra noted Haviland did not. It was another small victory and one Madame Aguillard was well aware of. But she was not a woman who admitted defeat easily. She put a confiding hand on his arm. 'There will be cards for Monsieur Gray and ladies for Monsieur Carr. I have some especial friends who would like to meet him particularly and I'm sure you and I can find something special for you, too.'

Alyssandra wanted to skewer the woman for her audacity. She watched Haviland step back, freeing his arm from the woman's touch. 'I appreciate the invitation, but I must respectfully decline.' He offered no reason. The conversation mopped up after that with polite small talk and Madame Aguillard wandered off to join other groups.

'She'll be back,' Alyssandra said as the woman took her friends and left.

Haviland gave her a small, private smile. 'Well, what I'm interested in is right here.'

But for how long? They started walking, a slow, steady stroll, taking in the lush greenery of spring, the pleasant, warm air of the day. She was thankful for the silence as they strolled. Her mind was whirling and she needed a minute to think. How did she fulfil her promise to watch Haviland? How did she keep him from asking too many questions? How did she keep herself from rushing headlong into this forbidden attraction while not losing Haviland in the process? Or worse, losing herself? It would be too easy to capitulate to his charm, to set herself up for heartbreak when he left. How to balance all this?

The audacious Madame Aguillard might be routed for now, but the lesson was learned. Haviland was a person of interest to the women of Paris and a healthy male in his prime. Madame Aguillard might not be to his taste, but he wasn't a man used to being alone. It had crossed her mind as she'd watched Madame Aguillard jockey for position that if she didn't claim him, someone would.

Maybe the real question to ask was how much was she herself willing to risk? Could she have it all? Could she reach for the pleasure Haviland promised, the escape he offered to explore with her, and still preserve her secrets? It was already the end of April.

'How long will you be in Paris?' She cocked her head to look up at him, letting her eyes give away a little of her contemplation.

His eyes danced in response. 'Long enough for you to take me up on my offer. Changed your mind already, have you?' He paused. 'All teasing aside, we plan to stay until June, unless Nolan offends any gamblers or Brennan angers any husbands. Then, it will be sooner.'

'Your friends sound delightful.' She had six weeks at most. Surely she could keep her secret and have her pleasure, too, if she dared.

He nodded. 'They are. The very best of friends a man could hope for, actually. Perhaps you'll get to meet them.'

'Then where will you go?' She shouldn't feel so empty at the prospect of him leaving. Her strategy depended on him leaving. She couldn't keep up this ruse for ever. He would go on to other places, other women, and she would still be here, her world much smaller than his and likely to remain so. *Don't think on it. He is here now, yours now if you encourage him. He's already made his offer, he is just waiting for you to accept.*

'My friends fancy a summer in the Alps, climbing the peaks.' He shrugged, and she thought she sensed some reluctance there.

'The Alps don't appeal to you?' They reached a fork in the walkway, and she gestured that they take the path to the right.

'The Alps do, just not as much as Paris,' he admitted. 'They are not known for their fencing *salles*. But it is on the way to Italy and Italy appeals a great deal.'

'Is it the *salles* alone that give Paris its appeal?' She might be guilty of fishing for a compliment here, but flirting was a way to keep the conversation light.

Haviland smiled. 'The *salles d'armes* are big part of it, but I love the coffee houses, the intellectual discussions. When I'm not at Leodegrance's, Archer and I sit for hours in the Latin Quarter, listening to the debates, joining in sometimes.'

'Surely you have that in London?' She shot him a sideways glance.

'I suppose we do. Soho is awash with artists and foreigners bringing their own flavour to the city, but it's not a place I am able to frequent often.' Wistfulness passed over his features and was quickly gone, but not missed. 'Perhaps it's not the city I love so much as the freedom I have in it. No one has expectations of me here.'

She gave a soft laugh of understanding. 'Le Vicomte Amersham has to keep up appearances?' There were places she no longer frequented, too, because life required otherwise. She thought about his comment regarding escape. Paris was about freedom for him. She'd been surprised a man of his background didn't already consider himself free, that he found it necessary to leave his home to taste freedom. She'd always thought money and power were the keys to freedom, and he seemed to have plenty of them. She and her brother had struggled to keep what little they had of either.

'Where does fencing fit with all of that?' She risked probing a little further.

'Fencing is a gentleman's art. A man should how to defend himself adequately.' It was a rote answer, the kind fencing instructors gave to build their student base.

'You've attained enough skill to have stopped ages ago.' She wouldn't let him get off with an easy answer.

He stopped walking and faced her, eyes serious. 'If you want to know, it's about freedom, the chance to prove myself on my terms and no one else's. Skill cannot be inherited, it has to be worked for, it has to be honed to perfection and that is something only a man can do for himself.'

'I know.' Her answer was a whisper. She did know. Better than he thought because that was how she felt every time she picked up a foil, every time she faced an opponent on the piste. How would she be able to keep her emotional detachment when he looked at her like that? Spoke to her in words that echoed in her heart? She swallowed in the silence. 'Come, the fountain I want you to see is just up here.' The layers were coming off. But his layers weren't the only ones being peeled back. She'd not bargained on the fact that exposing him would also mean exposing herself.

It was quiet beneath the shade of the leafy canopy overhead, the sound of trickling water growing louder as they approached the end of the path. 'This is the Medici Fountain, one of the prizes of our park.' Her voice was quiet out of reverence for the solitude.

'It's beautiful.' Haviland spared a glance at the stonework, but his gaze rested on her and she had no doubt his words hadn't been for the fountain alone. 'Is this what you wanted to show me?' His eyes dropped to her mouth, silently encouraging.

'And I wanted to show you this.' She stretched up on her toes, arms wrapping around his neck as she brought her mouth to his. This time there would be no mistake about who was kissing whom and who had started it.

Chapter Eight

It was both easier and more difficult to fence Haviland on Thursday, two days later. Alyssandra had not bargained on this. She would have thought the sensation of kissing him would have waned by now. And, most certainly, fencing him should have been easier. After all, this time she knew what to look for in his attacks from the experience of having opposed him before; knew how he'd hold his body, how he'd move, how fast he'd be. But the distraction of him, of knowing that body and how it felt pressed to hers, was mentally overwhelming. No wonder Eve was not to have eaten from the tree of knowledge.

It took all her concentration to think about *flèches* instead of kisses while knowing full well he did not share the distraction. How could he? He thought he was facing her brother. He had no idea she was behind the mask. Yet, she sensed he carried his own distraction, too. The timing of his movements was off and he was dropping his shoulder more than usual.

Even so, it took her longer than she'd planned to defeat him. With a rather large sense of relief, her button pierced his shoulder in the same place. She put up her foil, nodding to Julian, and turned to make a quick departure as she had on Tuesday. Today, Haviland was ready for such an exit.

'Wait, aren't you going to explain to me how you do that?' he called before she reached the door. 'That's twice now, Leodegrance. There must be something you look for.' She did not turn. She kept moving. She could see in her mind the scene playing out behind her: Haviland stepping forward instinctively, wanting to follow her out, and Julian stepping between them. She could hear Julian as she slipped into the hallway.

'*Monsieur*, you were distracted today. Your movements were like an amateur's. *Mon Dieu!*' Julian picked up the instruction with a rapid cataloguing of Haviland's mistakes.

It was not unlike the discussion awaiting her in the viewing room. She had barely taken off the mask and tugged her hair out of its tight bun before Antoine voiced his disapproval. 'You weren't concentrating!' He turned his chair from the peepholes with a fierce turn, his features grim. 'If this is what one kiss has done, it is too dangerous! He nearly had you today.'

Alyssandra shrugged, trying to give a show of nonchalance. It wasn't what one kiss had done, it was what one moonlit garden, one afternoon stroll, a rather charged flirtation up against an oak tree and another kiss at a fountain had done. 'If he had, we would have told him it was planned, part of the lesson to work on something or other.'

'That's not good enough,' Antoine snapped. 'You are supposed to be *me*. My reputation is on the line when you fence like that.'

It was true. Antoine would never have been distracted by thoughts of hot kisses or by anything for that matter. One of his many skills in fencing was his single-minded focus. Once, during a championship match, a fire had started outside but Antoine had been oblivious to all of it—people screaming, the fire brigade throwing water—until he'd defeated his opponent. It had become part of the legend surrounding him. She would never have that level of concentration. Privately, she wasn't sure it was a great loss. She'd rather see a fire coming.

She gave her brother a patient smile. 'Everything ended as we wanted. Shall I tell Julian to instruct him on his dropped shoulder tomorrow?' It would pacify Haviland and keep him from charging out of the room demanding answers from an opponent who wouldn't speak to him.

Antoine nodded, calming down. 'I'll tell Julian myself. We need to meet afterwards anyway.' He paused. 'I think I must apologise. It was wrong of me to ask you to stay close to the *vicomte*. I never meant for you to jeopardise your virtue. I thought you would be safe with him. I should have known better. I've seen enough of them come through the *salle* on their Grand Tours. They're all looking for the same thing. Your charming *vicomte* isn't any different, much to my regret.'

But he *was* different. He talked of freedom. He had offered escape, not a bawdy roll in the sheets. But how did she articulate those things in terms that wouldn't worry Antoine? 'I'll manage him. I'm not fool enough to lose my head over a kiss,' Alyssandra said tightly. 'I think I will change and go home now. I have a few errands to run on the way.'

Alyssandra changed quickly in her brother's office, her movements fast and jerky as she pulled off her trousers and slid into half-boots and a walking dress, mirroring the rapid, angry thoughts rushing through her mind. She wasn't mad at Antoine. She was mad at herself. He was right. Today's lesson had teetered on the brink of disaster. She'd nearly been too distracted and a second's distraction was all it would have taken. At the first opportunity, she'd failed to maintain the professional objectivity she'd promised herself.

He was right, too, about the uselessness of encouraging Haviland's interest in her. Nothing good could come of it outside of preserving their secrets. She had seen rich, titled heirs just like him come through the *salle*. The Grand Tour was supposed to be a time of intellectual enlightenment for young men, a chance to learn about the highbrowed philosophies that governed other cultures and countries. Alyssandra suspected that was simply the justification wealthy families gave for sending young Englishmen abroad to rut and gamble and drink so they couldn't cause trouble at home.

Alyssandra grabbed her pelisse from a hook on the back of the door and her shopping basket. It was hard to imagine Haviland fitting the standard mould, however. He looked to be a few years older than the usual fare they saw. Most of those men were in their early twenties and far too young to appreciate any of the cultural differences they might encounter. In contrast, Haviland had a polished demeanor to him, a sophistication that could only be acquired with experience. And the way he'd talked about freedom in the park hinted at depths behind those blue eyes. But that changed nothing. Even if he turned out to be different than the usual passer-through, what could he offer her but a short *affaire* and a broken heart? He would leave. They *needed* him to leave.

Perhaps a short affaire *is best. What do you have to offer him or anyone for the long term? No one will want to take on an invalid brother-in-law,* the wicked argument whispered, tempting. She'd been so focused on Haviland, she hadn't spent much time thinking about her part in this equation. Alyssandra pushed open the door leading into the back alley behind the *salle* and stepped into the afternoon light. She couldn't leave Antoine in the immediate future. She might never be able to. Didn't Etienne prove as much?

'Alyssandra!' The sound of her name startled her out of her thoughts. The sight of the man who called it startled her even more. Haviland leaned against the brick wall across the narrow alley, his coat draped over one arm, his clothes slightly rumpled as if he'd changed in a hurry. He stepped towards her. 'I didn't mean to frighten you.' He took the basket from her arm. She could feel the heat of exertion through his clothes. He had indeed made a quick departure. How had he managed to escape Julian?

'I came down to bring my brother lunch. I just dropped it off.' Alyssandra improvised and gestured to the basket to give the fabrication credibility. 'Shouldn't you still be working with Monsieur Anjou?' According to the schedule, he was supposed to be with Julian for an hour to give her plenty of time to change and leave the building without *this* happening. Not that it mattered, she reminded herself. He didn't suspect anything. It wasn't unusual for a sister to want to bring her brother lunch.

'I had enough fencing for one day.' Haviland shook his head and gave a half smile. 'The lesson didn't go very well. Monsieur Anjou assures me I wasn't concentrating. I didn't stay long enough to hear everything else I did wrong.'

'Perhaps you weren't,' she teased, looping an arm through his and beginning to walk. It did occur to her that Julian and her brother were still inside. If they concluded their meeting, they would come out this door—this discreet door that hardly anyone knew about or paid attention to. She needed to get Haviland away from the exit before something happened she couldn't explain away.

'Your brother got me in the same place he got me on Tuesday, right in the centre of my shoulder. I must be doing something to leave myself open for it.' Haviland looked back over his shoulder towards the door. 'In fact, I was hoping to catch your brother afterwards and speak with him.'

She'd guessed as much. She gave him an exaggerated pout. 'I'm not sure that's what a girl wants to hear—that you've come looking for her brother, but not her.'

'I didn't know you would be here.' He smiled back and gave up on the door.

'Now that you *do* know, perhaps you'd like to accompany me on a few errands?' She told herself she was doing this for Antoine. If she didn't, he would exit the building sans mask, hefted in the arms of his manservant, and Haviland waiting to witness it. Haviland would learn the error was not in Antoine's face, but in his legs. Yes, all this was to protect the great ruse. But her pulse still raced at his nearness, at the thought of spending the afternoon in his company.

This would be new territory for her. She had not been in the company of such a gentleman. Most of her encounters had been at balls and soirées—in short, events that were heavily scripted, where everyone was expected to be on their best behaviour. She'd never been out in public, at a 'non-event' where there was no script except for the one the participants wrote between them. It was a new kind of freedom, and Alyssandra liked it. Even without the requirements of a ballroom, Haviland was solicitous. He carried her basket. He didn't show impatience when she debated, perhaps overlong, which bread to purchase at the *boulangerie*. He held the shop doors open for her.

He walked on the far side of the pavement to shield her from any traffic.

It was all done effortlessly. Alyssandra hardly noticed, so easily were these little tasks performed. Maybe she wouldn't have noticed at all if she'd come to expect such treatment. As it was, it was new to her. Etienne had never had an opportunity to do these things for her. Their meetings had always been at events or carefully chaperoned in her home. Antoine might have done such things for her if he could have. But this was clearly not new to Haviland. These choices were ingrained in his being and it was intoxicating, a further reminder of his polish, his sophistication. This was no boy wet behind the ears. If he was this polished in public, how he must shine in private.

She shot him a saucy, sideways glance, wanting to flirt a little. 'You're very good at a lady's errands. Is this part of your "persuasion"?'

He laughed. 'A master never tells his secrets.'

'I can think of other ways a gentleman might prefer to spend his afternoons,' she teased.

'Really?' He gave her one of his raised-eyebrow looks. 'I can't.' He could melt ice with that look.

What was it the old wives said about flattery? It got you everywhere? There was definitely some merit in that when done right and, in her estimation, Haviland was doing it right indeed. It was hard to resist his charm even when she knew she so obviously should.

They crossed a street, skirting the edge of the gardens. They were just a few streets from the *hôtel*, and a few streets from the end of her glorious afternoon. Shopping had never been this much fun. Her stomach growled. Instinctively, she pressed a hand to her middle, trying to squelch the embarrassingly loud reminder that she hadn't eaten since breakfast and not much at that. Breakfast had been a hard roll and cheese.

'Are you expected back soon?' Haviland asked, his hand falling to the small of her back, guiding her towards the park entrance instead of home. 'I was thinking we might stop and try some of that bread you debated over for so long and some of that cheese. Maybe even some of that wine if you don't mind drinking straight from the bottle.' His motions suggested he was not expecting any resistance.

She liked that—confidence in a man was always attractive. Not Julian's over-confidence, which was really a combination of ego and arrogance, but the assumption that he knew they were enjoying their time together and would mutually like to continue it. She was also wary of that confidence. She'd not forgotten he'd given something up to be with her this afternoon. Maybe he thought this would be another avenue for getting what he wanted: a meeting with her brother. She'd warned him about such a ploy once before.

They found a patch of grass away from the path in enough shade to keep their eyes from being blinded by the sun. Haviland made to spread out his coat for her, but she declined with a laugh. 'I'm not so delicate as to need something to sit on. The grass is fine.' To prove it, she sat down and tucked her legs beneath her. She welcomed it actually, this chance to sit on the ground and just be.

Haviland reached into the basket and took out the wheel of cheese. 'You might as well take out the sausage, too,' Alyssandra said and then realised the flaw in their impromptu picnic. Bottles could be drunk out of in the absence of glasses, but they absolutely could not sit there and simply bite off hunks of sausage and bread with their mouths. 'Oh, no! We don't have a knife.'

Haviland grinned and dug into his pocket. 'Yes, we do.' He flipped open a small silver knife. 'It won't be elegant carving, but it will do.' In that moment, she didn't care. It was enough to watch this man smile, to know that he was smiling at her, enough to cling to the knowledge that he'd been interested in her before he'd known who she was.

Haviland sawed through a slice of bread and cheese and handed it to her. *'Bon appétit*, Alyssandra.' His blue eyes twinkled. Good lord, he was handsome but that didn't mean she wasn't cautious.

She tilted her head to study him. 'Why are you doing this?'

Haviland bent his knee in a casual pose. 'Does there have to be a reason?'

'There usually is.' She didn't particularly want to know it, but she would probably be better off in the long run knowing it now instead of later.

Haviland chewed his bread. 'You know. Persuasion. I made you an offer of pleasure and escape. The offer is still on the table.'

'I already rejected it,' she reminded him.

Haviland arched a dark brow. 'You didn't mean it.' He leaned closer, over the basket of food between them, his hand cupping her cheek. His voice was a low whisper against her jaw. 'You kissed me at the Medici Fountain. That's the most unlikely rejection I've ever had.'

She closed her eyes and let herself drink in the scent of him, the touch of his hand against her skin, his voice a caress at her ear. 'Then there's this electricity that jumps whenever I'm near you, like it's doing now. That's not any form of rejection I've ever known.'

She drew a deep breath and let herself pretend it could be real a moment longer before she uttered the words that would break the spell. 'Does that electricity have anything to do with wanting to meet my brother? Do you think seducing me will gain you an introduction to the famed Antoine Leodegrance?'

She expected him to rear back, expected him to take her words as a blow to his honour. It was what a gentleman would do, lie or not. No gentleman in good conscience would admit to such a thing. Haviland did neither. His mouth found hers, his lips brushed hers.

'Is that what other men have led you to believe? What fools.' He breathed against her and deepened the kiss until she wanted to forget that she needed to refuse him, that she needed to exercise caution. Too much too soon and perhaps he wouldn't come back having had all he'd come for, or perhaps it would push him to ask his insatiable questions. 'You don't want to turn me down, Alyssandra, you're just not sure how to accept.'

Maybe just this once, she could indulge. She knew her boundaries, after all. Perhaps she was making too much of a fuss over it. She leaned into him and gave over to the kiss, over to him, part of her mind remembering how far back they were from the public path. There was no one to see. His hand was in her hair at the back of her neck, massaging, guiding her into the depths of his mouth. He tasted of spicy sausage and fresh bread, of sun and grass, and of Paris in spring—hope and heat and possibility.

Alyssandra reached for his cravat, tugging him to her, letting him press her back to the cool grass. His hands bracketed her head, his body half lay against hers, her arms about his neck. Madness welled in her, want surged at the feel of him hard against her stomach. The madness was in him, too. Amidst this desire it was easy to believe this wasn't about Antoine, after all, but about her and about him. A hand slid up her rib cage, cupping a breast, and she gave a sweet moan and arched against him. There was only pleasure for a moment, before it exploded into chaos.

'*Bâtard!* Get off her, you English swine!' A booted kick seem to come out of nowhere, catching Haviland in the stomach. He groaned and rolled, staggering to his feet as she scrambled to sit up. Her first instinct was to grab a weapon, anything. Haviland's knife was on the ground beside her. She curled her hand around the tiny hilt. If only she had her épée.

Haviland was still bent double, but his fists were

up, and he moved to stand between her and their attacker. There was no need for his chivalry or her puny weapon of a penknife. She recognised their attacker as he drove his fist into Haviland's jaw.

'Julian! Stop!' Alyssandra screamed, but neither man was interested in listening.

Chapter Nine

Haviland's head snapped back, taking the force of the blow. He vaguely registered Alyssandra's scream, but he was too enraged to heed it. He charged like a bull, burying his head into the midsection of the Frenchman. Julian went down, Haviland on top of him, delivering a few equalising punches.

'Haviland! Enough!' He was aware of hands tugging at him, trying to pull him off Julian Anjou. Alyssandra's hands. Some of the rage ebbed out of him at the realisation she was safe. There was no need for more violence unless Anjou chose to jump him again. He rose, straddling Anjou and dragging him to his feet. From the look on Anjou's face, Haviland wasn't so sure Anjou wasn't going to do just that.

'What do you mean by attacking a man without warning?' Haviland barked.

'That is hardly the greater crime here! You were all over her!' Julian roared. Haviland released him with a shake. It was a mistake to let Julian go. It gave the man a chance to focus on Alyssandra. 'And you!' He jabbed a finger her direction. 'You let him. That makes you a—'

Haviland stepped between Julian and his view of Alyssandra. 'I'd advise you to stop before you say something you regret.' His voice held unmistakable steel. He wouldn't mind punching Julian again—the slightest provocation would justify it.

Julian backed away, throwing one last threat at Alyssandra. 'Your brother will hear of this and he won't be pleased.'

With Julian gone, he could focus on Alyssandra. Haviland turned towards her. She was pale, but not entirely from fear or shock. There was anger in her eyes. 'Alyssandra, I am sorry—'

She cut him off sharply. 'Do *not* apologise. Neither one of us is sorry about what happened, only that we got caught. An apology makes at least one of us a hypocrite.'

True as that was, he knew better and to carry on so in a public place was unconscionable. One moment he'd been stealing a kiss, the next, things had progressed far beyond what he'd intended, but not beyond what he minded. Although perhaps he *should* mind if the consequence was getting hit in the face. His cheek was starting to throb now that the adrenaline had receded, and his lip was split.

'Julian had no right,' Alyssandra insisted, still fuming as she gathered up their picnic.

'Doesn't he?' Haviland crossed his arms and leaned against the tree trunk, watching her, thinking. He knew so little about her and yet he'd risked so much in those unguarded moments. 'It seems to me that he felt he did. Is there an understanding between the two of you?' He'd not considered that. Up until now, he'd been focused on her as merely the sister of his fencing instructor. He'd not thought of her as belonging to another. An Englishwoman would never have invited his attentions the way Alyssandra had if she was claimed by another. Maybe that was his mistake. This was France, after all, the country where husbands begged guests to flirt atrociously with their wives.

She stood and faced him, hands on hips, looking gorgeously defiant. Her hair had come down and now it hung in a long chestnut skein over one shoulder. 'There is an understanding between Julian and me, but not the sort you think.' She slid the basket on to her arm and handed him his discarded coat. 'Thank you for the afternoon.' Her tone was terse, perfunctory. 'Now, if you'll excuse me? I have to go home and clean up this mess.'

'I'll come with you. Perhaps I can explain.' Haviland shrugged into his coat. His split lip and bruised cheek could wait. He owed her this much. A gentleman didn't let a lady face scandal alone even if the scandal wasn't likely to leave the house.

She gave a harsh laugh. 'What do you think you'll explain, exactly? It's not as if Julian misunderstood what he saw. No, I don't think an explanation would improve the situation.' She stepped away from him, her voice quieter now, but no less sharp. 'It would be best if I did this alone. I am sorry if that thwarts your plans yet again to meet my brother. *Au revoir.*'

It didn't occur to Haviland until after she'd disappeared from sight that he might not see her again. Ever.

'She doesn't trust me,' he groused to his friends in the common room of their apartments, a cold rag held to his cheek.

'And you don't trust her. She hid her identity from you on purpose,' Archer reminded him, handing over another cold rag to replace the one he held. 'It seems you have something in common.'

'She thinks I am using her to meet her brother. Even today when I offered to walk her home and explain, she refused on the grounds that I was manipulating the situation into a meeting.' Lucifer's stones, he'd made a mess of things. He'd never been so ham-handed with a woman before. Usually, he was discreet, masterful, charming. His *affaires* were smooth associations. Women could and did trust his lead.

Brennan snorted from his corner of the room where he lounged casually in a chair, his shirt open, his waistcoat undone. It was nearing evening and he looked as if he'd just risen. 'What did you think you were going to explain? The angle of your tongue in her throat?'

Haviland threw him a quelling look and winced. It hurt his face to move. 'Don't be crass. It's not funny.'

'I disagree.' Brennan laughed. 'It's hilarious. It's the sort of the thing that happens to *me*, not you. I am going to enjoy the shoe being on the other foot. Thoroughly.' He pushed himself out of the chair. 'If you'll excuse me, I have to get dressed. I'm anticipating a busy night at Madame Ravenelle's.'

'Stay in the Marais, Bren,' Haviland cautioned out of habit. He couldn't go with Brennan tonight, and Brennan was in the routine of slumming in the more dangerous parts of the city. At least in their more aristocratic neighbourhood, Brennan would be safer. Although 'safe' was always a relative term when it came to him.

Brennan clapped him on the shoulder as he passed. 'I can take care of myself, old man. Don't worry. Take care of you. You'll have quite a bruise in the morning. I'm an expert at these things.' Then he grinned. 'Was she worth it?'

Haviland chuckled even though it hurt. 'Yes.' God, yes, she'd been worth Julian's fist in his face. Julian would look worse, though. It was a male sort of consolation.

Nolan raised his head from his book. 'She was worth it? Truly? I find it interesting you would say that about a woman you don't trust. It is as if you are saying "I trust whatever you are keeping hidden from me will not be damaging to me".'

'*This* is exactly why I like horses.' Archer sighed. 'Horses don't require cynicism. Your thoughts on human nature are so uplifting.'

Nolan shrugged. 'I'm sorry if the truth offends you. Humans require more cynicism than others in the animal kingdom.'

'More than wolves? I would have thought...' Archer began.

Haviland stood, grabbing a spare rag to take with him. He didn't particularly want to hear what Archer thought. He wasn't up to listening to Nolan and Archer debate wolves, horses and humans. He wanted to retreat, nurse his cheek and think in the privacy of his room where his friends couldn't voice their well-meant opinions.

Alyssandra Leodegrance had him spinning. She was beautiful and intriguing. It was the latter that concerned him most. What drew him to her? Where did the intrigue come from? Some women could naturally affect an air of mystery. Was she one of them or was there truly a mystery about her?

Haviland lay on his bed, eyes closed, his thoughts turning inward. He suspected the mystery had to do with what she wanted with him. She wanted him and yet she didn't. It was as if she was afraid to get too close. Her actions where he was concerned were things of contradictions. She'd signalled him to approach at the musicale, she'd gone into the garden with him knowing who he was. She'd kissed him knowing that, too, and yet she was reluctant to accept his offer for pleasure in full.

Today had followed much the same pattern. She'd spent the afternoon with him and then pushed him away when they had to confront the consequences of their brief indulgence.

He knew what Brennan would say. *She's using you for sex, reeling you in nice and slow until you're mad for her and nothing more. That's every man's dream. Embrace it.* It wasn't quite *his* dream, particularly. His dream was freedom. His dream was choosing his own destiny. A thought came to him. Haviland's eyes opened slowly, as if opening them too quickly would cause the idea to evaporate. Suddenly, he knew why she intrigued him. She'd not been selected for him by someone else. He'd chosen her. She was his choice alone.

Julian Anjou chose to remain near the long windows in the main foyer of the Leodegrance *hôtel* while he waited for Alyssandra to return. He schooled his anger, focusing instead on the green expanse of the back garden. Perhaps a nobler man would contain his emotions better, but he was not that man. He was a man who had pulled himself up the social ladder rung by painstaking rung with the talent of his sword. He might look like a gentleman on the outside after years of cultivation, but inside he was a scrapper from the streets and a desperate one at that.

So close and yet so far as the expression went. He had free access to the elegant, generations-old *hôtel* of the noble Leodegrances, he worked side by side with the *vicomte* himself. His own mother had been a washerwoman. She would have been beside herself with her son's success. But it was not enough for him. He understood how fragile his elevated status was, how precarious. He was not permanently bound to Antoine Leodegrance in any way and yet all his own status rested on Antoine's. Should the *salle* fail, should Antoine be exposed, Antoine would survive it in some fashion, reduced though it might be. But he would not. No one would care where he landed. Fencing instructors without references were cheaply come by.

Behind him he could hear the front door open and Alyssandra's voice as she passed her pelisse to a waiting footman. He turned from the window and watched her face pale when she saw him, but she did not try to evade him or his reason for being there.

'He will be gone in six weeks, what harm can come of it? I'll never see him again,' she said baldly, her dark eyes meeting his in challenge. She joined him at the window, unafraid. She was far too bold. If he was Antoine, he would have taken a strap to her and demanded obedience. This latest adventure of hers could ruin them all and for what? For a roll in the grass with an Englishman? For momentary pleasure? There were far safer ways to achieve those ends.

Julian exhaled, letting his mind clear. Anger would not endear him to her and that's what he needed—endearment, and if not that, at least tolerance. 'When I suggested we use feminine wiles to keep him from asking questions, I was not suggesting we use yours.'

Images from the park began to stir in his mind where he'd trapped them. He'd rather not think of her as he'd seen her this afternoon, her hair loose, her face flushed, her eyes closed, savouring her pleasure, the Englishman pressed against her. And that sound she'd made, that mewl of unmistakable delight. He wanted to be the one who offered her those pleasures. He could, too. If it was pleasure she was after, he had more than one talent to his repertoire. It might be time to remind her, get her to reconsider what he'd once offered her.

'I'm surprised you're here.' Alyssandra ignored his remark. Her tone was cool, but not entirely. There was concern beneath it. 'I didn't think you'd really tell Antoine.'

'And hurt him like that?' he queried. Alyssandra was a loyal creature. It would be worthwhile to stir that particular pot with a little guilt. 'Do you know what that would do to him?' Julian replied. 'He will not hear it from me that his sister was playing the harlot in the park.'

'Of course not.' Her words were filled with acid. 'It hardly suits your purposes.' She made to move past him, but Julian wasn't done. His hand shot out and gripped her arm. She was not going to walk away from him as if he were a servant, as if he didn't wager his fate every day on the twins Leodegrance. He deserved her respect.

'What are you running from? Are you afraid of what I'm going to say? Are you afraid I'm right? Only a coward would walk away and leave things unsettled.' Julian knew just where to poke her. She was a temperamental one, any dare would spark her tenacity. She wouldn't walk out of a room where her courage was in doubt.

She wrenched her arm free. It was the only defiance she could afford and he knew it. 'There is nothing you can say that would frighten me.'

'I hope so.' Julian softened his tone. He didn't want her angry, he wanted her confused, wanted her to doubt her attraction to the Englishman. 'It's not my intention to hurt you, Alyssandra. We are family, the three of us, we're all each other has. We all guard the same secret for the same reasons. The truth is, the Englishman is just using you. I'm not telling you anything you don't already suspect. He wants to get to your brother and you're his best chance.' He reached for her chin, trapping it between his thumb and forefinger, forcing her to meet his eyes. 'In your heart, you know this is true. He tried to follow you out of the salon today, thinking to speak to your brother. He was waiting in the alley for your brother today, not you. You were a surprise.'

'How did you know he was out there?' Alyssandra jerked her chin away, the answer coming to her before he could supply one. 'You followed me.' Her eyes flashed with accusation.

'I followed *him*,' Julian corrected. 'He left his lesson early, walked out on me, in fact. I suspected what he was up to and I was worried.' They were standing toe to toe now. The world had narrowed to just the two of them. He was conscious of the rise and fall of her breasts, of the scent of her. He had not been this close to her in ages. It was arousing even to fight with her. But he had to be careful. He didn't want to engender danger or she would never come to him.

'And you kept following us. You spied on us the entire afternoon! It's the only way you could have known where we were at.'

She was making him look obsessed. That was not the image he was going for. 'I was protecting you,' Julian answered swiftly. He dropped his gaze to the floor as if to appear humble, perhaps momentarily vulnerable before he dissembled. 'Your brother is not the only one who cares for you.' It had the desired effect. She closed her eyes and gave a tired sigh.

'Julian, we've been through this—' she began.

He held up a hand to stall her words. 'Don't say it, Alyssandra. I cannot stand by and let you throw yourself away on an Englishman who will offer you nothing. You are too fine, you deserve better than that and *I* know it. I doubt your Englishman does.' He left her then by the windows to ponder his warning, his offer, and strode off down the hall.

It was time to make his next move. He needed to speak with Antoine and start laying his groundwork. He just needed Antoine to take up his suit with Alyssandra once more—perhaps this time it would succeed. When he'd approached her before, it had been three years ago, during the early stages of Antoine's accident. In hindsight he could see it had been too soon. She hadn't been nearly desperate enough. She was full of hope that Antoine would recover. Frankly, so was he. But those hopeful days were long past. He wondered if Alyssandra had admitted her brother would never walk again. There would be no miracle. She needed to start planning the rest of her life. He needed to convince her he was part of that plan. Together, they could keep the charade up, the salon running until a son of their own could take over.

Who better to leave the *salle* to than Alyssandra's husband, his very own brother-in-law? If that happened, Julian needn't wait for a son to establish his claims. He could claim it outright. Truly, how long would Antoine last? Cripples didn't live long healthy lives and he'd already put in three years.

He knocked on the door to Antoine's study and stepped inside. 'I need to speak with you. It's about Alyssandra.'

Marriage to Alyssandra would solidify his dreams. He was so close and one damn Englishman wasn't going to get in his way.

Chapter Ten

'Alyssandra needs a husband.' Julian had meant the words to shock and they had. Antoine looked up from the papers spread before him, worry and confusion on his face. 'What? Why? Is she all right?' His instant concern almost made Julian laugh. Antoine was such an easy puppet to manipulate. Mention his beloved twin and he melted. It even took him a moment to notice. '*Mon Dieu*, Julian, what happened to your face?'

Julian took the chair on the near side of the desk, shrugging off the reference to his purpling eye. 'Just a small accident after you left the *salle* today. It is nothing. It looks worse than it is.' He reached for the decanter on the desk's edge. Sometimes Antoine took a little brandy for the pain. He helped himself to a glass. They'd become equals, partners, over the past three years. Older than Antoine by seven years, Julian had painstakingly cultivated the complex role of mentor, friend, uncle-cum-older brother when the case demanded it. Antoine had bought into it whole-heartedly first during his grief over his father's death and then in the throes of despair after his accident. Today, he was claiming that role to the hilt: taking a chair without permission, helping himself to the brandy—an equal interacting with another peer.

'It's time she marries,' Julian repeated. 'A husband, a family, is what she needs. She's twenty-eight. Most of her friends have long since wed.'

'I know.' Antoine's eyes were thoughtful. 'I've been thinking about it for a while now. Perhaps it's time to give up the ruse and accept the fact that I will never walk again. We could sell and Alyssandra could go on with her life.'

Julian interrupted abruptly. This was not where he'd imagined the conversation heading. If Antoine were to sell, it would be devastating to him. 'Why not have the best of both worlds?' he prompted in silken tones. The *salle d'armes* was Antoine's other weak-ness. It meant the world to him. He must be worried indeed about Alyssandra if he was willing to con-sider giving it up. 'Keep the *salle*, you can "retire" if you like, but let Alyssandra and I run it as husband and wife. I am offering myself as a husband for her.' He said it quietly, humbly, watching Antoine's eyes lose some of their softness and become shrewdly as-sessing.

'You?' Antoine said.

'Yes. Who better? I have been with your father and with you. All total, I've spent twelve years in the service of your family. I have known Alyssandra since she was sixteen. I have been with you through death and through despair. What better than to have your sister marry your friend and keep your father's fencing legacy, *your* fencing legacy, alive? Some day, there may even be a nephew to look after that legacy.'

Antoine smiled at that, as Julian had known he would. Family was important to Antoine. 'What does Alyssandra think?'

Julian shrugged. He chose his words carefully. This answer had to be handled delicately. 'She's a wild creature. I don't know that her opinion is the one that matters most here. She may not know what is best for her over the long term.'

Something affirmative moved in Antoine's brown eyes, and he gave the most imperceptible of nods. Julian pushed his advantage. 'I fear her head may be turned by the Englishman. He is a fine figure of a man,' Julian offered. 'But I think it is nothing more than a sign of how lonely she is, how ready she is to move on with her life. It is too bad Etienne DeFarge has wed.' The reference to Alyssandra's old fiancé would make Antoine feel guilty.

'I like the Englishman, although I'm not sure of his motives. So many of them are just passing through,' Antoine said tentatively but it was enough to ring alarms.

'I'm sure North is a fine man. He's a real man's man. The other men at the *salle* seem to enjoy him,' Julian put in blandly, wondering what Antoine was thinking. He took a swallow from his snifter, hoping Antoine would elaborate.

'He has desirable qualities; a title in England, wealth, good manners,' Antoine mused out loud. Julian wanted to argue the last. Those manners had his hands on Alyssandra and his tongue in her mouth. 'Alyssandra is not without recommendations of her own. He would be a good match for her, and the *salle* could use him.'

Julian felt his insides freeze. He'd been right not to tell Antoine about the park. It would be all the provocation Antoine would need to start negotiating a marriage. He'd not counted on this. Antoine agreed with him on marriage, but not on the groom, and now Antoine was thinking of giving the Englishmana place at the *salle* too. Julian's ego didn't like that one bit. He was the senior instructor and he didn't like to share, which was precisely what he'd be doing.

Julian gave a sigh. 'That's a nice fantasy, Antoine, but I don't suppose it will work, do you? He's a viscount, heir to an earldom. He's not going to want to *work* as a fencing instructor.'

Antoine was far too quick to clarify. 'Of course not! He would be an owner. If he married Alyssandra, I could leave the *salle* to them and you certainly. I could retire and you could carry on. He could show up and offer instruction whenever he felt like it, make it a hobby for himself. He's talented enough.'

Julian took a healthy swallow of brandy. This was getting worse by the minute. It would be complete torture to have to answer to Haviland North at the *salle* every day, knowing North was going home to Alyssandra every night. He'd have to live every day with the man who'd taken everything from him. That was a lot of 'everys' and it was not to be borne.

'I think you're forgetting one thing.' Julian gave a sad half smile as if commiserating with Antoine. 'He'll want to go home some day. He'll have to go home when he inherits. There wouldn't be much good in that for us.' This was the second time Antoine had mentioned retiring. It was a bit disconcerting.

Antoine nodded his head. 'Well, still, it's a nice fantasy to think of Alyssandra with him, happy, safe, secure. I think she fancies him, and he'd be a fool not to fancy her.'

There was nothing left to say. Antoine seemed determined to ignore his own offer and now was clearly not the time to push it. Julian could only hope a few of his doubts would take root in Antoine's thoughts. Meanwhile, he needed a secondary plan. Alyssandra could not marry a man who wasn't there, nor could Antoine hire a man who couldn't fence well. It might be time to call in a few favours from the streets. With the tournament nearing, there would be ample opportunity to eliminate Haviland North.

Haviland was not going to let one Frenchman stand in the way of his training. Or maybe two Frenchmen depending on how Leodegrance had taken the news about the park. Haviland couldn't imagine him taking it well. He squared his shoulders as he entered the Leodegrance *salle d'armes* on Rue Saint Marc.

He was unsure of his reception. Perhaps it was good news he had yet to receive a challenge. He had no desire to fight a duel with the master. For one, the outcome would be uncertain at best. He had yet to beat the master in their lessons. And two, fighting a duel abroad over a foreign woman was exactly the type of scandal his family had prodigiously avoided for generations. His father would be appalled if news of such a thing reached English shores. It would validate all the reasons his father wanted to keep him close to home. 'Going abroad to sow wild oats suggests there's something wrong, something that can't be aired in public at home,' he'd argued on more than one occasion when Haviland had brought up his desire for freedom.

Inside, the *salle* was busy, filled with the clash and slide of steel on steel. It was mid-afternoon and all three fencing salons were busy with clients, pupils and day guests. The sight brought a smile to his face and he allowed himself a moment to drink it all in. Whatever else the reclusive Leodegrance might be, he'd certainly made a little world for himself here. From the moment Haviland had first entered the *salle*, he'd felt the energy of the place. To his right was the long day salon with its medieval shields and antique swords decorating the walls to set a tone of respect. This was the place where clients could pay by the day to use the services of the *salle*. Haviland had noticed the price was slightly more than the other *salles* in the city, but perhaps that increased the prestige. The fee included the use of the *salle*'s changing rooms and its weapons for those who didn't have their own.

In the centre was the large main salon for members

only. It looked more like a ballroom with its two enormous chandeliers at either end. Weapons and fighting equipment through the ages adorned these walls too, interspersed with silver cups set in niches bearing testimony to the greatness of Antoine Leodegrance and his father before him. The elegance, the trophies, the historic weaponry only a noble family would possess were all subtle, or perhaps not-so-subtle reminders that the fees for this club were well worth it.

Not for the first time, Haviland felt a stab of envy for the eccentric Leodegrance. This *salle* was his. It might have been his father's before him, but he'd maintained it through his hard work and his talents. It was a different kind of accomplishment than simply inheriting estates others ran for you. To do what you loved every day and see those efforts grow into a place like this, now that would be a legacy.

The third salon was smaller than the other two and more private. This was where Julian held his lessons, where Leodegrance met with the elite pupils. He would go there later and seek out Julian for his latest lesson, but for now he'd join the other members in the main salon.

The others present were glad to see him. Of course, they were unaware of the contretemps in the park. Haviland soon found himself engaged in a few bouts, helping another member master his *in quartata*. During his time here, he'd discovered he had an aptitude for teaching. Helping others with their fencing was something he enjoyed doing. 'Don't turn too far,' Haviland instructed. 'Turn to the inside, bend at the waist and get your left foot behind you so you can deliver a counter-attack. Perhaps if you moved your feet like this.' Haviland demonstrated.

'Too much footwork! Do you want to fence like an Italian, Pierre?' Julian's harsh tones broke in, scolding the younger man although Haviland knew the scold was directed at him as well. Haviland turned to face the surly senior instructor. He stifled a smile. He'd been right. Julian did look worse. True, he was sporting a bruised jaw of his own but that could almost be overlooked. There was no overlooking Julian's purple eye which stood out against his paler skin. 'You fence like the Italian school.' Julian spat the words in disgust at him. 'In the French school, it's all in the wrist.' *If you were a real Frenchman and not some upstart* Anglais, *you'd know that.* Haviland could almost hear the hidden derogatory message being spoken out loud.

'Are you ready for your lesson?' Julian queried coolly. The question was designed to remind everyone just who was the instructor and who was the pupil. 'Although it looks as if someone already gave you one.'

'And yourself?' Haviland enquired politely. 'Did someone give you a lesson, too?' There were a few nervous snickers from those who'd gathered around to watch. Julian's talent might have won him respect from the members, but his cutting wit hadn't won him many friends. Left with no response, Julian narrowed his eyes to a glare.

In the private salon, Julian set to the lesson with

brisk efficiency. 'Today, we will study the methods of the Spanish school.' He began pacing the floor with an occasional flourish of his rapier. 'We have a few Spaniards coming to the tournament and no doubt they will be eager to show that their methods are superior. If at all possible, you must have some ability to anticipate their moves. If you have done your reading, you will know that Carranza's *La Destreza* system has been the leading influence on Spanish swordplay for nearly three hundred years.' This was said as a challenge, as if to expose an intellectual weakness.

Haviland decided to go on the offensive. He picked up his foil and joined Julian's circling so that now they circled each other. 'The primary difference between the Spanish and Italian schools is that the Spanish focus on defence whereas the Italian school focuses on attacks,' Haviland answered. He'd done his homework. One of the many aspects he liked about the salon was the clubroom, an elegant gentleman's gathering place where fencers could meet for a drink or take advantage of the excellent library lining the walls. The library contained nearly every known treatise on fencing from all the major schools in Europe and even a few texts on the katana from Japan.

'Very good.' Julian gave him a begrudging nod. He stepped back and went to the weapons cupboard, unlocking it with a key and pulling out two rapiers. He handed one to Haviland. 'Then you will also know these are Spanish rapiers. You are not required to compete with one, but you should know what kind

of weapon your opponent is using, how it manoeuvres, how it feels in his hand.'

Haviland took the blade, noting the difference in
design. The Spanish rapier had a cup hilt that covered the hand. He tested it, giving a few experimental
thrusts. It was lighter and shorter. It would definitely
have an advantage in a longer bout where arm stamina might become an issue, but it would also be at
a disadvantage against the reach of a longer French
blade.

They worked throughout the lesson on the Spanish
defences until Haviland was sweat-soaked. Whatever
he thought of Julian Anjou, the man knew his fencing. 'Will I see Leodegrance on Thursday?' Haviland
asked casually as they put their blades away.

'I do not know. He has not told me if he has time.'
Julian did not look at him. It was impossible to know
if he was lying. 'He is very busy organising the tournament. There is much to be done.' He gave a shrug.
'There is plenty you and I can work on in the meanwhile.' Julian gave him a hard look. *Jusque à demain.'*

'No,' Haviland said with quiet fierceness. 'We are
going to talk about her. We are not going to pretend
Leodegrance is too busy to meet with me because of
the tournament and we are not going to pretend you
didn't ambush me in the park yesterday because I
was kissing her.'

Julian's face was a study of subdued anger. 'You
misunderstand the situation. We are not talking about

her because doing so would validate the absurd idea
that you have any claim on her.'

'And you do?' Haviland took an unconscious step
towards Anjou, his body tensing, fists clenching.

'I have been with the family for years. I will be
with them long after you've left,' Julian said tersely.
'If you would exit the room, *monsieur le vicomte*? I
have another lesson.'

The situation was deuced odd. Haviland took a
chair in the clubroom close to the bookshelves, nodding for the waiter to bring him a drink. It wasn't
that he *wanted* to fight Leodegrance in a duel, but
it did appear strange that there'd been no outrage on
the man's part. If he had a sister, he'd have been furious. The family would have required marriage. Yet
Leodegrance was acting as if nothing happened. Had
Julian told him?

Ah. Haviland took a swallow of the red wine. It
was starting to make sense. Julian hadn't reported
the incident for exactly that reason. Seeing Alyssandra married to an Englishman wasn't what Julian
wanted. He wanted Alyssandra for himself. That's
why there hadn't been any repercussions. Antoine
Leodegrance didn't know.

'*Monsieur*, a message.' The waiter extended a
salver towards him bearing a single folded sheet of
heavy white paper.

Haviland took it and thanked him, waiting until
the man left before he read it. A little smile played
along his mouth, he could feel his lips twitching with
it. He was to meet Alyssandra at Madame LaTour's

salon that evening. It was further confirmation Julian hadn't told Leodegrance. She'd never be allowed out of the house otherwise. A silver lining indeed, although not without an edge of madness to it. Alyssandra Leodegrance had proven to be dangerous to his health. Surely, there were far easier seductions to be had.

She must be mad to seek him out so boldly. Alyssandra wove a path through the guests crowded into Madam LaTour's Egyptian-themed drawing room, discreetly searching the room for any sign of him. Dancing had started and the sidelines were a crush of people as room was made for the dancers. It was early yet, far too soon to conclude he hadn't come. Although, such a conclusion was within the scope of possibility. Why should he come? The last time she'd invited him to come with her, he'd ended up with a bruised jaw and publicly brawling. She doubted the handsome, mannerly Viscount Amersham had ever resorted to public brawling. He'd known how to bloody his knuckles, though. So many gentlemen were useless outside the *salle d'armes*. But he'd known how to use all that muscle in practical application. He could defend a woman. Not that she needed defending. Still, it was nice to know he could. And, more importantly, that he *would*. A woman would be safe with him in all ways. Perhaps that was why she'd risked the invitation. She would be safe with him, body and honour both.

Alyssandra slipped outside onto the veranda at the

first opportunity. The fresh air was welcome after the heat of the drawing room. It was a chance, too, to escape the gossips. Julian might not tell Antoine about the park, but that didn't ensure the gossip tonight wouldn't reach Antoine's ears if someone saw her with the Englishman. It stood to reason that if she was with him, Antoine must condone him as an escort. Anyone who knew them well knew Antoine to be a socially reclusive but protective brother when it came to her welfare.

Alyssandra unfurled her fan, this time a white one painted with pink roses to match the rose of her gown. She would rest here for a moment and go back inside to dance with friends and to wait. And to see. If he would come.

'I knew I'd find you out here.' His voice was low and sensual at her ear, his hands at her shoulders ever so briefly. She could smell the vanilla and spice of his soap. All men should smell this good. She closed her eyes for just a moment to take it all in in her mind before he stepped back.

'How did you know I'd be outside?' She turned with a smile, her eyes skimming his face for signs of yesterday's altercation. It was hard to see any damage in the dark. She had seen Julian, though, and it made her cringe. She didn't like thinking of Haviland being hurt because of her.

'I would know you anywhere.' It was a lie, of course. She fooled him enough times in the practice room. In there, he had no idea who was behind the mesh mask. He grinned and she could make out the remnants of his split lip, but just barely.

She reached out her fingertip to it. 'Ouch!' Haviland scolded, jerking his head back.

'Does it hurt?'

'Only when people touch it.' He laughed and then turned serious. 'Am I to understand your brother remains unaware?'

'Yes. It doesn't serve Julian's purposes to bring yesterday to Antoine's attention.'

Haviland nodded. 'I figured as much. Still, I don't like secrecy or the idea that we have to sneak around. It seems deceptive. Perhaps I could call on him and formally ask permission to take you driving in the park or to escort you to these sorts of gatherings.'

Her stomach clenched. *This* was hardly deceptive. She could only imagine how he would feel about *the* deception. *If* he ever found out. Another thought came to her. 'I think the sooner you can accept the fact that my brother will not meet with you, the sooner we can move forward.'

'We're back to that again?' Haviland's eyes darkened, his body stiffening. 'You insult my honour to imply I am using you for an entrée.' His mouth came down close to her ear, the harshness of his voice roughly erotic. 'You know damn well I wanted you before I knew your name.'

'How do I know that hasn't changed?'

'*You* sent me the invitation.' He growled, his teeth nipping the lobe of her ear, sending a delicious trill down her spine. 'Now it's my turn. There's a carriage parked at the kerb, pulled by two matched greys. If you believe me, get in. The driver knows where to go. He will wait only fifteen minutes.'

Her throat went dry at the implication. One choice and everything would change.

Chapter Eleven

Get in the carriage. Don't get in the carriage. It was somewhat amazing how one simple decision could set in motion a series of significant events. But she'd been making 'simple' decisions about Haviland North since she met him: going to Madame Aguillard's musicale, unfurling her fan, taking a walk in the gardens. All were simple decisions and all had led to this moment of choice. Would she make one more simple decision that would move her forward on this path?

Her feet registered the decision before her mind. She was already moving towards the entrance before she fully realised the import of the decision. What she meant to do was reckless. She'd had a lover before, but not an *affaire*. She and Etienne had been together two years. They'd meant to marry. They would have, too, if not for Antoine's accident. An *affaire* was terminal. There would be an end—such a liaison *began* with that assumption in mind. It was the end that contained the risk. How would it end? With her heart still intact? With Haviland angry and knowledgeable of the deception that had been perpetrated on him? With Haviland happily naive to the drama around him and moving on to his summer in Switzerland?

Alyssandra came up short at the top of the steps leading down to the kerb, partygoers moving about her as people entered and exited the mansion. The carriage was there, an expensive, shiny black-lacquered vehicle complete with glass windows and lanterns. Two greys pranced in their traces, eager to be off. Seeing tangible proof made the decision real. Twenty more feet and there'd be no turning back.

The decision might be reckless, but that didn't mean it hadn't been thought out. Being with Haviland would mean far more to her than it would to him. He would go on to be with other women, she would be one of many to him if she wasn't already. A man like him must have women begging for his attentions. But she would live on this for ever. The coachman pulled out a watch to check the time, and she felt a surge of urgency. He was getting impatient. Had fifteen minutes passed already? What if she missed the carriage?

Then she would miss it—her one chance to date at experiencing true, unbridled, physical passion. She didn't hold out much hope there'd be other opportunities. Tonight had been Haviland's gauntlet thrown down. There would be no more arguing over trust and motives. If she did not take the carriage, he would not ask again. All would be settled between them whether she liked that settlement or not. Haviland North was not a man to be toyed with. Nor was he a man who tolerated having his word challenged.

Alyssandra hurried down the steps. It was time to be reckless. What had caution ever done for her anyway? The coachman nodded at her approach. A footman waiting at the kerb lowered the steps and helped her in. It all seemed so disturbingly normal when she felt as if the phrase 'I'm off to a clandestine rendezvous' was scrawled across her forehead.

The interior of the carriage bore out its external luxury with plush grey-velvet seats and matching draperies held back with maroon ties. But the carriage was disappointingly empty. Haviland was not inside. She supposed discretion demanded he be picked up at a separate destination a distance away from the venue, but she was disappointed all the same. Now that she'd decided to take his invitation, she wanted that invitation to begin right now.

She didn't have to wait long. The carriage pulled over three streets later to pick up Haviland, who managed to look urbane and quite comfortable with these arrangements as if he had assignations all the time. For all she knew, he probably did. He certainly *could*, anyway.

Haviland took the rear-facing seat across from her and gave the signal to move on, a rap of his walking stick on the carriage ceiling. He reached under the seat and drew out a thick lap robe of luxurious fur. 'Are you cold?' He settled the blanket across her knees. The warmth felt good and helped to quiet her nerves. Spring evenings and pending anticipation had their own special brand of chilliness.

'I thought we would drive for a while and enjoy the evening. Then, I have some place I would like to show you.' Haviland reached under the seat and pulled out a basket this time. 'I have champagne and if we drink it now, it should still be cold.'

His dexterity was nothing short of amazing. He managed to pop the cork *and* pour two glasses without spilling while the carriage moved over the rough cobblestones of the Paris streets. 'Years of practice.' He handed her a glass with a wink, and she had the feeling that 'years of practice' referred to far more than pouring champagne.

'Pour champagne for women in carriages often, do you?' she teased, sipping carefully from her glass.

Haviland laughed and had the good grace to look slightly abashed. 'I am hoist by my own petard, as the expression goes. Can I just answer "maybe" and leave it at that?'

'Absolutely. A gentleman with a bit of mystery to him is far more intriguing than an open book.' She smiled and risked clinking her glass against his—a difficult manoeuvre to accomplish in a moving carriage without spilling. She liked him this way; more relaxed, less intimidating than he was at the *salle*. It was the way he behaved around the men in the members' salon. She'd seen him in there on occasion working with others. He was a natural leader even in casual circumstances. It was how he'd been the day he'd come on her errands, as if a mask had been stripped away. When he was with Julian and even with 'her brother' he was different. In those lessons, he exuded a formality, an intensity that was as magnetic as his casual charm. She wondered which persona he'd bring to the bedroom.

'As is mystery in a woman, up to a point.' His eyes held hers, blue and intense over the rim of his glass. *Mon Dieu*, those eyes of his could sell a line. 'I think the mystery lures a man in, but after a while, he wants to know more and that desire for knowledge outweighs the desire for mystery.' That was the urbane rake in him delivering a practised line for certain—a remark designed to compliment and pursue, to bring a woman into his circle of sophistication.

Even knowing it, she couldn't stop a thrill of excitement from racing down her back. Still, she would not be an easy conquest. She might have agreed to this assignation and they both might be fully aware of the evening's intended conclusion, but she didn't have to be a quivering blancmange just because he was handsome and silver-tongued beyond reason.

Haviland looked out the window. 'Pont Neuf. Right on schedule. I thought we could take a walk. It's still just early enough in the evening to be safe out.'

Alyssandra laughed. It was only ten o'clock, early by Parisian standards. 'The streets aren't truly dangerous until after midnight. Surely, London streets are no different.'

Haviland jumped down to set the steps. He reached out a hand to help her down. 'They're wider though. For such a modern city, Paris has the narrowest of streets. I think a medieval merchant could walk through town and find the city unchanged in many regards.'

'I think that's true of most European cities.' Alyssandra stepped down onto the pavement. 'You will find Florence much the same.' She thought she detected the fleetest of grimaces. In the gaslight, it was difficult to be sure. It might have been a trick of shadow and light. 'You are going on to Italy, are you not?'

He smiled, and she felt sure the grimace had been nothing more than shadows. 'It is one of my greatest wishes.' He tucked her hand through his arm and signalled the driver to meet them on the other side of the bridge. They began to stroll, joining other couples taking the evening air. She had not been out like this for years and it was intoxicating; to be out with this man, in this place. The Seine was dark below them, smooth and still, the gaslights lining the stone vestibules of the bridge, casting a kind light on everything around them.

'I meant it, a few minutes ago, about trading mystery for knowledge.' His voice was low, weaving privacy about them even in public. 'Tell me about yourself, Alyssandra. Have you always lived in Paris?'

'The Leodegrances have a country home in Fontainebleau. We were raised there, but we've lived primarily in Paris since I was eighteen.' No need to mention that living in town allowed them to close up the country house and economise. The beautiful home in Fontainebleau was too big to keep open for just two people. It was enough of a financial commitment to live in the family *hôtel*.

'The *salle d'armes* occupies a great deal of your brother's time, but what about you? What do you do all day?'

'It might surprise you, but my days aren't much different than yours.' She offered him a coy smile and stepped into one of the vestibules, out of the flow of pedestrian traffic. She didn't want to lie to him, but she wasn't above distracting him when questions became more akin to an interrogation.

'*You* might be surprised what I spend my days doing.' His words were husky. His eyes darkened, his gaze falling on her mouth. 'I think about doing this.' His mouth took hers in a firm press of a kiss, and then another one. 'And this,' he whispered against her mouth. His hands fell to her waist, drawing her against him, his touch low and intimate on her hips where his thumbs imprinted themselves through the thin chiffon of her gown.

In the distance, she could the hear strains of a roving musician's violin. Haviland heard it, too. 'Perfect,' he murmured against her throat. He began to move in a slow circle of a dance, his hands still at her hips, his lips still at her neck, her ear, her lips. She moved, too, her arms lifting about his neck, her body swaying with his. This was like no ballroom waltz or indeed like any dance she'd experienced. This was intimate and close. This was bodies pressed together, the hard planes of him against the soft curves of her. This was two people falling into each other.

She could drink in the whole of him; she could taste the lingering fruity tang of champagne in his mouth, smell the spice and vanilla of his soap, feel the power of him where their bodies met. Her fingers dug into the depths of his dark hair, her body hungry for every inch of him.

This was precisely what she'd wanted when she'd issued her invitation: to forget who she was for a while and a man who could help her do it. Tonight was for her, not to talk about Antoine, or the *salle*, not to think ahead to the next day's lessons. It was just to enjoy, to feel alive again.

The music ebbed as the violinist passed into the street beyond the bridge. Their dance ended. She rested her head against the wool of his jacket, reluctant to step back just yet. Here on the bridge, surrounded by strangers who were too wrapped up in their own lives, their own romances, she was anonymous. She could do as she pleased in a way Antoine Leodegrance's sister never could.

'I know a place we can go.' Haviland's voice was low at her ear, whispering temptation.

'Yes.' Her own response was not more than a whisper of its own. She hoped it wasn't far. They crossed the remainder of the bridge in silence, hands interlaced, his grip firm and warm, her body awake, every nerve on edge, alert and raw to even the slightest sensations. She *needed* satisfaction.

In the carriage, they drank the rest of the champagne. The ride was short. The carriage came to a rolling halt and his eyes met hers over the empty glasses, the intensity of his gaze proof he was as primed for this as she, his eyes two intense blue flames, his body taut with wanting. It was flattering in a primal sense to be desired by such a man.

Haviland handed her out and she looked up at the building in question. It was an elegant building in a prestigious neighbourhood. 'Your place?' she asked quietly. Only a man for whom prices were no object could afford quarters like these.

Inside matched her expectations—expensive carpets, airy rooms in a city that was cramped for space. Behind her, Haviland lit a lamp. 'This is the common area, my room is this way.' She liked the feel of his hand at her back, confident and strong, as they made their way down the hall. He pushed a door open revealing a room dominated by a tall four-poster bed with carved pillars and dressed in pale-green damask linens. French doors on the side led out to a small garden.

Haviland left her for a moment to shut the door and set the lamp down on the bureau. It was a beautiful room for seduction, for making love. She wandered to the bed, a hand reaching out to caress the coverings. A decorative pillow covered in satin and trimmed with dangling crystal beads lay in the centre of it. Useless, but beautiful. They hadn't had such luxuries at the Leodegrance *hôtel* for years now. The heat in her began to build again, subdued momentarily by the intermission of the carriage ride. The bed conjured a thousand fantasies on its own, of rolling entwined among the rich fabrics.

Haviland turned towards her, playing the host. 'Would you like something to drink? There is more champagne. We've fallen in love with it, all four of us, and laid in cases. Perhaps something to eat? Our cook always leaves something in the larder.'

She shook her head, locking eyes with him.

He gestured to the two chairs set near the French doors. 'We could talk.'

Alyssandra let a smile slip across her face as she crossed the room to him. She let her hips sway. She pressed a finger to his lips before he could say another word. She kissed him once on the mouth, hard, and then stepped back, pulling her hair free of its butterfly clip in one deft movement. She let it fall, her tongue running across her lips. 'I don't want to talk, Haviland.'

Chapter Twelve

'*I don't want to talk, Haviland.*' Good Lord. Was there a more seductive line in the whole world? His entire body was on full alert. He watched her hair fall and his groin hardened. He shouldn't be surprised. *She'd* sent the invitation after all.

'Alyssandra.' His voice was a rasp, made hoarse by desire.

A knowing smile spread across her face. She knew precisely how she was affecting him, the vixen. She wet her lips in a slow, passing lick, her eyes locked on his. 'Shall I undress you first?'

She didn't wait for an answer, but moved towards him. Her hands rested at the waistband of his trousers, her fingers warm against his skin where they curled inside the band, tugging at the tails of his shirt until they were free. Her hands moved beneath the fabric, sure and confident, sliding up his torso, over his nipples. Her touch was a hint of the intimacy to follow, of being skin to skin. But the most searing aspect of her play was her eyes—dark flames that held his with a bold message: *I know what I'm doing to you, I want to watch you come apart under my hands, under my mouth.* He would, too, Haviland had no doubts of that. It was just a matter of when.

He cupped her face between his hands, taking her mouth in a full kiss. She answered aggressively, her teeth sinking into the tender flesh of his lower lip, her hands working his shirt open, pushing it from his shoulders. Then her hands were on him, on his chest, her thumbs stroking the nipples they'd so recently glided over in an effort to divest him of his shirt.

He kissed her hard, his hands taking possession of her waist, his thumbs reaching to stroke the underside of her breasts, sending a bold message of his own. He would be no passive lover. She could not play him without consequence. For every stroke, every caress she used to heighten his arousal and prolong his desire, he would apply himself in equal measure. His arousal would become her arousal, his waiting would become her waiting.

She gave a little moan as his tongue found hers, their mouths hungry, devouring one another as desire spiked. He could feel her breaths come shorter, her excitement rising. Her hands were rough at his waistband, fumbling with his trousers, her movements no longer focused, premeditated strategies of arousal. He knew a moment's pleasure at having distracted her, of knowing her desire for him was no longer a calculated thing, but something organic that was taking on a life of its own.

The moment was short lived. Her hand closed about his length, firm as she began to stroke him. She had the advantage just now. Haviland could not remember a time when he'd been handled so boldly, so enticingly. She pushed him with a gentle shove into the chair waiting by the French doors, kneeling before him, pulling his trousers down his legs. She ran her hands along the sensitive skin of his inner thighs, spreading him for more pleasure. Her eyes glittered mischievously before their gazes broke and she dropped her head between his legs. She took him in her mouth with a dilettante's skill; slowly at first, her tongue laving his head, her mouth sucking before it travelled his length inch by sensual inch.

He gripped the arms of the chair, fighting the urge to slide, the urge to explode. Her fingers squeezed the sac behind his phallus, and he nearly lost the fight. But losing would mean ending this and he was loath, oh, so loath to see this glorious torture end. And yet his body was priming to return the favour, such as it was. He wanted this—her mouth on him, her hand on him—but he wanted her beneath him, too, wanted her writhing as he did, wanted her eyes to go dark, wanted moans to escape her mouth in acknowledgement of what *he* could do to her, for *her*.

His eyes were shut tight, his senses overwhelmed when his body began to pulse, his balls drawing up tight. He felt her warm mouth leave him so she could catch his release in her hand. Once, twice, three times, four, five, he convulsed against her palm. His breath came ragged and short and when he looked at her it very nearly didn't come at all. He'd expected the smug superiority of a victorious woman, but the look she wore was one of amazement, the classic lines of her face soft with awe as if they'd witnessed something significant together, *done* something significant together.

Haviland leaned forward, taking her face in his hands, and kissed her softly in recognition of it. 'I am naked and you are not,' he whispered against her cheek. 'We must rectify that immediately.'

Laces loosened, silk slid. Alyssandra could not have said when her dress had fallen, or when her undergarments joined it in a heap on the floor. All of her senses were riveted on the feel of his fingertips against her skin, the pressure of his mouth on hers. It was a wicked sort of heaven to press against him, skin to skin, to feel him rise hard and strong against her stomach without any barriers between them.

He swept her up into his arms in a slow fluid motion and made the short journey to the high, gloriously bedecked bed, depositing her amid the luxurious pillows as if she were a precious gem. 'All the better to see you.' The gravel of Haviland's voice sent a tremor of anticipation through her.

'And you, too.' Alyssandra tucked a hand behind her head and held his eyes before letting her gaze drop slowly down the length of him. The lamp favoured him with light and shadows, showing off the carved perfection of his torso, the sculpted muscle of his abdomen, the masculine contours of his lean hips with their defined, square bones. 'A man can be such a beautifully made creature.' Haviland North was definitely that. Years of physical exercise had created the masterpiece standing in front of her.

'But you, Alyssandra, you are a goddess.' He came to the bed then and stretched his length down beside her. She fought a moment's self-consciousness. This was so much more intimate than standing naked together. Then they could only *see* the other's face. But now, he could see all of her, could reach all of her and he did. Haviland's fingers started a slow journey down her body, drawing heat where he touched her, drawing desire.

Haviland North was a tactile lover. With him, it was all about touch, how he could make her *feel*, and she revelled in it; the feathering caresses that ran from breastbone to navel, his fingertips light and sensual on her skin; the deeper, firmer touches when he cupped her breasts, his thumbs passing over her nipples, coaxing them to erectness much as she had for him earlier. Had it felt like this? This exquisite friction?

Alyssandra arched, hips lifting to him, her body asking for more and for less. There must have been an end to this heat, this slow burn that existed somewhere between torture and pleasure. Her legs opened in invitation, and he settled between them, rising up over her, the muscles in his arms taut with the effort and the discipline of pacing his desire to hers. Their eyes met one more time, one last time. He was looking for consent, waiting for it, she realised, when many men would have been hasty in their lust and seen to their own wants first. Alyssandra gave the signal. She wrapped her arms about his neck and took him full on the mouth, leaving no doubt as to what she wanted.

He thrust, and her body welcomed him, stretching, accommodating as they took up the rhythm, finding one another in the motion of joining and parting only to join again, each time more intensely until the rhythm consumed her, defined her. Nothing existed outside of this. There was only Haviland, there was only pleasure and it pushed her, *he* pushed her with each stroke towards some unknown cliff.

This pleasure, brilliant as it was, was unsustainable. It would end. She knew it empirically. They could not keep it up for ever. Haviland's shoulders were sweat-slicked with effort, her own legs strained from wrapping about him, but unwilling to release him. And yet it built, achieving the unattainable. She heard herself cry out, a series of sobs strung together between ragged breaths, desperate and satisfied at once. She felt the muscles of his arms tighten where she gripped them, felt his body tense, his muscles gathering themselves, her own body matching his. He gave a hard, final thrust and pushed them both into completion, into fulfilment.

This was new territory. It was her first coherent thought when she could think again. Long after Haviland had rolled to one side and taken her against him, his arm slung comfortably across her hips, she'd simply *felt*. She'd felt the rhythm of their breathing start to slow, their bodies start to cool, a hundred other sensations, not the least being the irony of feeling such completion while feeling as if her body had shattered into a thousand crystal shards, each a shining point of light.

Her body had awakened and it was greedy. Having discovered this place where nothing mattered, nothing existed but pleasure, her body wanted to stay. But to stay, it would have to happen again. Could it? Clearly it didn't always happen. It had never happened…before. She gave a little moan and pushed the thought away. There was not room in this bed for memories or for comparison. Or for hopes. Tonight existed in a vacuum, one time only.

'How are you?' Haviland's voice was at her ear, warm and comfortable as if they were more than acquaintances who'd found temporary pleasure together.

'Fine. I was just thinking,' Alyssandra murmured, turning over to face him.

'Don't do it. Thinking is dangerous.' He smiled at her, the sight of it warming her. Probably because he did it so seldom, not a genuine smile, anyway.

'You're very handsome like this.' Alyssandra pushed a strand of dark hair back from his face.

'Like this? Do you mean naked?' Haviland chuckled.

She shook her head and smiled. 'No, just being, I don't know, relaxed, as if the mask you show the world is off and you're very simply yourself.'

His eyes drifted away from her, and she felt a

moment's anxiety over having gone too far, which seemed absurd in the extreme considering what they'd already done tonight. A simple observation shouldn't tip the balance. Yet when his eyes strayed back to hers, she knew it had.

'Do you know me so well after an afternoon and an evening spent together?' His tone carried a hint of sharpness beneath the quietness.

She met the challenge and placed a hand against his chest. 'I know how you look when you kiss me and there has been plenty of that.'

'How is that?' The fire was starting to stir in his eyes again. He was going to forgive her intrusion into his privacy.

'Like a man who could be happy,' Alyssandra whispered and decided to push her advantage. She pressed against him and kissed him, effectively distracting them both from any chance of dangerous thinking. She didn't want to contemplate what lay beyond this night, nor did she want to contemplate why Haviland was so very private. 'Private' was often a polite euphemism for secrets. People who were private had something to hide. People like the Leodegrances.

Chapter Thirteen

This was going to be complicated. It was the one thought Haviland's mind kept returning to as the sky began to lighten outside the carriage windows. Alyssandra drowsed against his shoulder even though the drive to the Leodegrance *hôtel* would be a short one. Neither of them had been overeager to leave his warm bed and they had in fact already lingered longer in that haven than was prudent.

Paris had been waking up around them, or going to bed, depending on one's perspective, when they'd finally dressed and slipped out the gate at the back of the garden. He didn't think Archer and Nolan had come home yet, but he hadn't wanted to risk going through the common room. If the milkmaids and early vendors were out, his friends wouldn't be far behind. There were a few carriages like his out, too, taking the wealthy home from a night of revels. It was not at all odd to be out this time of day—and night— but there'd been no question of waiting any longer to see her home. They'd escaped her brother's detection over the kiss in the park, but that would look like a minor infraction if he caught them after tonight. Nor had Haviland wanted to encounter his friends. Nolan would most likely still be drunk and Archer would ask too many questions.

It wasn't that he was afraid of them or of Antoine Leodegrance. He simply didn't want to share. He wanted to keep Alyssandra to himself. She shifted in her sleep and murmured something softly incoherent. He looked down where her head rested against his shoulder. She was beautiful even in her sleep, with all that hair falling over her shoulder in a silky curtain of caramel, the sweep of dark lashes against her cheek.

He was already planning when he could see her again and how. After tonight, he knew that once would not be enough. That was the complicated part. There were the logistics, but there were also the ethics. How long could he go on seeing Leodegrance's sister without telling him? She was of an age to make her own decisions, but Haviland felt something of the cuckolder to face Leodegrance across the fencing *piste* while pursuing the man's sister behind his back, regardless of her age. Although it might be best if Leodegrance remained oblivious. The man would want to know his intentions and those were hardly classified as honourable.

Despite the concerns, Haviland knew it wouldn't stop him. Tonight had been heady stuff indeed. It had been hard to tell who was seducing whom. They'd been partners in pleasure. The result had been explosive and satisfying. The result had also been dangerous—it had created an intimacy, that if pursued, would eventually make demands of its own. There were already signs of it. *When I kiss you, you look like a man who could be happy.*

She saw too much and he could not give her that part of himself. She wanted to know him, but therein lay the rub. If she knew him, she wouldn't want him. How could he tell her he was expected to return home and marry Lady Christina Everly? Not only was he expected to marry, but it was a match he'd known about since he was eight years old. He could not plead ignorance.

But neither could Alyssandra, on different grounds. She was no blushing English virgin expecting marriage. She'd come to him for pleasure, not a proposal. She'd come to him tonight knowing full well what could happen and she'd certainly initiated a fair share of it. One night did not qualify as an *affaire*. However, the longer this went on, expectations *would* form, a consequence of intimacy that went beyond physical pleasure. It occurred to him that just as he'd never indulged in a purely self-motivated pursuit of a woman, neither had he indulged in a free-standing *affaire*. It was different than dealing with mistresses where the terms and expectations were less emotional and far more defined. The carriage pulled to a halt and Haviland gave Alyssandra a gentle shake. 'We're here.'

She lifted her head and gave him a drowsy smile that had him wishing the driver could take another turn around the city, but the sky was already considerably brighter than when they'd left his rooms. He jumped down and helped her out, insisting on watching her all the way to the door when she refused to let him walk her any farther. He doubted Antoine Leodegrance was awake this time of day, but the servants would be up and servants would talk.

'Goodnight, or should I say good morning?' She gave him one last smile and turned to go before it became too difficult. He wanted nothing more than to haul her back to his rooms and lock the day out. Haviland caught her arm before she could slip away. There was at least one detail they could settle that would make the rest of the day tolerable. 'I have to be at the *salle* this afternoon, but this evening, where can I find you?'

She gave him a coy smile. 'I'll send you a note.'

Haviland arched a brow. 'It's to be a puzzle, then?'

Alyssandra stepped away, dancing backwards with a little trill of laughter. 'I have it on good authority you like a woman of mystery. *À ce soir*, Haviland.'

Haviland folded his arms across his chest and leaned against the carriage, watching her until she disappeared. Even the Leodegrance home was private in the extreme. A high stone wall set it apart from the street, making the house accessible only through the arch that led into the inner courtyard. Certain she was safely inside, Haviland climbed back into the carriage for the lonely drive home.

Only he wasn't alone. She had not left him entirely. The carriage smelled faintly of her soap—lavender and lemongrass—as did his coat where she'd rested against him. The seat was still warm from her body, *he* was still warm. It was something of a novelty to realise he wanted her again, or was it that he wanted her *still*? After a night of rather thorough lovemaking, he would have thought he was ready for a respite, not just for a chance to recover, but to reclaim his space. He'd always been happy after a night with a woman's charms to be back in his space, to have his privacy. He enjoyed women, but he didn't need them clinging to him every second of the day. He liked an independent woman. But this morning he'd not been ready to let Alyssandra go.

Back at the rooms, Brennan had returned, looking entirely unkempt. Most of his clothes were draped over a chair instead of on his person, a sure sign he'd had to make a quick exit from somewhere. Apparently, he wasn't in any great danger, though, because he'd stopped for breakfast. French rolls, cheese and a block of rich creamy butter were laid out on the dining table.

'Just getting in?' Brennan said around a mouthful of bread. He motioned to an empty chair. 'I'll have Guillaume bring coffee.'

Haviland gave a tired smile, the night catching up with him at last. 'Thank you, but I think I'll go to bed.'

Brennan winked. 'I've already been there tonight, twice in fact.'

'You can tell me about it later.' Haviland tried to

laugh, but it came out as a yawn. He didn't know how Brennan did it; up all night, every night, and always cheerful as if his personal life didn't teeter on the edge of disaster.

Haviland knew what he'd find before he opened the door to his room. The carriage had been fair warning, but he was still unprepared for the lingering effects of her scent in the confines of a closed space. Lavender and lemongrass mingled with the musk of sex. She was everywhere in his room, *they* were everywhere. Haviland smiled to himself and tugged off his boots. All the better to dream of her. The only problem with getting up so early was that it took night that much longer to come. He had nothing to do except wait for her note and go to the *salle* for another lesson at three. But that was ten hours away. Until then, sleep could help. He lay back on the pillows amid the rumpled sheets, eyes closed, and let the dreams come.

Archer woke him shortly after one. 'You've slept the day away, lazybones. Don't you have to be at the *salle* for lessons at three? And…' He stopped there and grimaced. The grimace had all of Haviland's attention. 'You have a letter from home.' He held up the letter as proof.

Haviland groaned. 'Leave it for me. I'll read it after I get dressed.' He'd slept too long. He should have been up at noon. He rolled out of bed and did a quick wash. Anything more would have to wait until tonight—some time after fencing, but before he went out. The letter kept creeping into his periphery. He'd best get it over with. Shirt half-buttoned and feet still bare, Haviland picked up the letter and ripped it open. It was from his mother. The handwriting was a collection of neatly regulated loops. He sighed and slouched into a chair.

My Dearest Son,
    I hope you are well and that you are finding Paris lovely. I appreciated the one letter you sent upon arrival...

He could hear the rebuke in that for not sending others. She would want a full accounting of the parties and the fashions. He felt guilty. He should have written. It would have been the dutiful thing to do, but he'd wanted to keep Paris to himself.

    I have been busy with the Marchioness of Dunmore. We have begun plans for the wedding. It will be a Christmas affair at the abbey, the Dunmore family seat. We've decided to make the most of the holiday season and greenery.
    The abbey will look stunning all done up with boughs and berries and garlands. Christina and her mother have met with the dressmaker and selected the fabric for her gown. I have seen it; it's an ice blue that shows off her eyes and her hair to perfection. You will have the most beautiful bride in the ton.

He stopped reading.

Archer came in with a small tea tray. 'I thought you might want to eat before you left.' His eyes flicked sideways to the letter. 'Bad news?'

'It's from my mother. It's always bad news.'

Archer sat down and poured him a tea cup. 'Don't say that, Haviland. She loves you in her way and at least you have a mother.'

Haviland took the tea cup, regretting his words. 'I'm sorry. You're right, of course.' He nodded to the letter. 'You can read it if you want. She sends her love to you, it's down at the bottom.' He reached for the small decanter of brandy Archer had thoughtfully included with the tea tray and poured some in, giving time for Archer to scan the contents of the letter.

'It goes on for pages, but you get the gist.' Haviland sighed and eased back in his chair, one bare foot crossed over his knee.

'I can see that.' Archer gave him a shrewd look. 'It's really going to happen, then. You're going to marry Christina Everly.' He tried for a smile. Haviland knew he was trying to make him feel better. 'Congrats, old man. You'll be the first of us to marry and no doubt you'll have the loveliest wife of us all. Shall I tell Brennan and Nolan? We could go out and celebrate tonight, all four of us, when you get back from fencing.'

Haviland shook his head. 'No.' Getting three sheets to the wind with Nolan and Brennan was usually quite entertaining, but it wouldn't solve anything and it certainly wouldn't make his situation go away.

Besides, he had plans to be with Alyssandra, plans to escape.

Haviland got up and paced the room. 'I shouldn't complain. I feel like a petulant child when I think about all I'm resisting. Men would kill to have what I have.'

Archer didn't argue. 'What will you do?'

'I don't know.' Haviland pushed a hand through his hair and blew out a breath. 'I don't know what I stand for any more.'

'You have a little more time,' Archer said soothingly.

'A little.' Haviland looked out the French doors leading into the garden. There would be no petitioning his father for extra time now, his mother had neatly ruined that option with her wedding plans.

'I suppose this means you won't make Italy,' Archer said quietly after a while.

Haviland nodded his head, not daring to look back at Archer for fear emotion would get the better of him. 'I would have liked to have seen you race. It would really have been something to see you win the Palio, flying around the Campo.' It wasn't just the Palio he'd be missing. There would be no summering in the Alps, no second spring spent in Naples, no afternoons spent in the Italian *salles d'armes* of Florence. All the adventures he'd imagined would never be.

'Perhaps you can go as far as Switzerland with Brennan and Nolan,' Archer put in.

'Perhaps,' Haviland replied noncommittally. What would the point be? He'd just have to turn back.

Why not stay in Paris a little longer with Alyssandra? These were all horrible thoughts and there was no time for them, so in customary fashion whenever the subject of his future came up, Haviland pushed it away. 'I have to go, Archer, but I'll see you later.'

Archer rose, concern etched in his face. 'Will you be all right?'

Haviland tried to smile his reassurance. 'I'll be all right. After all, there is still a little time.'

She'd thought she'd have more time. Alyssandra stared at the list of clients on the desk in front of her. It was to be business as usual, although the idea of anything being 'normal' or 'usual' felt decidedly surreal after last night. It seemed even more impossible after seeing the list of the day's clients. 'Antoine Leodegrance' was giving three lessons today; the first two were regulars, young wealthy students from the university. They would be no problem, but the third name on the list held all of her attention. Haviland North.

'Is there a problem?' Julian leaned forward from his seat across the desk. They were alone in the *salle*'s office and she felt the absence of her brother's presence acutely. Antoine had not come in today. It was the first time she had seen Julian since their conversation after the park incident and he'd had a couple of days to recover. His black eye had faded to a yellow-grey halo, making it difficult for her to look at him and not remember who put it there.

'No,' Alyssandra lied swiftly. Of course she'd known she'd have to face Haviland again in the guise of her brother. She'd just hoped it wouldn't be so soon, not when she could still feel the delicious remnants of their lovemaking on her body. She'd hoped to have time to settle into it, into him. Leading a dual life certainly had its complications. 'Today, we have to tell North about his dropped shoulder. He'll need to control the habit for the tournament. This will give him two weeks to work on it.'

Keep it business as usual, she told herself one more time. This was good. If she could keep the conversation focused on the work at hand, perhaps she'd forget how uncomfortable Julian made her feel or how fabulous Haviland made her feel. 'Let's be clear on what I will need from you in the lesson today. I will need you to show him. I can't touch him.' Especially not now. Perhaps earlier with her full-face mask on, she could have touched him to demonstrate a point during the lesson, but not after last night. Surely, he would recognise her touch or she would do something to give herself away if she got too close. Better to maintain the aloof distance she'd already established in her relationship to him as Antoine Leodegrance.

'No, I suppose you can't.' Julian's response was snide. 'Hopefully you do understand in hindsight just how ill advised your little rebellion was. It has even jeopardised your ability to give a lesson.'

Alyssandra fixed him with a hard stare. 'Scolding does not become you, Julian.' For a man who insisted he had feelings for her, he certainly didn't understand her. He ought to know berating her would not prove to be an effective suit. She stood up to avoid giving him a chance to respond. She didn't want to fight with him. She had too much threatening to distract her without adding worry over Julian. 'It's time to change. Our first pupil will be here soon. I will see you in the private practice room.'

Changing did help to soothe her thoughts. The ritual of wrapping her breasts flat, of pulling on the trousers, worn loose enough to hide any telltale curves or lack of them under the guise that they provided freedom of movement, of putting on one of her brother's white shirts. She twisted her hair up into a tight bun and settled the mask over her head. Thirty years ago, her masquerade wouldn't have been possible with just a leather mask that covered the eyes, but the new invention of the full-mesh face mask gave her the social anonymity she needed. The genetics of being a twin gave her the rest.

Alyssandra opened the wall case and took out her foil, giving it a few experimental slashes. The grip felt solid in her hand. She could feel peace settle over her. All was right with the world when she held a blade. It always had been. She went through the eight parries, stretching her muscles to warm up. She moved about the room, calling sequences in her head: *Balestra flèche! Balestra lunge! Coup lancé!*

Her body took over automatically, letting her mind focus on the upcoming lessons. The first pupil needed to work on the pronation of his wrist while he executed parry three, *tierce*. The second pupil's lesson would focus on *coups d'arret*, stop cuts, as a way of improving his mediocre defence.

Alyssandra brought her exercise to a halt and blew out a breath. She felt good. Her body was primed, her mind was ready. Everything would be fine. Everything would be business as usual.

And it was. Through the first two pupils. Then Haviland stepped into the room. The air crackled, the tension ratcheted. The tenor of the room changed entirely or was it merely a trick of her imagination? His reserve was back, his polite aloofness in place. Gone was the man she'd been in bed with just hours before. What was he so determined no one see?

Haviland eyed Julian with a gaze that managed to convey respect and disdain all at once. Julian responded in kind. But Julian was far more wary. As he should be. Haviland could beat him. She wondered what would happen if the two met in competition at the tournament? If they both made the final rounds, they would most certainly face each other.

She smiled behind her mask. Two years ago at the tournament, *she'd* beaten Julian. Everyone had thought it was Leodegrance who had beaten him, but the three of them knew the truth and Julian had never forgiven her for it. Perhaps this year, she'd be facing Haviland instead.

That thought wiped the smile from her face. Facing Haviland would be dangerous in the extreme. Julian knew his duty: lose in the final on purpose if for some reason 'Leodegrance' couldn't win on his own. But Haviland would not be bound by any such compunction. *Couldn't* be bound without knowing their secret.

Julian stepped forward, explaining the structure of today's lesson. She had to pay attention. 'Master Leodegrance would like to open today's lesson with a bout. Then, after you lose, he would like to show you where your error lies and how to remedy it.' She thought he might have said most of that with too much relish, especially the 'after you lose' and 'where your error lies' parts.

Haviland gave a short nod in her direction. 'I will appreciate any instruction.' She approached her end of the piste and Haviland took up his position. Julian stepped between them and dropped the white flag. 'Gentlemen, *en garde.*'

Chapter Fourteen

En garde, indeed! It took all of Haviland's concentration not to see Alyssandra everywhere. She was in everything Antoine did, every move he made. Leodegrance's signature wrist flick was a damnable distraction today, calling to mind a flirtatious fan rather than the *fleuret* of Antoine's foil. That particular distraction nearly saw Haviland skewered embarrassingly early in the match. Then there was the smell—the light scent of lavender and lemongrass that wafted subtly whenever their blades made contact.

That was when Haviland realised how much danger his agitated brain was really in—they probably used the same soap or the laundress washed with the same soap. There were all sorts of reasons why Antoine carried the faintest scent of Alyssandra and none them validated fencing like novice. It didn't help that Leodegrance seemed edgy, jittery almost. His movements were fierce and confident, but less fluid than usual. Julian was revelling in his inadequacies.

'Get your arm up! Hold your frame!' Julian barked. *'Tierce!'*

Haviland used a *balestra-lunge* combination in an attempt to launch an attack, but he had no chance to execute it. Apparently impatient with the bout, Julian inserted himself between the two, seizing Leodegrance's foil in a lightning-quick move and stood *en garde* against him. 'Come now, *monsieur*. Let's see what you can really do.' His tone was grim, his eyes narrow flints of competitive fire. But it had the desired effect. There was nothing distracting about this opponent. Haviland's mind and emotions focused singularly on one aim—defeat Julian.

Julian was not easy to beat, even on a good day. Today he was especially sharp and indefatigable while Haviland was neither. They parried and thrust endlessly. Sweat ran. Haviland's arm ached. On the sideline, Leodegrance clapped his hands and halted the match after it became apparent it would go on until exhaustion. Julian stepped forward and lowered his foil. 'Now, *monsieur*, let's talk about your dropped shoulder. Master Leodegrance has analysed your technique and has noticed this as a weakness. This is when you are most vulnerable. You will recall this was how Master Leodegrance was able to defeat you every time.'

'Twice,' Haviland ground out in correction. Haviland was sure he didn't overlook the emphasis Anjou placed on *defeated*. The bastard was enjoying this too much. In standard odd fashion, Leodegrance stood silently on the side, watching while Julian conducted

the rest of the lesson. It was, however, the longest
Leodegrance had ever stayed in the room. Haviland
supposed that was something even if the master remained remote. The lesson ended only when Julian
and Leodegrance were satisfied he'd overcome the
tendency to drop his shoulder. He was sweaty and
exhausted, but *this*, he thought with a surge of satisfaction, was what he'd come to Paris for—to excel,
to acquire skills and knowledge he could not attain
at home and to attain it from experts whom he could
not access in London. Today of all days, with his
mother's letter fresh in his head, the reminder was
much needed.

Haviland wiped his face and hands with a towel
and headed for the changing rooms, trying to ignore
the old dilemma rearing its ugly head in his mind:
what to choose? Family honour or personal freedom?
Out of habit and practice, his mind sought to shove
the dilemma away, ignore it. No. He had to stop doing
that. Ignoring it solved nothing. Ignoring had only
led to this point: his mother was decorating for his
wedding and a girl he barely knew was designing her
wedding gown. Ignoring no longer meant avoiding.
It meant acceptance.

In the changing room he washed up and reached
for a clean shirt. He exchanged casual words with a
few others present and made his way to the club room,
feeling again that stab of envy for Leodegrance's accomplishment in creating such a place. He didn't want
to deprive Leodegrance of his achievement, he merely
wanted such a place too. Haviland felt at home here,

as if he'd found his place in the world at Sixteen Rue Saint Marc.

In the club room, he nodded at a few men he knew and settled in what was becoming his usual chair by the bookshelves. The waiter came with a glass of his preferred red wine. A new friend or two stopped by to ask his advice on parries. In between visits, he reviewed Agrippa's Italian treatise on fencing for his next lesson with Julian. They had moved on from the Spanish school to a quick study of the Italians and their love of offensive manoeuvres. But between the pages and the rich red wine, all the 'what ifs' he'd held at bay, hardly daring to believe in them, began to find their way forward in his thoughts.

The first was: what if he didn't go home? He'd certainly fantasised about that before, but always with some adolescent immaturity behind it: if he didn't go home, he couldn't marry Christina Everly. Beyond that, there'd never been any real clarity. Today, there was substance. What if he stayed in Paris? What if Leodegrance took him on as an instructor? If he performed well at the upcoming tournament, surely Leodegrance would find a place for him.

Haviland winced. Leodegrance might do that if he didn't run him through first for bedding his sister. He poured another glass of wine. What would Alyssandra think of him staying? They'd begun this mad *affaire* under the supposition that it was for escape and pleasure—two inherently short-term goals. The end had been implied since the beginning. If he stayed, that end could be put off. Would she want that? Would she want *him* if he came with reduced circumstances? He'd watched her subtly gauging the luxury of his surroundings the other night, her eyes noting the expensive carriage and the upper-class neighbourhood of his lodgings. She was used to living finely, she would not expect that to change.

That gave him pause. Haviland played with the stem of his wine glass. He'd never had to think about that before. Every woman he'd had wanted him because he had a title and was the embodiment of wealth. He supposed he'd still have a title, but it was unlikely his funds would be as extensive. If the Leodegrances wouldn't have him, he could always teach at one of the other *salles d'armes* or strike out on his own.

By his third glass of wine, the practicalities seemed less important than the vision of doing something. Practicalities would mean nothing, worries over the state of his relationship with Alyssandra would mean nothing, if he didn't take the first step and *decide*. In any situation there was always a choice. Sometimes those choices were just difficult.

What it came down to was this: could he live with that choice? Could he live with the choices his parents would make because of it? His father could not revoke the title, it was too much work. But his father would revoke the money. As much as Haviland felt the money acted as a stone around his neck, he'd never lived without it and the luxuries it brought. Could he do it? After three glasses of wine he thought he could, but it would require bravery and adjustment.

He poured the rest of the bottle and drank deeply, savouring the tannins on his tongue. He wished Archer was with him to talk, most of all to listen. Archer would understand the dilemma between family and self because he'd suffered under that burden, too. Only now, Archer was free. And Archer would be leaving them. The others didn't know. Archer would push on to Italy for the horse race in August, not stopping to play away the summer in the Alps.

It was something of an irony that the four of them had set out on this trip as one last chance to be together before they were pulled away by marriage and life, each to their own obligations, and yet, Archer was leaving and he was sitting here drinking wine, thinking of doing the same. Haviland chuckled to himself. It was a humorous and yet dangerous thought to think of Brennan and Nolan bashing about the Continent on their own, gambling and wenching their way south. Europe might never recover.

He was still laughing to himself over the image when the note arrived. There was a certain thrill at seeing the folded white sheet on the waiter's salver. Haviland unfolded it, marking its brevity with a quick scan. It contained only a single line; the address of the evening's entertainment. But it was enough to stir his blood and his imagination. Escape and pleasure seemed to be the watchwords of the day in some form or another.

Haviland smiled to himself. Alyssandra was not

above a little game playing, it seemed. An address, but no given time, no specified place of meeting. He would have to hunt for her. *If you want me, come and get me.* The message implied was clear. He would have to be in pursuit. She would not make it easy for him, only possible.

The evening's venue was another musicale the French were so very fond of, this one an effort to copy the début for the king, Louis Philippe, of Auguste Mermet's new two-act *opéra comique* at Versailles a week ago. It hardly mattered what was on the venue. Haviland doubted they'd stay for the entertainment. But first he had to find her—easier said than done considering the number of people present. It had almost been impossible to greet his hostess before being jostled along.

He looked for her first out of doors along the veranda just to be certain she wasn't there. He hadn't expected her to be—it would have been far too predictable, and she *did* want him to hunt her. He checked the crowded salon where the recital would be held and where most of the guests were gathered at this point in the evening. He checked the currently deserted card rooms, the refreshment room, the outdoors once more, this time strolling through the garden. He was certain she was here already. Musicales required a more prompt attendance than a ball. At a ball, one could arrive at one's convenience, but at a *musicale* one didn't dare arrive during the performance.

Haviland sat down on a bench to think. Where would she be? He looked up at the stone facade of the house, his gaze absently scanning the windows while he thought. Most windows above the second floor were dark. His gaze moved down to the second floor where the entertainment was. He watched people spill out of the wide doors and onto the twin curved staircases leading to the garden. He couldn't stay out here much longer without calling attention to himself. A lone man in a garden was highly suspect. He might as well just brand 'I'm waiting for someone' on his forehead.

A single lamp flashed in the window of a room at the end of the south wing. It had definitely not been there a minute before. A signal. For him. Haviland smiled and counted windows. Three from the end, seven from the main salon. He stood up and the light went out. The minx was watching him. She *knew* he was in the garden. It occurred to him to exact a little revenge of his own and make her wait. Perhaps he would sit through the first part of the recital. It would serve her right, but that would only punish him, too, and by now, the hunt had him fully primed for conquest. He was ready to flush his quarry.

'*You* have led me a merry chase.' Haviland shut the door behind him. She did not look up from her book at once, but he saw the twitching beginnings of a smile play across her lips. It gave him a moment to appreciate the surroundings and perhaps to ap-

preciate how well *she* fit those surroundings. She'd
chosen a comfortable room done in rich browns and
muted greens, part-library, part-sitting room with its
warm fireplace and collection of sofas and chairs.
She matched it perfectly in her gown of crushed gold
moiré, the firelight bringing out the tawny highlights
of her hair. His blood hummed as it hit him. She'd
planned this right down to the dress she'd worn. Planning meant he'd been on her mind. Planning meant
she was looking forward to this as much as he and
that could have some very scintillating consequences
indeed. His fencing match today proved he'd thought
of little else.

It was hardly to his credit to be so swept away.
He was made of sterner, steelier stuff when it came
to *affaires*. Among a certain set of a certain type of
London lady, he was known for his physical skill in
bed and his mental reserve. He was famed for his
ability to avoid sticky, emotional attachments. He
understood the import of physical pleasure remaining strictly physical. Yet here he was, eagerly anticipating this evening like a lovestruck swain. He was
only missing the roses and chocolates.

She looked up at last and he was aware of the heat
of her gaze slowly drifting the length of him. This was
how a mature woman flirted; boldly, directly about
her intentions. No shy maidenly glances to indirectly
communicate her preferences, here. Haviland swallowed, desire starting to ride him with some persis-
tence now.

'It's about time you got here.' She wore a thick

curl over one shoulder. She lifted a hand and twisted it about her finger. 'Haviland...' Her voice caressed his name with a sensual husk. 'Will you do something for me?'

Haviland gave a wolfish grin, liking this game very much. 'Anything.' He wanted to take her roughly, quickly, that gold gown hiked about her thighs. Maybe a hard, fast coupling would douse the fire that had been building throughout the day. Then they could slow down, could control the fire between them long enough to gradually warm themselves in it instead of burn with it.

Her brows lifted in acknowledgement of his boldness. 'Lock the door.'

The lock snicked quietly, ominously, in the silence of the sitting room. Privacy ensured, passion could ensue. He turned from the door, letting his gaze catch hers, let it communicate his wicked intentions; whatever happened next would be fast and it would be rough. Haviland crossed the room in three rapid strides, his hands gripping her hard by the arms, his mouth urgent against hers.

Her mouth answered his, her hands tore at his clothes, pulling out shirttails, tugging at cravats, words escaping her in little gasping fractured sentences. 'I want you, inside me, now.' Her teeth bit down on his lip. 'I've thought of nothing else all day, I've been wondering about nothing else all day.' She had the fall of his trousers free, her hand closing over him.

Haviland bore her back to the wall, lifting her.

'Wrap your legs about me.' The instruction came out hoarse, came out harsh with need. He pushed the fabric of her gown up high past her thighs, a fierce growl escaping him as his hands met bare skin. *Sans lingerie.* 'What a deliciously wicked thing you are, Alyssandra.' His voice was husky against her throat. He would not last long at this rate. Neither would she. Her curls were damp against his hand, the scent of her desire mingling with lavender and lemongrass. Thank goodness this was not meant to be a prolonged coupling.

Haviland braced her against the wall, his muscles taut with his need, and he thrust, hard, rough, fast, and still she urged him on. 'More, Haviland, more!' Alyssandra gave a low, guttural moan of sheer pleasure, her neck arched, her hair falling haphazardly about her in a wild cascade. 'Don't hold back, dear God, don't hold anything back!' She looked magnificent in her pleasure, she *sounded* magnificent; a woman owning her passion, crying it in her abandon and he hammered into her like a stallion, like the wild things they'd become, pushing them to pleasure's end. She screamed, and he gave an exhalation of primal release, the tautness leaving him, satisfaction filling him. More than satisfaction, although he didn't have a word for it, for this feeling that flooded him. His body knew only that the edge which had ridden him mercilessly all day had finally been dulled, finally been conquered.

They sank down the wall onto the floor in front of the fireplace, both of them boneless heaps. He lay on his side, finding enough strength to prop himself up on an elbow; so much the better to watch her recover. He'd never watched a woman recover before, never paid attention to the little changes as she transitioned back to earth. Alyssandra lay on her back, her gaze fixed on the ceiling. He watched her breasts rise and fall beneath her gown, fast at first, and then slowing as her breathing returned to a regular pattern, *le petit mort* giving way to the peace of satisfaction.

'I don't know if I got my wish or not,' she said after a while, her eyes still on the ceiling. 'Part of me had hoped it wouldn't happen again, that last night had been a random occurrence, a once-in-a-lifetime achievement.'

Haviland studied her in the firelight. He reached a hand out absently to push her hair back behind her ear, letting the tiny diamond studs she wore dance in the flames as he contemplated her words. 'Why would you ever wish that?'

'Because it was wonderful, because it had never happened for me. Did you know that?' She turned her head to look at him briefly. The brown eyes which had belonged to a confident temptress earlier were soulful now. There was a hint of vulnerability in them—but only a hint. Alyssandra was too stubborn to admit too much. He had guessed, of course. Her response last night had been so deeply genuine, so deeply amazed for her to have expected it, to have known what waited for them.

'And if it could happen, over and over again, it meant you were the one responsible for it; you and maybe only you could make it happen.' Desperation or perhaps hopelessness hemmed the edge of her voice although she tried to hide it. He knew she would not want to appear to be either.

What ifs began to hover on the periphery of his returning reason. What if he stayed? Staying would change everything. 'Leaving is a long time off,' he argued quietly. 'I have a month yet, maybe more, before we'll even think of such things.' He didn't dare say more. He didn't know any more, only that it was possible this didn't have to end. There were weeks to go and his friends seemed content enough with Paris. Archer would leave, no matter what. His dreams of the Palio demanded it. But Nolan was winning at cards without offending anyone and Brennan had found Paris full of willing females. Perhaps they wouldn't be in a hurry to move on. Yet. Perhaps it didn't matter what they chose to do. He might stay regardless.

She gave a half smile; half-hope, half-practicality. She'd heard the implication. 'Yet' would come no matter how he soothed. She hadn't had the epiphanies he'd had today. She was still thinking any delay was only temporary. It was the best he could offer for now. Who knew what the month would bring? Perhaps they would tire of one another by then and be glad to see the other go before the relationship could truly sour. It had been his experience that eventually all things did. Perfection didn't last, although it was hard to believe when he felt the way he did right now—sated and content.

She rolled towards him and they lay length to length, eyes meeting. 'Well, that's for later. Right now, we have a locked room. It would be a shame to let it go to waste.'

Chapter Fifteen

She'd only wanted to see him again as her lover, to see if the magic was real. Part of her almost hoped it wasn't. It would prove he was a man, as fallible, as ordinary as any other. But part of her had wanted to burn, wanted to be lit on fire once more. That part had got precisely what it desired.

And it still was not enough. Not by far.

It was as if her body was awake for the first time and, being acutely aware of that fact, it wanted to experience everything. She wanted to taste him again, feel him again. To imprint him again and again on her memory so her body would never forget what it was made for. Her eyes lit on the sideboard across the room, an idea starting to form. She rose to her feet, a little clumsy amid the tangle of clothes. Haviland's brows drew together, perplexed. She stayed him with a smile. 'Wait here.'

His body waited, his gaze did not. She could feel the heat of it with each step. Now that urgency had been satisfied, other wants, other desires, rose to take its place, the needs of a dilettante who wants to savour the experience, who is no longer in a hurry.

She turned, decanter in hand, her gaze perusing her lover with an intensity to match his. Just looking at him put a thrill through her blood. He was temptation personified in dishabille; his head propped on his hand, dark hair falling forward over one brow, one long leg bent at the knee. The fall of his trousers lay open, hinting provocatively at what lay beneath the loose billows of his shirttails. If he were to shift slightly to the right, perhaps there would be a glimpse, her mind thought naughtily. But, no, that would ruin the temptation. The secret was in the mystery, not the blatant revelation.

'I was just thinking how much I wish you were naked.' Haviland's voice was a gravelly drawl, each word a caress. Her breath caught. It was a wickedly daring suggestion; to be entirely naked in what amounted to a public room was audacious in the extreme even with the door locked. It only took one person to try the handle to confirm that something clandestine and private was occurring on the other side. And yet, they were far enough down the hall it was unlikely anyone would come looking. The odds were probably in her favour. Alyssandra set down the decanter and reached for the laces at the back of her dress.

She let the dress fall, her gaze riveted on Haviland and his response. His body went still. There was an ottoman close at hand and she raised one leg to it, untying the garter about her thigh and rolling down the silk stocking with deliberate slowness. Haviland shifted. Even at her distance, she could see the evidence of arousal assert itself against the folds of his shirt and it pleased her. She teased with her smile and rolled down the second stocking. All that remained was her chemise.

Alyssandra raised her arms, knowing full well the movement exposed her entirely below the waist as she tugged the chemise over her head. She had never been so daring. But Haviland brought out the boldness in her with his own audacity. They were alike in that regard, both of them cool and polite, aloof even among society, but behind closed doors neither balked at giving passion free rein.

His eyes devoured her, and she stood for him, letting him look his fill. Her hand closed around the neck of the decanter, and she began a seductive walk towards him, hips infused in the slightest of sways, hair tumbling down of its own accord to fall over her breasts in a riot of waves.

She set the decanter by the fire, letting the flames warm the glass, Haviland's eyes following her every move. 'Now,' she said, settling in the armchair. 'It's your turn.' A little smile played at her mouth as she borrowed his words. 'I was just thinking how much I wish you were naked.'

Haviland came to his feet and made her a bow, his tone full of mock gravity. 'Your wish is my command.'

His shirt went first. Dear lord, she should wish

more often. She'd seen him naked last night, but this was different. Last night had been a means to an end, a very intimate means. Tonight, the disrobing was an end in itself. His eyes were hot as he watched her watching him. He was stripping for her, putting himself on display for her as she had for him. There must be a name for this sort of erotic, two-way voyeurism, that raised such a specific heat in her. Her body ached, her breasts felt heavy with desire and she hadn't even touched him. He pulled off his evening shoes and made short work of his trousers so that he stood before her magnificently naked. Had a man ever looked so *beautiful*? Alyssandra felt a feminine moment of pride. Whispered speculations behind fans hardly did him justice and he was hers. *All* hers.

His blue eyes slid towards the decanter warming on the hearth. 'Did you want a drink?' His voice hinted at decadence. That suited her fine. She planned to be very decadent in the next few minutes.

She rose from the chair, her own tones husky. 'Yes, I did. Now, if you would lie down?'

'Stand up, take off my clothes, lie down. You are quite the tyrant,' Haviland scolded with feigned sternness but he complied, managing to look even more alluring horizontally in front of the fire than he had vertically. The firelight showed him to perfection. Years of fencing had honed his thighs to muscular solidity, defined the form of his arms and the lean length of his torso with its ridges and planes.

She straddled his legs and reached for the decanter, feeling the warmth of the glass beneath her hand as she pulled the stopper and wafted the decanter under her nose. She smiled at Haviland. 'Cognac. It's perfect.' Alyssandra tipped the carafe, trailing cognac along his rigid phallus.

'By Jove, have mercy!' Haviland groaned. 'That's divine.'

She gave a him wicked grin, eyes locking with his for a moment. 'Then what would you call this?' She bent to him then, her tongue flicking over the caramel rivulet.

'Paradise,' came the single hoarse word. It was probably all he could utter. Heaven knew she was nearly overcome with the pleasure of this intimacy as well. This was pleasure in its best and highest form, pleasure in the giving and in the receiving. Cognac and man combined to create salt and sweet on her tongue. Never had she found a taste to be so completely arousing, but this one was and it goaded her to extremes; she licked and sucked, bit and nipped, her hand squeezed, her tongue caressed until they were both groaning, her own breath coming in little pants as she brought him to climax, nearly as excited as he.

She held him then, with her eyes, with her hand as he spent, his own eyes holding hers intense with silent messages. Haviland raised himself up on his elbows. His gaze took on a mischievous cast, a spark dancing in his eye. 'Your turn.'

In a fluid movement he had her beneath him, their bodies pressed length to length before she could do more than register her surprise in a breathy gasp. He sat her astride, painting her in cognac, his fingertips brushing fairy-light circles around her breasts, tracing a line to her navel, leaving a thimble-sized puddle behind. 'I will smell like a drunkard,' she scolded half-heartedly. She was enjoying the feel of him too much to complain.

He leaned over her, stretching his body out above her, his mouth close at her ear. 'No one drinks cognac to get drunk. Cognac is for sipping, for savouring.' She gave a shiver at the words and their intent. *She* was for sipping, for savouring. His arms were taut brackets about her head as he slid down her, his tongue sipping and savouring as he went; breasts, sternum, navel, *ohhh!* She arched at the delicate sensation of his tongue dipping into her navel, of the pressure of his mouth covering it, creating suction as he drank the tiny sip.

Then he travelled lower, his breath warm against the damp nest of her curls. That was when she knew she was in danger of the worst sort—the danger of losing herself. It would be too easy to lose herself in this pleasure, to believe who she was, who he was inside this sensual *affaire* was the sum of them, the sum of her reality, when in fact this was a fantasy come to life for a short time. It was what she had promised herself when she'd actively begun this—if he was only here for a short while, what would it matter if she indulged? It could mean nothing and that had been the original beauty of her plan. But when he blew on her mons, when his fingers parted her folds and his tongue flicked over the nub of her clitoris, those rationales were paper dolls before flame, crackling to cinders. She raised her hips to meet his wicked mouth, to encourage it. She let herself burn. She would worry about the ash later.

She was hot and wet beneath his mouth, wanting him with a free abandon that was positively intoxicating if the heady scent of her arousal and the cognac wasn't enough to send him over the edge. *Again.* It wasn't as if he hadn't been over that edge twice already. Haviland steadied her, his hands firm on her hips as he felt her approach fulfilment. She gave a little scream, and he lifted his head to watch release take her, a shiver that moved down her body in ripples of pleasure, leaving peace in its wake. He liked this, he realised, as he stretched out beside her. He liked watching peace settle over her features— features that weren't usually at peace. Her face was constantly on alert, constantly expressive, constantly thinking about situations, weighing, assessing. But not in these moments. In these moments, her body *and* her mind were free.

She is like you in that regard. He balked a bit at the thought. It was far too provoking. He knew he *felt* that way, but did he show it? Did he *look* like that— all peace and contentment—after she finished with him? He knew the demons he needed respite from: the pressures of family, the title, the pressure to give his life to others, saving nothing of himself *for* himself. He knew precisely what he sought to escape. Did she seek to escape something as well?

It was hard to imagine. As a mature Frenchwoman, she had an almost unlimited amount of freedom compared to an Englishwoman. As a woman of noble birth, that social freedom was enhanced by her financial advantages. With her beauty she could attract any lover who appealed. And yet, her experience in that venue had excluded a certain level of quality up until now. Whatever lovers there had been in her past, they had been lukewarm at best in their abilities to sate her passions. Additionally, there seemed to be no apparent pressure for her to marry. From his perspective, she had it all. What could she possibly want to escape?

'What are you doing to me, Alyssandra? I'll be nothing but a shadow by tomorrow.' He gave a low laugh, but he was only half-joking. 'More importantly, whatever are you doing with me?' He understood he was an excellent catch by English standards—Christina Everly's family certainly understood that. But for a Frenchwoman who understood he was merely passing through? He was not quite an excellent catch for *that* woman.

Alyssandra's eyes dropped briefly to what was visible of his groin in the small space between them. 'What am I doing with you? I thought that was fairly obvious.'

Haviland gave his head a shake. If he wanted her to be brave, he had to be brave too. It was hard to be open when he'd spent so much of his life projecting a certain image even if it meant closing part of himself off. 'All teasing aside, Alyssandra, you know what I mean. Why me when there are so many better choices for a lover?'

She gave a throaty laugh. 'Better than you? That is doubtful. Every woman in every room you've ever walked into knows there would be few better.' She was serious now. He could see the change in her eyes—those brown eyes would remind him of cognac for ever after tonight. All of her would, in fact—from her eyes to the caramel of her loose hair resembling the shimmer of the liquor held to the light, and the taste of her where his tongue had slid along her skin.

He felt a moment's disappointment. 'I am a temporary lover? That is all?' He was nothing more to her than a warm body to service her needs. It was hardly different than what his family expected from him— stud service as Archer had once put it.

'Can you afford to be more than that to me? Can *I* afford it?' Her answer was sharp, those eyes of hers flashing, some of her peacefulness receding. She was on guard again, assessing again, as if every conversation was a duel.

Tell her your dreams, came the urging from his mind. But how could he? Those plans were too nascent, too fragile, as was their *affaire*, to bear the burden of his dissembling. Telling her his hopes meant also telling her about his past, about his obligations. And yet she was right. If he was to go on letting her believe all this was temporary, it was unfair to expect her to commit to the emotional aspects of a relationship if he wasn't willing to do the same.

But he didn't want to lose this. The way she responded to him, the way she physically made love to him, was far beyond anything he'd experienced with his mistresses, or anything he could imagine sharing with his bride who had made it clear to him last year during one of their two annual dances that sex would be for purely reproductive purposes.

Haviland pushed up and took to his feet. The bubble was coming off the wine of their evening. He'd rather take his leave before it had gone flat entirely, while he could still remember the warmth of her hands, the feel of her mouth and how incredible it had all been before words had got in the way. He'd asked for too much. She'd given him an honest answer. It wasn't her fault he didn't like it.

Alyssandra's hand reached up and curled around his, giving him a hard tug, her voice soft. 'I think you misunderstand me to your detriment.' She had all of his attention now. Just a few inches to the right and she would have been tugging something else. His member had the bad form to stir, apparently aware that those magic hands of hers were in close proximity. Damn it, he was trying to make a dignified exit.

Haviland looked down into her upturned face. She blushed, suddenly unsure of herself. Her dark eyelashes lowered. 'Come sit down. I'm not ready for you to go.' Her lashes flicked to the right ever so discreetly. 'And I don't think you are either, not really. You're just trying to salvage some pride that I never meant to damage.' She looked up again. 'Do I have the right of it?'

He didn't answer, *couldn't* answer. Answering would require telling her too much, telling her too many things he didn't talk about. And why? She was right, too, about expenses. There was a limit to what they could afford with each other. But he could sit and so he did, across from her on the floor, watching her draw a throw from the chair around her nakedness. The fire was starting to die and the room was cooler now. But she took his hands in hers and they were warm.

'You should know, I'm not in the habit of taking many lovers. I do not want you to think I am. To do so demeans me without justification. But it also demeans you. I would not want you to think so poorly of yourself as to define your merits strictly by your ability to perform in bed.'

Haviland wanted to say something but her eyes shone in earnest. If he interrupted her, he might miss something very important, so he remained silent and waited for her to continue.

'There has been only one other.' She looked down at her hands as if she feared he would find the confession shocking. Haviland watched her shoulders rise as she drew a deep breath. 'We were engaged. It was all very traditional. We courted for a year, our engagement was a year. We were to be wed the month after Antoine was hurt. We postponed the wedding, of course, but Antoine's recovery took longer than expected.'

'Longer than he was willing to wait?' Haviland finished the thought, grinding over the words with thinly veiled dislike. What man left a woman he was pledged to in the midst of crisis? Did the words 'for better or worse' mean so little to the man who had aspired to her hand? He hated, too, that Alyssandra was still protecting this man with her words, trying so carefully to not paint him with blame. *Longer than we expected.*

'Life flies by, Haviland. He is not to be blamed for wanting to reach out and seize that life any more than I am to blame for choosing not to. I chose to remain with Antoine.' She gave a wan smile. She leaned forward, taking his head between her hands, her fingers combing back his hair. 'You asked me what you are to me, and I shall tell you. You, Haviland North, are my escape.' She kissed him then, full on the mouth, and for the third time that night his body roused to her. He took her beneath him, bracing himself above her, sliding into her with the slow confidence of a lover who knew he had come home and was sure of his welcome, her words hovering on the periphery of his lovemaking. *You are my escape.* But he rather thought she had it backwards because he was more sure than ever she could be his.

Chapter Sixteen

What if she could be more than an escape? Did he dare indulge in all that she offered him, whether she understood she offered it or not? If he made his choice, this passion between them could be sustained beyond the confines of a purely physical *affaire*, he could give free rein to developing the emotional connection that simmered beneath the surface; the one they repressed so thoroughly because it had not been part of their original intentions.

It was the emotional indulgence Haviland debated with himself as the sun came up, throwing its spring morning rays into the courtyard of his apartments. He'd seen Alyssandra safely home after they'd unlocked the door of their impromptu lair and slipped through the ballroom, fifteen minutes apart to avoid notice that they were with each other.

She would be asleep in her bed by now and the very thought conjured images in his mind of her hair spread across a pillow; perhaps an arm thrown across the empty span of bed. These were images of peace and contentment and while they roused him, it was not in an erotic sense, but in a sense of comfort and a surge of protectiveness. He wanted to be in that bed with her; wanted to draw her against him, to feel the curve of her, wanted to match that curve to his, to feel the soft rise and fall of her breathing, wanted to watch the sun fall over her sleeping form and know she was his.

These were new feelings, *stunning* feelings in their own right when he took them out and examined them in the morning light, a cup of coffee at his elbow. These were not responses he'd had with any of his mistresses, not even the last one whom he'd kept for two years. Not once in that entire time had he contemplated anything resembling permanence with her. In converse, the permanence he contemplated with Christina was cold and empty. There were no images of sunlit mornings spent cradled together in bed, no images of nights spent behind locked doors indulging their senses until they were utterly spent to the point of exhaustion.

He'd come to France to fence, to escape for a time, and even to indulge in a physical *affaire* if it presented itself. He'd not come looking for this. But having found it, it compounded the decisions he had to make. Could his destiny include Alyssandra? Now, what had once only been a choice affecting him, now affected her. The equation of leaving his old life behind had just become more complicated and more tempting.

A door opened on the opposite side of their garden.

Archer stepped out, a banyan over an untucked shirt and breeches. His feet were bare, his hair tousled, all indicators he hadn't been out to ride yet. His hands were wrapped around a steaming cup of coffee—a habit they'd all seemed to pick up in Paris.

'Good morning,' Haviland called out in hushed tones. All four bedrooms opened onto the courtyard. If Nolan and Brennan were home, they'd just have fallen asleep.

Archer took the old wooden chair next to him and settled his long form into it. 'A good morning it is. The sun is out, our rustic garden is showing to its best, the coffee is hot and, if I don't miss my guess, something or someone has kept you from your bed. Would I be wrong in assuming it was Miss Leodegrance?'

Haviland sipped his coffee and chuckled. 'No, you would not be wrong.' He blew into the steam rising off his mug. 'Paris is everything I imagined it would be and more. Leaving will be more difficult than I anticipated. I suppose I hoped that being here would satisfy my cravings, not increase them.'

Archer nodded solemnly. 'Paris is a witch of a woman to be sure. She has spells aplenty, even for a horseman like me who prefers the wide-open downs of Newmarket. And Miss Leodegrance? I would suspect she's a large part of that reluctance.'

'There's not much point in pursuing her, is there? I would just have to leave her.' Haviland side-stepped the question.

Archer was too astute and would not be distracted.

'It seems to me you've already caught her and the real question is what to do with her.' He paused, his eyes locked on Haviland's. 'Don't look so shocked. I know she was here. I saw her with you the other night when you went through the courtyard. It seems you've chosen to pursue the lovely Alyssandra Leodegrance despite your misgivings about the future.'

Archer chuckled when Haviland refused to answer. 'I don't envy you, old friend. Now she's got you spinning and you haven't a clue what to do about it.' The silence stretched out between them before Archer spoke again. 'Unless, of course, you've already decided that leaving is your only option.'

Haviland gave a wry smile over the rim of his mug. 'You're more right than you know. She does have me spinning. But you're wrong about the other.' He did have some ideas about what to do about it, rebellious ideas as nascent as the morning itself. He drew a deep breath and tried them on out loud. What would Archer think? 'I was contemplating staying in Paris for a while longer.'

'And then go home?' Archer asked tentatively. Haviland knew they were both cautiously thinking about the letter. If he honoured his parents' plans and returned home in time for the wedding there was no opportunity to go to Italy and make it back, nor was there any reason to go on to the Alps.

'I thought I might try my hand at fencing instruction, maybe see if Leodegrance or some other *salle* would take me on.' This was the riskier idea to voice out loud. He was certain even Archer's tolerance would find the idea bordering on the insane. He did and they were his ideas. They were either crazy or courageous. He'd not realised before how very thin the line between the two could be.

Archer's face broke into a broad grin. Haviland had not expected that. 'Very good. Then you haven't decided to give up yet? I'm glad to hear it. I was worried yesterday that you might have acquiesced to the pre-ordained order of your life. I see there is hope still. You aren't the sort of man who'd ever be happy walking in another's path, but it won't be easy to carve out your own.'

'I know,' Haviland said solemnly. 'But thank you for the support, all the same.'

Archer nodded. 'It will take a brave man. What does Alyssandra think about all this?'

'I haven't told her yet.' Haviland looked out over the garden, not wanting to meet Archer's eyes. The longer he was with Alyssandra, the guiltier he felt about that particular secret. It wasn't supposed to have been relevant.

'So,' Archer began slowly, 'she doesn't know about Christina?'

'Originally, it didn't matter. This was just about escape, but somehow it's become something more.' Haviland shook his head. 'Alyssandra is like me in ways I can't explain, Archer. I know it hasn't been a terribly long time, but she's like a piece of my soul. She will be with me wherever I go, whatever I do for the rest of my life.' He paused to gather his thoughts. 'Being with her isn't about an escape any more. It's about for ever.'

Archer gave a low whistle. 'Then you love her?'

Haviland nodded slowly. 'I do.'

'You're going to have to tell her.'

Haviland knew what that meant. Telling her meant telling her everything. It would be his first major obstacle in his new life. He had to tell Alyssandra about Christina, about wanting to stay in Paris, and that he loved her, that she was the reason he wanted all those things. As hurdles went, he considered it a fairly large one and it would require a leap of faith perhaps on both their parts. But he would have to leap first.

When leaping, timing is everything. It was also true that there's never a perfect time for anything. As the tournament approached, Haviland's days were filled with fencing and practice. He spent hours with Julian and the ever-silent Antoine in the private *salle*, training until his arms ached. Hours more in the club room, poring over treatises, learning and relearning the other prominent styles: the offensive of the Italian school, the defence of the Spanish, even the German school.

His nights were filled with passion, with Alyssandra in his arms. There were candlelight dinners in the tiny bistros of the Latin Quarter where students gathered to debate the politics of the city, long twilight walks in the Tuileries Garden as nannies gathered up their children for the day, a few carefully arranged appearances at social events where they arrived separately. There were nights in his rooms with the French doors open to the evening, the light breeze billowing the curtains and flirting with the candlelight.

He was a new man in these precious days, a man come to life. This was a preview of what every day could be. He had purpose, meaningful direction that drove him out of bed every morning and every evening when he came into her that purpose was reaffirmed. He didn't need estates and a title to feel alive. He needed Alyssandra. He flattered himself that she needed him, too. That the intense privacy and reserve her brother imposed on her life by extent of his own personal choices receded when they were together. He would never know if he didn't ask her. With the tournament two days away, he was running out of time.

Haviland carefully picked his moment during the peaceful interval that comes between bouts of love-making when she lay in his arms, her head on his shoulder, and ventured his question in the candlelit darkness. 'Do you ever think of leaving it all behind?'

Her hand stilled on his chest where she'd been drawing idle circles. Not because he'd taken her by surprise, but because the moment she'd dreaded had arrived: the moment when he'd want more than she could give. She sighed, her breath feathering against his chest. 'Always. But to what avail? Antoine needs me. I'm all the family he has left. And frankly, without Antoine, I'm nothing more than an impoverished noblewoman alone in the world.'

She feared that day would come far too quickly as it was, but that was a fear she could not voice out loud to anyone—not to Haviland who thought Antoine only bore scars on his face, or to Julian, with whom she ought to have been able to share that fear. Julian would use that fear against her to compel her into a marriage with him that made sense only on paper, a marriage that alleviated all her practical concerns about her future, but answered none of her passion. Antoine would never walk. She'd seen the truth in the doctors' faces when the first year after the accident had come and gone without significant improvement. Paralysed individuals didn't usually live long lives. Their bodies weren't strong enough. Could she really expect Antoine to live to a ripe old age? Each winter required more and more effort to keep him warm and safe from the season's catarrhs.

'Surely your brother doesn't expect you to live your entire life for him? I know his accident was grave, but it is only scars on his face. It doesn't stop him from doing what he loves.' Haviland probed gently. From the things he'd shared with her about his family, he understood how sensitive the issue was. It was an issue of honour, after all. To leave was selfish. To stay was sacrificial. Both choices were extremes.

She went back to stroking his chest and tried for distraction. She didn't want to have to explain the truth about Antoine. 'What about you, Haviland? Do you think of leaving it all behind?' Of course, she had only the vaguest idea of what 'it' represented in the question. It was times like this she was struck by how much she cared for him and how little she knew of him.

In the nearly two months he'd been in her life, she knew him as a fencer. The identity she associated with him was wrapped up in who he was at the *salle d'armes*. He'd ceased being Viscount Amersham. He was simply Haviland North. She had difficulty remembering 'it' constituted a title, a fortune, a family, and those were just the things she knew of from rumour. Beyond that day in the gardens, he'd never spoken of them directly to her.

'Sometimes. A lot since I've been here, actually.' His confession surprised her and its implications made her nervous. Was it because of her? His hand played with her hair in a slow, relaxing stroke.

'What could you possibly *want* to leave behind?' She let her voice tease a little, trying to lighten the atmosphere.

'More than you might think. No one's life is perfect no matter what it looks like on the outside,' Haviland said. It was the most he'd ever offered about his life in England and yet it was hardly enough, a subtle reminder that for all the passion he'd offered her, for all the ways in which he'd offered himself, there was still a realm of secrets he was not willing to reveal.

'Would you tell me?' she ventured. 'You once asked me what I was doing with you. Now I want to know what are you doing with me. You could have anyone.' She could feel him tense beneath her palm. She gave a soft, sad laugh. 'I thought so. For all that we have shared between us, it is still not enough to trust the keeping of our secrets. We trust each other completely with our bodies, but not with our thoughts.' She might regret such reticence, but she understood it. She could not tell him about Antoine. It made her wonder, too, just how big his secrets were.

He stirred. 'It's not that. I find I'm afraid of what knowing will do to us. I don't want to lose you over it.'

'I'd rather have you try me and let me be the judge,' Alyssandra whispered. It was hardly fair. He would be disappointed in the end. He would tell her and she could not reciprocate in kind. His arm tightened around her and she knew a thrill of victory. He was preparing. She hoped she wouldn't regret it.

'You know most of it,' he began slowly. 'I'm a viscount, but it's a courtesy title on loan from my father until I inherit the earldom.'

She huffed. 'There's more to it than that, otherwise you wouldn't be so private about it.' But it was enough of a reminder to her that he could only fantasise about walking away from that kind of responsibility. She'd always thought English heirs had it a bit rough—their lives couldn't really start until their fathers died and that in itself was a rather morbid thought to contemplate—that their successes were predicated upon another's death. And then there was the pressure of enhancing the family tree with preferably male progeny.

She raised her head, a horrible thought striking. She knew his secret. 'Dear God, you're married.' It made perfect sense. He was older than most of the young, silly, Englishmen who set out from Paris on their Grand Tours. He was an heir, there were expectations. It explained his privacy.

'No!' he protested. 'I am not married.'

Their eyes held. 'But you will be,' she said slowly. She waited for the denial, but it didn't come. 'Who is she? Do you love her?'

'Her name is Lady Christina Everly and I hardly know her.' Haviland's voice was flat in the darkness. 'She is not my choice. I don't know that I will marry her at all.'

But she was his parents' choice, that much was clear, as was the 'it' she'd so desperately wanted clarified earlier. Leaving 'it' all behind for him meant escaping an arranged marriage, escaping a family that directed his life. She also knew what such a choice would cost him—most immediately it would cost him money and access to a lifestyle that he probably wouldn't appreciate until it was gone. The wealthy were like that, she knew. She'd been in that position of taking luxuries for granted when her father was alive. His death had impacted their finances, but they had recovered decently enough until Antoine's accident had cost them once more. Again they'd recovered, but it was a near-run thing and she was acutely aware of the luxuries she enjoyed today and their cost.

'Do you really have a choice, Haviland?' She could feel the anger rising in him. She'd not wanted their last nights before the tournament to end with discord between them. After the tournament she did not know how much time they'd have left. But she wanted him to see reason. He couldn't walk away, no matter how tempted he was. He would come to hate himself given enough time.

'I do.' His tone was grim. 'I can do what I want or what they want. I want to stay here in Paris with you. I was hoping to teach fencing with your brother or perhaps somewhere else. I'm sure if I do well at the tournament, I could be an asset.'

'But the cost,' she began softly.

'The cost is this: to let them choose means my freedom can be bought.' Haviland was fierce in his rebuttal. She'd not seen him like this, so intense, outside the fencing salon.

'Haviland, it will have a price either way.' She interrupted before he could give further vent to whatever idea he'd set his mind on. She didn't want to hear any more. Her own panic was starting to rise. This was what she'd promised herself wouldn't happen. 'We weren't supposed to get attached. This was to be an escape only.' She threw back the covers and swung her legs over the bed. She had to leave.

Haviland's hand tugged at her arm. Something in his eyes broke, the fierceness receded. 'Don't go. We have time. I am sorry I mentioned it. I did not mean to frighten you off.'

She realised then what his confession had cost him. He'd been afraid to share, afraid of what it would do to them, and she'd justified that fear after minutes ago assuring him she could manage it. Ironically, it wasn't Christina that she couldn't tolerate, it was everything else, the very idea that he was willing to throw it all over for her, and she couldn't possibly accept, couldn't possibly allow that level of sacrifice.

She sat down on the bed. 'I think it would be best

if I did. Haviland, these are big decisions. You have a lot to sort through. I think after you do, you will see that I simply represent your freedom. That won't be enough for me. I can't be—I don't want to be the woman you chose simply because you didn't want to choose another.' That much was true. This was all happening too fast. But it wasn't entirely the truth, just enough of a compelling excuse.

'Alyssandra, I haven't told you the rest. I haven't told you what I've decided to do.'

She cut him off with a shake of her head. 'Now is not the time. You need to keep your mind on the tournament. Nothing else. Promise me?' She feared what else there might be to tell. She was losing on all fronts. She'd lost the emotional detachment and now he wasn't leaving, the very thing she had been counting on to save the Leodegrance secrets and perhaps her heart. It was hard to love someone who was gone. Once he left, he would wear off eventually. She would get over him. But if he stayed? She might love him for ever.

He fell back on the pillows in acquiescence, and she tiptoed out of the room and into the garden. She'd got what she'd asked for—his secret. He'd kept it because it would definitely change the balance between them and it had. But she was glad to know. It made her choices no less difficult, but far more clear. He could not give up his world for her. He only *thought* he wanted to. But she could not allow him to give up everything for a woman who would only have to refuse him.

She knew what she had to do. She had to drive him out of town for both their sakes. She had to enter the fencing competition and defeat him, remind him of his place—just one more Englishman here on a holiday, having a holiday *affaire*, before going home to embrace his realities although it would break her heart to do it. Haviland thought he had choices, but Alyssandra knew she did not, and he didn't either, not really. She loved him too much to let him lie to himself.

Chapter Seventeen

'No, I will not have it! The risk is too much. What happens if "Antoine" is beaten *before* the finals?' Antoine pushed his chair around the large estate office of their home in agitation. 'We've always arranged it so that you simply have to fight once. You face the victor in the final. You have every advantage that way. You're fresh, while they have fought for two days. You've had two days to study them, while they have had no chance to see you in action.'

'Haviland North needs to be beaten before the final,' Alyssandra said, the bluntness of her words drawing Julian's attention from the window. Julian's eyes moved slowly over her face, their eyes locking in silent battle.

'Why is that?' Julian crossed his arms over his chest.

'Because he thinks to become a fencing master in his own right. If he can win the tournament, he could begin to establish himself. People would want to study with him. We cannot afford to lose students to him or to anyone.' *Because he thinks to stay here in Paris for me.* He'd not had to lay that specific plan out in so many words for her to have divined his intentions—foolhardy intentions. What sort of man gave up the things Haviland had to become a fencing master? Well, she knew the answer to that in part—a desperate man looking to escape the confines of an arranged marriage. One should never make decisions from a position of desperation. She had to stop him from embracing what would ultimately be a calamity for him. He would eventually regret this choice if he was allowed to make it.

Julian gave a cold chuckle. 'My dear, how do you know this? I must confess, it seems implausible. He's heir to a title and to a fortune. No rational man would consider making such a choice.'

'I just do,' Alyssandra replied tersely. At least Julian couldn't say too much in front of Antoine without implicating himself for having withheld information.

'Why not simply beat him in the final if he gets that far?' Julian gave a shrug. 'Have you considered someone else may defeat him in the preliminaries and save you the trouble altogether?'

'You've seen him train. What do you think the chances of that are?' Alyssandra scoffed at the idea. She strode to Antoine's desk where he'd been working on setting up the brackets for the tournament. His desk was littered with accepted invitations from swordsmen all over Europe. She picked up a few at random and shuffled through them. 'Ralf Dietrich and his German school? Ralf was fortunate to make the semi-finals last time. Luca Ballucci? He's good, but he's over forty and hasn't the stamina if he gets too deep into the tournament. Sven Olufson? He's been training in Italy. But he needs to. He's all show and no technique when it's required. He wins early matches against novices, but he can't stay with the likes of Ballucci.'

'I will stop North,' Julian said firmly. 'He won't get past me. Set him up in a match against me early in the preliminary rounds when no one is focused on a particular fencer yet.'

At least Julian understood her strategy: eliminate Haviland early before anyone could become enamoured of his skill. It was cruel, of course, but it would be better to have this whimsical dream of his thwarted at this stage when it wasn't too late for him to claim the life he was meant for. And with luck, Haviland would never know of her part in it. Her heart sank at the thought. This was one more secret to keep from him. It also meant giving him up was imminent. Even if she was the driving force keeping him in Paris, he would have no way to stay now.

Antoine's eyes slid away from her to Julian. 'Julian, I can't afford to risk you so early in the tournament. What if you don't beat him? I need you to advance to semi-finals at the least. Who wants to study at a *salle* where the senior instructor is defeated in the early matches?'

Alyssandra bit her lip, watching Julian process Antoine's concern. It wasn't often she and Julian were on the same side of an issue. That in itself was a flag for caution. 'You don't think I can do it?' Julian was incredulous. 'I've beaten him before, quite a few times before.'

Antoine played with a figurine on a side table. Her brother was planning something. She wished she knew what. He met Julian's eyes briefly. 'You haven't beaten him since he's been training privately with us.' It was a gentle but stern reminder. Antoine seldom reprimanded Julian.

'Training with *me*!' Julian corrected in outrage. 'Who better to know him than me? I spar with him almost daily. I'm the one who has worked on his *passata sotto* and his *in quartata*, with all of it.'

'And you've trained him well,' Alyssandra intervened. 'The sign of a true master is to create a pupil who is better than his teacher.'

Antoine's brown gaze was agate hard. 'But we cannot have that on display at the tournament. If North is to beat you, Julian, it can happen no sooner than the semi-finals. Enough discussion. I cannot afford to have either of you approach North before the elimination rounds are over. We will do it as we've always done it. Alyssandra, you will face only the winner of the semi-finals.'

'Antoine, please reconsider this,' Alyssandra began to protest.

'No buts. We will take our chances with his ability to set up a *salle d'armes* if indeed that's what he intends to do. Otherwise, if he's willing to work here, I'm certainly open to offering him a position. Still, I'm with Julian. The idea of any of this coming to

pass seems fairly preposterous given his background.'
Antoine wheeled himself towards the doors leading
outside to the garden with a stern look to them both.
'I am still the master and my decision is final.'

'So the Englishman has jilted you already?' Julian
barely waited for Antoine to move out of earshot. He
leaned against the desk, arms crossed, a smirk on his
mouth. 'You were so willing to spread your legs for
him, so willing to risk us all for your passing pleasure
and now you want us to risk everything once more
for your revenge.'

His crass words roused her temper, her anger bub-
bling. 'If that's what you think, you understand nothing.'

'I know you've been with him every night for the
last two weeks. I know you send him notes at the
club, arranging rendezvous.' What had he seen? *How
much* had he seen? The thought made her skin crawl.

Julian advanced. She stood her ground. She would
not give him the pleasure of seeing her retreat even
an inch. His hand cupped her cheek, cold against her
skin. 'After all you've put me through, I still want
you, you needn't worry on that score. Once the Englishman is gone, you will see reason. Antoine will
see reason when I explain it all to him.' He gave her
a hard smile, eyes glittering dangerously. 'Really, the
best thing you can do for my suit is to keep seeing
him. It gives my case more substance when I go to
your brother.' His thumb ran over her lip in a rough
caress. 'You needn't concern yourself with that just
yet, though. I will wait until North has gone so there's

no risk of Antoine insisting North be the one to make an honest woman of you.'

Alyssandra's jaw tightened at the intimacy. No, he wouldn't dare risk that. Julian was too great of a strategist to make that mistake. Haviland's presence in the city was the only thing holding Julian back. 'Take your hands off me.'

Julian raised his hands in a parody of surrender and stepped back. 'For now. But mark my words, you will be mine. I've waited and wanted too long. In your heart you know it's the right thing to do, the best way to protect Antoine and the life you are so well acquainted with. It would be a shame to throw all of that away. I don't think poverty would do you justice, Alyssandra.' He backed to the door and gave her a mocking bow.

Alyssandra held her rigid posture until he was gone before she sank into a chair, a hand pressed to her mouth. Her escape had become her prison. Julian had found the ultimate way to use Haviland against her. Her first inclination was to run straight to Antoine, to expose Julian's duplicity but she couldn't do that without exposing herself, too. When she was smaller, Antoine had always been her refuge. She had run to him with broken dolls to fix, with tears to dry. But she wasn't eight any longer and she'd become far stronger than that little girl had been. Their roles had become reversed. It was Antoine who needed her now. It would crush him to know the two people he trusted most had betrayed him.

She'd been aware of Julian's attraction to her for

some time now. After all, he'd already proposed once after Antoine's accident. At the time, she'd assumed he'd proposed out of a sense of honour, an attempt to make things right. But there was no honour in what he'd proposed today. Today had been blackmail pure and simple. It had been threats and coercion of the worst sort. Antoine thought he could trust Julian. How long had Julian simply gulled her brother and lain in wait for the moment to pounce? The moment to push his grander scheme?

What was that scheme? Was it solely a lust-driven obsession for her, or something larger? She knew only a little of Julian's background, that he'd risen from meagre beginnings. Did he aspire to take the *salle d'armes*? He'd never threatened to expose the great secret before.

That was without a doubt the scariest part of this morning's confrontation, the part that made her want to run to Antoine. Exposure would ruin them. But if Julian were the one to do the exposing, he would be able to separate himself from the damage. He could turn himself into the hero for bringing the deception to everyone's attention. Julian was a careful man—he would have given much thought about how to do it.

Alyssandra sighed. It was difficult indeed to fight a battle on two fronts. She had to keep Haviland from making a reckless decision that would destroy his future, while keeping Julian from destroying hers. As a woman kept behind the scenes, she had little power to thwart either of them. Not for the first time, she cursed her gender. It had kept her from proclaiming outright her excellence in a male-only sport, had kept her from finding a way to support her little family without resorting to a dangerous deception. If only she were a man—an independent man who wasn't under her brother's control like her incarnation of him was.

An idea began to form. She would have to be Antoine Leodegrance for the finals. But until then, she could be whoever she liked. Perhaps an anonymous Austrian come to try his skill. She knew very well that the tournament would take walk-in entries the first day. There was no guarantee she'd be paired with either Haviland or Julian throughout the tournament, but eventually, she would meet them and she would defeat them. She only hoped it would be soon enough to suit her purposes.

Admittedly her plan left a lot to chance. There was an easier way. She could simply tell Haviland. Perhaps there was a way to tell him without jeopardising her brother's secret. All she had to do was convince him she would not have him, that there was no reason to stay. It was testament to just how difficult that would be that she'd actually contemplated entering the fencing tournament as a more viable option. There was no 'simply' about it. He would be hurt. But in the final analysis of her options, it was the only one that left no margin for error.

Alyssandra called for her hat and gloves. It was best to get it over with before she lost her courage.

Damn her, she was going to *him*. Julian let the curtain to the front parlour fall. He paced the room, gathering his thoughts. He'd not expected this. His threat had been designed to force her into a corner, force her to realise she had no allies. The two men she might have counted on were of no use to her here. She couldn't tell Antoine without exposing herself and she couldn't tell Haviland without exposing Antoine, something her selfless little soul wouldn't conceive of doing. She would realise the only option left was to throw herself on his mercy.

He would be the man she turned to whether she wanted to or not. He would welcome her with apologies, with assurances that he'd only done this for her own good, to help her see reason and the foolishness of her headstrong notions. He would take her hands and kiss them, he would kiss her mouth, and she would give over to him, acknowledging his superior strength, his superior intellect with the acquiescence of her body. He would take her beneath him, roughly to make sure she understood who was in charge. Oh, yes, he had ways to make her understand that, pleasurable ways that had him rousing already at the prospect.

Those urges had to be subdued. He needed to think or the prize would slip away. He couldn't risk her spilling everything to Haviland North. Secrets only had power when no one knew them. If too many people knew them, or if the wrong people knew them, they weren't secrets any more, they became powerless little pieces of information. That's exactly what would happen if Haviland North turned out to be honourable. If not, it simply wouldn't be fair. If anyone was going to ruin the Leodegrances it was going to be him—he was the one who had put in the years, not some upstart English viscount who had stumbled into Alyssandra's bed on the conditions of his good looks.

Julian went to the small escritoire in the corner of the sitting room and wrote a quick note to two of his less savoury acquaintances. If his means seemed extreme, his ends would justify them. He wasn't going to give Alyssandra a chance to betray him. This next move was all his. She would be rather surprised to see that she had been outmanoeuvred.

There was movement at his open door. Haviland looked up, half-irritated over the interruption to his letter writing. 'Yes, Nolan?'

Nolan raised an eyebrow at his testy greeting. 'Don't kill the messenger. That's why I don't write letters home. It always puts me in a bad mood,' he jested. But Haviland thought there was truth to it. If he had to write to Nolan's father, he'd be in a perpetually bad mood, too.

Haviland sighed and pushed back from the desk with a penitent smile. He was learning that travel with friends meant never fully escaping them. It wasn't necessarily a bad thing. He and Archer had had several meaningful conversations. But it did take some adjustment. In London, he lived alone. 'I'm sorry, I have a lot on my mind before the tournament tomorrow.'

Nolan gave a knowing nod. 'In that case, you might be interested to know part of what is on your mind is also in the parlour. Are you receiving?'

Haviland gave a start. Alyssandra was here? He'd not expected to see her, especially after last night. They'd parted neutrally at best. He wasn't even going to the *salle* today. He would exercise in the garden instead. 'Did she say what brought her?' Something must have happened, something out of the ordinary and probably not for the good. Had her brother discovered their *affaire*? He was halfway to the door, shoving his arms through a coat before Nolan had a chance to answer.

Nolan caught his arm in caution. 'Gather yourself, man. Rushing to a woman's side makes you an easy mark. She'll think she can manipulate you. She didn't say, but I'd wager my last *sou* she's upset.' Nolan paused, his eyes going narrow in speculation. 'Dear God, Haviland, you don't suppose she's come to tell you she's with child? Make sure it's yours.' It was affirmation of Nolan's rather cynical train of thought that his mind went straight to sex.

Nolan's thought roused rapid speculation on Haviland's part. Had she? It wasn't outside the realm of possibility, although it seemed a mite early to know. They had not always been careful in slaking their need, the heat of the moment overriding caution at the critical point. Still, he didn't think she'd know. They'd not discussed it and it hardly seemed like something she'd tell him the day before the tournament if she only suspected it. Alyssandra was the sort to wait until she was sure about something. Even so, Haviland's reaction was not one of horrific withdrawal like Nolan's. Instead, a single line ran through his mind. *It would certainly make things easier.* She would have to let him stay.

Haviland stepped into the front parlour and she rose immediately at the sight of him, her hands gripping one another tightly at her waist, her face a trifle pale. Nolan was right. She was upset. 'Alyssandra, what brings you here? Are you well?' He offered a friendly smile, trying to ease her. Whatever she had to tell him, he wanted her to know it would be safe with him.

'Haviland, I'm sorry to impose.' She flicked a glance at Nolan who was hovering at his shoulder, making it clear about who was really imposing. 'Might we walk? There is something I've come to tell you.'

Nolan gave him a 'told-you-so wink' and earned an elbow in the ribs.

'There's a quiet park not far from here where we can expect some privacy.' Haviland gave Nolan a pointed look. But his insides were reeling. Nolan was so seldom wrong about people. He offered Alyssandra his arm, overwhelmed with the sensation that the moment he stepped out the door his life was going to change.

Chapter Eighteen

Haviland noted two shabbily dressed men in his peripheral vision three streets from the house. He told himself he was being overprotective. It was the middle of the day in a big city. The streets were busy and full of all sorts, workmen and shoppers alike. Two streets later, the men were still behind them, only closer now. They'd been subtly inching towards them. Haviland wondered what they might do, *how much* they could do in public. But he'd never been a man to rely on others to dictate his response. If he waited to act, it might be too late.

He tightened his grip on Alyssandra's arm, the subtle pressure urging her to pick up her pace, his tone low and measured. 'I don't mean to panic you, my dear, but I believe we are being followed.' She started to turn her head. 'No, don't look around. They're to the left, over my shoulder. They've just started to cross the street.'

Alyssandra kept her face forward, but he felt her body stiffen with awareness. Her eyes darted to the walking stick in his hand. 'May I assume there's something inside that stick of yours?'

'Yes.' Like most London gentleman, his walking sticks were sheaths for sword-sticks.

'Good. Then we have a choice. What will it be? Shall we make a run for it, or shall we see what they want?' Alyssandra was a cool customer beside him.

'I'd rather not place you in danger,' Haviland murmured a protest under his breath. But it seemed he had no choice in the matter. The men made their move as they passed an alley. One of them gave Haviland a rough shove into the dim corridor between two buildings, the other dragged Alyssandra away from him. Haviland stumbled, cursing himself for having waited a moment too long and giving these thugs the current advantage, but he had his sword-stick out when he recovered his balance.

His first thought was for Alyssandra's safety, but it was clear from the outset the men were here for him. One of them held her, but only to keep her out of the way, which was proving to be quite the challenge since she didn't intend to be subdued. The bigger concern was the other man advancing on him, drawing a sword-stick of his own. Interesting. That was most definitely *not* the weapon of choice for street thugs. Things were not what they seemed in this alley, but there was no time to contemplate the mystery. The man thrust his sword at him, trying to catch his blade and turn it aside. Haviland deflected him, but the move made it plain the man also had some training to go with his sword.

Haviland went into battle mode, his body and mind understanding this was not a practice exercise. This was a street fight and the rules of the piste didn't apply here. Nor could he be assured this man would stop at first blood. He must assume, and quite morbidly so, this man was out to kill him or at the least wound him. Haviland struck back hard and fierce, seeking to end the encounter as soon as possible. The longer it went on, the greater the risk of injury.

Haviland thrust at the man's unprotected shoulder, the tip of his weapon striking through the cloth of the man's shirt. A bloody rose blossomed on the fabric. The man ignored the attack and the pain with a growl, a knife flashing in his good hand. That was not what Haviland was hoping for. He'd been hoping to deter the attacker, not anger him to greater lengths. He had no knife to draw, but his opponent's wounded shoulder would equalise the fight. Haviland stepped back, the two of them circling each other, reassessing.

His opponent launched a furious offensive. Haviland was ready for him. He'd gauged correctly that his opponent would recognise time was not on his side. He was bleeding, his strength ebbing with every second. If his opponent wanted victory, he'd have to act quickly. Haviland struck again, this time on the wrist and the man howled in pain, calling for his comrade as he sank to his knees. Haviland knew a primal sense of satisfaction, the fight was nearly done.

He did not see the other man let Alyssandra go and charge him from the side. Haviland went down in a pile of stinking alley debris, the man on top of him, fists ready to do damage. But Haviland's reflexes were quick. He twisted, angling his body and eventually getting his hands on the man's neck in a throttle and a leg around him to offer enough leverage to flip him over. Haviland landed two well-placed blows to the man's jaw and the man went out cold.

He rose, staggering a bit, but ready to finish off the man with the sword only to discover there was no need. Alyssandra had picked up his dropped sword-stick. It had gone flying when he'd been tackled and now she had it trained on the bleeding man. He still held his weapons, his back pressed to the brick wall, but the man had no offence left in him.

'Alyssandra, give me the sword and I'll finish this.' Haviland moved beside her, his eyes never leaving the remaining man in case he tried a last desperate lunge. Hurt or not, his sword could put a gash in Alyssandra's side if she wasn't careful.

Alyssandra wasn't listening, her gaze intent on her quarry. 'I'll finish this *enculé* myself.' She stepped in a half-circle around the man, her arm extended, her blade poised straight at the man's throat. His fencer's mind recognised the elegant footwork, the positioning. She spat another curse in French and, with a quick movement of her wrist, divested him of his sword first and then changed direction to catch his knife. The tip of her blade returned to his throat. 'Now, tell me who sent you or I'll run you through.'

She would do it, too. There was something cool and thorough in her poise as she threatened their attacker. The man's eyes darted towards Haviland, his tone pleading. 'Don't let her hurt me.'

Haviland laughed and crossed his arms. 'Then tell her what she wants to know.' He stood at the ready— if it actually came to the skewering of this man, he'd intervene. No gentleman stood by and let a woman do his work for him, but Haviland was also a smart man. A smart man understood Alyssandra would not take well to being considered helpless. But that was something they'd sort out later. There'd been a lot of surprises revealed in this alley and not all of them lay with their attackers.

'I will give you until the count of three.' Alyssandra pushed her point against the soft part of the man's throat. 'One, two—'

'All right!' The man was nearly crying from the sword, his wound, his blood.

Alyssandra stepped back, the sword point still held at the ready. 'Tell us.'

'Julian Anjou,' the man gasped and rushed on. 'It wasn't meant to be dangerous. We weren't to hurt you.' He was all but begging Alyssandra. 'Just the English fellow and just enough so that he couldn't fight at the tournament.' He scowled, making it clear he thought the shoulder wound was entirely too much.

Alyssandra paled and dropped her sword arm Haviland wondered if she knew how exposed she was in those seconds. He stepped up and closed his hand over hers, taking the sword-stick. 'Go, *allez*, take your friend with you. Tell Julian Anjou the next time he sends thugs after us, it will be even worse.'

Haviland slammed his sword into the sheath of his hollowed-out walking stick for emphasis.

He followed the man with his eyes until he was gone, dragging his friend with him. 'Did you know about this?' Haviland turned to Alyssandra. 'Was this what you came to tell me?' His tone accused them both—she and Julian. His earlier speculations seemed foolish now. She had not come to tell him about a child. His stomach knotted. Now that his mind had time to think it through there was room for conspiracy; she'd not been frightened by their approach, she'd not been in any danger. Her struggles, even her bravado with the blade later could have been for his benefit, an attempt to absolve her of any complicity. He spat the last words at her, advancing until he gripped her shoulders, his eyes narrowed. 'Or did you come to lure me out?'

'I knew nothing about this!' Alyssandra cried indignantly, trying to shake off his hands. His words cut her cruelly. There was so much to think through it was hard to get her thoughts sorted; Julian had attacked Haviland and—*mon dieu!*—Haviland accused her of being part of it. 'How could you think such a thing? If I was part of it, why would I have pressed him for a name? I would have sent him off before he could expose Julian's plot.'

She shoved at Haviland's chest, her anger starting to replace her shock. He stank of alley garbage, his immaculate clothes ruined, and she'd been so very frightened for him. All she wanted to do was hold him, even with the stench, to reassure herself he was unhurt. How could she want a man who doubted her loyalty? She could only rail at him.

'How dare you! How dare you question me after what you put me through?' She gave her emotions full vent. 'I felt real terror when that man drew a sword against you.' She'd also known a fierce primal thrill in seeing Haviland advance on him, showing him no quarter. 'And when you fell.' Her anger broke, her voice trembled. She'd only had a few seconds to act. She'd not thought about the implications, she'd simply grabbed up the sword and done her part. 'I wasn't about to stand by and watch you die in an alley. Does that sound like I was Julian's accomplice?' Yet she understood she was asking him to believe her on very little evidence. She had her secrets. She could not truly blame him for believing the worst. He was a worldly man.

She tilted her chin up in a show of defiance, locking eyes with him. Perhaps it didn't matter if he believed her. She was sending him away regardless. She just hadn't imagined it happening this way. She'd rehearsed her speech on the way over and nowhere had she written in that script 'alleyway' or 'smell of rubbish'. Maybe, too, her pride was at stake. She didn't want him remembering her this way, with doubt and cynicism. There were other memories, better memories, to take with him when he went.

His eyes softened, his hands dropped from her shoulders and he sighed. 'You're right, of course. Forgive me?' His mouth opened and then compressed into a grim line. 'No, I won't make excuses for my conjecture. I will simply apologise.'

He bent his head to hers, foreheads touching, and they stood that way for a long while in the privacy of the alley. She'd sought him out today to let him go and now she wanted nothing so much as to keep him close. At last she spoke, saying the only thing a girl could under those circumstances. 'Haviland, will you do something for me?'

'Mmm? Yes, anything.' She could hear the laughter in his voice. 'I believe I've told you that before.'

'Good. I need you to take a bath.'

They made their way back to Haviland's apartments, heads held against the stares they acquired. Haviland looked atrocious and smelled worse. A few ladies even put handkerchiefs over their noses as they passed. But Alyssandra stared them down while Haviland laughed and called her a tigress. She didn't care. Haviland was unharmed and that was all that mattered. Other things would matter later, but for now this was enough.

'We were attacked by ruffians,' Alyssandra said curtly, meeting the eyes of his travelling companions when they entered the front parlour.

'Lovely cologne, Haviland,' the one called Nolan teased, but Archer, the one she remembered from the soirée, rose without remark and called for a bath. 'I'll have the tub set up in your room, Hav. Shall I tell Renaud to attend you?'

'No, I'll see to him.' Alyssandra was brisk and efficient, marching Haviland across the room, trying to pretend she didn't see the looks exchanged between his two friends.

'Are you sure you aren't hurt, Hav?' Nolan called to their retreating backs. 'Seems like you might have lost your balls.'

'We're ignoring you!' Haviland answered as they slipped into his room and shut the door behind them.

'Your friends care for you.' Alyssandra helped him out of his coat and bent to work on his boots. A valet would have the devil's own time getting them polished after today's events.

'We've been together a long time.' Haviland let out a sigh as the boots came off. 'Since we were boys in school, actually.' He flopped back on the bed. 'This may be the last time we all go gallivanting together, our last great adventure before…' His voice trailed off. She knew what he was thinking. Before marriage came to each of them and they took up the responsibilities of husbands and fathers and, in his case, heirs. She tugged at his hand. 'Up with you, before the water cools.'

The tub had been set up in front of his doors leading to the garden and it made a fairly romantic picture with the white-gauze curtains billowing softly in the afternoon breeze as a backdrop. Haviland stripped out of his trousers and sank into the water with a grateful sigh. 'That feels nice.'

'This will feel nice, too.' Alyssandra picked up a cloth and the bar of soap and began to scrub, heedless of the water soaking her dress. The muscles of his arms rippled under her hands where they passed over him. He lay back, giving her free access to his chest and lower. She washed the most intimate parts of him, stroking him with the warm, wet cloth, feeling him come alive in her hand.

'I dare say my own baths aren't nearly this exciting,' Haviland drawled when it became clear they were heading for a wet conclusion.

She leaned forward, pressing a kiss to his mouth. 'I should hope not.' She rose from her knees then and held out a thick towel. 'Shall we get you dry?'

'And then we'll get you wet, unless you're wet already?' Haviland's hot eyes raked her, and heat pooled inside her as he rose from the tub, all dripping, muscled male. He could turn her to a puddle with a simple look. She would miss that when he was gone.

'You're a naughty man, Haviland North, for all your outward show to the contrary,' she teased, kneeling to dry his legs and work her way up.

'An honest one.' Haviland choked out the words as she wrapped the towel about his phallus and stroked.

'There, that should hold you long enough to get you on the bed.' She could see he was disappointed, that he'd harboured hopes of her using her mouth on him. 'Maybe later.' She gave him a wink and worked the back of her laces free until her dress gaped about her. 'I want you inside me first.'

Her dress fell, and Haviland swept her up in his arms. 'And so you shall have me.'

This was better; having him over her, having him in her, her legs wrapped about him, holding him tight.

It was far better than the threat of the alley, the fear of losing him, the hatred of his doubt. She slid against him, encouraging him with her body. She didn't want to leave this room. She wanted to stay locked inside for ever, where Julian Anjou's jealousy couldn't reach them, where the outcomes of tournaments wouldn't dictate their futures, where they had no secrets between them. There were no secrets in sex, in this bed.

In these moments she could forget what she'd come here to do. She could forget that a suitable lady waited with his estates in England as part of his duty, or that she could never have him because she owed her brother her loyalty above all else.

He came into her hard, and she moaned her desire, her desperation, to hold on to this feeling for ever. 'I don't want to give this up.' Recklessly, she spoke the words out loud before she could take them back. 'I want every spring afternoon in your bed and every autumn night.'

'And the winter? The summer?' Haviland nuzzled her neck and nipped at her ear, his body still warm and joined with hers, neither of them in a hurry to part.

She stretched into him. 'I'll want those, too.'

The magic of the afternoon was taking them both, washing away the fear and doubt of the alley as assuredly as the tub had washed the grime from his body. 'I meant what I said last night about leaving it all.' He pressed kisses down the column of her throat, slowly, randomly. 'If I win the tournament, you can have them. *We* can have them.'

She put a finger to his lips. 'Shhh. Don't talk about it. Don't jinx it.' She shifted beneath him, and he rolled to his side. She felt the absence of him too keenly.

'Then perhaps we should talk about other things.' Haviland's hand caressed her hair, his touch as soft as his voice at her ear. 'Such as why Julian would go quite so far as to hire thugs to attack me in an alley and how is it that you held a man at sword point with the efficiency of an expert who had done it before?'

Alyssandra drew a deep breath. The moment of truth had come. But which truths to give him?

Chapter Nineteen

'Julian and I quarrelled over you. He sees you as a threat at the tournament.' All true, if vague. 'My brother hosts this tournament every two years. For the last two tournaments, Julian has been the one to win the coveted prize of facing Antoine in the finals. It's a great coup for our *salle*, to have our senior instructor do so well.' The first time, Julian had actually faced Antoine. It had been just a few months before the accident. The second time, it had been her behind the mask.

'He's grown complacent, then? He expects that spot will always be his?' Haviland chuckled.

'Just the opposite, I think,' Alyssandra said seriously. Julian could not be taken lightly. But if Haviland did take him lightly, it was her fault. She could not tell him everything. 'I think he's had a taste of success and wants more. He sees possibilities, but he also sees how fragile the string is they hang by.'

Haviland's arm shifted from about her and he rolled to his side, facing her. 'Anjou grows ambitious.

But for what? Or is it for whom?' Something primal and fiercely male flickered in his eyes. 'I've asked you before. You were not forthcoming, but I did not press because the nature of our relationship did not necessarily require it. But things have, ah, progressed since then. What is Julian Anjou to you?'

'He is my brother's friend. He's not forsaken Antoine since the accident. He's kept the *salle* running. I do not know how we could have managed without him.' But another phrase leapt to mind, too, without prompting: *secret keeper*. She'd understood that for a long time. But it wasn't until now, with Haviland beside her, that the phrase took on a different meaning. Before, it had been a term that connoted loyalty, if nothing else. One who kept another's secrets was loyal, trustworthy, a protector. But the reverse was also true. Secret keepers had power, leverage. They could just as easily be destroyers as protectors. That was what Julian had become with his threats this morning—a destroyer. One word and he could bring down Antoine's work of a lifetime and she'd given him the power to do it.

'Do you feel indebted to him, then?'

'No.' That, too, was true. 'Julian had been a junior instructor at the *salle* under my father, even though he's older than Antoine by several years. But he was a hard worker and very talented. My father's death was very sudden and a bit sensational.' She paused, wincing.

'You don't have to tell me,' Haviland soothed.

She probably didn't, but she would. 'I shouldn't

mind, it's been eight years now and all is well. The brief scandal has passed. He was duelling over his mistress on a bridge. When I say on a bridge, I mean on the very rim of it, the railing, the wall's edge. My father was famed for his balance, and that was part of the challenge—to duel on a strip no more than ten inches wide. He fell and drowned. It wasn't here in the city, of course, but news like that travels with all haste.'

She shrugged. 'Antoine and I were young, only twenty. But Antoine was already a champion. The question was whether or not being a champion was enough to keep the *salle* open. Would instructors stay under Antoine's leadership? Would pupils stay? Would new ones come? That was where Julian stepped in. For the first three years, it was Julian's leadership that saved us. Instructors were willing to follow him and he convinced them that Antoine was worth following as well. It helped, of course, that Antoine won several tournaments and developed a reputation of his own.' She sighed. 'Does that explain what Julian is to me?' She didn't know how much more truth she could give him.

'I suspect Julian disagrees with you on the owing piece.' Haviland studied her with consideration.

'He's been made senior instructor. He is literally the face of the *salle* since Antoine can no longer perform that function,' Alyssandra protested.

'That's well and good but it's you he wants, it's you he believes he's entitled to.'

Alyssandra looked down, unable to meet his gaze.

'I know he thinks that, but he's not entitled to me. I'm not available to him.'

Haviland lifted her chin. 'Is that why you quarrelled this morning? Did Julian send men after me because of the tournament or because of you?'

'Perhaps both.' She would never be able to sell the lie at close quarters. 'He knows our association did not end that day in the park.'

She watched anger light Haviland's eyes like a flame travelling a fuse. He understood the implication. 'The bastard had us followed,' Haviland ground out. 'I should call him out.'

Alyssandra could think of nothing worse. She pressed a hand to his chest. 'That would solve nothing except to bloody you both and call my brother's attention to things he need not worry over.' The very last thing she needed was Antoine dragged into this. He would insist on marriage if he knew. She didn't want Haviland to recognise that. At this point, Haviland would think that played into his hand perfectly. 'Promise me, whatever happens between us, I want it to be our choice, a choice made just between the two of us.'

Haviland picked up her hand from where it lay on his chest and brought it to his lips. 'I promise.' Perhaps it was unfair to have manipulated him, when she knew full well how much he valued a sense of his own freedom of choice. He would not deny her the same, at least in theory. He might feel very differently about that once he realised what her choice would be, what her choice could *only* be.

'Does this mean you've thought about what I said last night? I had hoped when Nolan told me you were here that you'd come because you had.' Hope flickered briefly in his blue eyes. She hated to disappoint him.

'No, I came to warn you, and, as I recall, we promised not to speak of those things until after the tournament,' she reprimanded lightly. She was only buying herself time, but it would be enough time for him to rethink his choices.

Haviland sighed in resignation. 'I will hold you to that promise. We will talk about it. Nothing can be decided until we do and I am not a patient man. If you won't tell me that, then tell me how is it that you are so skilled with a sword?'

His tone had turned playful, a sign that he felt the danger had passed—Julian had been explained to an acceptable extent. Haviland could understand misguided passions and male jealousy. She'd spun that tale well and it was full of truths even if it omitted others like the power of the secret Julian held and what he'd threatened to do with that power.

What he *didn't* understand was that this new question he asked was the more dangerous one by far. It represented the heart of the secret. Alyssandra moved her hand down his body, finding his phallus already beginning to stir again and closed her hand around it. She gave him a coy smile. 'Is it so hard to believe a fencing master like my father would not train his daughter, too?' She could tell him that much.

'I trained alongside Antoine when we were growing up.' She matched her words to the rhythm of her hand on him so that he wouldn't want the story to go on too long. 'My father felt a girl should know how to defend herself.' But that was as far as his enlightenment went. A girl, no matter how talented, could not compete, could not train at the *salle* with the other fencers. She would always resent him for that limitation as much as she loved him for the other. 'I still train with Antoine.' Another truth that would lead to a misconstrued conclusion. She was starting to understand one didn't have to lie to create subterfuge.

'Really?' Haviland seemed impressed. 'Perhaps you and I should train together some time.' She could tell from his voice his attentions were drifting away to other pleasures. That was probably for the best since the only response her mind could seem to make was *we already have*.

'You've failed? Two of you against one in an alley and a man taken by surprise at that?' The two men, already giving every appearance of having been beaten to pulps, stepped backwards, giving Julian space as he took a vicious swipe with his sabre, slicing through the fabric of a stuffed dummy in one of the *salle*'s training rooms.

He was to give a sabre lesson in a few minutes, the last one of the day, although he was hardly in the mood after hearing the news. He would have enjoyed handing them a beating if they weren't so battered as it was. To begin with, they were late. He'd expected them much earlier. That had been the first sign they'd fallen afoul of trouble. How long did it take to deliver injury in an alley? Fifteen minutes? They'd been gone since noon and it was nearing six. Anger pulsed through him. These idiots had failed in their very simple task! He took another swipe, enjoying the satisfaction of their fear.

'He was better with a sword than we thought,' the one with the bandaged shoulder said with a hint of accusation in his tone as if he believed he'd been led astray.

'I warned you he was good. Surprise was your best element.' Julian cursed freely. He'd given them every advantage and yet they had failed.

'You didn't warn us about *her*. You said nothing about her being a sword-wielding bitch.' The bandaged man spat. 'She put that blade to my throat and that was *after* he stabbed me and blood was running everywhere.'

'And she kicked me and bit me and scratched me,' the other man sporting a purple jaw complained.

'Bested by a woman? Tsk, tsk,' Julian scoffed. 'I'm not sure I'd be bragging about that.' He stopped his angry stabbing and stared at each of them. 'Is there anything else you'd like to tell me?'

The men looked down at their feet. 'No, we'd like our money, please, and we'll be off.'

A cold fear uncurled in Julian's belly. These men hadn't just been beaten. They'd been thoroughly whipped. What had the one said? Alyssandra had held him at sword point? He didn't know them personally, they were arranged for him by an old friend from the streets—they owed him nothing in terms of loyalty. If circumstances were dire enough, they would not feel compelled to die to keep his secrets.

Julian whipped the sabre up, pressing the point of the blade into the stockier man's belly. They needn't know a sabre was for slicing, not piercing. All they needed to know was that blades were sharp and Haviland had already taught that lesson for him. '*What* did you tell them?'

'Nothing! We swear,' the other man avowed hastily.

Julian gave an evil grin and pushed the blade harder, watching the man gasp. 'I am not sure your friend agrees with you. Maybe you would like to try a different answer?'

'He told them your name,' the man with the sabre pressed to him confessed, ratting out his 'friend' with apparent ease. 'It wasn't me, I swear that's true.'

'No,' his companion sneered. 'You couldn't do anything. That gentleman had laid you out cold with his fists. It was just me trying to fend for myself, trying to get us both out of there.'

Julian gave a cold chuckle. 'Don't lay it on too thick. I doubt you were a veritable hero in the alley. You gave me up quick enough. I'd say your loyalty could use a little polish.' He put up his sabre. 'Go on, get out.'

'But our money, sir?' one of them managed to stammer. Clearly he'd not frightened them enough.

Julian made a threatening gesture with the sabre that sent them scurrying towards the door. 'I don't pay men for failure and I certainly don't pay them for betrayal. Get out if you value your lives.'

Alone, Julian sat down hard on a crate of equipment, head in his hands. What did he do if he valued his own life? He couldn't simply just 'get out'. His whole livelihood was tied to the *salle*. Would Alyssandra go to Antoine and expose him? Would it be enough to turn Antoine against him? Antoine had always been his unwitting champion—dear, young, impressionable but ungodly talented Antoine. He'd recognised the vulnerability and the skill in the young *vicomte* from the start and he'd used it to win Antoine's friendship. The boy he'd been had been so desperate to give it after his father's death and the man he'd become needed him so much now. Perhaps the need would allow Antoine to forgive him.

If Alyssandra ratted him out. Perhaps she wouldn't. How could she without exposing herself and her little perfidy? There was some hope in that. What would Antoine do if confronted with his sister's *affaire* with an Englishman versus his friend's attempt to mitigate the Englishman's presence in all of their lives? Perhaps he could sell his actions as those chosen out of misguided loyalty for Antoine?

The door to the training room opened. Julian rose and took a moment to compose himself before turning. It would be his student come for the sabre lesson. '*Bon soir*, Monsieur Delacorte. I am just...'

His words died. Alyssandra slammed the door shut and strode across the room, trousers tight across her hips, shirt tucked into the waistband emphasising the fullness of her breasts. Another time he might have given those charms more appreciation, but at the moment all of his rather considerable appreciation was fixed on the sabre in her hand.

'En garde.' Her face bore no expression as she took up the position, a sure sign of the depths of her fury. Good lord, there was a reason men didn't teach women to fight. Sometimes they got angry.

Julian matched her position, his own eyes narrowing. Perhaps this was the perfect time after all to teach her a lesson about what happens to a woman who overreaches herself in a man's world. He executed a couple of feints to see what she would do. 'Come for a lesson, have you?' He parried her initial attack. 'Straight from your lover's bed? I have to inform you I do have a lesson shortly.' He barely dodged a slice at his right side.

'Then I hope you'll have enough time to get cleaned up.' She deftly sidestepped his blade. She'd become good. He'd not faced her with sabres for a while. Damn her father for training both his children in the art of all the blades. She was as gifted as Antoine and it didn't matter the sword—rapier, épée, daggers, sabres—the Leodegrances were born with a talent for them all in their blood.

She lunged, and he was too slow. Her blade sliced through the sleeve of his shirt. Fabric ripped. 'You tried to kill him today.' They circled, Julian dancing back from the edge of her sword.

'Killed is far too strong a word, my dear. A scratch, a nick, is all. But even that didn't succeed.' He tried

to sound more nonchalant than he felt. The truth was, he didn't know exactly how far Alyssandra was willing to go. Was she intent on blood? On murder? Murder was doubtful. He didn't think she had it in her. Most women didn't. Did she intend an injury that would take him out of the tournament? That was his worst fear. He needed that tournament to boost his own importance.

Julian launched another offensive with his blade and with his words. 'What sort of man sends a woman to beg in his place? If he's spoiling for a fight, he should face me himself.' He gave a smirk. 'Or are *you* his rendition of an alley thug? Makes us even, I think.'

'He did not send me.' Alyssandra went for the other sleeve, slicing it down the centre. If he wasn't careful he was going to end up looking like a vagabond for the lesson.

Blades met in a resounding clash, steel and bodies came together, the strength of the other's arm pushing their blades into the air. He grinned. He had the superior strength here. His strength would outstrip hers. He pushed her to the wall, their arms still raised above their heads, sabres still locked. 'You were foolish today, Alyssandra, to let him see your skill. He might start to suspect there is something afoot. How do you think he'd feel if he knew what you'd been up to? Masquerading as your brother, duping people, duping *him*, into spending sums of money on lessons with "Antoine Leodegrance" when in reality they were only fencing a girl?'

'You wouldn't dare tell,' Alyssandra ground out

with effort. He'd keep her pinned a little longer, make her sweat, make her think about what she risked, make her see that she needed him and his protection.

'Wouldn't I?' Julian mused. 'I could destroy you.'

'And I could destroy you. What do you think my brother would do if I told him about the alley? About the threats, that you are not so loyal as you pretend. You are loyal only to yourself and you will betray him the moment it is beneficial to you.' Alyssandra's eyes flashed, and his groin tightened. She was magnificent in her temper, all fire when cornered. That would make some rousing bedsport.

'Your brother will think what I tell him to think. He will believe me when I give him penitence for my actions and tell him it was out of concern for him that I resorted to drastic measures,' he sneered. 'He will not believe you, an ungrateful sister who would risk us all for the sake of a short-lived *affaire.*'

'I hate you,' she spat, arms showing the first signs of trembling. She would have to surrender soon and she would hate that even more.

'I know you do. But that won't matter in the end.' He relished the thought of her capitulation. He would wait for her to break, wait for her to admit defeat. He pressed against her, taking advantage of her weakening arms, knowing full well his erection would be evident.

'Me faut retourner à la pute qui m'a accouchée,' he muttered to his opponent.

Alyssandra moved, he could feel her muscles bunching for a last try. But her last try had nothing to do with their swords. Her knee came up between them, taking him sharply in the groin. She gave him a shove that put him on the floor, doubled over with pain. She strode past him.

He heard her open the door and say to someone in the hall—probably his lesson, dammit— 'Give him a moment to collect himself.'

He would get her for this. He would give her one last opportunity to redeem herself. If not, the time had come to reveal the Leodegrances for the frauds they were.

Chapter Twenty

The *salle d'armes* was a crowded, bustling hive of activity when Haviland arrived the morning of the tournament. Outside, the street was bursting with energy. Vendors, sensing a profit to be made, had gathered with their wares and were doing a brisk business. He stepped inside and let the excitement of the atmosphere engulf him, let the anticipation of competition override his rage towards Julian Anjou, let the thrill of facing other excellent swordsmen from around the Continent dull the complexities of wanting Alyssandra. Now was not the time to have his mind distracted by either rage or lust.

At either shoulder were Archer and Nolan, who had come ostensibly because they were eager to see the tournament. But Haviland suspected they'd come out of concern for his safety. He didn't truly believe Julian would attempt anything at the tournament. For one, it was too late in the game. Anything Julian wanted to do to him could be attempted on the piste

should they meet. For another, it was far too public a
venue to get away with anything covert.

He flexed his grip around the handle of his long
sword case and approached the entrance table. Today
was the day he proved to himself just how good he
was. More than that, he had a chance today to prove
how worthy he was of his dreams. Were they dreams
only? Or was there reason to hope in them?

Haviland recognised one of the young men at the
table as the student he'd helped with his *balestra*. The
young man saw him and smiled. 'You'll be entering
rapiers, no doubt.' He nodded at the case in Haviland's
hand. The competition featured all nature of swords,
but the rapier was the premiere event given that it was
Antoine Leodegrance's speciality. As a result, it was
also the most heavily entered event. Haviland nodded and pushed forward his entrance fee.

'We have both changing rooms available today,'
the young man said. 'And we're using the day guests'
salon as a warm-up centre. All the matches will take
place in the main salon.' He nodded to Nolan and
Archer. 'Your friends can find seats in the stands if
they hurry.'

Haviland parted company from Nolan and Archer
and headed to the changing rooms. Compared to the
bustle in the *salle*'s lobby, the changing rooms were
quiet, but only relatively so. The rooms were crowded,
but the energy was friendly as men stripped out of
street clothes. Most would fight in trousers and shirts
covered by padded vests for protection. Haviland recognised a few of the other more advanced clients of

the *salle* among the crowd who'd come to compete and went to join them.

'Is this all of us who've come to champion the *salle*'s good name?' Louis Baland, who'd been one of the first to befriend him when he'd arrived in April, clapped Haviland on the back in welcome. 'The six of us will make good showing, but isn't Anjou coming?'

'I hope not. I don't stand a chance against him,' Jean-Marc, a sandy-haired man with laughing hazel eyes, complained good-naturedly. Haviland liked him. He was a strong fencer in practice, but he lacked the competitive urge to win when the match was on the line. 'I just want to make it further than I did last year before I have to face Anjou. It's a shame to have to fight him all year and then have to face him in the tournament, too. We should be exempt. I think I'll propose that to Leodegrance for next year,' he joked.

'North here can take him. I've seen him do it,' another, Paul Robilliard, put in. 'I'd say North is a great favourite in this tournament. The odds on you in the stands are good. I can arrange a go-between if you want to wager on yourself,' he added quietly.

Haviland politely declined. He knew some of the fencers wagered on themselves to lose in order to make money. But he wasn't here to win money. He wanted to win something far grander.

'There's Anjou.' Jean-Marc directed their attention with a discreet nod of his head.

Julian Anjou sat alone in a corner, dressed only in tight buckskin trousers. He was shirtless and impressively well muscled. Louis snorted. 'Showing off his physique to intimidate us, no doubt.' Julian's pale hair was severely pulled back away from his face. His eyes glittered as he acknowledged the group with the slightest of nods, but he made no move to join them. 'He likes to be alone before he competes.'

'Do you think he can stand up?' Jean-Marc queried, his face breaking into a knowing grin and the group laughed. 'Have you heard, North? Delacorte showed up for a sabre lesson yesterday and Alyssandra Leodegrance had kicked him in the balls.'

'Everyone knows he's been sweet on her for years,' Louis put in. Haviland barely registered that last remark. He was still groping over the first one.

'What was she doing here?'

Louis laughed. 'We don't know, but whatever it was, she was wearing trousers and she was mad, mad, mad. Delacorte says there were two sabres in the room when he got there. Maybe they were duelling?' It was clear he didn't take his own suggestion seriously. The men laughed, but Haviland's mind was racing. She'd left his bed and gone straight to the *salle* to confront Julian. And not to just confront him verbally. She'd done it with a weapon.

Over him.

These men could think it was a lovers' spat between Alyssandra and Julian, but Haviland knew better and part of him was shamed by it. It was not her place to defend him. If anyone was to confront Julian, it should be him. He'd hoped to have the chance to settle things on the piste. Apparently, Alyssandra had beaten him to it. He was going to have stern words with her when he saw her next.

The announcement came that the first rounds were posted and the changing room disgorged as everyone surged into the main salon for their matches. He had to put Alyssandra out of his mind and focus on the task at hand, which apparently would be a fencer from Spain.

This would be a defensive match. His mind immediately emptied of everything except the pages of the treatise, images of the lessons flashing through his head in review—the triangles the Spanish school loved, the geometry of the steps. Haviland found a quiet space and took out his rapier, practising with a few experimental lunges and stretching his muscles. He could feel excitement building inside himself and did his best to control it. Too much adrenaline could leave one breathless, or cause one to go out too recklessly. Haviland closed his eyes and drew deep breaths, imagining the match to come, seeing himself execute flawless attacks and strong parries.

They were calling for his match when he opened them. 'On the centre piste, Mr Haviland North will face Señor Julio Navarra.' *Mr Haviland North.* He drew another breath, his heartbeat steady and controlled now. Haviland North would fight this tournament, not Viscount Amersham. He hadn't been Amersham for weeks now, not since he'd crossed the Channel. His father would say he was being selfish, but Haviland would argue he was being free. Haviland stepped to the piste, exchanged bows with the officials and his opponent and took up his stance. The officials gave the signal and everyone at the eight pistes lining the salon took up their *en garde* positions.

Fighting in a large arena with other matches going on around you took some talent and some experience not always acquired in practice, Haviland soon realised. It took far more concentration to simply block out the matches on either side of him than he'd expected. During practices in the main salon, there were any number of bouts going on haphazardly at one time, but the randomness of those bouts was hardly distracting. In the beginning, the synchronisation of the matches was the distraction as they went through many of the same opening strategies at the same pace. There was a beautiful symmetry to it that addicted the eye, but it would also see him eliminated embarrassingly early if he wasn't careful.

Haviland took deliberate stock of his opponent, using the early moments of the match to assess the quality and speed of Navarra's moves. Navarra was a man of middling height and years. Grey streaked the temples of his dark hair and his moustache. He was perhaps in his early forties, but his physique was well maintained. Haviland would have the advantage on him when it came to reach and to stamina, but he was not arrogant enough to discredit Navarra's superior knowledge of the Spanish strategy. He needed to go on the offensive immediately and initiate the French school, force Navarra to fight outside his comfort zone.

* * *

Ten minutes into the match, Haviland caught him off guard and executed a *flèche* to his right line, earning a direct hit and five of the ten points needed to win the bout. They resumed their *en garde* positions, the Spaniard given the opportunity to initiate the first offensive movement. It would be a chance to also initiate the Spanish line of attack, but Haviland used a strong riposte to take control and land his second direct hit to the man's upper shoulder.

At the declaration of victory, Haviland felt a surge of excitement pass through him. It was only round one, but he was focused now, his thoughts centred on the tournament. He would not fight again for a few hours, but he remained on the floor of the salon instead of joining Nolan and Archer in the stands. He removed his gear and went to watch the second round of matches, to study whoever his next opponent might be. The match featuring a late entrant from Austria intrigued him. The Austrian was slim and tall, with elegant movements that were beautiful to watch as well as deadly, delivering lightning-fast defeat to his opponent. Impressive, Haviland thought. Afterwards, he came forward to compliment the Austrian, but he had disappeared into the crowd, gear and all. It was to be expected. Haviland knew from experience in some of the London tournaments that some fencers enjoyed socialising between matches and exchanging tips on technique while others preferred to slip away to a quiet spot to think and to plan. Still, he would have liked to have met the Austrian.

* * *

Alyssandra locked the door of the private practice room behind her and slipped off the mesh mask. She unbuckled the leather protective vest and breathed a sigh of relief. Her first match had gone well. She'd been fast and decisive, the first match of her round to conclude. She'd been able to slip out unnoticed and that had been her plan. The Austrian, Pieter Gruber, had done well.

Haviland had done well, too. She'd discreetly watched his match against Navarra. It was no surprise Haviland had won. Navarra was fifteen years Haviland's senior and limited in his ability to adapt to the different schools of strategy. Julian had won as well, but he had done so meanly and harshly. His match had not been pretty. He was under-matched against a young boy from Belgium. Julian had made him look ridiculous, using complicated moves and unnecessarily difficult attacks. Julian could have beaten him just as easily with straightforward efforts the boy was at least likely to recognise.

His choice was a testament to the depths of Julian's anger, however. She'd shamed him yesterday and he was determined to exercise his superiority. Perhaps she'd misstepped. It did occur to her belatedly that she ought to have left Julian alone, poking a sleeping dog and all that. But part of her could not simply ignore what he'd done and that part had begged for confrontation. In truth, she was more than a little frightened as to what Julian might do to her and to Antoine. Would he go so far as to expose them publicly? Or would he opt for a more private blackmail over public ruination? Which one would offer him more? Either would destroy Antoine.

She buried her face in her hands. What a mess she'd made. In her attempts to protect her brother, she'd become the instrument of his ruin and he didn't even know. Her conscience asserted itself. *It's not fair to keep this from him. It's his future that will be ruined, and he'll never see it coming. At least you've seen this evolve from the start.*

She'd been selfish and prideful, wanting Haviland for herself, thinking herself worthy of a little pleasure to hold the long empty years at bay. She'd even convinced herself Haviland was safe. He would move on and pose no threat to her. Yet, she'd not been able to keep him secret. She'd provoked Julian and turned him, once an ally, into a powerful enemy. Worse than that, she'd not been able to keep her heart free of entanglement. Giving up Haviland would destroy her just as assuredly as Julian's betrayal would destroy Antoine. But keeping Haviland would be the utmost in selfishness. He was a titled lord, not meant for her. Satisfying her wants would hurt both her brother and him.

There was a rattle outside the door, the click of a key in the lock. Alyssandra took a panicked step backwards. No, she would not panic. She had an alibi—she was merely practising—and she already knew who would be coming through the door. Only Antoine had a key.

She was right about the latter. She was wrong

about the former. Antoine rolled himself into the room, his face thunderous. 'What the hell do you think you're doing, *Pieter Gruber of Austria*? Did you think no one would notice? No, let me rephrase that, did you think *I* wouldn't? Why are you doing this? Do you know what you risk?'

'Risk? What about you, rolling around in these back corridors? What if someone sees you?' It was an entirely non-responsive answer to his barrage of questions.

'I am perfectly fine. I will ensure no one sees me. What is going on? I thought we'd decided you would only fight in the final,' Antoine reprimanded.

'*You* decided that.' This was another piece of her pride coming back to haunt her. She'd flouted her brother's authority in order to assuage her damnable pride. She could protest all she wanted that she'd entered to keep Haviland from winning so he wouldn't throw away his future on her, or that she had done it to keep Julian from hurting Haviland on the piste.

But deep inside those weren't the only reasons. She'd done it for herself, because she wanted to prove to herself just how good she was without her brother whispering her opponents' weaknesses in her ear, without having her brother study those opponents ahead of time with her through peepholes, to fight without the assurance that Julian would lose in the final to preserve the name of Leodegrance.

'Yes, I decided that. It is what makes most sense.' Antoine gave her a hard stare. 'You do understand that being unmasked is more than just public embarrassment, don't you? It can be construed as fraud and that is a crime, a punishable crime, Alyssandra. The longer our masquerade goes on, the more people we'll have duped and the more criminal it will look to the public.'

'No one is going to tell.' It was a brave lie. So much for telling her brother the truth. She would shut Julian up herself if she had to.

Antoine shrugged. 'I don't worry about telling as much as I worry about discovery.' He gave her a pointed look. 'What if Pieter Gruber is exposed to be a woman and my sister at that? And of course you'll have to forfeit if you make the final or even the semi-finals because you can't fight yourself.' They were arguing technicalities now because the larger issues were too difficult to face.

'If you're worried about discovery, help me maintain my disguise. How did you know it was me?' Alyssandra asked.

'The way you move. You move like I do...' Antoine paused. 'I mean, the way I used to.' His tone softened and for the first time she could see the pain it must bring him to plan the tournament, to see the matches and not be able to participate. The knife of selfishness dug deeper into her gut. 'Only someone who knows you well would see it.' He grinned, trying to hide his hurt. 'Besides, I'm your twin. I'm supposed to know things like that.'

Antoine reached a hand out for her. 'Maybe we should give it all up after the tournament. We could sell the *salle*. Maybe Julian could buy it? We could retire to the country house and forget all this. I'm not going to walk again. There's little sense in continuing the masquerade. It would only take one last lie—that I have sickened in the interim—to explain the wheelchair. Then I could go about as myself at my will and so could you.'

'How long have you been thinking about this?' These didn't sound like impromptu plans born of a sentimental moment.

'A few months. I didn't want to say anything until I was sure of myself, and then lately, things have been a bit off between us. My fault, I fear. I know you're lonely. I know you gave up Etienne for me.' Rage and sadness infused his features. 'If only that accident hadn't happened, if only I'd not taken that jump without knowing what was on the other side.' His fist came down hard on the armrest of his chair. His eyes sparkled dangerously with tears. 'I've ruined both of our lives in a moment of foolishness.' Is that what he thought? How selfish of her to have let him see her moment of weakness, to have let him see any ounce of resentment that she was tied to him for life. He was her brother, and she loved him.

'No, not at all,' she was quick to answer. She could not handle Antoine's tears. They were rare things indeed and she was ill equipped to cope with them. He'd not wept when the doctors had brought him the news of his legs, he'd not cried when their father had died. She would promise him anything to forgo those tears. She didn't like the idea of selling to Julian—it would make him a fixture in their lives, but perhaps it would neutralise the threat he posed. She squeezed his hand meaningfully. 'Let us get through the tournament and we will be gone, off to a new beginning.' Even if it would be a new beginning without Haviland. Nothing had been decided between them and now it had been decided for them.

Chapter Twenty-One

By the next day the field was considerably narrowed. All events had concluded except for the foil competition, which was moving into the quarter-finals with eight fencers left. The stands were full. The unknown Austrian, Pieter Gruber, had quickly garnered a following of those awed by his footwork and wrist play. Julian Anjou had turned his matches into blood sport in his last two bouts the day before. While such behaviour was inappropriate, especially from an instructor who ought to have known better, it did bring spectators.

The athletic Englishman, Haviland North, was bound to meet one of them in the quarter-finals and the spectators held their collective breath, both loath and eager to see which of the three would fall first. The fates spared the audience until the semi-finals. All three would advance, but a pairing now was inevitable. It would be North and Anjou on the centre piste second, Pieter Gruber and the Italian master, Giovanni Basso, first.

Haviland stood at the edge of the floor, studying Basso and Gruber. He would meet one of them in the final round before facing Leodegrance. Three matches to go. The tournament was not only about skill, but about endurance. He'd fought five matches yesterday and, thinking positively, he would fight three today. Nolan and Archer were in the stands again and Brennan had come, too. Nolan was making a fortune on wagers. He was glad for it. His friends might need the money as they continued their tour without him. If all went well, that is what he meant to happen. He meant to stay in Paris, but he couldn't force them to wait.

That was putting the cart before the horse, and Haviland quickly shoved the thoughts away. There was only room for thoughts of this match and the next. The quickest way to failure was to look too far ahead. Gruber was undeniably good. If he'd wagered, he would have picked the Italian simply on reputation and years of study. He'd seen Basso duel yesterday and had been suitably impressed. The man was good and Pieter Gruber was an unknown. Gruber had apparently come alone. He had no friends here and had not travelled with a fencing group. Haviland knew, he'd asked around.

But for a man whom no one knew or ever heard of before yesterday, there was something oddly familiar about Gruber. His face was covered and, with the leather vest and protective padding, it wasn't possible to really tell what Gruber looked like. The familiarity was in the rhythm of his movements, in the fluid grace of them. Haviland gave up watching Basso and studied Gruber.

There! That arm motion. He had his answer. Gruber moved like Leodegrance and eerily so. It was more than the way someone might study another and pick up that person's gestures. Haviland had never seen such a successful mimic, but 'mimic' seemed to be inadequate to truly capture what he was witnessing. This was ingrained, innate. Gruber advanced aggressively and gave a turn of his wrist, the motion disarming Basso and bringing the match to a close.

An unreal conclusion asserted itself: Gruber was Leodegrance. No one could so precisely match another and the odd habit of disappearing immediately after his rounds fit Leodegrance's reclusive personality. But why? Leodegrance had no reason to duel covertly at his own tournament.

Another image settled in its place—a woman with a fan, a woman with a sword-stick pressed against a thug's throat in an alley. A woman who had gone after Anjou with a sabre and kneed him in the groin if rumour was to be believed. Snippets of their last conversation came back to him, words that hadn't fully registered. *We were both twenty when my father died.* Alyssandra was a twin—a twin who had trained side by side with her brother. She would need the anonymity of the mask. Women were not permitted and it would certainly do Leodegrance no good if she were discovered.

That did not answer his question of motive, however. Why would she do such a thing and risk her brother's credibility? Whether he thought it was ridiculous or not, the tournament would be disgraced and that could hardly be what either of them wanted. Alyssandra had made no secret of the fact that the *salle d'armes* supported them financially.

You will have to face her to get to Leodegrance. He would have to face her. It seemed to be a bit of twisted irony that the woman he loved would be his last obstacle. She would quite literally be all that stood in his way. Had that been why she'd done it? Or was there someone else, something else she was protecting? Maybe he was overthinking it. It might be nothing more than wanting to prove herself. Had she finally had enough of living in her brother's shadow? If so, her reasons for wanting to compete were not much different than his own: freedom, pride in personal accomplishment, the desire to show the world for a brief moment he was more than the sum of his title and wealth—things that had come to him as an accident of birth, nothing more. He understood those reasons well enough.

He felt a presence close at his shoulder and stiffened. It wasn't a friendly presence. 'Have you figured out Pieter Gruber's little secret?' The voice carried a smirk. It was Anjou, and his proximity made Haviland want to do violence. How dare the man saunter up to him as if he hadn't ordered an attack on his person two days ago, as if he hadn't faced Alyssandra with a sabre. Haviland didn't like imagining what had transpired in that room to cause Alyssandra to go for his groin.

'Keep your distance,' Haviland growled.

'Or you'll what?' Anjou was all casual insouci-
ance. 'Draw your foil and start our match early? Get
ejected from the tournament for foul play?' He gave
a laugh. 'I don't think there's anything you can do to
me right here. Perhaps you'd like to save some of that
vengeance for the piste? I know I will.'

It galled Haviland to think that anyone watching
them would think they were acquaintances, friends
even. But Anjou was right. Haviland couldn't touch
him here as much as he wished otherwise without
sacrificing what he'd worked so hard to achieve. Perhaps Anjou was hoping he'd lose his cool and be dis-
qualified.

Julian changed tack, nodding towards Pieter
Gruber, who was exiting the floor yet again, to hide
in seclusion until he was called. 'She's a fool, of
course. After I beat you, I'll beat her and perhaps
teach her a rather public lesson about interfering in
the games of men.' Julian smiled coldly, his intentions thinly veiled. He meant to expose Alyssandra.
Had he thought that through or was anger talking?
Surely he'd harm himself in the process.

'You won't beat me,' Haviland answered, keeping his gaze forward. He would not give Anjou the
satisfaction of looking him in the eye. 'You haven't
beaten me for some time.' And now, knowing that
Alyssandra was at risk, he certainly couldn't allow
it. Julian facing Alyssandra would be disastrous. He
was hunting revenge for last night and possibly more.

There was far more bad blood between Alyssandra and Julian than she'd alluded to.

Julian shrugged, unconcerned. 'I'll take my chances all the same.' He paused for effect. 'It's not me you should be worried about, you know. I am a straightforward fellow. You know exactly where you stand with me. I don't like you. I want you gone. Defeating you is the fastest way I can get rid of you. But Alyssandra is a different matter. She's not been plain with you from the start. I know this because I know the real truths. I know what she hides from you.'

A cold finger ran down Haviland's back. Julian was merely trying to get a rise out of him. Julian would like nothing better than to pierce his calm and distract him. Unfortunately, it was working. He could not discard this latest probe as the jealous lashing out of a thwarted suitor. Julian was not spinning lies in the *hope* of hitting a target. He was spinning truths knowing full well they would hit a target.

He'd known there were secrets, things to hide. Privacy meant secrets and one did not get much more private than the Leodegrances—Antoine with his odd habits in the lessons and Alyssandra and her penchant for withholding information. She had done so since the beginning when she had not disclosed her name until it was too late. She'd kept him hidden, too, not wanting him to call at the house and conduct a proper courtship, not wanting him to address her brother. She'd not told him she was a twin or that she fenced.

What else hadn't she told him? What had there

truly been between them besides great sex? Sex so good that he'd believed there was something more, something worth fighting for, breaking free for. It was horrid to think, after all his years of practising detached physical affairs, that he'd fallen into the trap he'd tried so hard to avoid. And he'd fallen unaware.

The announcer called for their match. 'Are you ready?' Julian sneered. 'I'll take you apart a piece at a time.'

'And risk being thrown out of the tournament yourself? You were warned yesterday one more infraction would see you expelled. Leodegrance won't tolerate it,' Haviland said coolly.

Julian scoffed. 'Leodegrance will do nothing, he *is* nothing, that's how little you know. Are you familiar with the concept of smoke and mirrors, North? Do you think this is the first time Alyssandra has masqueraded as a man? She's rather good at it—too good at it, don't you think?' He strode off to take his position at the end of the piste, waving to the crowd who cheered as he passed on his way to be helped into the padded vest and mask waiting on his side of the arena. Then it was Haviland's turn to step forward, to take the adoration of the crowd. He raised his arm in acknowledgement, smiling, wiping away any trace of unease. He would not give Julian the satisfaction of knowing what his insinuations did to him. Julian would not win any game with him, mental or physical. But, by Jove, did he really mean what Haviland thought? That Alyssandra was *the* Leodegrance? But how could that be? She couldn't be both Pieter Gruber and Antoine Leodegrance in the prize round, assuming she won the match between them. And she might win. If Julian was right and she was the face behind the mask during his lessons, he had never beaten her. Would she lose on purpose to preserve her identity or would she win to prevent him from achieving his goal? Did she care for him so little that she would thwart him in such a manner?

Haviland let the piste assistants help him into the equipment. Where was his foil? It should have been back from cleaning by now. He never let his foil out of his sight and it made him nervous not to have it now. At the last minute, a boy acting as squire ran up with his foil.

Haviland's hand closed around the grip of his foil, letting the feel of his weapon centre him. He had to empty his mind. A full mind was what Julian wanted. Julian would like to turn him against Alyssandra. What was he going to put his trust in? Julian's viperous tongue or Alyssandra's passion? He took an experimental swipe with his foil, exhaling a breath, purifying his thoughts with the exhalation. He closed his eyes. Words could lie, but the body couldn't. For now, he would simply believe in her.

'I don't believe Julian's presence in the prize round is a foregone conclusion this year.' Antoine pressed his eyes to the peepholes. He could only see the match from one end since the stands erected for the occasion obscured viewing the matches from the sidelines. 'What do you think, Alyssandra? North or Anjou?

This might be the highlight of the tournament. The crowd is excited. Listen to them.'

Alyssandra joined him in the locked room, glad to see he was in better spirits. 'Haviland will beat him,' she said tersely. He had to. The alternative was too disastrous to think of. She had gone too far with Julian the night before. She thought of the note she'd received after her match, tucked into Pieter's gear. Julian had made his intentions clear. She was frightened of what he might do to Pieter Gruber on the piste if she gave him the chance. He would not care if he was ejected from the tournament. No one would even pay attention to his infraction if it revealed Pieter Gruber was a woman and Antoine's sister besides.

'Haviland? Is that how it is these days?' Antoine looked away from the match to study her. 'That's a long way from Viscount Amersham or Mr North. When he first came, he was merely the Englishman to you.'

She met her brother's eyes, unwilling to hide any longer. Too much had been hidden for too long. 'Don't worry. It's a temporary *affaire*, nothing more. It will end shortly.' When she beat him and prevented him from winning the tournament and he realised his dreams weren't worth his future.

'Why would it end? Does he not care for you?' Antoine asked carefully.

'He's not in a position to offer for me, if that's what you're thinking.' Alyssandra busied herself with looking through the eyeholes, but that only put Haviland firmly in her view, most particularly his backside in her view.

Antoine was silent for a moment. 'What position would that be?'

'He's on a Grand Tour with his friends. He plans to go on to Italy and study there.' It was the safe answer. She couldn't bring herself to say the rest—that there was a woman expecting to marry him back home in England. Never mind that he didn't love her, or that she didn't love him. And certainly never mind that Haviland had declared his plans to be otherwise. He wanted to stay in Paris, wanted to stay with her. Haviland would do his duty because his honour demanded it and in a fight between his honour and his freedom, honour would win. Alyssandra would see to it even though it hurt. The woman she would be sending him back to would never know him, never know how he looked when passion took him, or how he danced on bridges in the moonlight. He would never do those things with that woman. Those memories belonged to her alone.

'Perhaps he needs a reason to stay,' Antoine mused. 'If you gave him a reason, he might be persuaded. I know I told you to be careful with him, but since you weren't...?'

Alyssandra scolded softly, 'He already questions why a man with scars would need his sister so much. I think Haviland staying is the last thing we need.'

'But the first thing you need,' Antoine countered. 'You care for him.'

'I care for you more.' She looked away in order

to end the argument, her attention going back to the match. It was as close as she'd ever come to admitting out loud just how deep her feelings for Haviland went. 'Watch, Antoine. They're about to begin.' She sent up a prayer that Haviland be safe. Julian would stop at nothing, but surely Haviland knew that and would be on his guard.

Antoine wasn't ready to let it go. His voice was quiet beside her. 'But if you could have him, would you want him?'

Yes and always, her heart answered silently. But it was an impossibility. If he knew what she'd done, Haviland would never forgive her deception. He would never accept a relationship that had been begun with the intent to conceal secrets.

Chapter Twenty-Two

'I think I'll start with your heart. Oh, I forgot, I already have,' Julian sneered and parried. But Haviland knew the words were an attempt to regain ground. He was giving Julian no quarter and it showed. He meant to end this bout as quickly as possible. The sooner this was over, the sooner he could get to Alyssandra. Until he saw her, Julian's words could have no power.

Haviland made a hard thrust, catching Julian's blade. It should have turned Julian's foil aside, but instead he felt a tremor run up the length of his own blade. It caught him off guard, giving Julian an opening to advance. Julian brought his foil across Haviland's in a strong sweep. Haviland was ready for him, but his weapon wasn't. His blade quivered, undeniable proof something was wrong. Haviland parried, blocking the move, but Julian could see the blade was in distress. He struck again and again with the same sweeping thrust, hammering on the weakening foil. Each blow taxed the strength of Haviland's arm in his attempts to keep the foil steady and recover fast enough to meet the next onslaught.

Reality sank in. At this rate, the blade would break and soon. Julian had seen it weakening and was shamelessly exploiting that fact. He was going to lose. Haviland moved to launch one last offensive, but his blade hadn't the strength. On the next thrust, it met Julian's foil and snapped five inches from the hilt in the place Julian had been relentlessly catching. He could hear the crowd give a collective moan of disappointment, a few gasps of disbelief. For the fraction of a second he, too, was caught up in the disbelief staring at the broken foil. But Julian wasn't done yet.

Julian didn't stop for the broken blade. Even though the officials had immediately stepped forward to call the match, Julian carried on his attack, driving for Haviland's shoulder. Out of instinct, Haviland blocked with his foil, but a broken weapon was no match for Julian's speed and wrath. The buttoned tip of Julian's foil pierced the padding at his shoulder in a legal touch. 'Now I've won on points. No one can claim otherwise,' Julian hissed under his breath as the officials had them separate and return to their own ends of the piste. The officials conferred together briefly. One official stepped forward and proclaimed the outcome of the match to the crowd.

'Victory in the second semi-final round goes to Julian Anjou on the grounds that his opponent is unable to continue. The final touch to the shoulder will not be counted.'

Down the length of the piste, Haviland watched

Julian's face mottle. That was not the decision he was looking for. He'd wanted a decisive victory, one that nobody could question. He didn't want anyone to think that, but for the broken blade, the outcome might have been different.

The crowd applauded, but the applause lacked some of its earlier excitement. For them, the outcome of the much-anticipated match up had been anticlimactic and in some ways inconclusive. There was a small commotion at the officials' table where the matches were set and another announcement was made. Pieter Gruber had forfeited his place in the final. The tournament would move straight to the prize round—the chance to directly face the tournament's renowned host, Antoine Leodegrance. The match would be held in an hour, giving the victor time to recover and it would be fought with rapiers, Antoine Leodegrance's famed weapon of choice. Julian tossed Haviland an 'I told you so' look while the crowd murmured its surprise and disappointment in rising volumes.

Haviland felt his gut clench. The forfeit seemed to confirm all that Julian had hatefully intimated. Alyssandra was playing a dangerous masquerade. And now Julian had what he wanted: a chance to prove himself in public once again as the great instructor, a man who might dare call himself Leodegrance's equal. But if that was no longer enough, he had a chance to expose Alyssandra. Of course, he'd have to choose. Julian couldn't have them both. Perhaps Julian's own ego would keep Alyssandra safe in the end.

Haviland stepped from the arena. He looked down at the snapped blade still in his hand, his fingers running over the rough break. His fingers suddenly stalled and he brought the blade up for closer inspection. Blades *did* snap due to rust and misuse, but he took impeccable care of his. He examined the exposed cross-section and swore under his breath. This blade had been tampered with. There was a notch where Julian had hammered away until the blade had given. There had been only one time when the blade had been out of his sight and that was when it had been taken for inspection before the semi-final. Since the semi-final was fought with personal blades, they were always examined. If Julian was willing to go to such lengths to ensure victory and reach the final it was further proof Julian meant to do the Leodegrances harm. What Julian had done was tantamount to a declaration of war.

Julian had made his choices. He had his own choices to make as well. To go and bow to duty or to stay and pursue his freedom here? That would depend on Alyssandra. Had she used him for pleasure alone? Was there truly nothing between them to build a future on? Maybe in the end, this hadn't been any different than his other affairs. He'd just wanted to be so much more than a temporary bedfellow with a title, a phallus with a fortune.

It was hard to think of their time together that way. Perhaps that's why he'd been so eager to set aside seeking those answers from Alyssandra. He'd had excuses aplenty to wait. The affair was short term, the affair was physical only, there was the tournament to concentrate on. But now, those items did not apply. There was no longer a reason to wait. The tournament was over. He had lost.

Dear God, Haviland had lost! Alyssandra set back from the viewing holes with a sigh of disbelief that mirrored the crowd's. She'd had not been prepared for that. The depths of her disappointment, her incredulity, revealed to her just how much she'd counted on Haviland's victory, how much she'd come to rely on him.

'It's hardly his fault,' Antoine said, sounding as disheartened by the result as she. 'Foils snap. It happens. It is rather unfortunate. If it's any consolation, Julian looks displeased too. The officials are announcing the decision.'

Julian wouldn't like winning on a technicality, but he would take it gladly. He'd been losing up until the point Haviland's blade had weakened. Under the circumstances, he couldn't have wished for better if he'd arranged it. That thought made her sit up a little straighter. Had he? Could he have had Haviland's weapon tampered with? A man who hired thugs in alleyways would not shy away from notching a blade. 'Antoine, you don't think Julian had anything to do with the blade breaking, do you?' She said the words carefully. It was a bold accusation to make.

Antoine looked aggrieved by the suggestion that one of the men in his *salle d'armes* would be capable of such treachery. 'Blades break,' he said firmly.

It was easier for him to believe that statement than she. He didn't know what she knew. Julian had done violence to Haviland on two occasions.

She was about to delicately push the subject matter when a loud call in the corridor pierced the shelter of their little room. Someone was calling her. Not someone, Haviland was calling her. And he was calling her *by name*.

Alyssandra shot a worried glance at her brother. Haviland was in the hall, *shouting*. She could only hope there was no one nearby to hear. What was he thinking? If he had known how much she needed to preserve her identity, he wouldn't be outside shouting her name. *Or maybe he didn't care*, came the niggling thought. Maybe he knew and was beyond discretion. 'He's come for his reckoning.' Alyssandra stood and swallowed hard. Haviland had every right to be angry. Her secrets were a betrayal of all they'd shared. It would be better this way, to let him leave her in anger. But it wouldn't be easier.

Antoine furrowed his brow, cocking his head to listen. 'That doesn't sound like an angry man.'

Alyssandra disagreed. It sounded like a man who'd come for answers, and she couldn't quarrel with that. In her heart, she knew she'd treated him abominably, sharing with him only the intimacy of her body when he had shared his mind with her, opened himself up to her. *You didn't have a choice. You had a brother to protect*, came the old argument. But it did little to soothe her.

Haviland was pounding on the doors now. They

could hear the heavy thump of his fist on the panels as he came closer. 'I will go out and meet him. I will try to protect you,' Alyssandra promised. There was no way out of this viewing room except through the door. 'If Haviland gets through the door, there's nothing left to hide.' She drew a deep breath. She was so tired of secrets, but it was almost over. She had to face Julian on the piste and then it would be done. She and Antoine could go to the country and put this chapter of their lives behind them. One more match, one more victory. She had to stay strong now when they were so near the end.

She stepped into the corridor, Haviland spying her immediately. He stopped. His features collected themselves into aristocratic coolness. He looked as he did when she'd first met him: calm, unflappable, untouchable, as if the world did not dare to bother him with its petty troubles. Almost. He'd not stopped to change after his match. He was dishevelled, dressed only in breeches and shirt showing signs of sweat. His dark hair fell forward over his brow. He'd come straight to her. It was either a sign of how deep his anger went or something else she dared not name. Naming it would make it all that much harder to let him go.

'Are you Pieter Gruber?' he asked in even tones, his eyes locked on hers, waiting, watching for the truth unflinchingly. Perhaps it was good he wasn't yelling wild accusations and calling her every slanderous name known to womankind. If he was, it would make it easier to sell a lie because she wouldn't care about his reaction.

'Is that what Julian told you?' She could be cool, too, even though she was hot with worry, hot with desire, beneath the surface. Just looking at him here in the dim corridor made her want him, made her want to die from the knowledge she might never have him again, never lie beside him again. Once he figured it all out, and she was sure he would now that he was so close, he wouldn't want any part of her. He might even for a while hate himself for being duped. She'd never wanted that, never meant for that to happen. 'I saw the two of you talking before the match. Is that the sort of poison he was pouring in your ear like the snake he is?'

'*He* was talking.' Blue eyes flashed at the insinuation he and Julian had somehow made up.

'You were listening. Apparently.' Maybe if they could fight over something, she wouldn't have to answer the question.

'I'm sorry that you think I'm a man who would be served his opinions by a man who has little credibility to recommend him,' Haviland parried, arms crossed, eyes darkening dangerously. Her attack had been thwarted and now it was time for him to go on the offensive. 'I had already made up my mind. Once I saw Pieter Gruber use his wrist I knew it was you. I know how your body moves, all grace and glide. I know what your body looks like, what it *feels* like. Did you think I could be in bed with you, or run my hands over your naked body, and not know you?'

His words were a rough caress. She did not miss the scold in them for underestimating him. But they were not meant only to punish. He was teasing her with pleasure, too, using words to conjure hot images, to kindle the heat in her belly. To what end? To lure out her last secrets? Could she trust him not just for herself, but for her brother? It wasn't always for herself that she held back. She would find a way to live with the repercussions, but she could not assume that Antoine would. And what would trust result in? Would it be worth it? Or would he leave anyway, disgusted with her for one reason or another?

'Yes, I was Pieter Gruber and, yes, it was selfish and risky. But I deserve a chance to prove myself and I did. There was no man my equal,' she said defiantly. Perhaps this truth would distract him from the larger one.

He raised a brow as if he doubted her confession. 'Is that truly why you did it?' He started circling her, and she started to move clockwise, refusing to let him stalk her.

'You think it isn't?' she challenged. She was more comfortable quarrelling than disclosing. This was more familiar territory. She'd been quarrelling with Julian for years. She knew how to protect herself here.

'No, I don't.' Haviland was cool. 'If it was, you wouldn't have forfeited the final. You would have *enjoyed* besting Julian, you would have been *thrilled* to be taking the stage in the finale against your brother. What better way to make your point than to face the great Leodegrance and perhaps even best him? And yet, when the moment came to prove yourself against truly great talent, you bowed out. That makes little sense. Only a coward would falter at the last, afraid to seize greatness for themselves.' He paused. 'I did not take you for a coward, Alyssandra.'

Those clipped, crisp English tones, so superior, so all knowing, provoked the tiger in her. She had to tread carefully here and not give that rash tiger free rein or she'd be saying too much. There was nothing to say so she fell back on her strategy of questioning to distract. 'What exactly do you think explains it, then?' They'd started circling one another again, crossing foot over foot as they stalked.

'I think Pieter Gruber and Antoine Leodegrance are the same person, making it impossible for them to face each other in the finale.'

'A woman masquerading as her brother? Do you hear how absurd that sounds?' She wanted him to reject the proposition for himself before she had to affirm it. 'Now, consider this: the brother is regarded as the finest swordsman on the Continent.'

Haviland was not daunted. 'Consider *this*: his sister is his twin and was trained beside him by their father.' He paused and cocked his head. 'It seems less far-fetched now, coupled with the fact that the brother suffered from an accident three years ago.' His features softened. He broke his circling and stepped across to her, his hand going to her cheek. 'Did he die?'

She could see that storyline spinning across his face, pity and sorrow mixed together. It was an explanation that made sense to him, an explanation his code of honour could forgive: her father dead, her brother killed in an accident, a young woman suddenly left alone to fend for herself so she turned to her inheritance—a *salle d'armes*, her own formidable talent and her family name. And Julian had supported it for his own gains, waiting for a time when he could strike out for himself or marry into it.

'No, he didn't die.' The words were in her mind, but she'd not been the one to speak them. She watched Haviland's eyes move past her to the door she blocked. The voice spoke again. 'I'm Antoine Leodegrance and I'm very much alive.'

They both turned and stared at the man in the wheeled chair. For once she had the luxury of seeing Haviland caught entirely off guard. This was too much for even his noble hauteur. She knew with a certainty that whatever pity he'd felt for her was gone, replaced with something indecipherable.

Haviland stared. Two simultaneous thoughts flashed. Antoine Leodegrance did *not* have a scarred face. Instead, he had a face that very strongly resembled Alyssandra's, high cheekbones and all, right down to the chocolate-brown eyes. Secondly, he was in a wheeled chair. It was not scars that prompted his privacy, but that fact that he couldn't walk. Antoine smiled in the wake of the stunned silence. 'Perhaps this isn't best discussed in the hallway. Alyssandra, if you would please help me inside.' He gave his attention to Haviland. 'This chair can do some amazing things, but backing up is not one of them.'

'Of course,' Haviland said automatically, still trying to take it in as he followed the Leodegrances inside. Alyssandra was pale and, for the first time since he'd known her, she was visibly unsure of herself and unsure of what to do next. She shot him a glance he wasn't meant to see and realised where the uncertainty came from. She didn't know what *he* would do next. Perhaps she was right to carry that uncertainty. What would he do next? He had the feeling that this revelation should change everything, but he didn't know how. Was he supposed to stop loving her because her secrets were revealed?

Antoine pulled out a pocket watch. 'There is still forty-five minutes before the match. I think there is time for our tale.' He looked at Haviland. 'But I'm sure, at this point, you've figured out an accurate sketch of it.'

He had. His original thought was not far off except for Antoine's role in it. He wasn't dead, but he was incapacitated and it had fallen to Alyssandra to literally become the legs of the *salle*. The masquerade was ingenious in many ways, making the most of their shared likeness and their shared talent. Haviland had understood that aspect well enough the moment Antoine had opened the door. It was the details he was lacking.

Antoine gave Alyssandra a small smile full of affection, his attention riveted on her as he began. 'I love my sister, Mr North, and she loves me. So much so that she has dedicated her life in recent years to my care and well being to the detriment of her own.'

His dark-brown gaze swivelled to Haviland. 'You are aware that slightly over three years ago I was hurt in an accident. You might even have heard that it was a riding accident? I'm not sure how much news of that nature would be of interest in London. I took a jump stupidly, not knowing what was on the other side. It was muddy and slippery and my horse landed badly. I was thrown and this is the result.' He gestured to his useless legs. 'The doctors were hopeful the damage wouldn't be permanent and, under that assumption, we took up the masquerade. Alyssandra could be me for a few months. We could keep the *salle* open and it would be business as usual.'

He shook his head, a shadow crossing his face for the first time. 'But the months became a year, the doctors became less optimistic. A year became two years. Alyssandra's fiancé lost hope that she would ever leave me, ever feel free enough to marry and have a home of her own. He broke with her.'

He paused and looked down at his hands. 'I think that was when I started to realise I had to end the masquerade for Alyssandra's sake. I was going to be tied to this chair for the rest of my life, but it was not fair for her to be as well. But these things take time and timing. I couldn't just close the *salle* and disappear. There are practicalities to be met. What would we live on without the membership fees?' Antoine said apologetically as if the delay in acting on his thoughts had needed explanation.

'It is not a sacrifice to be with you,' Alyssandra inserted swiftly, fiercely when he paused. 'You do us both little credit to talk about yourself that way.'

Haviland smiled. That was the woman he knew,

selfless and giving. Some of the worry inside of him began to ease. Despite his comment to the contrary, he had allowed himself to be influenced by Julian's words more than he'd cared to admit; perhaps not in the way Julian had intended—that she was a master plotter, a woman of covert, insincere attentions—but in a more personal way. He'd doubted Alyssandra's feelings for him, doubted the quality of their intimacy.

Julian had failed on both accounts. The masquerade had not been wrought out of duplicity but out of love, out of a need to protect themselves and each other. Haviland saw the underlying message in Antoine's apologetic remark. He was Alyssandra's brother, he had to provide for her. And Alyssandra recognised his pride demanded it. He saw now why the masquerade had been maintained. Alyssandra was protecting her brother's pride while he protected their livelihood.

'But now it has to end,' Antoine continued. 'She cannot do this indefinitely. After the tournament, I will look for a buyer and sell the *salle*. We will remove to our country house in Fontainebleau and start again somehow. Perhaps it is what should have been done from the start. Now, Monsieur North, you know our little secret.'

It was a request for judgement. Haviland knew what Antoine was asking. Antoine wanted to know what would he do with their secret? Would he expose them here at the last with them so close to escaping detection? More importantly, what were his intentions towards Alyssandra? Haviland understood, too, that Antoine had taken an enormous risk in what he shared. Men did not take such risks unless they felt that risk was somehow justified. Antoine must be very sure of him.

Was he that sure of himself? He let his gaze rest on Alyssandra, lingering on the fall of caramel hair, the sharp jut of her chin, the depths of her dark eyes. There was sadness in them and he wished he could take it away. There was little doubt in his mind that he'd been the one to put it there in the first place. He was starting to understand Alyssandra's choices.

It occurred to him in the silence of the room that he'd been wrong. All along, he'd viewed the tournament as the watershed, the event that would define his future. But it wasn't. Winning the tournament or taking third as he had done, didn't change anything *for* him and it certainly hadn't changed *him*. It had merely been an exercise, a chance to show off an accomplishment, but nothing more. *She* was his watershed. What he did *with* her, what he did *for* her, would define his future. She had given up her secrets for him. Would he give up his family for her? Not for a fencing salon, not for personal freedom, but for her because she was his freedom, his dream. But the time for such an announcement was not yet.

'I think Alyssandra needs to prepare for her match,' Haviland said at last. 'Monsieur Anjou must not be underestimated.' She needed her mind on Julian, not on him, not on any emotional turmoil. He tore his gaze from Alyssandra to give attention to Antoine. He bowed. 'You have done me a great honour with your revelations. Your secret is safe with me. When the tournament is over, we will speak again.'

Walking out of that room past Alyssandra without touching her was the hardest thing he'd ever done. He supposed he could have stayed. Antoine would have allowed the company, but he sensed Alyssandra and Antoine needed time alone, perhaps not solely as brother and sister, but as coach and athlete.

Knowing didn't make passing her easier. He wanted to stop and kiss her, wanted to tell her a million things to watch for, how to fence against Julian, how Julian preferred to go for the right line on his opponent. But he recognised those things served no purpose. A kiss would distract her, and she already knew how to fence Julian. She'd been fencing him for years. Anything he might tell her she already knew.

At the door, Antoine called out to him, 'Do not worry, Monsieur North. Julian is no danger to her. He knows his part. There is just as much glory for him in losing the finale, if not more. A defeated Leodegrance is bad for business and Julian depends on that business as much as we.' He smiled confidently.

Haviland wished he were that sure. Julian might know his part, but Haviland wasn't at all certain Julian would play it. He shot a glance at Alyssandra, counselling caution. Antoine would have to be told about Julian's perfidy, but now was not the time. By Jove, he did not want Alyssandra to go out there. Every instinct protested against it. What sort of man let his woman go out to face danger?

Alyssandra held his eyes, firm and unwavering. *I*

will be fine. I've done this a hundred times. He had his answer. A brave man. A man who trusted in her abilities. She was not outmatched. She'd beaten *him*, hadn't she? It had been her behind the mask conducting the lessons, meting out the defeats until she'd helped him correct his dropped shoulder. Perhaps, too, he could do her more good out there, where he could keep an eye on Julian. He gave a short nod as he opened the door. 'I'll see you both afterwards.' This was a different kind of bravery, a different kind of honour. But Alyssandra would tolerate nothing less. It would take some getting used to.

'He's coming back.' Antoine smiled triumphantly.

Alyssandra returned his smile. She hadn't the heart to ruin his happiness. Antoine thought everything was solved. And it was, in a way that had nothing to do with his disclosures to Haviland. 'You should have told me you meant to tell him everything,' she said, reaching for her gear. She would have to go soon.

'I didn't know myself that was what I intended,' Antoine confessed. 'When I heard him out there, I knew I had to tell him. He loves you, Alyssandra. It's in his voice, in the way he looks at you. You love him, too, I think.' His voice softened, and he looked young again, the way he looked before pain marked his days. 'Maybe he's the reason Etienne wasn't meant to be the one?'

That brought tears to her eyes. 'You're a hopeless romantic, Antoine.' She brushed at her cheeks and shook her head. She had to tell him. 'Maybe he does love me, but nothing can come of it.'

Antoine cut her off. 'You're the daughter of a French *vicomte*, you're a lady in your own right. There's nothing wrong with your birth. You're perfectly acceptable—'

'Antoine, listen,' she interrupted. 'It wouldn't matter if I was the Queen of England. He's promised to someone else. It's been arranged since they were children. Two families are counting on him to fulfil the contract when he goes home. He's an honourable man, Antoine.' She couldn't tell him the rest, that Haviland wanted to stay in Paris, wanted to teach fencing, wanted to be with her. Antoine would hope too much.

The news crushed him. She could see the life go out of his face. Oh, she hated doing it to him. 'Then he should not have dallied with you.' Antoine's voice was grim, bitter.

'Don't blame him. We started it, you and I, with our subterfuges. And I proved less resistant to his charm than I would have thought.' Perhaps she should feel regret over having waved her fan that very first night. But she didn't. She would lose Haviland, but she wouldn't lose the memories.

Antoine relented, but remained unconvinced. 'I guess it was all for naught. I thought if he knew, if he understood...' *He would forgive her and the path would be clear for him to propose and everyone could live happy ever after.* Antoine didn't need to finish the sentence. She knew his thoughts, knew how his mind worked.

'It's not all in vain.' Alyssandra picked up her rapier. 'I will finish this tournament and we will have a new life.' She bent down and dropped a kiss on her brother's forehead. 'All will be well, you'll see.' Eventually it probably would. She'd got over Etienne. She would get over Haviland, she promised herself. But it would take a long time and it would hurt. It already did.

Antoine's hand closed over her wrist. 'Wait, why is North worried about Julian?'

She smiled brightly, too brightly, and pulled away. 'I do not know. I will beat him.'

The bitch would not beat him. Julian stood on the sidelines of the piste, waiting for the final to be called. He couldn't notch her rapier, as well. He caught sight of Haviland shouldering his way through the crowd and moved to intercept him. He had something for the Englishman too.

He made sure to stand next to North on the sidelines. 'What a day this will be. First I beat you and now I'll beat your woman.'

To his credit, North refused to be drawn. 'You didn't beat me. You notched my blade.' His tone was low and calm, his eyes straightforward, never straying from the curtained cubicle where Alyssandra must be right now getting ready. 'Did you notch hers? If not, she'll beat you.'

Julian smiled. He was going to mess with North's mind until the Englishman was paralysed with fear. 'Two broken blades in two consecutive rounds against me would be far too suspicious. No, I have something better for her. Shall I tell you what it is?' Just then, his page ran up to him, delivering his rapier. 'Ah, and here it is. Thank you, my boy. You didn't touch it, did you?'

'No, sir.' The boy nodded and ran off.

'Good lad, because if he had...' Julian leaned towards Haviland with an air of confidentiality '...he might be dead. I poisoned the tip, you see.' He watched Haviland's jaw tighten. 'I think it adds a little excitement to an otherwise dull sport, don't you? Really, what's the point of fighting with only wooden fleurets to pierce one's chest? It's like knife fighting with dull blades, firing guns without bullets. It's much more exciting this way.' He held up his blade to the light. 'It's cobra venom, it's invisible. All I have to do is knick her arm or leg. It won't matter if it's a legal touch or not. The result will be the same. I just have to give the poison a chance to work. The surface of the skin isn't enough, it has to enter the bloodstream.'

Then it would just be he and Antoine. He might not have the security of marriage any longer to bind him to the family without Alyssandra, but Antoine would need him for ever, would need the quality of his name to keep the *salle* drawing high-paying customers because to all the world, Antoine Leodegrance would be dead. Best of all, Antoine would never know what he'd done. It would be a shame to lose such a beauty, but she had made her position plain and refused to budge when she'd come after him with that sabre.

'You can tell her if you want to. There's time.' Julian smirked at Haviland's silent outrage, his fists clenched at his sides as he realised there was nothing he could do in a crowd. 'Or do you think it would distract her too much to know? What you have to ask yourself is will she fight better knowing her life is on the line or better if she was ignorant of the fact? It's your very own roulette game. Or maybe you don't care either way. You know, she has played us both, North. She's led me on for years. Maybe you've finally figured out she came to you only to protect her brother. She flirted with you so you'd stop asking questions about the two of them. She's done nothing but deceive you. If you didn't want to tell her, I wouldn't blame you.' He gave Haviland a little nod. 'If you'll excuse me, I need to get ready for the final.' Julian was through waiting. Fortune favoured those who took action and it was going to smile on him in about twenty minutes.

Chapter Twenty-Three

Murder! Haviland let the horrifying knowledge gal-
vanise him into action. There were mere minutes in
which to act. His mind raced ahead of his body as he
pushed his way through the crowd gathering on the
floor for an up-close look at the bout which would
take place on a raised stage. There was no time to go
to Antoine. Even if there was, there was no guarantee
Antoine could do anything to stop the match without
revealing himself. Neither could he go to Archer or
Nolan in the stands. He'd never make it through the
press of people to reach them and still warn Alyssandra.

His mind had already resolved that issue, too. He
impatiently elbowed aside a few bystanders that refused to move. The crowd was nearly impossible.
He wouldn't risk playing with her mind because she
wasn't going to fight. He needed to take her place.
The crowd would be expecting a man anyway. With
a mask on, he doubted they would see anything but

what they expected to see—Leodegrance on stage, at a distance from them.

Haviland turned sideways and edged through the people congregated at the foot of the stage. There were curtained cubicles set on either side for garbing up. She'd be there, but she'd already be garbed. As the champion, she'd be stage left. She was there, practising with her rapier—one of the *salle*'s premier blades. Haviland had seen them under lock and key in the glass case of the private instruction rooms.

'Leodegrance…' he began, careful not to use her name in case they were overheard.

She stopped mid-lunge, startled by the intrusion. He strode towards her, a hand to his lips, warning her to be silent, to do nothing to give her away, although he suspected she was far better at that game than he. Close enough to whisper, he delivered his news. 'Julian has poisoned his blade. Likely it's the tip, perhaps part of the blade itself. Definitely the fleuret.'

He wanted to rip the damn mask from her face, wanted to see her reaction, but it was far too risky with a crowd just feet away beyond the curtain. What was her reaction? Did the news frighten her? 'He means to do murder.' Motives didn't matter at this point. All that mattered was that Julian not have a chance to do it.

'Give me your helmet and your rapier.' Haviland's tones were stern, leaving no opportunity for argument. He didn't want her to feel there was a chance to contest his decision.

She backed up, shaking her head. She risked low, fast words. 'You will not die for me.'

'I don't mean to die. I am safer out there. Julian means to murder you. He'll recognise me, but no one else will. Perhaps he'll swap out his rapier or perhaps he won't even try if it's not his intended target,' Haviland reasoned. 'Who will protect Antoine if you fall? Who will protect the *salle d'armes*? Julian will have everything he wants with you gone.' He did not give voice to the rest of that argument. If Julian did succeed in harming him, it would accomplish nothing, move none of Julian's avaricious goals closer to achievement.

'Haviland, you have a family, people counting on you,' she argued. 'You simply can't throw yourself away.'

'Neither can you. I will beat him,' Haviland answered swiftly. They were running out of time. He could hear officials taking their places, the rustle of papers and the murmur of conferring voices. He ran his hand down the side of her mask as if it were her cheek. 'And when I get back, I mean to marry you if you'll have me.' He hadn't meant to do it quite that way. He'd meant for there to be champagne, roses and candles. But the words tumbled out, a promise that he had not been daunted by her brother's disclosures, nor his family's expectations, nor would he be daunted by Julian's poison. After all, Julian's rapier would never pierce his padding. Julian would have to go for a very specific mark on his arms or legs.

Haviland smiled, his world shrunk, the crowd

noise faded. Thoughts of Julian and poison receded. There was only the two of them in their tiny curtained alcove. 'Do you want to marry *me*? There's no reason you can't any more. You don't have to protect Antoine from me. It's just up to you. Can I be enough for you?' It might have been the bravest question he'd ever asked.

'What about Lady Christina? Your family? Wanting and being able to are different things.'

Haviland pressed a finger to her lips. 'Your decision is not about them. What about you? What about us? *You* are my priority. It doesn't have to be us or them, but that will be their choice to make. I've already made mine.'

'My brother...' she began.

'I have a plan for him, too,' he breathed, his mouth close to hers, close enough to silence her with a kiss, long and full. Barely a day had passed since they were together, but it felt an eternity. His body was hungry. He wanted to touch her, taste her, hear her little sighs as they took pleasure in each other. 'Don't worry so much.' He pushed back her hair, his hand cradling her head. 'I love you, Alyssandra. That's the best reason I can think of for getting married. That and the fact that it makes it official: you are not alone any more.' He pressed his forehead to hers. 'I am learning that sometimes being brave is about trusting others to do right by me. Perhaps you need to learn that lesson, too.'

Outside the curtain, the announcer began his speech. He went through the standard rules; the bout would be fought with weapons from the *salle* itself, making the rapiers identical so there would be no technological advantage for either side. Haviland didn't listen further. He was too intent on the woman before him. One more victory and he could focus on what was truly important.

He took her face in both hands and kissed her one last time. She reached up and put the mask over his head. She bit her lip and then it all came in a rush. 'Watch out for Julian's—'

'Right-side attacks,' he finished speaking for her and they laughed together. 'I know.' She needed something to do, something to take her mind off the bout. 'I need you to change your clothes and go up into the stands. Find my friend, Archer Crawford, have him go for the inspector. Then tell your brother. I want you with him. I need to know you are safe.'

It was time to go. The announcer was making introductions. The crowd's momentum was starting to build. He heard Alyssandra behind him. 'Keep your shoulder up.' He smiled to himself and climbed the steps to the stage, hearing the words that went unspoken in that four-word phrase. Alyssandra loved him. A man waited with a poisoned blade, but all was right in the world.

The world slowed. Alyssandra pressed her eyes to the peepholes in the viewing room. She'd done all Haviland had asked of her. There was nothing left to do but watch. She'd rather watch from the stands, but she'd been conspicuous enough when she'd gone up to find Archer. This was not a venue open to female attendance and she'd promised Haviland she'd stay with Antoine in case…in case the unthinkable happened.

Beside her, Antoine was still as stone, shocked to his core at Julian's betrayal. Even now, she thought he didn't quite believe it. But he believed *her*. Julian had been wrong about that. She sucked in her breath as Haviland avoided a graze of Julian's blade on his sleeve. Julian had recognised immediately his opponent wasn't her, but it had not deterred him as Haviland had hoped.

Haviland retaliated with an aggressive move that brought their blades close together, crossed and tangled. But Julian was strong and he pushed back. Both blades spun out of their competitors' hands, landing on the floor. 'No!' she cried out, grasping for Antoine's hand. She felt anew the panic of having a front seat to a man's murder. The man she loved. He was going to marry her. *If he survived this*. Had she sent him to his doom?

On the floor, there was a scramble for the blades. Then it hit her. The blades were identical! How would they know? It would be a relief if Haviland came up with it, but a horror, too. Would Haviland kill Julian? Would he have a choice? She'd not sent him to be a murderer any more than she wanted him murdered. The scene on the floor had turned violent. Ignoring the officials' call for a break while rapiers were reclaimed, Julian tackled Haviland. The two went down and the piste became a brawl; punching, kicking, rolling as they grappled with each other awkwardly through the thick padding of their vests and masks. Julian was trying to rip the mask off Haviland's face.

'No!' Alyssandra exhaled as they rolled dangerously close to one of the blades. Exposure wasn't the only risk Haviland ran out there. It would be too easy to be accidentally pricked. But the brawl couldn't last long—already she could see the officials moving in to separate them, but not fast enough. The two had scrambled to their feet, coming up with rapiers, although it was impossible to tell who had which. One look at Julian's ashen face suggested, however, that *he* knew.

'Haviland has the blade,' Alyssandra whispered. It should have relieved her to know the blade was out of Julian's hand, but it had just the opposite effect. Haviland had to fight carefully, had to consider every strike.

'He should use the *passata sotto.*' Antoine scowled when an opportunity to score passed. 'He could come up under Julian's blade and strike at Julian's flank.'

'And risk killing Julian?' Alyssandra responded. 'All it will take is a nick of the blade.' Haviland was in an impossible situation. Then Julian made a sudden move, a startling turn in an attempt to disarm Haviland. She saw it all in slow motion. Haviland threw up his arm to ward off the unorthodox move, his blade catching Julian's sword arm, slicing into the sleeve of his shirt. Julian went to his knees, rapier clattering away, his other hand gripping the sliced arm, red showing on the fabric of his shirt.

Alyssandra fought back a scream and raced from

the room. She did not care who saw her. She knew only that she had to get to Haviland. He would need her. Haviland's mask was off when she reached them and he was kneeling beside Julian, gripping the man's shoulders. She fell to her knees beside Haviland on the floor. But there was little she could do.

Julian was dying, writhing and cursing on the floor, and it was a horrible sight. Julian was the enemy, he'd threatened her, but it was not in her nature to enjoy death. 'We have to do something!'

'I need a knife!' Haviland shouted. 'I need someone to hold him.' A knife materialised and Haviland ripped apart Julian's sleeve, careful to avoid contact with the blood.

Julian screamed at the sight of the knife against his flesh. 'You don't need to kill me any quicker, the poison will do it soon enough.'

Alyssandra fought to hold his shoulders, watching in fascination as Haviland scored an 'x' over the tiny scratch with the knife and pressed his mouth against the wound. He sucked and spat, sucked and spat again. Over and over until the crowd had gone silent, the mass panic ebbing. Nolan and Archer made their way to Haviland's side with the inspector while officials began to usher spectators out.

'I need a bandage,' Haviland said, hoarse from his labours. Alyssandra grabbed up a piece of ruined shirt and handed it to him. He tied it around the wound site. 'I think you'll live, Anjou.'

He'd saved Julian, his enemy. Alyssandra stared at him with admiration, her heart filling with love all over again as if she didn't have reason enough to love him. Not many men would make the effort on behalf of a man who would have willingly killed them. She went to him, letting him wrap a warm, strong arm about her. Archer and Nolan helped Julian to his feet. But they weren't out of the woods yet. There would be explanations—why hadn't Antoine Leodegrance been under the mask? Why had the blade been poisoned? The whole situation was starting to unravel. It would only take a few words from Julian to expose everything in a very public fashion.

'You should have let me die.' Julian shook off their hands and snarled at Haviland with such vitriol that Alyssandra nearly recoiled.

Haviland met his hatred coolly. 'You owe me a life and I want Antoine Leodegrance's. That is a fair trade for what I've given you today.' He was asking for a confession and for protection of Antoine's identity.

Alyssandra watched the last bit of honour stir in Julian's eyes. 'You shall have it.'

The inspector stepped forward, and Nolan made introductions. 'Inspector Bouchard, this is Alyssandra Leodegrance, the *vicomte*'s sister.' Nolan gave her a cheeky grin. 'Miss Leodegrance, this is Inspector Bouchard. He and I play cards on occasion.'

Alyssandra smiled back. Everything was going to be all right.

And it was. Especially later that night as she lay in Haviland's arms, candlelight dancing about the room, her body and mind sated from desire fulfilled. As soon as they were able, they'd come here and retreated from the world, making love in a celebration of life both past and future. She'd almost lost him today to the slightest prick of a rapier, proving how dear and precious each moment was and how small the obstacles one raised to their own happiness could be when weighed against what one had to gain.

She stirred in his arms, turning to face him. 'I love you.' She'd missed the opportunity to say it today and it had almost been her last chance.

'I know,' he murmured drowsily.

'You don't know,' she argued playfully. 'I didn't say it until now.'

He nuzzled her neck. 'Yes, you did, when you told me not to drop my shoulder. That's how the great fencer, Alyssandra Leodegrance, says "I love you".'

She laughed. He had understood after all. 'Out of curiosity how does Haviland North say "I love you"?'

He rolled her beneath him, and she gasped. 'Don't you know? With his mouth, with his eyes, with his hands. Perhaps it would be better if I showed you.' And he did, beginning with a trail of hot kisses that ran all the way to the damp curls between her thighs and ending with their bodies joined in a star-splitting climax that left them exhausted...until the next time.

Epilogue

When Haviland North, fourth Viscount Amersham, imagined his wedding it had always been in a big church filled with hothouse roses and hothouse people, a useless white runner on the aisle for the bride to walk upon once before it was thrown out, and an icy, beautiful but remote woman he hardly knew floating towards him in another useless piece of expensive frippery while he stood straight and immaculate at the front, showing not a single emotion. But now, when he pictured his wedding, what lay before him was not that. It was better. Much better.

The little church in Fontainebleau was turned out with simple vases full of late spring flowers, looking its best even though the wedding was attended by only seven people counting the reverend and his wife, Nolan, Brennan, the bride and groom and the bride's brother. The wooden floor was bare of any decorative runner and the woman walking towards him drew every emotion he possessed to the fore of his mind.

He was certain they were written on his face for all to see. The only item this wedding shared with his original vision was that the bride was beautiful. But that was where all similarities ended. Alyssandra was radiant in a gown of buttercup yellow that made her skin glow and her caramel hair shine. She vibrated with life as she looked at him, love in her eyes. She was his—his partner in all things.

And there were a lot of things to partner. In the time before the wedding, he'd encouraged Antoine not to sell the *salle d'armes*, but to keep it in the family by turning it over to him. Antoine would be able to live in the country while he and Alyssandra divided their time between Fontainebleau and Paris. Alyssandra would pioneer fencing classes for women in the private instruction rooms of the *salle*. But all that would be after their honeymoon in Italy.

The only sad note for Haviland today was that Archer had left the previous week, going ahead to Italy to prepare for the annual horse race in Siena, the Palio. But they had said their farewells with promises to catch up with him there as part of the honeymoon. Antoine met Alyssandra at the end of the aisle and placed her hand in Haviland's, the aisle not being wide enough to accommodate both of them and his chair. Country life agreed with him, Haviland was pleased to note. Or perhaps it was the housekeeper they'd hired to open the house. Haviland thought she'd rather taken a fancy to the *vicomte*. Either way, Alyssandra need not worry about leaving Antoine for their wedding trip.

In the month since the tournament much had been settled. Julian had been sentenced to house parole in Lyons so that he would not be a constant reminder in their lives. But Haviland's parents had not been one of the things settled. His father had written a vituperative letter deriding his decision to marry elsewhere and to stay there. He had expected that. However, there had been a surprise. His mother had enclosed a private note wishing him happiness. There was hope in that direction, then. And he was optimistic that, given time and eventually grandchildren, his parents would relent. He didn't hate them, he just loved his freedom more, loved Alyssandra more than even that.

The reverend began the service—where Nolan had found a Church of England man in France he didn't know. He didn't bother to question it. The reverend intoned the words, 'with my body I thee worship', and Alyssandra beamed up at him, mischief sparkling in those dark eyes. 'I'm already thinking about tonight,' she whispered naughtily.

Haviland raised an eyebrow. 'Really? Tonight? Is that the best you can do because I'm already thinking how I will worship you this afternoon.'

She blushed, and the reverend coughed. Haviland didn't mind. He was *alive*, he could feel it in his bones. He'd set out on this journey with all his hopes pinned on Paris, and Paris, the city of love, had not disappointed.

* * * * *

RAKE MOST LIKELY
TO THRILL

For Judi and Don and Nina and El Dorado Farms.
Thanks for helping Catie find Sharper Eagle.
There is no finer love than a girl and her horse.

Chapter One

The Antwerp Hotel, Dover—March 1835

There was going to be blood. It had become a forgone conclusion the moment the teamster brought the whip down across the hindquarters of the Cleveland Bay straining in the traces of the overloaded dray. How much blood, and whose, remained to be seen.

Archer Crawford had not stepped outside in the predawn darkness looking for trouble. Indeed, he'd been trying to avoid it. Inside, his travelling companion and long-time friend Nolan Gray's card game was starting to take a turn for the worse. But it seemed trouble had found him anyway. He could not stand idly by and watch any horse abused. From the looks of this horse's ragged coat, this wasn't the first time. But it might be the last if Archer didn't intervene. The teamster's whip fell again, the beefy driver determined the horse pull the load or die trying. The latter was highly likely and the horse knew it. The Cleveland Bay showed no fear. He merely stood with resignation. Waiting. Knowing. Deciding: death now, or death pulling a weight more appropriate for two.

The whip rose a third time, and Archer stepped out from the hotel's overhang. In a lightning move, Archer's gloved hand intercepted the thong of the whip and he wrapped it about his wrist, reeling in the teamster on his high seat like fish from the river. 'Perhaps you might try a sting or two of this lash yourself before delivering it to your animal.' Archer gave the whip a strong tug. Each pull threatened to unseat the teamster. The man leaned back in his seat, trying for leverage.

'Let go of the whip or come off the seat!' Archer commanded sternly, his eyes locking with the other man's as he gave another compelling tug.

'This is none of your business,' the teamster growled. 'That horse has to earn his keep and I do too.' But he released his end of the whip—forcefully, of course, probably with the hopes the force of his release would send Archer sprawling in the mud. But Archer was braced. The abrupt release did nothing more than seal his opinion of the man: bully, brute.

Archer wound the whip into a coil around his arm. 'Not with loads that are best drawn by a team of horses.' Archer jerked his head towards the horse. 'That horse won't finish the day, then where will you be?'

The man seemed to recognise the logic but his mouth pursed into a grim line. 'There's nothin' to be done about it, if you'll be givin' me my whip back, guv'nor, I'll be on my way.' The hint of a threat glimmered in the man's eye and he began to make his way down off the seat. That was the last thing Archer wanted.

He had a boat to catch within the hour. There was no time for fisticuffs. Archer was fast and light on his feet, thanks to hours of practice at Jackson's salon, but that didn't change the fact that the teamster outweighed him by two stone. Leaving on his Grand Tour sporting a split lip and black eye didn't exactly appeal.

The horse whinnied and stamped in the traces, his head rolling towards Archer as if in warning. The big man stopped a few feet from Archer and held out his hand. 'The whip.'

Archer grinned. 'I'll trade you for it. Give me the horse.'

The man spat on the ground. 'A whip for a horse?' His tone was derisive. 'That seems a bit unequal to me.'

'And for whatever is in my pocket.' Archer patted the pocket of his great coat.

'Maybe your pocket is empty.' The teamster's eyes narrowed. 'Show me.'

Archer nodded, careful to keep his body between the teamster and the horse. He could feel the horse's nose nudging his shoulder blade, perhaps in encouragement. Archer held up a gold money clip to the street lamp, letting it catch the light. He turned it, showing off the collection of pound notes folded together. 'It's fair. You can buy two horses for what's in this clip.' He was not going to doom another horse to the same fate simply by freeing this one.

Archer tried to assess the man's reaction. Money was usually the fastest way to settle a dispute, even if it wasn't the most moral. He waved the clip again in the beam of light. Behind him, he could hear the clatter of an oncoming coach, probably the one that was to take him and Nolan to the docks. He was running out of the time. 'The whip and the clip for the horse,' Archer pressed. What was there to think over? The man was letting pride get in his way.

'All right,' the man said gruffly, taking the money clip out of Archer's hand in a rough swipe. He jerked his head towards the horse. 'He's yours now, you unharness him.'

Archer had the horse free in short measure. There was triumph in knowing he'd rescued the animal from a certain fate, but what was he to do now? The coach he'd heard was indeed theirs and the driver was waiting. He had ten minutes to see the horse settled. He led the horse by a rope bridle towards the hotel's stable, sneaking a peek through the hotel's long street-front windows at Nolan. The situation inside didn't look good. Nolan and the other card players were standing. One of them was gesturing wildly at the cards and money on the table. Ten minutes might be a generous estimate.

Inside the stable, Archer roused the ostler, issuing rapid-fire instructions. 'This horse needs to be boarded.' He plunked down some coins on a small crude wood table. 'This will keep him until you can deliver him.' Money helped the ostler rub the sleep from his eyes. It was more than what was necessary. 'When the horse has been rested, have a boy deliver him to this address.' Archer pulled a card from a coat pocket. 'The man there will pay well. Here's additional money for the journey.' His nearest friend was a day's ride from Dover, but it was the best he could do under the hasty circumstances. Archer hoped the promise of more money would be enough to ensure the ostler didn't sell the horse instead of deliver it.

The sounds of commotion drifted in from the front of the hotel. That would be Nolan. Archer ran a friendly hand across the horse's ragged coat. The animal had been beautiful once, strong once; with luck he would be again. He dug in his pocket for more coin. Money was all he had to keep the horse safe. Archer pressed a third round of coins into the ostler's hand. 'This is for you, as my personal thanks for your efforts, one horseman to another.' Perhaps an appeal to the man's ethics would be enough. There was no time for more. The commotion was demanding his attention now. Archer gave the ostler a nod and strode into the courtyard, aware that the horse's eyes followed him out.

In the darkness, he almost collided with Nolan who was moving at a near run. 'Archer, old chap! Where did you get to? We've got to go!' Nolan seized his arm without stopping and dragged him towards the waiting coach, his words coming fast. 'Don't look now, but that angry man behind us thinks I cheated. He has a gun, *and* my good knife. It's in his shoulder, but I think he shoots with both—hands, that is. It wouldn't make sense the other way.' Nolan pulled open the coach door and they tumbled in, the coach lurching to a start before the door was even shut.

'Ah! A clean getaway.' Nolan sank back against the seat, a satisfied grin on his face.

'It doesn't always have to be a "getaway". Sometimes we *can* exit a building like normal people.'

Archer straightened the cuffs of his coat and gave Nolan a scolding look.

'It was fairly normal,' Nolan protested.

'You left a *knife* embedded in a man's shoulder, not exactly the most discreet of departures.' If Nolan had been discreet, he would have stopped playing two hours ago. The other players could have respectably quit the table, their pride and at least some money intact. But then he never would have had a chance to save that horse. 'You got away in the nick of time.'

Nolan merely grinned, unfazed by the scolding. 'Speaking of time, do you think Haviland is at the docks yet?' They were scheduled to meet two friends at the boat this morning to begin their Grand Tour. 'I'll wager you five pounds Haviland is there.'

Archer laughed. 'At this hour? He's not there. Everything was loaded last night. There's no reason for him to be early. Besides, he has to drag Brennan's sorry self out of bed. That will slow him down.' He and Haviland had known each other since Eton. Haviland was notoriously prompt, but he wouldn't be early and Brennan was always late.

'Easiest five pounds I'll ever make,' Nolan said something more, but Archer had leaned back and closed his eyes, blocking it out. He wanted a moment's peace. Between angry teamsters, rescued horses and irate gamblers, the late hour was starting to take its toll. Sometimes, Nolan wore a person out. Provoking a fight on the brink of departure wasn't exactly Archer's idea of *bon voyage*.

Still, whether he agreed with Nolan's choices or not, it was his job to have Nolan's back just as it was Haviland's job to have Brennan's. He and Haviland had divided up the duties of friendship years ago at school when it had become apparent Nolan and Brennan weren't entirely capable of exercising discretion on their own.

Back then, what couldn't be tamed had to be protected. These days, Nolan did a pretty fair job of protecting himself. He didn't need defending as much as he needed what one might call *support*. That was the gentlemanly way to put it. Needing a duelling second would be another.

It was times like this morning when Archer appreciated horses. He understood them, preferred them even. It was horses, in addition to his long-standing friendship with the others, that had provided the final, but not the only piece of motivation to leave Newmarket. Perhaps there were new breeds waiting for him in Europe, breeds he could send back to the family stud.

His father had charged him with purchasing any exciting prospects he could find and had given him *carte blanche* to do it. But Archer knew what that charge really was. It was his father's way of apologising. His father was very good at apologising with money. It was easy to do if one had a lot of it and his father, the Earl, had bags of it, rooms of it even. He'd never understood his family wanted more from him than his money or what it could buy. Not even at the last had he understood that and Archer had had enough of his father's aloof, uncaring reserve, enough of the coldness. He was off to seek warmer climates, warmer families: his mother's people in Siena.

Archer had never been so glad to be a second son.

His brother was the heir. He, as the eldest, was confined to the estates, whereas Archer had been given the stables, the racing string and that had been the avenue of a convenient escape when Haviland had delicately proposed the tour last autumn. He could be in Siena for the Palio, the town's grand tradition in the heat of August. He could be with his mother's family, horse breeders like himself. Perhaps that was what drew him most of all, these people he'd never met, only heard about in letters over his childhood; his uncle Giacomo, the breeder whose famed horses had won that race more than any other, a chance to be part of something great, a chance to keep the vow he had made to a dying mother. Her dreams and his promises were all he had left of her now.

There was the rustle of Nolan shifting, his body leaning forward to look out the window. 'I don't think he followed us, not with a knife in his shoulder,' Archer muttered, eyes closed. He heard Nolan's body relax once more against the squabs. Not quite relaxed, he amended. He could *feel* Nolan staring at him, those grey eyes boring into his head in a very one-sided staring contest. He would *not* open his eyes, he would not, would not, would not... Archer's eyes flew open. He couldn't stand it. 'What?'

Nolan crossed his arms over his chest, a wide smile taking his face. 'Archer, why is there a horse following us?'

'A horse?' It was Archer's turn to look out the window. He stared, he squinted, he looked at Nolan and then back out the window. It couldn't be. But it was. The Cleveland Bay he'd rescued was cantering down the road behind them. *Right* beside them, as if he knew Archer was inside the coach.

'I sort of rescued him this morning while you were playing cards,' Archer explained. What was he going to do with a horse at the docks? He couldn't take the beast to France with him. It would hardly be fair to make the poor horse endure a Channel crossing or to make him walk from Calais to Paris. He needed good food and rest. That didn't mean the horse's efforts hadn't tugged at his heartstrings. Nolan might laugh at the notion horses could and did communicate with their owners, but Archer had seen too many examples to the contrary. A horse's loyalty was not to be taken lightly. Horses would give their lives for the people they loved.

Their coach turned in to the docks, the horse slowing obediently to a trot to match the pace. Archer jumped down the moment the coach stopped. The horse still wore the rope bridle, but thankfully no lead line dangled dangerously at his hooves. Archer held out his hand and approached slowly. 'Easy, boy.' The horse blew out a loud snuffle, flecks of foam at his mouth. The running had started to wind him. A horse like him should be able to run for miles, but poor nutrition and hard labour had taken their toll on his natural endurance. They had not, however, taken their toll on the horse's sense of a good man. The horse stood patiently, letting Archer put a hand on his long nose and another on his neck.

Archer stroked the sweaty coat and spoke in soft, reassuring tones. 'I've got a good home for you. The ostler at the hotel is going to take you there after you have had a rest. There are green pastures. You can run all day and eat orchard grass.'

'He doesn't understand you, Arch.' Nolan chuckled, coming to stand on the horse's other side. 'He sure is a game fellow, though, to chase after you. Smart too. You've got to respect that.'

And wonder at it. Archer leaned his head against the horse's neck. People only left when there was no reason to stay. He knew that perhaps better than anyone. His mother had kept him bound to England when he would have left perhaps years ago. Now she was gone and so were his reasons. Were horses any different?

Archer walked the horse to the back of the hired coach and tied him on behind. He gave instructions to the driver and a few coins to deliver the animal back to the mews at the Antwerp Hotel. The ostler would be expecting him. He gave the horse a final pat. 'Trust me,' he whispered. 'Everything will be fine.'

'Except that you will be five pounds poorer.' Nolan gestured with a laugh towards a tall, dark figure standing alone on the pier. 'Haviland's already here. I told you he would be, and look, he's got his fencing cases with him. He couldn't be parted from them for even a night.'

Archer gave an exaggerated grimace and handed over the money, more concerned about the fact that Haviland was *alone*. 'Where's Brennan?' Nolan called out as they joined Haviland.

'Did you expect him to be here, scholar of human nature that you are?' Haviland teased and then his tone tensed. Archer could hear the worry. 'I had hoped he was with you.' Haviland motioned to the boat. 'We have to board. The captain is ready to leave. There's no more time. I was worried I'd be sailing alone.'

'Well,' Nolan said cheekily, 'we were rescuing horses.'

'And throwing knives at people's shoulders. Don't forget the knives part,' Archer added crossly. He was tired, concerned about the horse and Brennan. It seemed an ominous note to leave on. Perhaps it was an omen that he should stay behind? He could take a few days and deliver the horse himself to Jamie Burke over in Folkestone. He could find Brennan. They could catch a boat together. It was a sensible solution. He should offer...

No, he told himself firmly. He wasn't going to give in to the excuses no matter how practical they seemed. He'd put this off long enough, put others' needs ahead of his own long enough. He was getting on that boat. Perhaps he prevaricated out of cold feet at the last. If he took this step, there would be no turning back. His step would be larger than the others. He was going to find a new life, a new family.

The trio boarded the boat reluctantly and took up positions at the rail, their eyes glued to the wharf, each of them lost in their own worries about Brennan. The glances they exchanged with each other all communicated the same thought: What could have happened? Brennan had been with them last night at dinner. It wasn't, Archer knew, a matter of *where* Brennan was, but a matter of whether or not he was safe. Nolan tried to keep everyone's spirits up by wagering on Brennan's arrival, but to no avail. By the time the anchor's chains began to roll up, there was no sign of their fourth companion.

Archer bowed his head to the inevitable. Brennan wasn't coming. It wouldn't be the same the trip without him. It might be a whole lot safer, but it would lose something all the same. Wherever Brennan went, there was life and fire, he made everything exciting.

A blur of movement on the wharf caught his attention. Archer lifted his head. Beside him, Haviland saw it too. It was Bren! Haviland began shouting and waving madly. Brennan was running full tilt without his coats, white shirttails flapping like sails in the growing light. Haviland sprinted the length of the boat, yelling instructions: 'jump,' and 'don't jump here, it's too wide, jump at the back of the boat where it hasn't left the dock yet'. The back of the boat was flat for loading and there was a section that sported no railing. It would be Brennan's best chance.

That was when Archer realised Brennan wasn't alone. In his excitement, he hadn't noticed the two men racing behind, one of them armed. There was something more too. Behind the men was a horse, thundering past them, jumping knocked barrels, headed straight for Brennan and the drink. That wasn't just any horse. That was *his* horse. Archer exchanged a look with Nolan and they dashed off after Haviland.

The stern of the ship was chaos. Haviland was yelling, Brennan was running, the horse had pulled up alongside him, matching his pace to Brennan's, but the two men in pursuit were gaining. As long as they kept chasing him, they couldn't get a worthy shot off. It was when they stopped that worried Archer and that would be soon. There wasn't anywhere else to run. The ship had nudged away from the dock, leaving a gap of cold dark water between itself and the pier. Archer gauged the distance. Even with Brennan's speed, it would be close. Not close enough. Bren would need some help.

'Get on the horse, Bren!' Archer shouted into the wind, gesturing wildly towards the animal. It would be beyond dangerous. What if the horse refused to jump? What if they both missed the boat deck? Like him, Brennan had been born to the saddle. If anyone could do this, it would be Bren. There was no other choice unless Bren wanted to face pistols. Haviland and Nolan joined him in the wild charades. They held their breaths as Brennan Carr grabbed mane and swung himself up on the running steed. He put his feet to the horse's sides.

They leapt.

They landed.

Just barely.

Another foot and they would have missed. The shock of the landing and the uneven movement of the deck beneath him brought the horse to his knees. Archer and Haviland raced forward.

Brennan rolled out of the saddle. Haviland was there to catch him, but Brennan pushed him down with a rush of incoherent words. 'Stay down, Hav! Arch, the horse, keep him down!'

The first bullet whined overhead, missing Haviland by inches. Archer crouched beside the frightened horse, using his words and his hands to keep the big animal from becoming an accidental target.

Now that they were all safe, Archer wished the boat would move faster. There was suddenly not nearly enough space between them and the dock. It wouldn't surprise him to see Nolan's man from the hotel show up. Everyone else was here, even the horse. Thanks to Nolan and Brennan, the morning had got off to quite a start.

Assured they were out of range, the foursome picked themselves up cautiously, brushing off their clothes and exclaiming over Brennan. Archer exchanged knowing glances with Haviland. It was going to be quite a trip with those two along, but Haviland was smiling as England disappeared. Archer nodded to the reins in his hand. 'I'll go speak to the captain about where we can stable this boy.' As he moved off with the horse, Archer could hear Nolan drawl at the rail, 'The real question isn't where you've been, Bren, but was she worth it?'

Brennan's laugh drifted over the wind, as if the mad chase had been a simple lark, as if there hadn't been bullets fired. 'Always, Nol, always.' Sometimes, Archer envied Bren and Nolan their nonchalant ways, not seeming to care too much. They were proof that perhaps the unexamined life was underrated.

There was a makeshift stall above deck where the horse would be relatively safe. The Channel crossing was short. Just twenty-one miles of water separated England from France, but the water could be rough. Archer didn't want to risk the horse doing further injury to himself, so saw the horse installed and ran a hand down each of his legs to make sure there'd been no damage from his leap.

Satisfied the horse was no worse for his morning adventures, Archer placed a hand on the horse's neck. 'I guess you'll need a name if you're going to stay with me.' Archer thought for a moment. 'How about Amicus? It means *friend* in Latin, and you were that today. You stood Brennan in good stead when he needed you.'

'Especially since Cleveland Bays are carriage horses.' Haviland's voice was quiet behind him. Archer shrugged. He'd long since stopped caring if anyone heard him talking to the horses.

Archer smiled and stroked Amicus's long nose. 'Especially because of that.' He gave Amicus a considering look. 'I wonder if you might have been a hunter once, boy? It looked like you knew what you were doing when you made that leap.' Fearlessly, as if he'd taken hedges and logs, heights and wide spreads, before. Cleveland Bays were the preferred carriage horse of royalty, and Archer knew a few breeders who enjoyed riding to the hunt on them.

Haviland stepped up beside him and petted Amicus. 'Why do you suppose he did that? It was an extraordinary leap. I know horses that would have balked. He could have been killed.'

Archer gave Haviland a solemn look. 'He decided England could no longer hold him.'

'Like you, old friend?' Haviland ventured. 'Are you still determined to do this thing?' Nolan and Brennan might not know of his choice to stay in Italy, but he'd confided in Haviland.

Archer nodded. 'And you?' Haviland had done some confiding of his own. Archer wasn't the only one using this trip as an escape.

'Yes. I want to taste some freedom, I want to know

my own power, to see what might have been before…' Haviland shrugged, his sentence dropping
off. Haviland didn't have to say it. Archer knew how
that sentence ended: before he had to go back and
give himself in an arranged marriage to a woman
who did not inspire his passions.

Archer silently thanked the heavens again that
he wasn't firstborn. He at least had choices. He just
had to make them. He and Amicus had something
in common. He too had decided England could no
longer hold him.

Chapter Two

The Pantera Contrada, Siena, Italy—early July, 1835

Tonight, nothing could hold her! Elisabeta threw her head back and laughed up to the starry sky. She let the wildness loose, humming through her blood in time to the musicians playing in the Piazza del Conte as she and her cousins drew near to the neighbourhood's centre. There was already a crowd gathered for the celebration and they were jostled on all sides by good-natured merrymakers filling the narrow streets. She didn't care. The press of people only added to her excitement. Tonight she was going to dance until her shoes were worn through and then she was going to dance barefoot. She'd dance until the sun came up!

It was her first real party since coming out of mourning and she was going to enjoy it, no matter what, which was no small thing in light of what had transpired this afternoon. Elisabeta grabbed her cousin Contessina's hands and swung the younger girl around in a gay circle. 'I'm going to do something scandalous tonight,' Elisabeta declared, watching Contessina's pretty brown eyes widened in shock.

'Do you think that's wise? Papa just announced—'

'Especially because of that!' Elisabeta cut her off. She wasn't going to think about *it*—the fact that her uncle, Rafaele di Bruno, the *contrada*'s *capitano*, had bartered her off in a proposed marriage to Ridolfo Ranieri, the relative of another neighbourhood's *priore* in order to secure an alliance for the all-important Palio.

Like her first marriage, it was not a match of her choosing and it wasn't fair. Five years ago at the age of seventeen, she'd served her family and married the very young Lorenzo di Nofri. It was meant to be something of a dynastic connection for the family, and her feelings had not been considered. Then, Lorenzo had died after three years of marriage and she'd dutifully but begrudgingly done her year of mourning for her adolescent husband.

Now, at the very first decent opportunity, she was to be married off again. This time to a man in his late forties, more than twice her age, heavy and gouty from rich food and wine. Where would the chance for a family of her own be in that? Elisabeta forcefully shoved away images of what would be required of her to produce a child in that alliance. There was no place in this evening of celebration for dark thoughts.

She deserved better although her uncle disagreed. He was quick to point out she was lucky to marry again at all. She was no fresh virgin like Contessina, but a widow who'd been tried in marriage and hadn't managed to prove her fecundity. Who would want such a woman? She should be honoured by the Priore of Oca's attention and the chance to serve her family's greatness.

The Piazza del Conte came into view and Elisabeta pulled Contessina forward with her to take it all in: people, music, lanterns lighting the piazza like a magical fairyland. Celebrations like this were being held all over the town tonight, with every neighbourhood, or *contrada*, hosting its own party. It was Siena at its best and she'd missed it sorely in the years of her marriage spent in Florence. She'd missed her family, the festivals and, perhaps most of all, the horses.

It wasn't that Florence didn't have festivals or that Lorenzo's rich family didn't have horses, but they weren't hers and she was seldom allowed to work with them. Returning to Siena had been like coming alive again, which made the proposed marriage seem all the more cruel: to live again, only to face another sort of death.

Contessina tugged at her arm, slowing her down. 'What will you *do*?' she asked with a hint of worry.

'I don't know—*something*.' Elisabeta laughed. When the inspiration came she'd know it. Spontaneity was best left unplanned. 'Maybe I will dance with the next man I see!' Elisabeth announced, but that was hardly scandalous to her way of thinking. She'd have to do better than that to be truly scandalous. She'd made the remark mostly to shock Contessina, who loved her dearly, but didn't always know how to respond to her exuberance. Her uncle ran a strict household.

'You can't!' Contessina whispered a warning. Contessina's own dancing partners for the evening had already been arranged by her uncle and her brother, Giuliano. Even though it wasn't a formal ball, Contessina's partners were to be respectable young men from appropriate households in the *contrada*. 'What if the next person you saw was someone from Aquila?' Contessina dared to breathe the name of their rival *contrada*.

Elisabeta threw her a smug smile. 'I would even dance with an Aquilini.' She would too, but that was hardly likely. There would only be men of the Pantera *contrada*, her family's neighbourhood, here tonight. No one would dare venture away from their own neighbourhood celebrations. Still, stealing a dance was hardly the type of scandal she was thinking of, it was far too tame.

'What about your husband? What would he think?' Contessina was almost aghast at the thought of disobeying male authority. Her father had ordered her life to perfection. She had lived sheltered and protected to ensure she made a good marriage. Contessina had never thought to question the dictates of her parents. She was a good daughter and she would do what she was told.

Not so Elisabeta. She had played the good niece once. She was not ready to do it again, if ever, and certainly not to the fat cousin of the Priore of Oca, no matter how rich he was or what benefits it might serve the family when it came time for the Palio.

'He's *not* my husband yet. The engagement isn't even official,' Elisabeta said sharply, irritated with the conversation and what it signified. 'Perhaps I'll find a way out of it,' she teased, but she was only partially joking. If she could find a way out, she would.

Ridolfo terrified her with his beady, lecherous eyes. It was clear how he saw her: another thing to claim, to put in his treasury of earthly possessions. She did not relish the idea of being any man's slave, but especially not his.

'How would you do that?' Contessina, her brow knitting in contemplation, took her seriously. 'I can't see how it's possible unless you were to take a lover.' Contessina blushed as she said it. It was likely the most scandalous thing she could think of, an idea gleaned from conversations she wasn't supposed to overhear when her mother gathered with the other women of the *contrada* to exchange gossip.

Elisabeta gave her cousin a wicked smile. 'Exactly! What a perfect idea.' The thought held merit, just the sort of scandal she was looking for, but the list of candidates for such an affair was horribly short. She scanned the piazza, selecting and discarding the men of the *contrada*. 'Fabrizio is too old, I think I'd like someone younger, with more stamina. Alberto is young but he smells like garlic.' She wrinkled her nose.

'No!' Contessina was truly shocked now. 'I only meant to tease, to demonstrate how impossible it is.'

'How impossible what is?' Contessina's brother, Giuliano, sidled up to them, throwing an arm about his sister. He was handsome and wild, always in the throes of a grand affair, but life was different for a male. No one would condemn him for such promiscuity.

'Getting out of her engagement,' Contessina supplied.

Elisabeta moved to his other side and looped her

arm through his, feeling mischievous. 'Contessina suggested I take a lover.'

'I did not!' Contessina blushed furiously.

Giuliano's dark eyes sparked with mischief of their own. 'Ah, a last fling before settling down? A widow could do it, but not one who is affianced to another.' Giuliano thought for a moment. She could see her daredevil cousin puzzling it out. 'It could be pulled off, though, as long as you were discreet and the man you chose wasn't an enemy.' That meant not a man from Aquila or from Torre, the enemy of her would-be husband's neighbourhood.

Contessina looked frantically at them, waiting for them to give in and say they were only joking. 'Stop it!'

But Elisabeta didn't think she would stop. Why not take a lover? Perhaps just for the night? Perhaps it didn't have to be publicly scandalous, just a private interlude for herself. She deserved it and she'd been alone for so long. Even if her marriage had not been an intensely passionate one, she missed Lorenzo's presence. Was it so wrong to want one night in the arms of a strong, handsome man? To seek a little comfort, a little pleasure? No one had to know unless she wanted them to.

'Who would it be, Elisabeta?' Giuliano's playful pressing fuelled her madness. She would do it if the right man presented himself. Surely there must be one…

Elisabeta looked out over the piazza, towards the arch that marked the boundary of their *contrada*. Her breath hitched. It was as if the saints had conspired to present temptation and scandal personified. A man stepped through the arch. His height alone would make him stand out in any crowd—add to that those shoulders and it made for a remarkable sight. Good lord, they were broad, and that face! Even at a distance, the angles and planes were striking against the rich dark brown of his hair. It was longer than most of the men's present, skimming his shoulders and falling errantly over his right brow. She cocked her head and gave Giuliano a playful stare. This man wasn't a rival from an enemy *contrada*, he was something even more dangerous, a stranger, a man of unknown origins and family. That didn't make the man dangerous, it made him exciting, and it made him exactly the man she was looking for.

Did she risk it? It would be daring, even for her, but that was what tonight was for. The town's general spirits were high. The first Palio of the summer was behind them, her uncle victorious, his attentions already turned towards the Palio in August, and tonight people had gathered to celebrate the strawberry harvest: La Sagra del Fragole. Elisabeta doubted she'd be the only person present who allowed themselves to be swept away by the magic of a summer evening. Decision made, Elisabeta spoke her verdict.

'Him.' Her eyes studied the newcomer. 'I choose him.' Most definitely him. She wasn't the only one who'd noticed him, though. The attention of most of the feminine eyes in the crowd had gone his direction, she noted. He was *that* sort of man, the type who could command the female population of any gathering. The real issue was whether or not she could get there first. She would have to move fast. Signora Bernardi was closer and already edging near.

Elisabeta straightened her shoulders and tugged the square neckline of her gown lower, letting the tops of her breasts swell against the tightly laced bodice, to Contessina's dismay. She didn't have to reach him first, but she had to make her intentions known, had to convince him she was worth waiting for. She flashed Giuliano a competitor's smile and crossed the piazza, hips swaying, head held high.

Chapter Three

She was the kind of woman men crossed rooms for, or piazzas in this case, and she was headed directly for *him*. Archer couldn't say he didn't see her coming. How could he *not* see a woman like that; all those shiny black curls cascading down her back, the almond-shaped eyes that tilted ever so slightly at their corners as if they were always full of mischief and mystery, and the gown that set off the rest of her to perfection. The white of her shift peeked enticingly over the square bodice of a pale-green overdress laced over the full, rising curves of her breasts to a tight, slim waist before flaring out into provocatively swaying hips. The knowing smile on her lips suggested it was deliberate. She knew precisely what she was doing and what she wanted. At the moment, that was him.

The thrill of the hunt surged through him. Quicksilver eyes locked on his, and he held her sharp gaze, his own eyes communicating the unspoken message: *invitation accepted*. On his periphery, he was aware of women falling back, their interest averted by the advent of this woman's approach. She had staked her claim. If she meant to hunt him, she might be in for a surprise. Like any stallion worth his stud, Archer would be dominated by no woman.

She held out her hand, and he felt the full force of her attentions. 'Dance with me.' Not a question, then, she was too bold for that, but a summons, and he would honour it. Archer took her hand. That was where her supremacy ended. In his experience, a bold woman wanted a bold man and he could be that indeed, a commanding stallion to her flirty, teasing mare.

Eyes unwavering, he led her into the dance and fitted his hand to her back, swinging them into the polka without a word. Who needed words when they had eyes like hers? A body like hers, that communicated everything she thought and felt? She gave him a toss of her glorious dark head, tipping it up to meet his. Archer grinned, and she answered with a wide smile of her own, her eyes sparkling with the thrill of the dance.

Archer swung them into the turn and let the energy of the music claim them, his hand confident at her back as if it belonged there, as if they had done this before. He knew how to dance, how to navigate a crowded space, and she knew it too, recognised his skill and delighted in it, just as she was revelling in the sheer joy of the dance. The joy emanating from her was nearly intoxicating. She danced with her heart, her very soul, and it fired him, drove him to reckless abandon.

At the edge of the makeshift dance floor, he manoeuvred them sharply, bringing her up against him with the force of the turn, and did not relinquish her to the decency of distance. The pulse at her neck beat hard from the dancing and possibly from something more. She laughed up at him, confirming the latter. She felt it too, this surge of wildness, this connection between them although they'd not spoken a word— the dance was too fast, they were too breathless for conversation, too in love with the moment to contemplate the use of words.

What moments they were! Archer thought he would remember them for ever. It was an odd sensation given how many moments made up a lifetime, thousands upon thousands, most to be forgotten. Why these moments with a stranger who had lured him into a dance with only a smile and a touch? What made them different? What made them more valuable than all the other moments?

The music was ending. He took them through one last turn, his body memorising the soft curve of her hip where it met his, the straightness of her spine beneath his hand, his eyes discreetly taking in the rise and fall of her breasts beneath the tight-laced bodice just as he was aware of her gaze taking in him, studying his neck and throat where his shirt lay open. This was summer magic at its finest: a beautiful woman in his arms to enjoy the music and dancing with, a starry sky overhead, an arduous journey complete. He felt quite the king in these moments. Archer tilted his head to the sky and gave a howl of primal victory. And he knew.

He knew why he would remember these moments; because he was so alive in them, *she* was so alive in them. They were breathing hard and laughing, drinking in the simple pleasures of music and dance beneath a starry sky, the summer air warm around them. Did life get any better than this? His hand lingered at her waist in no hurry to set her apart from him and he thought that indeed it just might get better. His eyes drifted across her face, resting briefly on her lips. This woman was no stranger to pleasure, not with that body and those eyes, and the way she looked at him—with boldness and invitation. The rest of the piazza might as well have melted away for all that he noticed anything but her.

Archer's voice was low and private when he spoke, his gaze lingering meaningfully on the sensual curve of her lips. 'Who are you, *bella signora*?' They were the first words he'd spoken to her. She would know now that he wasn't Italian. She would hear it in his accent. Not just a stranger, then, from a neighbouring town, but a true outsider. Maybe it didn't matter where he was from for what they wanted of each other. 'My name is Archer.'

'Elisabeta.' She returned his signals, letting her own eyes wander over his mouth. Arousal stirred hard. She had understood the negotiation. She had consented. They were to be Elisabeta and Archer. No last names, no true way to trace the other once they parted. There would be no strings, no ties that would bind them beyond the immediacy of the affair.

'Well, *Archer*...' she smiled up at him '...you are just in time.'

Heat intensified in his groin. 'In time for what?'

She gave him a coy glance. 'For strawberries.' Elisabeta crooked her finger and beckoned with a 'come-hither' smile that left him aching. 'Did I mention there would also be cream?'

The innuendo was not lost on Archer. He was going to come all right. Between the dancing, the warm summer night, the elation of having arrived at his destination at last and the seductive beauty in his arms, his body was fully primed for more intimate thrills. He had every reason to celebrate. It had not been an easy journey from Paris on his own. He'd had to leave before Haviland's rather sudden wedding. He'd given up the summer in Switzerland with Nolan and Brennan. There'd been no choice. Time had been of the essence if he wanted to make Siena in advance of the August Palio. He'd known from the start he'd never make the first one in July.

Travel had been rough, the Italian inns rougher. But, oh, the journey had been worth it the moment he'd passed through the city gates, seen the town lit up and festivities under way, as if the party was just for him. He'd stabled Amicus, left his bag at the livery and headed for the central piazza, hoping to find someone to direct him to his uncle's. The piazza had been quiet, but he'd followed the music to this neighbourhood and found more than directions. He'd been in this piazza less than five minutes when this dark-haired beauty had pulled him into the dancing, all fire and beauty in his arms, her quicksilver gaze flashing with life and exuberance, her body moving into his as if they were made for one another. Dancing with her had been effortless, just as following her across the piazza was now. He had no doubts where this was heading: to the food tables and to a quiet space in the dark beyond the lights.

Archer's stomach growled, and he grinned. There was no choice to ignore it. Elisabeta smiled and passed him a plate. She gestured to each dish and offered an explanation, pleased when he nodded. While all of his friends had been studying French, he'd been studying Italian. His mother had seen to it that he had Italian tutors. It was paying off now, even if it was just to bring a smile to this woman's face.

'Risotto alle fragole, polenta con fragole, ravioli...' She rattled off the dishes, taking a serving for herself as they went. At the end of the table stood an enormous vat-like bowl of strawberries and tubs of cream alongside various tortes. *'La torta!'* Elisabeta beamed back at him over her shoulder, silver eyes gleaming in delight.

Archer took a healthy helping of everything. The smells alone would have been persuasion enough to try the new foods, but Elisabeta's smile stole any reservation he might have had. The way she looked at a man, the way her eyes lingered over him in appreciation, he would have eaten slugs for her. There was wine to pour from casks after that and slices of hearty dark country bread to add to his burgeoning plate.

She led him to a quiet spot off the piazza where the lantern lights didn't quite reach and the music didn't quite preclude conversation. There was privacy in the darkness. 'It's the strawberry festival, in case you haven't guessed,' she said between bites. 'We celebrate it every year. Most of the dishes of the evening are made with strawberries.'

'It's delicious.' Archer took another mouthful of the risotto. It truly was. The food was rich and warm. He'd never tasted anything as good as this, not even the fine food of Paris could compare. He took a swallow of wine, letting his tongue savour the full-bodied flavour, a perfect complement to the meal.

When his plate was nearly empty, she took it from him and set it aside. Her voice was a sultry whisper in the night. 'Now for *la dolce*.' She dipped a strawberry in the small pot of cream and held it to his lips. 'Lick,' she commanded as he took the berry between his teeth, laving the sweet cream with his tongue until her eyes locked with his and her lips formed the very erotic word: 'Bite.'

Two could play this game, as he knew she very well intended. Archer plucked up a berry and swirled it in the cream before he offered it to her, his own voice offering a seductive invitation of its own. 'Suck.'

She took the berry in her mouth, her tongue flicking across his fingers where he held the fruit, her eyes never leaving his, the message in them plain, *you're next*. Archer's throat went dry. He was going to love Siena, he just knew it.

Chapter Four

He would be an exquisite lover, and who would know what they had done? Who would care? He would just be passing through. He could give her something of pleasure to carry into her marriage. Elisabeta leaned towards him on their narrow bench, her eyes caressing his mouth with their gaze, offering him a moment's preparation before her lips slid over his. She tasted him, tempted him—or was she tempting herself?

His mouth answered hers, hungry for more, his body straining in acknowledgement that they were not private enough for 'more'. Elisabeta drew back. It would be up to her to initiate, this was her territory. 'Perhaps a walk? There's a lovely fountain not far.' It was a ruse, an excuse to seek that privacy, to be alone, and her heart thundered in knowledge of it. There would be more to come with this man.

'Which direction? I'll go first.' His concern for preserving at least a facade of decency spoke to her. Here was a man of experience.

'To the right.' She motioned to the street veering

off from the piazza. 'It's not far.' She watched him slip into the night and counted the minutes in her head before following.

He'd gone deeper into the curving street than she'd anticipated. There was a moment when she thought she might have misread him, where she thought he had taken the opportunity to disappear. Then the whisper came in the darkness. 'Elisabeta!' An arm reached out to seize her about the waist, dragging her into a curve of a little alcove. She gave a startled yelp as he spun her about and drew her against him, his mouth stealing a laughing kiss. He felt as a man should, all heat and hardness where their bodies melted together.

'What took you so long?' He was grinning in the darkness. She could hear that grin in his words as his hands rested at her waist, so comfortably, so naturally as if they were long-time lovers well used to one another's bodies.

'I didn't expect you to go so far.' Elisabeta twined her arms around his neck, her hands fingering the ends of his hair where it brushed below his collar.

'I was looking for the perfect spot.' His mouth was at her neck and his words came between kisses along the column of her throat, his mouth latching over the pulse beat at its base, sending a trill of excitement down her spine.

'For what?' She managed to breathe, although she could guess, and the guessing made her giddy with excitement. She was thankful to note there was a wall at her back should she need it. At this rate, her legs wouldn't hold her much longer. This man was a consummate artist in the craft of *amore* with his subtle touches, the lingering of his gaze, the temptation woven in his kisses.

'For this.' His mouth returned to her, his body pressing hers to the rough brick of the wall. She was fully protected here by the breadth of his shoulders and the height of his body. They blocked her from view should anyone stagger down the street or come looking for privacy of their own.

She should have *known* such a master of the art would not resort to a base, rushed, dark-alley coupling, or be carried away by the heat of the moment and his own need. She should have been *ready*. The kisses to her neck, to her throat, should have primed her, warned her that here in the privacy of the dark and the quiet of the night, the music and noise of the festivities far behind them, these moments would be different than the frenzied excitement in the piazza. But still, the kiss took her unawares.

This kiss was a long, languorous exploration of her, his tongue probing and tasting, his mouth opening to encourage her to do the same, and she did. She tasted the remnants of rich wine on his tongue, smelled the last vestiges of his morning *toilette* beneath the sweat of the day, the scents of a man. Wherever he'd come from, he'd come on horseback. The smells of leather and horse were evident too, on his skin, and most pleasantly so. She preferred a man smell like a man than a flower garden. A man's scent should above all be an honest representation of him.

As should his body. There was honesty aplenty in that dark alcove. His want was in evidence, his erection hard at her stomach where their bodies met. He was not alone in that evidence, only more obvious. There was wetness at her core, an ache that rose in her, demanding to be assuaged. He nipped at her lip, tugging at it gently, and she moaned, her body pressing into his, her hips grinding in suggestion against his.

Archer groaned his response into her mouth, his kiss becoming possessive, the slow tempo between them quickening, turning primal. His hands bunched the folds of her skirts, pushing them up. 'Let me lift you.' The command was hoarse with need.

His hands slid under her, cupping her buttocks and hefting her to him, her legs wrapping around his waist as he balanced her between himself and the wall. Her skirts fell back, her private flesh bare against him. She felt the hardness of him through the barrier of his trousers, the contact erotic, and she moved on him in instinctive response.

She was rewarded with a fierce nip at her ear and the feel of the strong muscles that held her, trembling. 'You will have me spilling like a green boy.' The rasped warning was both caution and accolade and it spurred her on. The heat and frenzy was returning, stoked to life once more. Her hips sought him again, but he had other ideas, better ideas.

He shifted his weight, his hand finding the core of her, his palm pressing against her mons until she cried out in pleasurable frustration. She was far beyond it being enough. But he knew. 'I can make it better,' he promised against her throat, his fingers parting her folds. His breath hitched as he felt her wetness, found the tiny bean of her pleasure and began to stroke. Her pleasure was exciting for him, she realised. The knowledge that her delight roused him was intoxicating, heady, and she gave herself over to it, fuelling them both, driving them both towards the cliff of madness. She reached for him, her hand taking him through his trousers as he stroked her. *Dio caro!* The man was big, and long and, oh, so deliciously hard.

Elisabeta worked the fall of his trousers open. The best way to tell him what she wanted was to show him. Her hand found the naked length of him, and he gave a low, guttural groan. 'You will kill me yet, Elisabeta.' Her name was a groan on his lips, his body straining.

'Take me,' she whispered fiercely at his ear. She too had become primal in these moments. She had never been so lost in the madness of lovemaking before, had never been this far and yet something more loomed on the horizon of this pleasure. All reserve, all rational thought had been stripped away by his hands, his mouth.

'Yes,' Archer rasped and the response was immediate; the slide of his body into hers. She was tight but ready, the slickness of her tunnel easing his way until he was fully within her. There was the glorious sensation of stretching, accommodating. Then he began to move, and she with him, her hips matching the thrusting rhythm of his body, slowly at first, the pace growing with their intensity.

Moans and gasps became the sum of her vocabulary, his body the sum of her world. She muffled those gasps against the fabric of his shirt and still he brought them closer and closer to the undefinable something that lay just over the edge of madness. All she had to do was…

'Let go, Elisabeta,' came the hoarse command. 'Let yourself go, we are nearly there.' The words came in pants and broken fragments, but that he had any power of speech at all was miraculous to her— she had none. He gave a final thrust, and she let the madness take her entirely. She was over the cliff, claiming pleasure in its fullness, her heart pounding, her pulse racing, and Archer was there too, his own heart pounding hard against hers, proof of his efforts spilling against her thighs, a hot reminder of glorious life.

She rested her head against the brick of the wall, Archer's head on her shoulder, his own shoulders heaving from his exertions. Her hands were in his hair, absently stroking, soothing. Her mind was still in an incoherent fog where thought came in incomplete scraps. What did she know of such things? She'd known nothing of this pleasure before tonight, only that it hypothetically existed. How was she to have known it would be so bone-shattering? Her experience was limited to the adolescent skills of a fumbling but well-intentioned virgin. Later, her marriage bed had known the comfort that comes with familiarity, but never this overwhelming pleasure that left her drugged; sapped and satisfied all at once.

Curiosity began to ignite as reality slowly settled on her. It made one wonder. If this man's lovemaking could be incredible up against a wall in a dark alcove of a city street, what would it be like in a feather bed? What would it be like with a woman he *knew* or perhaps even truly loved?

No, she couldn't let her mind travel that direction, not even under the excuse of this pleasurable fog. To know the answer to such a fantasy meant knowing him, learning his last name, his history, his people. She was not looking for that. She could not have that, it was far too much temptation. Her uncle had promised her to another. What a cruel temptation it would be to know he was out there in the world somewhere and to have the tools to find him, while being married to the *priore*'s gouty relative. There was only hurt down that path, and shame.

The thought of shame sparked too the reality of what she'd done. For all of the nuances he'd provided with his laughter, his touch, his sexy knowing mouth, his intimate possession of her body, for all that he'd never made her feel that this was a cheap encounter or she was nothing more than a *troia*, there was no disguising what this was: sex in an alley with a stranger. *Extraordinarily* good sex, apparently, and with a *very* handsome stranger, but adjectives didn't change the blunt truth. She'd set out to act scandalously and she had.

Archer's head moved against her shoulder and he set her down slowly, as if warning her legs they would need to stand on their own. He moved away from her long enough to restore his trousers. In the dimness, he was even more attractive after sex than he was before, if that was possible. His hair fell rakishly in his face as he concentrated on his clothes, his hands sure and competent in their tasks. She'd never found a man's hands sexy before, but even in the dark, his hands carried a certain quality to them, she'd thought as much when they'd danced and eaten. Those moments in the piazza seemed a lifetime ago.

'Elisabeta.' His voice was soft in the darkness,

his face close to hers, his eyes half-shut. One arm bracketed her as he leaned against the wall. His lips touched hers in a light brushing, not a full kiss. He was formulating ideas, deciding what happened next. She couldn't allow that. She gathered her reserves.

'Archer,' she answered in equally soft tones, her hand gently cupping the firm line of his jaw. She wanted to touch him until the last, to give her body every chance to remember him. 'I have to go.' With that, she ducked under his arm and ran into the night.

Just like bloody Cinderella in the children's tale. Archer took a few steps forward into the street after her, but he stopped himself. Women who fled without provocation didn't want to be followed. He would not make a fool of himself by running after her. Or worse, put her in danger of discovery. Elisabeta, if that was even her name, was gone with not even a glass slipper to trace her. If Nolan was here, he'd tell him he'd got a fair bit luckier than the prince. That poor fellow had only got a dance after flirting with her all night. To which, Archer would acerbically remind him it *was* a children's tale after all. As such, it was also a tale of true love.

Sex in an alley wasn't true love, not even close. It wasn't meant to be. Yet nothing in the encounter had been casual. Archer leaned against the wall, his active mind imagining the brick still warm from her body. He'd had casual sex before. It was physical and fast, a game for the moment, a way to pass the time at a ball or masquerade. The arousing quality of those liaisons usually came from the heightened risk of discovery. Certainly, those qualities had been somewhat in evidence tonight. A street was public no matter how dark. But there had been more. Even now, arousal gave an insistent stir at the memory of her head thrown back at the last as she claimed her pleasure, her hair spilling, her breasts thrust forward against her bodice, her cries of release, the squeeze of her legs, holding him. Never had he seen an abandon so complete, so beautiful in its naturalness.

She had been stunned, surprised when it had come. He'd had the sense in those moments that while she was no virgin, this was new to her. New seemed an apt but inadequate description of what he'd seen in her face, felt in her body. His ego preened at the thought. He'd given her that exquisite release for the first time. It was silly, he hardly knew her, but he prided himself on putting a woman's needs at the centre of his lovemaking. It was what had made him one of London's rather more successful lovers.

And yet, his body hadn't been without its own pleasures there against the wall. His body hummed for more of the same even now with having achieved repletion. Once was apparently not enough. Then again, perhaps it was understandable. He'd been on the road and alone for quite a while.

He was going to be alone quite a while longer too if he didn't put this fanciful nonsense out of his head and find his uncle's house. He'd left Amicus at the livery near the *campo*, the town centre, with plans to return for him once he'd located his uncle's home. He'd had no desire to tramp through narrow cobblestone streets with a horse in tow, in the dark, looking for a home he wasn't familiar with. His best bet would be to return to the party and ask for directions to Giacomo Ricci's home in the Torre neighbourhood.

Archer shoved off the wall and began walking back to the festivities. His other best bet would be to put his Cinderella out of his mind. He wasn't here to fall in love; he was here to make a new start, to help his uncle with horses for the Palio and to fulfil a promise to his mother. Taken together that seemed quite enough to keep a man busy without a woman to complicate things. The mysterious Elisabeta would have to remain just that—a mystery and a memory.

Chapter Five

'*La famiglia è la patria del cuore*! Family is the country of your heart. Of course you've come.' Giacomo Ricci rose from his chair and came to embrace Archer, kissing him on both cheeks the moment Archer entered the *loggia* where a late breakfast was being served the next morning.

'*Buongiorno, Zio.*' Archer bore the effusive greeting as graciously as he had last night after finding his uncle's *contrada*, Torre. It hadn't been far from the town centre, just to the west of where he'd come from. Everyone had known his uncle and it had been easy to find Giacomo among the throng of revellers. Apparently each neighbourhood had been hosting its own celebration.

His uncle had kissed him publicly and spirited him away to his home where a new party commenced as he was introduced in whirlwind fashion to cousins, spouses of cousins and their offspring. There had been neighbours and friends after that, all eager to greet him and kiss him. He'd never been kissed by so many men in his entire life. Archer couldn't recall the last time his father had kissed him. Had his father *ever* kissed him?

Archer filled a plate with bread, cheese and fresh strawberries and took a seat at the table where he could look through the arches of the *loggia* into the street. The *loggia* was open by design, so that people passing by could wave to his uncle or stop to conduct brief business or even partake of some food. He knew enough from what his mother had told him about her home that the arrangement spoke to the power and position of her family in the *contrada*. To be seen with Giacomo Ricci was important. It was the sort of news people would share over dinner later in the day.

For now, though, Archer was thankful the *loggia* was empty and the streets quiet after a boisterous night of festivities. He was still reeling from last evening. His uncle retook his seat. 'Did you sleep well? I want to take you around the neighbourhood and show you everything, have you meet some peoplc.' His uncle's eyes shone with warm pride as he paused, gripping Archer's hand firmly. 'I cannot believe you are here at last, my sister's son, here in my own home.'

Archer felt his throat tighten unexpectedly at the warmth and sincerity of his words. 'I cannot believe it either. I wish it had been sooner. I promised her I would come.' These were promises only his brother, Dare, knew about, promises he'd made that last day in his mother's final hour and not spoken of to anyone, not even Haviland. He and Dare had been with her, all three of them simply waiting, knowing the end was so very close, that all the sunshine, all the open windows letting in the crisp autumn afternoon, couldn't hold back the inevitable. She was going on without them. They were grown men. They should have been able to handle the reality. But Archer's own throat had been tight with emotion as it was now.

'What did you promise her?' his uncle prompted gently. Archer struggled to find words to tell this man he knew and yet didn't know. 'She said, "Promise me you will go to Giacomo, Archer. Go to my home. I think you will find what you're looking for."' He was looking for so much. A father figure who could replace the one his father had become, a place of his own where he could be his own man as opposed to the second son, where he could live his own dreams among the horses.

'This is a pilgrimage for you?' Giacomo asked quietly.

'In part,' Archer confessed. 'I come here to honour her, to remember her, to know who she was before she was my mother. But I have also come here for the future, for *my* future, to see what I can be.' His mother had not told him explicitly to stay in Siena, but the idea suited him, this concept of striking out on his own and under his own power.

His uncle smiled, his grip on Archer's hand tightening. 'The past and future are often intertwined in this way. She was right to send you to us. You are a good son to honour her and you shall be like a son to me.' Even if the past ten hours weren't enough to confirm it, Archer knew from years of letters how his uncle and his wife had despaired of any children of their own.

Archer could see now, surrounded by the big brick home of the Riccis, how disappointing it must be for his uncle not to have the home filled with children.

His uncle was a well-built man, tall in the tradition of the Riccis, but his temples were greying and his years for child rearing had passed. He was a local statesman now, his days consumed with running the family cloth business and training horses. Archer understood now with vivid clarity how his mother's last wish had been a gift for him and for her brother. Even facing death, she'd thought about what would be best for the family, for others. He would not fail her.

Giacomo was smiling now, already planning. 'There are people I want you to meet, places I want you to see. I'd like to show you around the *contrada* today if you're up for it.'

'I would like that, if it's not too much trouble. I can show myself around,' Archer offered. Perhaps there was a chance of running into Elisabeta. But he would like it in other ways too. It would give him time to spend getting to know this uncle of his. The warmth of his uncle's welcome was overwhelming, the sincerity and emotion of it touched him. It reminded him of his mother, of the warmth she extended to everyone she met. She had been a generous woman in the way that his uncle was a generous man.

His uncle waved an adamant hand in the air. 'No, no, it's not any trouble. You are one of us. Everyone must understand that.' Archer nodded graciously. His mother had warned him, had she not? In an Italian family, one was never alone, never 'forced' to make one's way on one's own. His uncle was not done with his plans. 'Perhaps tomorrow, we can ride out to the country and see the horses. It is why you've come, isn't it? Your mother mentioned you loved the animals in all of her letters.'

Archer smiled. Ah, this would be easier than he could have hoped. His uncle understood. 'It is. I am interested in the Palio. I want to be part of it.'

Giacomo beamed and laughed out loud. 'And so you will! I am the *capitano* this year,' he said proudly. Archer felt the man study him for moment, dark eyes assessing. 'Maybe I could appoint you as one of my *mangini*.' He nodded as if the decision was made. 'Yes, you would do nicely and it would give you a chance to learn about the race.'

The *mangini* were supporters of the *capitano*, his lieutenants in seeing his commands carried out. Archer knew it was a position of honour, but it was not what he'd hoped for himself. Archer leaned forward, holding his uncle's eyes, amber-brown like his own, in all seriousness. 'The honour would be mine. I will serve the *contrada* however I may, but I had hoped to offer myself to you as a rider.' Surely his mother had mentioned his skills in that regard if she'd mentioned him in the letters that had been exchanged over the years.

'A *fantino*?' his uncle asked before shaking his head. 'It is not possible. The riders are not from the *contradas*, or even from Siena.' He gave another wave of his hand. 'It makes it too difficult to arrange the *partiti*. It simply isn't how it is done.' Perhaps he saw Archer's disappointment. He gave a gentle smile. 'Everyone in the *contrada* is part of the Palio and you will be too, you will see. I will need you as a *mangini*, someone to help me with the Palio arrangements.' He nodded, affirming his satisfaction over the arrangement.

It was not what Archer had wanted. He'd come all this way to ride in the Palio. He'd given up Haviland's wedding to make the journey on time. But his uncle was done with the subject for the moment. He sat back in his seat. 'You have your mother's eyes, the Ricci eyes, and her chin.' His tone softened and lowered. 'My sister, your mother, was a beautiful woman. She stole hearts wherever she went, your father's included, and his was not an easy one to steal. But he saw her and it was all over for him. I remember that summer as if it were yesterday; the grand English earl had come to Siena for the races to see the Italian champions, and he went home with a wife, the most beautiful woman in Tuscany.'

He gave a nostalgic sigh. 'It was a heady summer, watching Vittoria in the throes of her courtship. It was a time full of victories and romance, and now the earl's son has returned.' He smiled benevolently at Archer. 'Perhaps we will find you a wife too? Someone worthy of a Ricci, no?'

Archer tried to refuse politely. 'My path is unclear to me. I don't know that I'd be much of a catch at the moment.' He didn't need his aunt and the troops of his newly introduced female cousins matchmaking for him. Marriage was the last thing he wanted. He'd just gained his freedom, he didn't need a wife. And yet his reckless conduct in the alley last night suggested he needed something. Had last night been about sowing wild oats, or had it been about a desire to make a connection?

His uncle drummed his fingers on the table, a

knowing gleam in his eye. 'Young men all think they know what they need. I know, I was a young man once too. That's why young men have female relatives. Women can see what a man needs better than he can himself.' His eyes moved to Archer's empty plate. 'If you're finished eating, let us be off.

'Have I completely overwhelmed you?' Giacomo asked as they stepped out into the street and the sun.

Archer laughed, shading his eyes and appreciating the easy camaraderie that flowed between him and his uncle. He'd missed his friends during this last leg of the journey, even Nolan's goading and endless wagers. It was good to be back among people he could trust. 'You mean despite the fact that you've tried to get me married off in less than a day? And you've appointed me to be a *mangini*? Overwhelmed hardly begins to describe it. I am overcome with your generosity.'

'That doesn't please you?' Giacomo asked as they turned towards the *contrada*'s central piazza.

'It does please me, it's just that I had hoped to ride,' Archer confessed. He would be honest with his uncle. The sooner his uncle learned he was determined and wouldn't accept no for an answer, the better. 'Although I understand to be a *mangini* is a great honour,' he added, not wanting to appear insulting.

'Ah, I know the feeling. I would have loved to have ridden but it isn't how it's done for the Palio,' his uncle commiserated. 'The *fantini* don't come from the *contradas* themselves. It's no matter.' Giacomo shrugged. 'If Torre wins, you will still be a hero.' He gave a mischievous wink. 'The women will go crazy for you since you were part of the negotiation team that helped us win.'

They came out of the street into the piazza with its fountain. It was busier here, people starting to go about their daily errands. Although, Giacomo informed him, that wouldn't last too long once the afternoon heat peaked. Everyone would retreat behind shuttered windows into cool stucco rooms for siestas. 'My favourite part of the day with your *zia*.' He gave Archer a knowing look. 'In the evening everyone will come out again for strolling, *la passegiatta*, do you know it?'

He didn't wait for an answer. 'Everyone strolls within their neighbourhood or in their allied neighbourhood.' He pointed to a banner hanging on the wall of one of the tall buildings surrounding the piazza. It depicted an elephant in the foreground, a tall tower in the back, done in crimson. 'That's our symbol. We are Torre, the Tower.'

'Does neighbourhood matter so much?' Archer asked, thinking of Elisabeta and the neighbourhood he'd wandered into last night before finding his uncle.

Giacomo threw back his head and laughed. 'The *contrada* is *everything* if you are Sienese. You are *born* into the neighbourhood. If you ask anyone who they are, they'll tell you their neighbourhood first, city second. If you know someone's neighbourhood, you know everything about them; who their allies are, what they do; most of us in Torre are in the wool trade. You know where they live, you know who their enemies are.'

'Enemies? Really?'

'Oh, yes.' Giacomo was in earnest. They strolled

the perimeter of the fountain, stopping occasionally to greet people and exchange a little news. 'Valdimonte's enemy is the Nicchio Contrada, Aquila's enemy is Pantera and so on. Our enemy is Oca, which is rumoured to be striking an alliance with Pantera. Pantera won the July Palio.'

Archer did his best to follow Giacomo's conversation. It was a lot to take in, especially in a second language. English families and English neighbourhoods were far simpler entities by contrast. He wondered which neighbourhood he'd stumbled into last night? Would that make Elisabeta an ally or an enemy? 'Do *contradas* ever intermarry?'

Giacomo gave him a keen look. 'Of course, but during the Palio, husbands and wives often separate and go home to their own neighbourhoods.' He grinned and wagged a finger at Archer. 'You will learn. It's the *contrada* above all else. My Bettina, though, your *zia*, was the old *priore*'s daughter so we are never separated.' There was no mistaking the pride in Giacomo's voice in having married a Torre woman. This was a new world indeed, his mother's world, Archer reminded himself. She'd grown up in the *contrada*.

Giacomo clapped him on the back. 'Do you have your eye on a pretty *signorina* already? Perhaps you refused my help because you have spied a pretty girl for yourself?'

Archer was tempted to tell him about Elisabeta, but thought better of it. If she had been from an enemy *contrada* it would only make trouble if he pursued her. Anyway, he wasn't looking for a permanent relationship. But that didn't stop him from thinking about her as they stepped into a few shops to meet some of the family's especial friends. Was Elisabeta out in her neighbourhood doing errands? Talking with shopkeepers? Was she with friends? Another man?

Had he merely been an escape for her? Maybe he'd merely been part of a fantasy or the madness of the summer night? She'd not wanted to be followed. There were only so many reasons for that; none of them suggested she was unattached and free to make her own decisions. He *should* let it be and accept it for what it was: a few glorious moments. Yet, the thoughts persisted. Where was she? What was *she* doing? Archer chuckled to himself. He knew already he couldn't just let it go. Against his better judgement, he was going to find her.

She was picking petals off a rose like a silly school girl. 'He loves me, he loves me not.' The foolishness made her laugh. Elisabeta snipped the roses and put them in her basket. To be honest, love had nothing to do with it. All right, then, she amended: he lusts me, he lusts me not. Even here in her uncle's garden in the full light of day, thoughts of last night managed to bring a blush to her cheeks and a heat to her body that had nothing to do with the sun. Those thoughts made her want.

More.

Of him.

Pleasure once tasted was proving to be a potent elixir with a power, she suspected, to addict. Once was not enough. What a lovely addiction that would be. What an unexpected one. When she'd sought out her stranger, she'd not expected this wanting as a consequence. He was to remain a stranger, a man to whom she had no ties. But she'd come away with a name and a longing to have him again. Already, she was wondering if that name would be enough to find him. Over breakfast she'd reasoned an English name couldn't be terribly hard to find among all of these Italian names. Nor was Siena so big that she wouldn't be apt to run into him if she went to the city centre often enough. Surely, those odds would be in her favour if she chose to exercise them.

By the time she'd wandered out to the garden to pick flowers, the issue was no longer a question of finding him, but a question of did she truly want to? Her curiosity said yes. It was her curiosity that had driven her to distraction this morning with its questions filling her mind: Where was he now? What was he doing? Had he woken to thoughts of her? Had he dreamt of her? Did he too regret their veiled identities?

Then again, perhaps it was better to wonder than to know. The pleasure he'd offered might only have been the luck of the night, the work of the stars and summer magic. Surely such pleasure was not commonplace? It most certainly didn't happen all the time. She'd lived her entire marriage without it and she would likely live through another without it, proof enough that Archer's pleasures could not be conjured on a whim nor by just any man or woman. It would be a shame to have him again only to be disappointed by the ordinary nature of their lovemaking. Better to let him become memory.

'Cousin! There you are. I've been calling for you.'

Giuliano came striding down the path, playful mischief sparking in his dark eyes. 'Have we been daydreaming over our handsome stranger?' he teased. 'You were quick to disappear last night.'

She gave Giuliano a saucy grin in return, her good spirits making her reckless. 'I told you I'd have him.'

Giuliano leaned in close, a grin on his face. 'And did you? Have him?'

Elisabeta gave him a light punch on the arm. 'You're wicked. Besides, a lady never tells.' She paused and gave him a considering look. 'What of the lovely Widow Rossi? Did you have her?'

Giuliano groaned and had the good grace to look down at the ground. 'Point taken.' But a moment later any penitence he felt over probing into her personal affairs had vanished. 'Will you see him again?'

Elisabeta shrugged and moved on to a new collection of flowers, trying to keep her actions nonchalant. She did not want to give too much away to Giuliano. He was reckless and there was no telling what he might do. 'Of course not. We didn't exchange enough information for that.'

Giuliano followed her, far too astute in the games of *amore* to take her response as a direct or even accurate answer. His voice was low now, his tone compelling. 'But would you? If you could?'

Elisabeta fixed her cousin with a cool stare, trying to keep her pulse from racing. 'What do you know?'

'There's an Englishman in town. There was word of it when I ran my errands this morning. He's the nephew of Giacomo Ricci, the horse trainer who lives in Torre.'

The information was better than a name and it was

worse. She could find him, she knew who his people were and where. But it didn't help her cause. Her eyes held Giuliano's and a silent message passed between them. Both of them were serious now. Love stopped being a game once the *contradas* were involved.

She could go to Archer. But did she dare? Beside her, Giuliano gave a short nod. 'It's probably best your answer is no.' The Oca *contrada*'s sworn enemy was Torre and while that might not matter to her uncle, it would matter to her future husband's *contrada*.

'Then why did you tell me? I do not think of you as generally unkind,' Elisabeta scolded quietly. Perhaps it was far crueller to know she could not have him. It was not like Giuliano to tease meanly.

He ducked his head. 'Forgive me. Last night you said you were desirous of avoiding your engagement. I thought only to give you a choice, Cousin.'

'Your father would never forgive me.' Elisabeta played idly with the stems of the flowers in her basket.

'My father need not know,' Giuliano countered. 'You have done your duty for the family in marrying Lorenzo. You may even do it again in another marriage very soon, but in the interim, perhaps you owe yourself some pleasure?' The argument was so very compelling, maybe because it was the same argument she'd made with herself. To hear it validated by another made it all the more persuasive.

'No one can know,' Elisabeta said out loud, more to herself than to Giuliano, but it was Giuliano who replied.

'He is English. He is not one of us. He will leave.

He will be a thousand miles away. While you think it over, say you'll come with me to see the horses for the August Palio. Father wants me to go out to the farm tomorrow.'

Elisabeta barely heard the invitation. She was too focused on the unspoken rationale. *No one will ever know.* Suddenly the risk seemed minimal against all that stood to be gained. Only two questions remained: Did she dare? What would she risk to see Archer again? And perhaps more importantly, what did it mean to her and why? What had started out as a spontaneous dare had taken on something much deeper and more significant if she cared to explore it.

Chapter Six

Archer didn't dare press his uncle's decision immediately. No man liked to be countermanded outright. Challenging his uncle would hardly be the way to ingratiate himself to his new family. But he could make an effort to change his uncle's mind about the Palio. Archer kicked Amicus into a trot to pull up alongside Giacomo, determined to start on that good impression today at the horse farm.

If his uncle could see him handle the horses or see him ride, his uncle would change his mind. Seeing was believing after all. His uncle had nothing to go on in reference to him except his mother's letters and mothers were inherently biased. Based on that, Archer understood his uncle's reticence to make him a rider.

'Tell me about this beast of yours, *mio nipote*,' his uncle said as Archer pulled even with him. The traffic had lessened on the country road. They were able now to ride side by side and enjoy some conversation. 'He's a fine-looking animal, strong through the chest.'

'He looks much better these days,' Archer agreed. Even considering the rough travel from France, Amicus had blossomed from good care and affection. He told his uncle the story of Amicus's rescue and his heroic jump on to the boat, keeping his attentions covertly alert to his uncle's reaction.

'No!' Giacomo cried in happy disbelief. 'That's incredible.'

Archer patted Amicus's neck. 'It is incredible. But he's an incredible horse. He had two months to rest in Paris and I worked him with a fine group of riders while I was there. Paris has a surprisingly strong group of enthusiastic riders. I had not expected it. They were a pleasure to train with and I was able to give Amicus some more refined skills. He'll make a good hunter.' Although he intended to stay in Italy, Archer still wanted to make the trip north to the Spanish riding school in Vienna. It would be a treat to see Amicus join their training regimen and it would be a good opportunity to look for new horses. He shared as much with his uncle. 'Perhaps next year's Palio horse will be among them.' He winked.

'Could be. We haven't had a horse from that far away for quite a while, but it wouldn't be unheard of.' Giacomo nodded, the idea becoming more interesting as he thought about it. That had to be a good sign, a sign that he could trust his nephew as an assessor of horses. One step closer. Archer had no intentions of taking no for an answer on the Palio. Just because his uncle thought he wasn't going to ride in the race didn't mean he was going to accept that decision any more than he was going to accept the mysterious Elisabeta simply disappearing into the night, lost to him.

He'd come too far to let these challenges get in his way. He was going to ride in the race. He was going to find Elisabeta because he wanted to, and Archer Crawford was a man used to getting what he wanted.

'We're nearly there. The farm is just over the hill.' His uncle gestured ahead of them. 'Let's be clear on what we're looking for today. This man is a horse breeder. He's bred more winners of the Palio than anyone else currently living. I train them, of course, but they spend their early years with him. I've had two horses in his care since they were yearlings. They are four years old now. I want to see if they're ready to be recommended for the race, but I also want to see which other horses might be brought in either by Torre or by the other *contradas*. We are not the only ones who use him.' This was to be a test, then, of his skill, Archer thought. His uncle would listen to his opinions and decide if he knew his business. But the visit was more than a test for him. It was also a subterfuge.

Checking on the two horses was merely the surface of his uncle's agenda. Archer saw that immediately. This was a reconnaissance mission. They were here to ascertain the level of competition. 'I understand,' Archer nodded. He was enjoying this easy camaraderie with his uncle, finding it a novel contrast to the terse, succinct conversations he had with his father. His father rarely asked for opinions. The man just gave them. But his uncle seemed to genuinely care what his opinion might be. 'This is not all that different than wandering through the Newmarket stables during race week to see the other horses.'

Giacomo gave a friendly laugh. 'That's where you're wrong, *mio nipote*. At Newmarket, it is straightforward; a man races his own horse with his own rider. Anyone who wants to enter a horse can as long as they can pay the entry fee. Not so, here. We have to make it more dramatic. We can recommend horses for the Palio, but we do not control which horse we get. We do not enter a horse for Torre, our horse is drawn for us, assigned to us, out of the final pool of horses. All we can do is recommend the best horses possible for that pool.'

That was news to Archer. He was starting to see that his mother's stories of the great race had left out certain details. It was easy enough to do. When one lived in a particular milieu, there were nuances that one took for granted and assumed everyone else did too. 'I think I understand, but give me an example.'

Giacomo grinned and warmed to the subject. 'Consider the horse that won the July Palio, Morello de Jacopi. He is owned by Lorenzo Jacopi, but the Pantera Contrada drew him for the race. It doesn't matter what *contrada* Jacopi is aligned with, if any. For the race, the horse is Pantera's. If the horse is selected again for the August Palio, another *contrada* might draw him.

'Hopefully us.' Giacomo leaned in although there was no one on the road to hear. 'He's the best-looking horse this year and I think we could put a better *fantino* on him than any of the other *contradas*.'

The remark wounded Archer although he knew

it wasn't his uncle's intention. He could be that rider if his uncle would give him a chance. 'If the horse has proven himself by winning, surely he's an immediate choice for the August race,' Archer put in.

'You Englishmen are always so direct.' Giacomo laughed. 'You're thinking just like your father, that speed matters. It does to some extent. But now, you must think like an Italian, like a Sienese. If we all know who the fastest horse is, the race is less exciting. Why race if the outcome is certain?' He gave Archer a sharp look, daring him to debate the proposition.

For all that his mother had taught him about her city and her language, she'd not taught him that. Archer had no answer. 'First you tell me a *contrada* doesn't enter its own horse and now you tell me the race isn't about speed? I'm afraid it all seems a bit counter-intuitive.'

'It's like this,' his uncle explained, clearly revelling in the chance to delve into the intricacies of the great race. *This* Archer was prepared for. His mother had told him that for many in Siena, the mental exercise of the Palio was raced all year. 'Every *contrada* should have an equal chance to win the Palio. To that end, the horses are selected to give everyone the best chance for an equal race. Obviously, horses who are hurt or not in good physical condition are not considered. They would obviously put the *contrada* who raced them at a disadvantage. But also, a horse who is too good might give a *contrada* who drew it an unfair advantage. When the *capitani* vote for the horses that should be in the drawing, we vote for the horses that will create the most equal race.

The horses that are chosen for the honour are neither too fast or too slow, but just right. They fit well with each other.'

The fastest horse didn't race? That sounded crazy to Archer but he did not dare to say it out loud. It would be imprudent to question a centuries-old tradition. Who was he to say it was wrong? It was merely different, *vastly* different than the straightforward tradition of speed he'd been raised to.

'Of course, a good *fantino* isn't going to let a horse go all out in the trials if he's too fast,' Giacomo put in cryptically. 'There are ways to ensure your horse fits in.' Good lord, Archer thought. This wasn't a horse race, it was a chess game. Based on the statistics, Torre played the game well. His uncle's *contrada* had won the Palio eleven per cent of the time over the past three hundred or so years. Many of the successes of the past twenty years had been his uncle's doing as the *contrada*'s *capitano*.

The farm came into view, a lovely spread of flat green pasture fanning out before them with a brownbrick farmhouse rising in Tuscan style in the background. The age-old desire of man to claim land and to make it his own surged within Archer, so compelling was the scene spread before him. *This* was what he wanted—a home of his own where he was master, not of the land necessarily, that was rather egotistical, but master of himself and his destiny, where his children ran alongside the horses in the grass, where his sons and daughters would ride bareback through the fields, where he worked hard each day and retired each evening to a table full of fresh country food and a wife to warm his bed and his heart.

It was an entirely fanciful notion. He had some of that in Newmarket but there, he was always the earl's second son and the stables had been part of the family long before he'd taken over. There was also the issue of wealth and social standing. There were appearances to keep up at Newmarket. He could not muck out the stalls or work too closely with the stable hands. He could hand out orders, design breeding programs and instruct the riders who exercised the Crawford string. But that was all. Heaven forbid his father heard his son had been out riding like a common jockey or cleaning stalls. And his father always heard. How many times had he been told by the earl that gentlemen *rode* to the hunt? That they *bet* on the races?

They swung off their horses as the man they'd come to meet strode out to greet them. Michele di Stefano was a man of middling stature and easy confidence, dressed in farm clothes. There was handshaking and cheek-kissing, something Archer didn't think he'd ever get used to. He couldn't imagine Haviland ever kissing his cheek, although he could very well imagine Nolan doing it just to goad him. Nolan would like Tuscany with all its touchy rituals. Nolan was a great believer in the idea that people were more inclined to trust you if you touched them.

They tromped out to the stables and the paddocks where his uncle's two horses—both high-spirited chestnut beauties—were running the length of the fence. Giacomo and the man talked briefly before the man excused himself to see to other guests. For the first time, Archer noted how busy the stables were. They were not the only guests who'd come to see the horses. 'I see you're not the only one who thought to come out and view the horses,' Archer said slyly.

Giacomo elbowed him teasingly. 'Everyone is interested in making the race equal. There are three weeks until the horses are chosen. The *capitani* from the different *contradas* will spend the time travelling to the different stables looking for horses and *fantini*. Naturally, the *capitani* have been looking all year, but now that we've got one race behind us, we know what must be done for the next. We're looking to fill in gaps.' Giacomo lowered his voice. 'What that really means is that we're all looking for a horse to beat Jacopi's Morello.' This last was said with more seriousness than it had been on the road, a clear indicator that they were in earnest on this mission.

'Tell me, *mio nipote*, what do you think of the horses?' Here came the first test. Archer was ready.

'I think they run quite nicely, but at a distance that is all I can tell. Let's go in. I want to look at their legs.' Archer was already heading into the paddock, slices of apple retrieved from a pocket and at the ready in his outstretched hand, his voice low and sure. It was an irresistible invitation. Both horses wasted no time making his acquaintance.

Archer stroked their manes and played a bit with them before beginning his examination. He checked teeth and ran his hands down their legs, finding the bones strong and the muscles cool. 'They are in good shape. Now, how they'll do with a rider remains to be seen.' He brushed his hands on his riding breeches and stepped back.

'We should take them to my farm, then, to join the

others?' his uncle asked. 'I have riders there who will work with the horses we want to nominate.'

'Yes, definitely take them,' Archer said confidently, his blood starting to hum at the mention of a horse farm. He'd not realised his uncle had a place outside the one in town. 'Perhaps I could deliver them for you if you're busy?' He was suddenly anxious to see this place.

His uncle smiled and Archer grinned, laughing at himself. He had taken his uncle's bait quite easily. 'You're just like your father when it comes to horses, eager as a school boy.' His uncle clapped him on the shoulder. 'You may pick them up tomorrow and deliver them to our villa.' There was something else in his uncle's eyes too, something that said he had passed the first test.

'Just like my father?' Archer queried, not sure if he liked the sound of that. He'd spent most of his life trying to avoid such a comparison.

His uncle studied his face for a moment, his happy eyes sobering a little. 'Like he used to be the summer I knew him. I don't know the sort of man he became, but I know what he was like at your age.'

'And what was that?' Archer ventured, finding it odd and novel to think of his uncle knowing his father, knowing a man different than the one Archer knew.

A small smile returned to his uncle's face. 'A man who wasn't afraid to live, to embrace life. A man like you, who wasn't afraid to get his hands or boots dirty when it came to horses.' Really? Archer didn't know that man.

There was movement across the field, and Archer

followed his uncle's gaze as it flicked across the paddock to another holding pen farther out. 'Pantera's here. The *capitano* has sent his son and that niece of his to survey the competition. Rafaele di Bruno must be feeling the pressure now to win two. Wouldn't that be a feather in Pantera's cap to win both Palios in a single year? Of course, it won't happen.'

Giacomo uttered something about the statistical possibility of that being unlikely, but Archer didn't hear it. He was too focused on the woman across the field. He'd been ready to ride the breadth of Tuscany to find her and here she was. She could not have been delivered to him any more neatly.

'His niece is a beauty,' Giacomo put in idly. But Archer wasn't fooled. He'd better tread carefully. His uncle's next words confirmed it. 'Perhaps you might spend some time with her this afternoon if you're interested.'

Archer was interested, all right. She was perhaps even lovelier by daylight. Any worries he might have entertained that his perception of her beauty had been influenced by the night and the lighting were immediately banished. Her black hair was neatly coiffed beneath a straw hat that showed her profile to advantage; the curve of her jaw, the firm jut of her chin. She wore an exquisitely tailored riding habit done in blue. The white of her lacy jabot stood in striking contrast from the dark fabric, but even from here Archer could see that the jabot was loose, the neck of her blouse undone against the warmth of the day. She walked arm in arm with her cousin, stopping now and then to watch the horses and comment to their host. Archer imagined he could catch hints of her laughter. But thoughts of Elisabeta had to be set aside until later. There was work to do now. *Pranza*, or lunch, was to be served only after everyone had viewed the horses. There would be time to meet her then. He could possibly manoeuvre a place beside her at the table, perhaps a walk after the meal while his uncle conducted the rest of his business.

Archer's blood began to hum with the knowledge of her presence and with plans. He let a smile of satisfaction spread across his face. Today was shaping up quite nicely in terms of his goals. His uncle had been impressed with his story about Amicus and Elisabeta was here, standing a hundred yards away.

Chapter Seven

He was here! Elisabeta felt his eyes on her before she dared look for him. She didn't want to be disappointed. She didn't want to look up and see that she was mistaken, that her fanciful imagination had simply made up a girlish whimsy. You couldn't really feel someone looking at you and if you did it was unlikely to be the man of your dreams—for her literally the man of her dreams the last two nights. It was unlikely the man she'd been thinking of nonstop had suddenly materialised at a Tuscan horse farm. Her life didn't work that way. She wasn't that lucky. And yet, the illusion she was indeed that lucky was a pleasant one. She could maintain it if she didn't look up. She shouldn't look, she wouldn't look. Looking would shatter it. She would not commit the Orphean crime of looking.

She looked.

He was watching her.

She blinked in the sun and then feared the image would disappear. Perhaps she'd only seen him because she'd wanted to see him standing there. No, that was him. It was definitely him. She'd recognise that nut-brown hair skimming his collar, the set of his jaw and that kissable mouth anywhere, even at a distance.

Their host had left them to see to other guests and she was aware of Giuliano watching her too. Elisabeta averted her gaze, careful to school her features. A suspicion took root. 'Did you know he would be here?' She thought of Giuliano's request that she join him on this visit.

'It was guesswork only,' was all Giuliano would admit. 'We should go in for *pranza*.' He grinned and took her arm. 'I'm hungry, how about you?'

She was undeniably hungry. She only hoped forbidden fruit was on the menu. If it was, would she eat of it? All her hypotheses were about to be tested. She had a chance to see him again. Would she pursue it? Why did it seem to matter so much?

The meal was laid out at a long table beneath the trees for shade. Michele di Stefano's wife had outdone herself. There was a white cloth on the table, and an abundance of food; bowls of fresh pasta, trays of round mounds of mozzarella and sliced tomatoes, bowls of olives and loaves of bread to dip in the dishes of olive oil. And of course there was wine, the rich local red wine of the region.

Perhaps it was all in an effort to impress Pantera, Elisabeta thought. Pantera had won the Palio. It would be good to be in their favour. Or perhaps it was to impress the influential *capitano* of Torre and his nephew.

Elisabeta allowed her eyes to land on Archer as they took their seats. He had not been able to finagle the seat beside her. Giuliano had seen to it that it wasn't possible. 'It is better for your reputation,' he murmured, but she could hear the laughter beneath his words. He understood the irony of having arranged this opportunity only to keep her from Archer at the meal. 'Make him watch you, build his anticipation and wait for your moment,' Giuliano coached quietly.

'I can't decide if I love you or hate you,' Elisabeta said quietly, sliding into her seat at the benches lining the long the table.

Giuliano winked. 'You love me, Cousin.'

Elisabeta lowered her voice. 'I'll let you know after lunch.' She eyed Archer surreptitiously over the rim of her wine glass. Lunch was going to be... interesting.

'Would you like to go for a ride?' The question caught Elisabeta off guard, just when she'd thought she had successfully navigated lunch. She coughed and the wine she'd swallowed nearly made a reappearance in a most unladylike fashion.

'On a horse?' Her reply came out with a slight rasp as she dabbed at her mouth with a napkin. What was Archer thinking to make such a bold reference? Perhaps the real question was what was she thinking to infer the nuance was there to begin with? Lunch had been a polite, careful affair with conversation drifting between talk of horses and of goings-on in town. Both parties were careful not to give away too much while still appearing to be friendly.

Archer's dark eyes twinkled just for her. 'You do ride, do you not?'

'Yes, I do.' Elisabeta took a swallow of wine in the hopes of conveying a sense of normalcy. 'Is the bay in the courtyard yours?' She'd noticed the animal on the way to lunch. He was a magnificent creature.

'Yes.' Archer reached for another slice of bread. Elisabeta took consolation in having limited his speech to monosyllabic responses. If he was going to make references to riding or 'riding' as the case might be, she had to have some recourse.

Archer's uncle jumped into the awkward breach. 'It's quite a story how he came by that horse.'

'Do tell.' Elisabeta smiled at Archer, returning the mischief in his eyes with her own. 'I love a good horse story.'

It was a good story too, and a dangerous one. By the end of it, Archer was no longer a stranger, but a man she was beginning to know and respect, a man who shared her interest in horses. Such knowledge was the very last thing she wanted. It meant an end to 'no ties', but perhaps that concept had ended the moment she'd spied him across the paddocks. Maybe it had even ended sooner than that, or perhaps it had never truly existed at all. It might have just been a convenient rule to justify what she'd wanted to do.

Now she knew him. Here was a man who loved animals, who cared about their well-being as she did. It would have been easier to resist him if he'd merely tolerated horses or seen them as merely a means to an end.

Archer finished his story and rose from the table. He held out a hand for her. 'Shall we take that ride while the others finish their business?'

For protocol's sake, she waited for a consenting

nod from Giuliano, who was acting in the role of chaperon, something she only nominally needed. She was a widow after all, but his presence communicated to others that the family valued her, although her uncle would be appalled at the nature of Giuliano's chaperonage. In that regard, he was a miserable failure. They would laugh about it on the way home.

She took Archer's hand and let him lead her away from the table. His move had been nicely played. His offer appeared generous. The other men at the table would appreciate her absence so they could 'talk' without a female present, never mind that she knew more about horses than most, and Archer, as the outsider, was expendable to their conversation. It was only logical that he be the one to temporarily take over as her escort.

They took their own horses, of course. It would somehow be unfair if they rode any of the horses who might be eligible for the Palio in August. His bay was indeed magnificent and her mare whickered in appreciation.

'What sort of horse is she?' Archer asked as they turned on to the bridle path leading away from the paddocks.

'She's a Calabrese. They originated south of here, in Calabria as the name implies.'

Archer studied the horse as they rode. 'Probably cross-bred with an Arab? Her head is distinct. Perhaps another breed has been used too? There aren't any other strong Arab features. Arabs are smaller in build with a tighter body construction. The mare has a larger quality to her.'

He was musing out loud. She recognised the trait.

She often thought out loud when she looked at horses too, wondering what their antecedents were. 'Likely there's an Andalusian in her family tree somewhere.' Elisabeta patted her mare's shoulder. 'She's twelve, I've had her since I was seventeen.'

The mare had been a wedding present from her uncle for doing her duty by the family. The mare had gone with her to Florence and back again. The two of them had weathered the past five years of life together. She pushed the reminders aside. Talking of horses was better than calling up sad memories of the past. They would only lead to thoughts of a future she wasn't ready to contemplate, not with this handsome man beside her. But apparently the subject was depleted. Silence fell between them. They could not speak of horses for ever.

'I did not think to see you again.' Archer braved the topic, showing none of her awkwardness with the silence. Then again, he was not an awkward man.

'Did you want to see me again?' She wasn't sure how to interpret the remark. Was this afternoon a good surprise or a bad one?

'What a leading question,' Archer teased, fixing her with a merry stare, the amber lights of his eyes dancing. '*I'm* not sure how to answer for fear I might appear too desperate. Let's just say I'm not in the habit of women running off on me.'

He was far too handsome for his own good. Women probably threw themselves at him. 'Well, there's a first time for everything and all that,' Elisabeta responded with a laugh. Flirting with him, exchanging this teasing banter, was easier than pursuing the conversation in a more serious vein, but the question remained: What next? Was there anything between them worth pursuing? And the ever-returning question: Would she dare?

Her mare turned her neck towards the bay and nipped at him. The bay nipped back, causing each of the horses to sidestep. 'She's in season,' Archer commented, reining his horse to one side of the path until the big bay settled down.

'Most likely.' Elisabeta turned the mare in circles. *She's not the only one*, Elisabeta thought. She'd been hot since she sat down for lunch. Archer had the most seductive eyes, the most kissable mouth, she'd ever seen on a man. Every word he spoke seemed to conjure up hot images in her mind, reminders of their bodies entwined in the alley, and the possibility for more.

'Is there a place where we can run?' Spoken like a true horseman who thought of the safety of his mount first.

Elisabeta nodded. 'There's a meadow just ahead. We can gallop there.' She kicked the mare into a fast trot and moved ahead of Archer on the path. A run was exactly what she and the mare both needed.

At the edge of the meadow, Elisabeta let the mare go, let the wind take the hat from her head, her hair from its pins, the very thoughts from her mind until there was nothing but sky above her, horse beneath her. This was as close to flying, as close to freedom as she was ever likely to get. In these exhilarating moments it was close enough.

The thunder of hooves alerted her to Archer's approach, his bay coming alongside, his body stretched out in the gallop as they pulled slightly ahead, just enough for her to appreciate Archer's form low over the horse's neck, his body out of the saddle, his heels down in the stirrups, presenting a magnificent pose of man and beast in synchronicity together.

Her mare would have nothing to do with it. No stallion was going to outrace her. They pulled even and Archer flashed her a grin of sheer delight, content to let the horses sort it out between them. Or the meadow. The far edge of the meadow settled the race for them, declaring it a tie. The horses could not race safely any farther and both of them pulled up, breathing hard. Archer swung down from the bay and came to her side. 'Let's walk them.' He reached up, his hands at her waist to help her down, and she let the thrill of his touch run through her body.

The horses were more obedient after their run and walked patiently behind them along the shaded path. 'Speaking of first times, was it your first time in an alley?' Archer boldly picked up the threads of their conversation before their mad gallop. She'd hoped he'd forgotten.

'Now who's asking the leading questions?' she replied, but the bantering fun of earlier had disappeared between them. It was time to be serious. What did they know of each other? What did they *want* to know? 'Just as you are not in the habit of having women running from you, I am not in the habit of, um...' She cast about for a delicate word, not wanting to be crass.

'Alleyways?' Archer supplied. 'Then why? Why that night? Why me?' His voice was quiet in the still of the afternoon.

She could say she didn't know, but that would be

a lie and she suspected he would know it. He'd been different, safe, a convenient outlet for her anger over the betrothal and for her discreet rebellion. But he'd not been different enough, not safe enough and not nearly convenient enough. He was associated with an enemy *contrada* and the beloved nephew of its *capitano*. He was not going to go away as she'd first thought. She opted for a simple answer. 'I wanted you.'

'*Me?* Or what I could give you? A dance, company, *pleasure*?' He held her gaze, and she didn't look away. She let him see the honesty. Her eyes could confess for her what she dare not put into words.

His own eyes darkened in response. 'And now, Elisabeta di Nofri?' He'd added her last name to make a point; now that they knew more about one another; now that they were no longer strangers; now when she would have to think about why she wanted this. Once, it could be about rebellion and recklessness, but twice was something else.

She dared further boldness. She would think about those reasons later. 'Now, *Archer Crawford*, I want you still.'

But...

She didn't need to speak the 'but' for Archer to hear it. That one small word screamed in the silence of the trees around them. From here on out it would be different. The anonymity of the alley no longer protected them. The magic of the night, of two strangers coming together, could no longer prevail without also giving credence to other considerations. An affair was not impossible, but it came with consequences. She had family. He'd sat across the table from it at lunch, understanding full well what Giuliano di Bruno represented—a protective male presence who would not tolerate anyone dealing unfairly with a female associated with the family.

'You've only answered half the question,' Archer prompted. He took her reins and led the horses to a grassy patch and picketed them, hoping the action of doing something, of moving away from her, would encourage her to say more and encourage his body less. His mind understood the need for renegotiation, but his mind was holding on to that by the slimmest of threads while his body thundered with want and clamoured for satisfaction.

Whether she meant to or not, she'd been teasing him since lunch with those eyes covertly watching him over the rim of her wine glass, her mouth forming around a rich red berry not unlike it had the night they'd fed one another berries in the piazza. And now she'd confessed she wanted him still, wanted him again.

He could have her, his own rules would allow it. She was a widow and this was no romance. He'd not lied to Giacomo when he'd said he wasn't looking for a wife. He hadn't the time right now for romantic entanglements and all the effort a proper courtship required. His priorities lay with the Palio and starting his new life. A wife would come eventually, but not now. The lovely Elisabeta di Nofri wasn't looking for romance either, only company and pleasure. He could do that.

'You still haven't told me why that night.' He strode back to where she leaned against the trunk of a tree. Her hair had come down, a result of the ride, and her cheeks were flushed. The collar of her blouse was open, her jacket unbuttoned to her waist. Taken together, it created an enticing picture. Hell, yes, enticing. He'd just lost the battle and gone from 'possibly aroused' to 'definitely aroused'.

'I've answered the most important part of the question: Why you? Surely the rest doesn't matter.' She gave him a coy smile that took his arousal the rest of the way.

Archer braced an arm against the tree trunk, letting his eyes drift over her mouth. 'Maybe I disagree. Maybe I think the most important part of the question is "Why that night?" I do wonder why a beautiful woman would suddenly pick that night of all nights to wander off with a stranger for the *first* time.' That particular thought had kept him awake for two nights in a row. If it was not a habit, then why that night? What had happened to compel her to take what could only be viewed as a *rash* action? 'What you did was reckless. There has to be a reason.'

She gave a throaty laugh. 'Recklessness has a reason? Are they not the antithesis of each other?'

'I think one spurs the other on.' He was pressing her for an answer. She looked away, uncomfortable with the conversation, but he needed that answer before he could let things progress, before he could claim the kiss that lay inches away on those lips.

She had no such compunction. Elisabeta moved into him, sliding her mouth over his, a hand slipping under his shirt. He felt her touch against his skin, felt his body give in to the temptation. His hand closed around her wrist, his mouth broke from hers with a firm, 'No. Not until I have my answer.'

Her grey eyes hardened to flints. Ah, he *had* read her aright. The kiss had been a distraction, an attempt to make him set aside his questions. She was not pleased in having been thwarted. Her tone was sharp. She was not afraid to stand her ground. 'I doubt my answer will change your mind if you're determined to play the noble hero.'

Archer knew then it was going to be complicated. She'd been using anonymity as a means of protecting him. He could not be blamed for what he did not know. Neither could he be blamed for what he didn't understand. Perhaps she'd been using his status as a stranger for protection too. But Archer was not accustomed to hiding behind anyone's stratagems, female or not. He tightened his grip on her wrist so she would not be tempted to flee. 'I will not be used to cuckold another.'

'Nothing is officially decided.' She did not like his choice of words. Her chin went up defiantly. 'I've betrayed no one. Your honour is intact. I have not compromised you.'

Not yet, Archer thought. He wasn't compromised *yet*. Even though she'd spoken the words in defence, there was an admission in them too. His intuition had been right. There was someone. This was followed by the other realisation he'd shied away from since she'd run into the night. She'd used him, damn it, as an escape. Elisabeta di Nofri was a *femme fatale* of the first water. She might not make a habit of alleys, but Archer doubted he was the first man who'd been lured by her. 'Tell me, who is he?'

The only thing that kept his temper in check was the shadow that crossed Elisabeta's face as she uttered the words. 'There is a man my uncle wants me to marry for the sake of the *contrada*.'

'You are opposed to the match?' Archer asked, not willing to assume her brief facial expression told the entire story. Duels were often created that way.

'I wasn't asked.' Elisabeta's tone was fierce, her grey eyes flashing her indignation. She yanked her wrist from his grip, and Archer let it go. Her own temper had the better of her now and he let her stride about the clearing, venting her wrath.

'I am to be bartered again in service of the family, this time to an old gouty man, without even my permission given. My uncle is the head of the house and the *contrada capitano*. It is his right to do so.' Her eyes had gone from flashes of indignation to full fires of righteous anger. Archer could feel their heat from where he stood, his body firing along with them.

Elisabeta was not done. She marched towards him with forceful steps until they stood toe to toe like two boxers at the line. 'I am supposed to be honoured by the opportunity to grace his bed and let his fat, hairy body rut over me for *his* pleasure.'

Archer was not unmoved by the vivid crassness her words conjured. She would be wasted on such a man. She would never throw back her head and embrace her passion as she had done in the alley with him.

Her eyes narrowed in challenge. 'I've had a young boy barely able to do his duty and now I'm to have an old man. So if you want to stand there and condemn me for seeking a little pleasure, so be it.' Her voice broke at the end. 'All I wanted out of life was one good man.'

'And you shall have one.' Archer's response was swift, his voice hoarse as he seized her about the waist and drew her to him, his mouth claiming hers in a rough vow of its own, tasting her anger, her desperation and, somewhere beneath it, her hope and that was the fire he stoked and fed. She would have a good man for the moment at least. He would see to it. He could not give her for ever, but he could give her pleasure for the now.

Chapter Eight

Pleasure for now. Elisabeta gave herself over to the kiss in all its rough, hungry glory. At the eye of her angry tirade was desperation and she gave herself over to it, let it drive her recklessness. She was desperate for so much; desperate to forget, desperate to see if the magic between she and Archer was still there.

Heaven help her, it was and it transported her out of desperation into seeking. In Archer's arms she was no longer reacting, but actively seeking…something, the elusive, explosive end of pleasure, and so was he. She gave a soft moan and pressed against him, revelling in the feel of his erection and that he made no gentlemanly attempt to hide his arousal from her. She was not alone in this; she was not the only one affected so thoroughly by the fire he conjured between them. It was heady knowledge to know she had a partner, that it wasn't all just for her. She didn't want pity of any sort, certainly not the sexual pity of a handsome man.

She ran her hands up under his shirt, drawing her

thumbs across the flats of his nipples, feeling them pucker at her touch, and then down again over the rippled ridges of his abdomen, wishing she could see what her hands felt. He must be exquisite naked, this well-made man of hers.

Yes, *hers* for the moment. That was the promise communicated in the meeting of their mouths, the caress of their hands. Her hands reached the waistband of his trousers. They belonged together for the moment. She reached for him through the fabric of his clothing, running her open palm along the hard ridge of his stalk. He gave a deep groan, his mouth pressing against the column of her throat as he shuddered his appreciation.

His response drove her on. She wanted to give him pleasure, to take his delight further. She caught his eyes, a dark, deep amber that reflected the depth of his arousal. Her hand stalled on his phallus as she whispered, 'Let me give you pleasure.'

She flicked open the flap of his trousers, her hand closing around the hot, hard flesh of a man. Oh, this was heady indeed, the feel of this virile man in his prime and knowing he desired her. Elisabeta stroked down from the tender tip of him and up, and then again, and again until she had a rhythm that had his tip wet and his breath coming in ragged pants. She felt his body clench, heard him give a long groan as his body gathered itself for its release and then it took him, sweeping through him in a shudder as he spent, her hand still clutched around him.

Their eyes held as his body finished and a thrill passed through her at what she saw there: awe. The experience had shaken him as much as it had shaken her. Perhaps *shaken* wasn't the right word. Δ, perhaps, was a better word. This was a shockingly bold and new intimacy for her and apparently for him too. It wasn't always like this. She knew it wasn't. And yet it had been like this twice with him now, this man she hardly knew.

He hardly knew himself. Archer handed her his handkerchief and took an unsteady step backwards, trying to regain his mental equilibrium. In the distance, he was aware of the soft nicker of the horses, a reminder that they'd been gone a while. People were waiting for them. 'I'll get the horses,' he offered to give her privacy in these moments of post-intimacy, and perhaps to buy himself time too, time to think through what had transpired.

These reckless encounters were not his usual style. Not only that, he hardly knew *her*. Perhaps that was the most reckless and surprising aspect. He'd been reckless before in the way young bucks about London are, but always with women he knew. There was a certain safety in that. He would not be ambushed for his recklessness by angry brothers or other males. He did not have that security here. Yet he'd found an overwhelming pleasure with her twice that was nearly beyond words, so different was it from his other experiences.

To feel her hand intimately on him had been exquisitely primal and private, something that would bind them together. In truth, being the sole recipient of pleasure in an encounter was new territory for him. In all his encounters, he was the one in charge of delivering pleasure for them both. There was a reason the London ladies who sought his bed had dubbed him the Rake Most Likely to Thrill, and he did, time and again. But today, Elisabeta had brought him pleasure that was for him alone without asking for pleasure for herself. Her pleasure had been giving him his.

That didn't change the fact he didn't know her beyond the pieces he'd gleaned from their conversations and, maybe most telling, from her rant in the clearing. Nor did it change the fact that while he'd known nothing of her, he'd been willing to offer her pleasure, to offer himself in the hopes of fulfilling her wish—*all I want is one good man.* That remark alone birthed more questions; clearly she was referencing her marriages both past and pending.

Archer took the horses by the reins and led them back to where Elisabeta waited, cheeks flushed, but her gaze none the shyer for what had passed between them. What he did know of her was that she was a bold woman with honest passions. He liked that. Honest passion often spoke of honesty in other dealings as well. A woman lived her truth in the expression of her feelings and that boded well for Elisabeta.

He cupped his hand and tossed her up on to her mare, neither of them in a hurry to race back to the farm, both of them content to leave the other alone with their thoughts. But Archer was unwilling to waste the entire ride in silence. How was he to learn of her if he kept the questions in his head?

Archer held a branch back for her so that she could pass along the trail. She smiled her thanks, and he took the opening in quiet tones that rivalled the stillness of the summer afternoon and the lingering intimacy between them. 'Was it bad? Your first marriage?' It was a bold question, but the two of them had done bold things together. She would tell him if he presumed too much.

Elisabeta gave a small smile and a shake of her head. 'No, we were just poorly suited for one another. We didn't know each other. We met for the first time at the wedding. Even the engagement was conducted by proxy. He was young, just fifteen. Neither of us was interested in being married, but we were interested in being dutiful, so we tried to make something of it. Perhaps we were even successful to a degree. After all, I missed him when he died. It might not have been a grand passion or a perfect marriage but we became friends, unified by the understanding that we were in this together. Perhaps in time, that friendship might have borne a grand love.' She gave a shrug that spoke eloquently of genuine regret.

Archer nodded solemnly, grasping implications of that regret, of all that she'd lost, of all she'd never had the chance to explore. 'I am sorry, but I'm glad it was not an entirely miserable arrangement for you.'

'No, not entirely miserable. Lorenzo tried his best to make me happy, but I missed home. I belong here with the horses. It wasn't so hard being married to Lorenzo as it was being in Florence. My darkest days were after Lorenzo died. Without him, I had no reason to stay. All I wanted to do was come back. It seemed for ever until his family agreed to let me return.' She paused and Archer sensed he'd reached the borders of what she would share. Then she added rather suddenly, holding his eyes in a brief, meaningful exchange. 'His family had hopes, you see.

They would not let me go until those hopes were fully quashed.'

Archer could imagine what those hopes were: that their beloved son had left behind an heir in his wife's womb. He could imagine too the pressure she might have been under to make those hopes come to life for them and even the cruelty she might have endured afterwards when those hopes were quashed. She was granted her freedom, but at what price to herself? The grieving family would not understand that in their disappointment.

'I am sorry,' he said again. She'd been so very young to bear those burdens. She was young still, too young to be bartered off in a second marriage, too young to be a widow. 'How did it happen?'

'A summer fever,' she said simply. 'All of us had gone to the family villa in the hills of Fiesole above the city, but Lorenzo had stayed in town to look after some business. He was always trying to prove himself.' She knitted her brow as if she were debating whether or not to tell him something. 'You have to understand Lorenzo had never been in good health. I think his family was eager for him to marry so soon in life because of that.'

Archer felt his heart go out to the young man he'd never know, a young man never destined to make old bones, as the expression went. A stronger man would not have been as susceptible to such a fever.

'It's hardly a subject for today.' Elisabeta gave a little laugh. Her cheeks flushed and she pressed a hand to them. 'I don't usually talk about Lorenzo to anyone. I must apologise for burdening you. You don't want to hear about all of that.'

'But I do, and I asked,' Archer protested. 'I have a lot of questions about you.' He said it lightly, not wanting to scare her away. She'd run from him once. Of course, she couldn't literally run this time. He knew where to find her. He had a name and an address. But there were other ways to run.

The fences of the outlying paddocks came into view. His time was running short. He was a man who believed in asking for what he wanted and he'd best get on with it. Archer drew Amicus close to Elisabeta's mare, his voice low. 'I have one more question. What next, Elisabeta? Will I see you again or is this the end?'

She lowered her gaze, her attentions focused overmuch on the reins at her horse's neck. 'I am promised to another.'

'That's not an answer,' Archer pressed. Perhaps he should feel guilty for being so bold, but she had confessed to being against the match, had confessed to wanting pleasure if only for the short term. If she wanted it, he would give her no quarter in neglecting to go after it. Perhaps, too, this was why London considered him a rake. He understood there were people who would not see the honour in his actions.

A true gentleman would give way in face of an impending agreement, but Archer would not give such an agreement, one made without the woman's consent, any sway. If she chose to honour the agreement, he would not gainsay her, but if that was not her choice, he would not be a party to forcing it upon her.

They were near enough now to make out the figures of his uncle and her cousin leaning against the fences. 'Elisabeta, when shall I see you again?' Archer asked once more, his tone urgent.

She kept her eyes forward, fixed on Giuliano, and raised her hand to wave, signalling their arrival. When she spoke, her voice was so low, Archer nearly missed it. 'There is a party at my uncle's home to celebrate the Palio victory. It will be a large party, a summer masquerade, with a lot of people in attendance.' She put her heels to the mare and spurred her horse on ahead.

They left soon after that, eager to be on the road now that the afternoon heat had started to cool and travel would be more pleasant. His uncle rode beside him, telling him about the afternoon discussions. Plenty of wine had been passed during those discussions. Archer half-expected to have to take the reins.

'Now, it's your turn, *mio nipote.*' Giacomo clapped him on the back, the suddenness of the gesture causing Amicus to jig. 'What did you learn this afternoon? Was Signora di Nofri full of information? Did you *pump* her for it?'

Archer tried to ignore the innuendo and the fact that he might have been set up. His wily uncle had wanted him to pursue her for information. 'I hardly know her. I doubt she has anything of worth to impart.' There was no lie in that. He did hardly know her. It wasn't as if he was denying having met her prior to lunch. Thankfully his uncle hadn't asked that.

'That's all to the good,' his uncle said. 'A woman should be loyal to her *contrada*. Signora di Nofri honours her uncle with her circumspection. If she was gossiping about his strategies and his Palio dealings with everyone, she would be a discredit to him and to the family.'

Uncle Giacomo leaned towards Archer in his saddle. 'However, while she is not sharing secrets willy-nilly, she might be inclined to share a little something if she knew you better. Pantera and Torre are not sworn enemies. Perhaps there is something we might cultivate there? It would be helpful to know what Pantera's plans are for August. Will you see her again?'

Archer thought of Elisabeta's rage over being married for a Palio alliance. No, he would not share that. It wasn't official. But there was something he could share, something he would need their help with if he was to see her again. Archer grinned at his uncle. 'It seems I've been invited to a party.'

His uncle raised an eyebrow. 'Torre hasn't been invited,' he said slowly, sharply, for a man who'd spent the afternoon drinking wine, his mind making lightning connections.

Giacomo's laughing eyes narrowed in contemplation. 'It would be good to know who was invited. Perhaps Oca? We could not possibly attend if Oca was invited,' he explained to Archer. 'Torre and Oca are bitter rivals. Pantera would not invite us both, but neither would they seek out Oca on purpose. Oca is not their natural ally and they had no dealings with Oca for the last Palio.' His uncle was thinking out loud, his ideas mixing with his explanation. 'Palio winners will invite those who helped them win to their parties; other *contradas* with whom they had *partiti*, or secret negotiations, will be rewarded with invitations.'

Archer laughed. 'I thought *partiti* were illegal? It's in the rules.'

Giacomo laughed along with him. 'My dear *nipote*, that's why they're *secret*.' Giacomo returned to his thoughts. 'Perhaps Pantera seeks a secret alliance with Oca?' He eyed Archer. 'You must go to this party, but be very careful. One Torre smuggled in with a mask will not be noticed, but more would stand out.

'Yes...' Giacomo chuckled '...you will crash the party, it will be your first official duty as a Torre *mangini*.'

These were exactly the machinations his mother had told him about. There was a certain adventurous thrill about crashing a party, something Nolan and Brennan would have thrived on. He was missing his friends right about now. He would have welcomed them with him. There was Elisabeta to consider too. He didn't want her compromised should the two of them be caught. At least this way, he wouldn't betray Elisabeta's secret. If Giacomo learned of the arrangement with Oca on his own, it wouldn't be Archer's fault. Besides, if it was official soon, everyone in the town would know of it.

Giacomo waggled his dark brows. 'You'll be able to spirit your pretty widow away to a dark corner without anyone being the wiser. Just think of all the trouble you can get up to with a mask on?'

That, thought Archer, was precisely the problem. There could be trouble aplenty.

Chapter Nine

So far so good, but there was still plenty of opportunity for something to go wrong. Archer adjusted his mask and surveyed the brightly lit courtyard of the di Bruno home. Like most well-to-do Italian homes, the di Brunos' featured a large, square, internal courtyard in the centre of the home that served as an al fresco drawing room surrounded by arched colonnades leading to the private internal rooms of the occupants. Tonight, that courtyard was full of masked guests dancing while others strolled the colonnades on the perimeter.

His job was easy. He just had to blend in. The sheer number of people present made it likely no one would even know he was here. It made him wonder how many other 'uninvited' guests were here too. He'd wager he wasn't the only one. But it also pointed out the flaw in his plan. If no one noticed him, perhaps Elisabeta wouldn't notice him either. How was she to spot him among so many? How was he to spot her?

What had started out as simply slipping into the

party had turned into a major reconnaissance mission. His uncle was using him to spy on the Pantera *capitano*. In hindsight, Archer saw now why his uncle had encouraged him to take Elisabeta out for a ride after lunch: it had been good for *contrada* business, just as accepting her covert invitation to the party was good for business.

Still, he was here and he had his own agenda for the evening aside from his uncle's: find Elisabeta. How would he do that among all these people and all these masks? He only had until midnight when the masks come off. Then he had to be gone. Archer scanned the room, considering what sort of mask Elisabeta would wear. There were glittery suns, and silvery moons, jet-beaded cat masks, a few long-beaked birds, half-masks and full masks of all varieties. He had wanted to send her a note confirming the masks they would be wearing, but Giacomo had been rankly against it, saying, 'If it's a trap, they will know who you are immediately.'

Archer wasn't used to such machinations. London ballrooms seemed rather straightforward by comparison. Then he saw her, a woman in a deep-red gown, wearing a red-and-blue mask in the form of a panther's head. It began to make sense; red and blue were the colours of the Pantera *contrada* and the panther their animal. The event was to celebrate the *contrada*'s victory, so it followed that the *capitano* as host would pay tribute to the *contrada* with this sort of symbolism. Probably the whole family wore panther masks and sported some combination of the *contrada* colours. Archer chuckled to himself. He was starting to think like Uncle Giacomo.

Archer approached. If he was wrong, the worst it cost him was a dance with a stranger. But he wasn't wrong. He would know her anywhere from the way she moved; all graceful confidence communicating in every step that she was a woman who knew what she wanted. Archer stepped into her path and bowed over her hand. *'Buona sera, signora.'*

Would she know it was him? They had not had time to arrange a signal greeting. No secret code word, no pre-identification of masks—he was doing this socially blind. It was not the way he handled his usual assignations. Brennan, of course, would thrive on the unknown, but Archer preferred preparation and plans. Fewer things went wrong that way. Fewer feelings were hurt. It seemed imperative that she know him, that she be able to pick him out of a crowd, as if that spoke to the quality of their relationship in some way.

Clear grey eyes met his through the holes of her half-mask, a smile taking her face in a recognition that had him stirring. If he hadn't known her before, he knew her now by that sensual mouth, that confident smile. *'Buona sera, signor.'*

Archer closed his hand about hers and led her to the dance floor. 'We should have planned this better.' He grinned, his spirits lifting now that he'd found her.

'What's the fun in that? You found me, didn't you?' She tossed him a saucy look as they joined a set for a lively country dance. Archer threw back his head and laughed. That confirmed it. She definitely wasn't safe and for the moment he didn't have to do anything about it except enjoy her.

Masks had their benefits, or maybe the benefit was

just simply being in Italy where the rules were different. No one seemed to care how often he danced with Elisabeta. Perhaps it was simply too hard to keep track of everyone in masks let alone who they partnered with. By the third dance, Archer didn't care what the reason was. He was intoxicated with her; with her laugh, her knowing looks, her sensual smile, the feel of her body moving in rhythm with his to the music, providing a powerful reminiscence of how their bodies moved together in other intimate rhythms.

Would they seek those intimate rhythms tonight? Was that all she wanted from him? These were the questions populating Archer's thoughts as they stepped from the dance floor, breathless from their efforts, and found their way into the darker realms beyond the colonnades. Others strolled here, oblivious to those around them. It would be easy to disappear from the throng, to slip into the shadows.

Elisabeta tugged him farther from the dancing, into a darkened foyer. There was no one about now and opportunity aplenty. Was that what she wanted? For him to take her against the wall? A hunger rose in him to have her in a bed, to have a night to linger with her, to see her naked beneath him and to savour it, no more rushed encounters pushing them at record speed towards pleasure.

Archer pulled her to a stop. 'Elisabeta, wait. Where are we going? What are we doing?' Two questions he was sure Brennan never asked a woman, but Archer had to know. The alley he could justify as a one-time occurrence, the heat of the moment. Her hand on him during their afternoon ride was harder to justify except for the fact that it didn't involve penetration. That was just indecent fun, with no consequences. There would be no justifying a third time. A third time was outside the scope of what constituted a random encounter. A third time constituted a relationship.

Elisabeta looped her arms about his neck, her body pressed against his, her voice sultry. 'We can go wherever you want, do whatever you want.'

A woman wanted him for sex and he was about to say no. Had the world turned upside down? Nolan and Bren would be laughing their asses off. The Rake Most Likely to Thrill was about to turn down a thrill of his own. 'Perhaps we should talk first. We can't keep doing this. Once, maybe, twice, but...' He didn't get to finish.

She put a finger to his lips. 'You cannot deny we have a talent for pleasure between us.'

He tried to speak around the press of her finger, to form the argument that having a talent for it didn't make it right. But she would have none of his protest.

'Shh, Archer,' she whispered right before she stopped his words with a kiss, a far more effective measure than a mere finger since the kiss stopped his words *and* his mind. It was impossible to think logically with her in his arms, firing his blood, firing his body, obliterating his thoughts. It mattered very little in the moment that she did not fit into his plans, his dreams, that he wasn't in the market for a permanent woman in his life. But he had his standards and the desire to bed her appropriately ran hot and fierce in his veins.

She reached for him through his trousers, but he

stayed her hands, his voice a raspy imitation of itself. 'I would have you in a proper bed, Elisabeta, if we are to be proper lovers. I would at least honour you in that way.' And then, because his body was driving this interaction and not his mind, 'Let me come to you tonight, after the revels.'

She relented, her forehead bent to his, her eyes downcast, her body pliant where it had been strung tight. 'I'll leave a candle in the window.'

'Come back to the party and dance with me until then,' Archer said softly. He took her hand, and they made their way back to the lights and the music in companionable silence. Much had been settled between them. They were to be lovers. The knowing of that took away the stress of ambiguity, of wondering if they would see one another again.

If he had not been so content, perhaps he would have noticed the man in the mask charging towards him. As it was, he saw the danger too late. The man yanked at Archer's mask, tossing his own aside as Archer's identity was revealed, a curse erupting from his lips. 'What the hell are you doing here? What are you doing with her?' He was older and heavy. Archer did not recognise him, but he could guess. This was Elisabeta's intended.

'Ridolfo, leave him be.' Elisabeta had removed her mask.

The man's gaze swung to Elisabeta. 'What are you doing with him?' he accused, lunging forward to drag her away. But Archer was faster, stepping in front of her, instinctively acting as a shield.

'Leave her alone,' Archer warned. 'I am here on my own accord.' It was true. She might have proffered an invitation but no one had compelled his attendance.

Ridolfo spat on the ground. 'Torre scum!'

'Stop this!' Elisabeta protested from behind him. She was trying to get around him to stand between him and her unofficial bull of a fiancé, but Archer kept her effectively blocked. He didn't trust Ridolfo, who seemed equally mad at both of them and he was not one to let any woman play his protector.

'What are you thinking to entertain this man under my nose? Do you think to play the whore in front of me? Oca will not tolerate such a blatant disregard for virtue,' Ridolfo snarled, a dagger flashing in his hand.

Archer reached for his in response. He'd thought his uncle too wary to suggest he bring one. Now he was glad for it. 'Watch your mouth when you speak of her.' If Ridolfo wanted a fight, he'd give it to him. They were drawing a crowd, the guests sensing a fight was inevitable.

Even Archer, new as he was to the machinations of the *contradas*, recognised the danger in this. A fight there might be, but not a fair one. Torre was on enemy ground here. He was outnumbered. Around him the guests started to shape a circle, forming into allies and enemies. If only he knew who the Torre allies were. This was going to be bad. There was going to be a brawl and he was going to be at the centre of it.

Over a woman.

There was a first time for everything. 'Elisabeta, go,' Archer warned, wanting her to find safety. Then he swung his fist straight for Ridolfo's jaw. It was the catalyst for all-out chaos. Fists flew along with a few chairs and quite a few goblets as the *contradas* engaged one another. Insults were hurled with punches all around Archer, but here at the centre of the fight, there was just he and Ridolfo. And their daggers. Ridolfo had no compunction about using his. His first swipe made it clear he was out for blood and a lot of it. The rules of first blood would hold no sway here. Ridolfo would stop only if he was knocked out cold and unable to fight. Archer set aside any hopes of fighting defensively. He had no desire to feel the cut of a blade. He danced backwards out of the way as Ridolfo made a mad slash with his dagger. The older man was slower on his feet. Before Ridolfo could recover, Archer swung at his chin with an upper cut. The big man went down. It was time to go.

And Archer went. Not because he was a coward or because he wasn't capable of more fighting, but because it made sense. With him gone, the fighting might stop. He took a step backwards towards the darkness of the colonnades and sprinted for the door.

He'd almost made it when the cry went up. 'There he goes!' The core of the fighting turned from the centre of the room to the door and as one, the mêlée surged towards him. Archer ran into the night, scaling walls and vaulting fences as the mob chased him. His dancing shoes skidded on the slippery cobblestones, he put down a hand for balance, readjusted and kept running. He was breathing hard now but he gave himself no quarter. He didn't want to find out what the mob would do if they caught him. He sped across the *campo* in the centre of town and hazarded a glance behind at the mob. They were closing in on him, but he was nearly there. The safety of Via Salicotto loomed in front of him, the boundary into the Torre *contrada*. The mob wouldn't dare take their chase into foreign ground. It was one thing to chase an intruder through the streets of Pantera, but quite another to invade a *contrada*.

He sped across the boundary and down a twisting alley, losing himself in the darkness. He heard a collection of disappointed yells go up behind him and knew the mob had given up the chase. But that didn't mean Pantera wouldn't seek vengeance. It would just take another form.

Archer bent over, catching his breath. This was the height of foolishness, being chased through the streets by a mob. It was something that would happen to Brennan. And yet, beneath the foolishness, Archer felt alive. The thrills of the kisses, the fight, the escape, were heady ones. There was some excitement lurking in the unpredictability of it all. It was unlike him. He was a planner. Elisabeta's laughing words came back to him: *Where would the fun be in that?* He hoped she would be all right, that Ridolfo wouldn't turn his frustrations on her.

There was no question of going back to Pantera tonight. The streets would be full of thwarted revellers looking for a fight and Pantera would be on guard. Did he even dare go to his uncle's? Would his uncle be angry? He'd started a fight and ruined a prestigious party. His own father would be appalled. It was one thing for his son to be famed for his bedroom exploits as a lover, but it was another for his son to be embroiled in vulgar scandals. Would his uncle feel the same way? Would his uncle ask him to leave? The full implication of what he'd done tonight, of what he'd caused, was starting to settle on him. He might have ruined his chances. Well, he was no coward. Archer turned his feet towards home. He might as well face his uncle and get it over with. Waiting never solved anything—it usually only served to make things worse.

Chapter Ten

'Well?' His uncle's face was stern as Archer entered the *loggia* and Archer feared the worst. The news had arrived just ahead of him, the bearer not having to dodge a mob in the streets. Archer could only imagine the report Giacomo had been given: how he'd thrown the first punch, how he'd drawn his dagger in defence of a Pantera widow, how he'd not been the least penitent when Ridolfo Ranieri had called his presence into question.

It was hard not to wince at the thought of it. But his uncle's next words surprised him entirely. 'Was she worth it?' Then his uncle's face split into a wide grin and his loud laugh filled the quiet *loggia* and spilled into the silent streets of Torre. 'Good God, *mio nipote*, you've the makings of a fine Ricci yet! Come have some wine and tell me all about it.' His uncle's eyes twinkled. 'I have heard part of it, but I want to hear your version.'

Three glasses of wine later, Archer was more confused than ever. What had struck him as singularly scandalous behaviour on his part had his uncle slapping his knee and eyes brimming with tears of mirth as if it was the best of larks. His uncle raised his glass. 'We'll make a Torraioli of you yet.'

Then his uncle sobered. 'But there is still the issue of the Widow di Nofri. You fancy her and they mean to marry her to our enemy. *This* is serious.' As if drawing daggers at a party and being chased into the night wasn't. He looked sternly at Archer. 'The *signora* is lovely. I understand the attraction. But she is not for you. She *cannot* be for you. Pantera will be our friend no longer. They have chosen to align themselves with our enemy.

'This will go down in our records as a conflict of equal fame with Pantera's interference with Aquila in the 1752 Palio. The friend of our enemy is also our enemy.' Giacomo tapped the side of his temple with his finger. 'The Torre memory is a long one. We will not forget.' He fixed his dark eyes on Archer. '*Mio nipote*, you have had your fun and there is no shame in it. Romance is part of life, is it not? But it ends tonight. For the sake of the *contrada* and peace in the streets, you must not see her again.'

The next moment he was jovial once more. 'Besides, I have good news. The horses Torre wants to volunteer for the Palio need you. I need you. I want you to start working them. There is less than two weeks before the drawing of horses for the race.'

He was to ride! The import of the news was not lost on Archer. If his uncle could see him ride in exercise, he might change his mind about allowing him to ride for Torre in the Palio. He was one more step closer to his dream. It seemed the fight tonight had done for him what his ability to ride had not been able to achieve: convincing his uncle to give him a chance with the horses. But he was too astute to not recognise there were other agendas here as well. This was also being dangled in front of him as a carrot. Should he not abide by his uncle's edict to leave Elisabeta alone, the honour of riding would be removed. There was the practical consideration too. If he was working the horses in the country, he would be effectively removed from the city. Those conditions would not be spoken directly, of course, and his uncle would deny those strings to his face, but Archer would know they were there.

His uncle walked with him to his room on the second floor. To make sure he actually went to bed instead of going back to Pantera? Or just because it was the fatherly thing to do? Archer was learning quickly that the family might love you, but they seldom did anything without multiple reasons.

'It was a good night.' Giacomo clapped him on the back. 'You did well. It is too bad about the widow, but we'll find you another woman if you want.'

'Of course,' Archer said because it was all he could think of to say as he bid his uncle goodnight. He shut the door behind him and leaned against it with a sigh. This was shaping up to be something out of *Romeo and Juliet*. Too bad he'd only paid attention to the Shakespeare plays that had horses in them. If Romeo had had a horse, he might have been better prepared for this turn of events; Ridolfo's attack this evening, his own crashing of a party, and now the potential of street warfare between the neighbourhoods, all over a forbidden woman.

Archer began to strip out of his clothes for bed. Why should he care if he saw Elisabeta again? He'd known her for a week and very little of her at that. His uncle wasn't asking him to end a dear friendship or to throw away the love of his life. Why did he feel as if he were? The evening was warm and he lay on top of his covers, naked and hard and wondering if a candle still burned in a certain window in Pantera?

There would be no candle tonight. Elisabeta stood before her uncle and Ridolfo without flinching. A fiercer tribunal she could not imagine. She'd been on her feet, answering questions for half an hour. Had she known who was behind the mask? How had someone from Torre got into the party? Her uncle had been ready to accept her vague explanations, it was a masked ball after all. Who was to prevent unwanted guests? But Ridolfo was not as easily pacified. He kept watching her with beady eyes, waiting to catch her in a lie. Ridolfo was sporting a large bruise on his face where Archer's fist had left its mark. It might be petty, but she took some satisfaction in that.

'Tell me again, had you met him before?' Ridolfo questioned for the third time.

Giuliano intervened from his position against the wall. He came forward. 'She's already told you. How many times do you have to ask? How was Elisabeta to know she was dancing with a Torraioli? She was merely doing her duty as a good hostess. If the Torraioli seemed taken with Elisabeta, who could blame him? It was hardly her fault. You seem taken enough with her, surely you can understand the attraction she might hold for another man,' Giuliano managed to sneer. 'Have you thought that perhaps you should blame Torre for this and not Elisabeta? You seem quick to condemn her, but not the man who gave you that bruise.'

Ridolfo snarled and turned to her uncle. 'Your niece is a harlot, no matter what she says,' Ridolfo accused from his chair at the table. She watched her uncle flinch. 'Do not sit there and tell me she is a dutiful niece because she would not have done this if she was. She does you no credit.'

'I am sorry, *signor*,' her uncle began, and she felt guilty for making him have to say those words. She didn't want him to beg a man like Ridolfo Ranieri. Her uncle was a proud man. He might not be as wealthy as Ridolfo, but he had standing in his own right. She had endangered that tonight with her daring invitation. She'd not thought...

Ridolfo brushed away the words as if they meant nothing. 'It is not your fault. She needs a man to take her in hand. Clearly, her first husband was too lenient with her.' His eyes flicked her direction, narrow and assessing as they looked her up and down, his fat sausage fists flexing and releasing. She willed herself not to look away, not to show him her loathing, her fear. He would punish the loathing and he would use the fear.

'I am her fiancé now, I should have the handling of her since I am soon to be her husband and her behaviour reflects on me,' he said, and her stomach went cold. She shot a glance at Giuliano who stood alert, his gaze encouraging her to stay calm.

'I shall see to her punishment. She will know who

her master is.' His eyes never left hers and her skin crawled with the knowledge of it.

Giuliano spoke up. He could risk being less diplomatic than his father. 'I do not think it is your decision. You are not her husband yet. The engagement has not even been formalised.' Giuliano's challenge drew his eyes from her, and she allowed herself to feel a little relief, but it was short-lived.

'If this is how she will behave in the interim, I want the engagement announced immediately and I want the wedding to take place two weeks after the Palio at the end of August,' Ridolfo announced, throwing down his terms like a gauntlet.

'It is too soon,' her uncle prevaricated. 'We need time to plan. We are so busy now with the Palio.'

Ridolfo fixed her uncle with a stare. 'Shall I tell my cousin the *priore* that Pantera does not mean to keep its word?'

Those were fighting words. Her uncle could not let them pass. He rose from his chair. 'We will keep our word.'

Ridolfo rose as well, sensing the interview was over. 'I will expect an announcement shortly.' He gave her an insincere bow. 'I will also expect planning your wedding, Signora di Nofri, will keep you too busy for further scandal.'

When he had gone, Elisabeta waited only a moment to launch her protests. 'Uncle, you cannot allow this. You see what kind of man he is.'

But her uncle held up a hand to stop her words and raised tired eyes to her face. 'No more, Elisabeta. Go to bed. You've done enough for one night. Giuliano will see you up.'

Giuliano took her arm and she allowed it until they were out of sight. 'Take your hand off me!' Elisabeta hissed, at the top of the stairs. 'I will not be escorted to my room like some sort of prisoner.' She was taking her temper out on him and it was unfair. Somewhat.

She fairly *burned* with angry indignation. If anyone shared responsibility for the debacle of the party, it was Giuliano. He'd encouraged this affair. He had arranged for them to meet again at the horse farm.

Giuliano opened the door to her bedchamber and stepped inside with her, his own anger simmering. 'Stop with this posturing, as if you're the wronged victim here.' His body vibrated with tension. 'I protected you down there. I gave nothing away, although Lord knows you deserve it for taking such a risk.'

She did have to give him that. He had stood up for her during Ridolfo's repetitive inquisition. Her uncle had sighed and accepted the story as truth because Giuliano spoke it. It wasn't implausible that events had happened as Giuliano stated. It wouldn't be the first time a *contrada* had stolen into another's party.

'I do thank you for that,' Elisabeta offered politely. 'You did protect me.' She astutely kept the thought to herself that in protecting her, Giuliano was also protecting himself. Uncle Rafaele would not like to hear of Giuliano's part in encouraging her association with the handsome Torre *mangini*.

Giuliano leaned against the door. He had protected her and in doing so had admitted privately, between the two of them, his own culpability in the fiasco. But she could see in the set of his body he wasn't ready to accept all of the blame. 'What were you thinking to invite him *here*…?' Giuliano began, his anger not yet spent.

'It was a masked ball. I didn't think he'd be discovered. He would have been well away by midnight. It was just supposed to be a few dances,' Elisabeta defended her decision with crossed arms. She might confess, but she wouldn't be penitent over it. She was not sorry she'd done it.

'Your future husband was in attendance. Surely, you had to know he would notice if you danced so often with the same partner, masked or not. If not that, he'd notice if you were absent for an extended time,' Giuliano pointed out.

'We weren't gone that long. Nothing happened.'

'You sound disappointed by that.' Giuliano pushed off the door and began to pace the room. He pushed a hand through his hair, and Elisabeta winced. That meant he was thinking, perhaps too hard and too much. She liked her cousin when he was more spontaneous. When he thought he became too responsible and that was dangerous, especially to her freedom. 'Is the Englishman worth so much you would risk dishonouring our family?'

'I do not want the marriage your father has arranged.' It was an indirect answer and it was complicated. Of course she didn't want to dishonour her family, but neither did she want to dishonour her freedom. 'When I am with him, I am alive. I am not a pawn, not someone else's currency to spend.' Could Giuliano, a young man raised with freedom and privilege, understand that?

Apparently not. 'The *priore*'s cousin is wealthy. You will have a nice home in town and a villa in the country. There will be fine horses. He is besotted with you. He will give you anything you ask for,' Giuliano reiterated the benefits. She'd heard them all before when the match had been first put to her. They were even less appealing now that she had Ridolfo's measure.

'Your answer disappoints me. I had hoped for better from you,' Elisabeta shot back fiercely. 'I get all that in exchange for what, do you suppose? Not for "free". It is not just about horses and the Palio, Giuliano. It's about me being with him for ever. His wealth does not make the prospect more palatable.'

'But the prospect of pleasure with the Englishman is more than palatable.' Giuliano countered. 'This is why I suggested him. Now, you have had your pleasure where it belongs, in the countryside, in an alley. But that's where it ends. Your *discreet* foray into pleasure does *not* take place in this house in front of the man you would marry or under my father's nose. *Those* are flagrant insults and not to be tolerated.'

Elisabeta swallowed. What she had done had been dangerous. She'd been lucky. Giuliano had been able to deflect the issue away from her downstairs tonight. She would not be punished. Giuliano had persuaded her uncle and fiancé any punishment that was meted out be directed at Torre and the Englishman. They were the ones responsible for what had happened, Elisabeta was merely a casualty. Yet, her mistakes did not validate being sold into marriage against her will.

'Perhaps Ridolfo will cast me off now,' Elisabeta said hopefully. Casualty or not, tonight had drawn attention her way and that was hardly a commodity valued in a politely bred Sienese woman of virtue.

It would be one good thing to come of the evening's travesty.

Giuliano shook his head. 'That's doubtful. If anything, tonight verifies for Ridolfo and the Oca *priore* that you are a beautiful, sought-after woman, a credit to their house. They are fortunate to have won such a lovely bride. Men want what other men covet. You heard Ridolfo—he is more eager than ever to move the marriage up.'

There was a scratch at the door followed by a whisper. 'It's me, Contessina, let me in.' Elisabeta sighed. Her room had become as busy as a posting inn. All she wanted was to go to bed and wallow in her misery and her memories. Giuliano opened the door, and Contessina slipped in.

'Are you all right? I came as quickly as I could,' Contessina said, slightly breathless as if she'd run up the stairs. Elisabeta smiled in spite of herself. The very proper Contessina had been eavesdropping. 'You are to be married early. I heard the news.'

Elisabeta felt panic start to rise. She'd done a fairly good job of convincing herself she'd have more time, until tonight and Ridolfo's announcement. Hearing Contessina say it made the reality far too real, far too close.

Elisabeta shot a desperate glance at Giuliano. 'Can't you do something? Can't you talk your father out of it? There is no shame to back out of the agreement, nothing has been announced. No face will be lost if it's not public. Ridolfo and Oca need not be embarrassed yet. We only dislike Torre on behalf of Oca. Torre is not our enemy,' she argued.

Giuliano shook his head slowly. 'You know I cannot. My father has made up his mind. Perhaps it will not be so bad, Elisabeta? Ridolfo is rich.'

'Yes, I know,' she all but shouted. 'He will deny me nothing as long as I reciprocate in kind.' She was tired of being told to endure, that the money was worth it, the prestige was worth it. Did no one see that this arrangement was nothing more than church-sanctioned prostitution—a woman taking a man in exchange for money? No matter what vows were traded, that fact could not be erased.

'Perhaps you should stay with her tonight, Sister,' Giuliano suggested quietly as he slipped from the room before she could strangle him. He thought she would run.

'I will. I will stay with you, tonight, Cousin,' Contessina offered sweetly. 'Let me brush out your hair. You will feel better.'

It was hard to be mad at Contessina. Elisabeta sat and let her take out the hairpins. There *was* comfort in the ritual and in Contessina's presence. The girl meant well. They all meant well. Her uncle, Giuliano. Her uncle had arranged one wealthy marriage for her and when that had failed, he'd brought her home and arranged another. Her uncle was fulfilling his promises to her father to see her taken care of for life.

She should not ask for more. She felt badly that she could not reconcile herself to this marriage, that she selfishly wanted something different. Sometimes she wished she could be more like Contessina who accepted; who did what she was told.

Contessina helped her into a nightgown and they settled into her big bed. She didn't want to desire the Englishman, but she did. To pursue him was to pursue folly and yet her gaze went to the dark window. Was he out there, looking up from the ground even now, waiting for a sign? Was her Englishman that foolish? To brave the streets tonight would be far too perilous. He would risk more than his safety if he tried to make his way back to her uncle's home.

Elisabeta tucked the pillow more firmly beneath her head and rolled on to her side. He was not down there. Coming back risked not only his safety, but her reputation. Archer had understood that tonight. His first inclination had been to protect her with his words and his actions. He'd drawn a dagger on *her* behalf and he'd been quick to take the blame upon himself, quick to divert any of that blame from her. Archer's own words had given Giuliano the grounds for his arguments later that night. A gallant lover was her Englishman and she could not have him not even once more.

Her uncle and even Giuliano, her champion, had made that request explicit. To see Archer again would undermine Giuliano's arguments regarding her innocence. It would make them both appear as liars to her uncle. More than that, to see him again would lead to blood. She knew how these family feuds went and a duel was where it was headed. The upcoming Palio had diverted that course of action for now. Plotting against Torre in the race would serve in the stead of duelling. But a duel would not be escaped if she were caught with Archer again.

She sighed, and Contessina rubbed her back consolingly. 'It will all look better in the morning,' Contessina comforted. What did Contessina know? Nothing went wrong in her world.

Elisabeta doubted it. Nothing would ever be better again. Seeing Archer again definitely involved no small amount of risk. But not seeing him again carried its own risk too. She had found a very private, personal sort of pleasure with Archer. She wanted to explore how deeply that pleasure ran, how long it could last.

Her cousin's hand stilled for a moment. 'Elisabeta,' she began tentatively, 'why does the Englishman matter so much? You hardly know him.'

Ah, but she did! She'd ridden with him, watched him with animals, danced in his arms, seen him vulnerable to pleasure as she held him intimately in her hand. How did she express that to Contessina? Elisabeta turned to face her cousin, taking the girl's hands in hers. 'When I am with him, I'm not alone. There's a connection.' The words seemed apt, if not inadequate. In truth, being with Archer was unlike anything she'd ever known.

Contessina's pretty face turned sad. 'You have us. You don't need to be alone.'

Elisabeta shook her head. 'It's not the same.' It would be so much easier if it was. Tonight, she was just beginning to realise that what had started out as a single venture into discreet sexual experimentation had moved far beyond that. Her curiosity had been satisfied. Pleasure had been achieved. Those had been her goals—to experience that which had eluded her in her marriage. Now that she had, the adventure should be over. But Archer had become more than a sexual partner.

Contessina was looking at her patiently, waiting for her to say more, to explain. Elisabeta tried the idea forming in her mind, the words coming slowly, her brain peripherally aware that her grip on Contessina's hands tightened with the intensity of her thoughts. 'What makes him important is that he makes me feel alive. He is *my* choice.'

He represented something she'd never had before—the liberty and the luxury to choose. The most significant events in her life were not things she'd chosen to happen to her. She'd not chosen to have her parents killed in a coaching accident. She'd not chosen to marry Lorenzo. She would not have chosen to marry Ridolfo on her own. She'd not chosen either of the men who had been or would be given sanctioned intimate access to her body. But she'd chosen Archer. He was the physical embodiment of her freedom. He was *hers* entirely.

'What are you going to do?' Contessina asked softly, perhaps divining the dilemma such an acknowledgement created—the personal good pitted against the greater good.

Elisabeta shook her head and gave her cousin a small smile. She had no answers and she'd kept the girl up too late tonight as it was. 'I don't know. But *you* should definitely go to sleep.'

Elisabeta blew out the light next to their bed and settled down to her pillows. It was a futile exercise. Her mind was too alive to find sleep immediately. Which risk did she take; the risk that exposed her family to Ridolfo's revenge and scandal or the risk that asked her to give up a chance at claiming her freedom? More than that, it asked her to give up the right to a choice. It would make her a pawn once more.

Chapter Eleven

Archer was a man who liked having choices. He'd grown up learning that while one must always consider others in one's decisions, ultimately a man's choices were his own. Not so in Siena. The individual respected the wishes of the family in theory *and* in practice. It was the one rule Archer could not entirely bring himself to live by. He would go to his uncle's villa and train the horses, but on his own time. He had something to do first. He would see Elisabeta regardless of his uncle's edict to the contrary. He was a grown man of twenty-nine, not a boy in leading strings who could be told what to do.

His conscience demanded no less. He could not leave the city without knowing Elisabeta was safe. If it had only been his own safety he risked, he would have gone back to Pantera last night. But he'd been astute enough to realise he jeopardised her as well. He would take his chances this morning in the hopes that his note had reached her. The route it had travelled was rather circuitous and relied on her cousin, Giuliano, giving it to her.

Archer paced the small upper room he'd rented on a street not far from the busy *campo*, checking his watch yet again. There'd been no question of trying to approach her publicly, not with the rumours of last night on everyone's tongue, nor without his uncle knowing. He doubted too that she would appreciate the attention either. But the confines of the room were chafing on him and waiting made him feel impotent.

He'd been here an hour already. It was market day and the streets were bustling with customers and vendors. Surely, if the note had reached her, Elisabeta would be able to slip away in the crowd. If she wanted to come at all. There was always the possibility that she'd decided he was too dangerous, or that she couldn't come. Archer wasn't sure which option concerned him most—wouldn't come or couldn't come. If Ridolfo, or anyone, had hurt her, vengeance would follow no matter what his uncle thought.

There was a quiet knock at the door, a whispered question of a name through the door. 'Archer?' He snapped his watch shut with a smile, his anxiety fleeing. She had come.

Elisabeta stepped into the room, flushed and breathless. Relief swamped him at the sight of her so vibrantly alive and unharmed. He'd been ready to feel such relief, but he'd not been prepared for the intensity. He had not realised just how worried he'd been. 'You're all right?' Archer crossed the small room and took her hands, searching her face, her eyes, to assure himself she was unhurt. 'I feared last night that Ridolfo might turn his anger on you after I left. I hadn't wanted to leave.'

She stepped into him then, her arms wrapping around his neck, her body pressed against his, wanting more from him than the touch of his hands on hers. 'You would have been hurt or worse if they'd caught you.' She kissed him, her mouth lingering on his. 'You should see Ridolfo's jaw. He has the most magnificent bruise,' she murmured.

'He'll get a lot more than a bruised jaw from me if he ever seeks to do you injury,' Archer growled fiercely. He bent to kiss her, but the tentative quality in her eyes stopped him. 'What is it? What has happened?' Had she been hurt after all?

She stepped away from him. 'You won't always be able to protect me.'

'Let me decide that.' Archer's answer was terse. He reached for her hands. 'I'm one of the best boxers in our London club. I've left more than a few opponents on the ground when the need arose.'

Elisabeta shook her head. He saw sadness in her eyes, which had been alive a short time ago. 'You can't fight a husband over his wife.' She paused. 'I am to marry him at the end of August, after the Palio. It was decided last night.' By others, not by her, that much was clear, but that didn't stop a cold pit of dread from spreading in his stomach.

He could feel her hands start to shake in his before he saw the fear take root in her eyes. She was starting to break, this beautiful, strong, woman who loved with abandon. 'I don't know what I'm afraid of most, being married to Ridolfo or of not having a choice in the matter. Perhaps it doesn't matter which I fear most. I am trapped either way. There is no place to run.'

'You can run to me,' Archer said in deadly, measured tones. He'd seen Ridolfo last night, a hulking, stinking ogre of a man whose only recommendation was his wealth and social connections. It wasn't that Ridolfo was a fat man that made him repellent. It was his lack of manners, his lack of regard for Elisabeta and likely for any woman that made him distasteful. Archer had been more than glad to take a fist to his face.

'I don't want your pity,' Elisabeta said solemnly. 'You hardly know me. You are not required to do anything, to feel anything...' Her words dropped off, her thought incomplete.

Archer felt his temper start to rise. 'Pity? Is that what you think exists between us? That night in the alley was pity? The horse ride was pity? Drawing a dagger for you in the middle of my enemies was done out of pity? It was done out of choice. I am not required to do any of those things. I chose to do them, *for you*.' He would do more for her too if she would allow it.

The rashness of that realisation struck him hard. How much more? Today, with her trembling before him, he was willing to do it all, to give her the protection of his name, of his body. That was the power of his anger at her for not understanding what had passed between them, of his anger towards Ridolfo who saw her as nothing but a possession, anger at her family too for not seeing what she needed or what they doomed her to with their plans. He turned from her and strode to the window, trying to wrestle his emotions into compliance. He had not counted on a reaction like this. Then again, he hadn't counted on a woman like this.

'I'm not a horse to rescue like your Amicus.'

'Of course you're not,' Archer answered sharply.

'But the premise is the same, isn't it? This is what you do. You rescue animals and people,' Elisabeta challenged. She was getting angry too and that fuelled his own temper. How dared she be angry when he'd made her such a generous offer of protection? She was the one throwing it back in his face, rejecting him outright. He was going to lose her before he'd really found her.

Archer turned from the window and let her see his anger. 'What did you come here for if you won't let me help you? Did you simply come to say goodbye?' He wanted to hear her say it and yet a part of him held out hope that she wouldn't. Coming had required a certain risk. Why would she take that risk if only to leave him again? It hardly seemed worth it.

'I came because you asked me to. I came because I wanted to. I didn't come to quarrel.'

'What did you come to do?' Archer asked, his words quietly cutting. Coming wasn't enough. 'Did you think to have one last romp in the sheets?' He gestured to the iron bed in the corner with its quilt. He tugged at his shirt, pulling it out of his waistband as he began to undress.

'Archer, stop!' Elisabeta cried as he tossed his shirt on the bed, standing before her half-naked.

'Oh, so you're *not* using me for sex? My mistake. I thought you were.'

'That's not fair!' Elisabeta's eyes blazed. She strode to the bed and balled up his shirt. She threw

it at him. Good, she was willing to fight. He was getting to her now, getting her to move past the paraly-
sis of her fear. It was what he wanted. She was no
coward, but currently she felt cornered. She didn't
know what to do, or what she was capable of doing,
and she wouldn't know until she tried. He knew all
too well from dealing with his father how it felt to
be cornered, to feel there were no options. He hadn't
known his power until the day he'd chosen to step out
of the corner. But that had come with consequences
too. What was she willing to risk?

'What is not fair is what you're letting them do to
you,' Archer replied. 'It's simple really. Either you
marry Ridolfo and accept it or you don't.'

'You forgot the part about what happens if I don't.'
Elisabeta's eyes narrowed. 'You forgot how scandal-
ised my family will be, or that I'll become a social
outcast, or that my uncle might be forced to send me
away. I would be exiled from everything I know. I've
already done that once. You can't possibly know how
it feels to be so entirely alone in a new world.'

Archer raised an eyebrow, challenging her assumption. 'Don't I? And yet here I am with a family I have never met, in a country that doesn't speak
English, a thousand miles from home.' He softened
his tone. They hadn't much time left. She would be
missed soon and he needed resolution. 'You wouldn't
be alone, Elisabeta. I would be there for you.'

Archer or Ridolfo. When the argument was boiled
down to that common denominator, the choice was
easy. The thought that she could have him made her
knees weak. This bold, handsome, kind man was offering himself to her. Not as a husband, she wasn't

that naive. There'd been no talk of marriage between them. They would be lovers—she would be his mistress. He stood there before the window, a veritable Adonis without his shirt, the sun behind him, representing everything she craved: pleasure, freedom, respect, choice. But to get it, she'd have to give up all she'd ever known.

Elisabeta moved towards him, daring to touch him since their quarrel began. She placed a flat palm against his chest, feeling his heart beat strong and healthy beneath her fingers. 'You do understand, Archer, that you represent everything I want as well as everything I fear.'

His hand covered hers, his eyes holding hers with their amber lights. 'Not everything you fear.' He smiled. 'I wanted to tell you that I am going to my uncle's villa in the country for a couple of weeks to work with the horses before the Palio selection. The villa is near San Gimignano, not far, I hear, from the di Bruno villa.'

Her pulse quickened, with hope, with the prospect of pleasure. She heard the implied invitation. In San Gimignano they would be anonymous. In the Chianti countryside they would be free to pursue the possibility of what they could be. They could buy themselves some time. *She* could buy herself time to consider what she would risk, what her freedom was worth to her. In those moments as they said farewell, Elisabeta could barely speak, so great was her gratitude. Archer had given back the one thing that mattered most right now—her choice. It gave her strength, strength she needed far sooner than she would have anticipated.

* * *

Ridolfo was waiting for her when she and her cousins returned from the market. He'd arranged it very neatly, intercepting them on the street before they gained the house. He fell into step beside her, forcing Giuliano to move ahead with Contessina on the crowded street. He had her by the arm, steering her away from Giuliano.

'They can manage without you,' he replied when she protested. 'You and I have unfinished business to settle from last night.'

'Where are we going?' She was instantly wary. He was leading her back down the street away from Pantera, away from the people she knew.

He smiled, showing all of his yellowing teeth. 'We're going to Oca, to my home. It occurred to me that you will be mistress of all of it and you've seen none of it. It's a big house. It will, however, require a woman's touch. You will want to make changes.'

'Shouldn't my aunt be with us? I am sure her advice would be useful,' Elisabeta suggested, not wanting to show any of the trepidation that surged through her. No one knew where she was at. She would run if she had a chance, no matter how childish that would look—a grown woman running in the streets. She couldn't imagine how she would explain such an action to her uncle but that was the least of her concerns at the moment. She counselled herself to stay calm. Ridolfo had done nothing now or ever to directly harm her even though he'd implied it last night with his talk of punishment, something she thought he'd enjoy meting out. Still, she had no proof he intended anything other than what he said. Perhaps he meant only to win her over with a display of his wealth. His was the nicest home in Siena after all.

Still, all the tapestries and fine furniture couldn't erase the heavy clamp of his hand at her back as he ushered her through the home, couldn't make up for the sour smell of his breath at her ear as he told her about each piece of art and how he acquired it. She was acutely aware of his closeness, of his touch, of her body's judgement on that: he was repulsive. Her body couldn't relax, she was on edge.

He saved the bedroom for last. It was a large, opulent room done in thick, heavy wood pieces that had been passed down for generations of Ranieri. 'It's done in the Turkish style,' Ridolfo boasted, waving a hand in the air. 'Everything here is from Constantinople.' His voice dropped. 'Even the bed linens are from a pasha's harem.'

His hand ran down her spine, and her skin crawled. 'I think you will come to enjoy this bed, if your behaviour with the Englishman is any indicator of your passion. I saw last night how I had misjudged you. I was waiting around, trying to be the delicate gentleman when, in reality, you were ready for a man. You have passion that needs to be spent.'

Elisabeta said nothing. He must have taken the silence as acquiescence. 'I assure you, there are ways we can help your enjoyment,' he drawled. He was playing with her now, she realised with a sick drop of her stomach. He went to a drawer next to the bed and opened it. He held up silken cords. 'Some tricks from the harem. You may prefer to be tied down, blindfolded, as you learn to take your pleasure in my bed. Being deprived of the senses can heighten that.' He drew out a jar. 'There are lotions too that I can spread on you before I enter that eases your passage. You cannot say I won't be a considerate lover. I have a physician on staff to see to your every need as well. You'll meet with him once our engagement is announced and he can ascertain your special needs.'

He gave the drawer a firm shove and approached her, forcing her to back up to the wall. She would not flinch. He would like that too much. He would have his victory. He'd brought her here to warn her, to punish her with words, with visions of her life to come in his house. His fat fingers gripped her chin roughly. 'You will never shame me like you did last night with the Englishman. I am to be the only recipient of your attentions. Once you are mine, I can do with you as I please. Whips, ropes, potions. Do you know how many nights I've lain in this bed imagining you in it? You naked before me, tied and helpless, rousing to me, begging me to give you release? And it will happen.'

Elisabeta spat in his face. 'I will never rouse to you.'

'You naive bitch!' He wiped at the spittle. 'You have no idea what I can make you do.' He gave her an evil look that nearly took the last of her resolve. 'The next time you think about your Englishman, think about this. The potions work, the drugs work. I can make you rouse to me whether you like it or not.'

He stepped too close, and Elisabeta saw her chance. She brought her knee up, hard and fast, thrusting it into his groin. Ridolfo went down, hands clasped over his privates and screaming expletives.

She didn't stop to listen. She ran through the streets, dodging vendors and passers-by. Her side ached as she tore through alleys and shortcuts to Pantera, not caring who cursed her as she bumped into them, or who called after her. She would not be safe until she reached her room. Upstairs, she bolted the door. Even then, with the heavy door and the bolt to keep out unwanted intruders, she wondered if she'd ever be safe again.

Ridolfo would get up eventually and he would come for her. He might not be able to tell her uncle what had transpired without implicating himself—after all, women don't knee men in the crotch without a reason—but he would come for her, he wouldn't let this pass without retribution. The longer his temper cooled the less severe that retribution might be. She needed to leave, needed to get out of the city. She needed time to think, to discover her options. She needed a friend.

You can run to me. The words came to her as she leaned her head against the strong oak of her door, her breath coming in gasps and sobs. Archer would keep her safe. He had given her all the power to decide her fate. Perhaps he might also have some ideas about what to do with that fate, or better yet, how to avoid it. A girl could always hope.

Chapter Twelve

If there was one thing Archer knew, it was horses. He could feel the heat in their legs if they were lame and which ones had 'kissing spine' when the girths were fastened. He could treat them too, and he did, spending hours massaging liniment into the muscled shoulders and strong backs of the horses at his uncle's villa in the Chianti countryside. The horses became his full-time occupation, along with waiting for Elisabeta.

Letting the horses absorb him was the easy part. Waiting for Elisabeta was not. Archer lay back in the grass and looked up at the sky, watching the first evening stars come out. This had become his night-time ritual—lying on the grass in front of the villa. It had only been three days since he'd seen her. Logically, he knew he couldn't expect her to appear so soon. She had arrangements to make, assuming she could get away. Would she choose to come? Even if she wanted to come, would she be able to? It was the thoughts of what might keep her in town against her will that bothered him most. Those ranged from the benign—being unable to arrange transportation, being unable to get out of whatever previously arranged social commitments she had—to the more harmful: being locked in her room, being forbidden to leave the house, being forced to endure the odious company of Ridolfo to please her family.

Restless, the early stars unable to hold his attention tonight, Archer sat up and reached for his whittling knife, another nightly habit. Sometimes, like tonight, he did some carving from the scraps of wood lying about the stable. He hadn't had much time to indulge his little hobby since leaving Dover. Now, he had time to spare. Keeping his hands busy also kept his mind busy, kept it off Elisabeta.

Archer laughed to himself. He should be careful what he wished for. There'd been times in the past four months he'd wished for aloneness. Now that he had it, he missed the companionship that had surrounded him since his trip had begun. In Paris, he had shared lodgings with the others. In Siena, he'd been surrounded by his uncle's family, cousins upon cousins, that had filled in the absence of his friends. He had not been alone for quite some time.

Now, he was alone and his thoughts had him all to themselves, a privilege they were exercising ruthlessly at the moment. Archer shaved off an edge of the wood with extra fierceness. Every thought went back to one central theme: what to do about Elisabeta? He'd meant it when he'd told her she could run to him. But what did that mean? In the heat of the moment he'd not thought about what he was willing to offer her, only that he would protect her. Certainly, she could claim the protection of his body.

But that was easy. It required the skill of his fists. It didn't require matrimony. The protection of his name, however, did.

Archer held the little carving up to the lantern light, the form of a horse starting to take shape. This was familiar territory. He'd been carving horses since he was a boy. A stable hand in his father's barn had shown him how, much to his father's displeasure. Whittling was not a gentleman's pastime. It had become a boy's quiet rebellion against his father, against rules that made no sense except to separate people from one another.

Even here in Italy, his father haunted him, intruding into his thoughts about Elisabeta. If he married her to protect her, it would mean going home, the one thing he did not want to do. Going home meant going to his father; it would mean making amends and facing the past. Not just facing it, but accepting it. Elisabeta had talked of the price of pursuing him, the price to her of leaving Ridolfo. Archer understood the price of her choice was considerable. But she was not the only one to pay. He would pay, too, for his offer. He would not be able to keep her and stay in Italy. Probably, he wouldn't have to marry her to be banned from Siena. Any association would be damning since both his uncle and hers, and her fiancé, had forbidden contact. Was the protection of a woman worth his dream?

That dream had become real to him in the days since his arrival in the Chianti countryside. He'd seen first-hand the possibility of his uncle's horses and the villa. This was the life he wanted. He loved the routine of his days here and already he was earning the respect of his uncle's grooms. He rose early before the heat of the day, oversaw the morning feeding and walked the stalls, checking on each horse. Over a group breakfast, he assigned each groom a set of horses to work out. He spent the morning watching those workouts and even riding himself. The hot afternoons were spent in the cool of the indoors at a desk, writing down his observations in a log that recorded each of the horses' progress. The evenings were his own spent under the Tuscan sky.

Archer looked up into the sky. It was fuller now, the stars having emerged in force. He could pick out the Plough and the Pleiades. In his mind, he could envision evenings like this with a child or two, or three, or even a horde of them beside him picking out constellations too, their mother holding the newest addition in her arms. He'd always a wanted a family, but it had been a goal for later. Since arriving in Siena, in spite of his plans to the contrary, it seemed 'later' was intent on being 'now'.

Maybe it was Italy that prompted such thoughts. His mother had warned him often enough with a laugh that in Italy family was the most important thing and it was infectious. One could not be in Italy and not feel that yearning. He'd not truly believed her. Or maybe it was Elisabeta that prompted such yearnings. He was missing Haviland. Haviland would know how to talk through this with him. For now there wasn't any more he could do. He'd made his move. Now he had to wait for Elisabeta to make hers. He hoped he wouldn't have to wait much longer. Perhaps in the morning there would be word…

* * *

She was not good at waiting. Elisabeta's pulse raced. Her horse pranced beneath her, picking up on her nervousness. She scanned the wide open space of the countryside, looking for Archer. He would have got her note this morning with his breakfast. If he was there. He could be out. There could be any number of reasons he was late or wouldn't show up. Had he felt this way waiting for her that day in Siena?

Perhaps he'd changed his mind? Perhaps he realised how foolish his offer had been up in that little room? Or perhaps she had truly convinced him she wasn't worth it, this woman whom he hardly knew when it came right down to it. Had he gone home and weighed the cost of his offer? Had he truly thought about what it would mean if she took it and concluded he would not pay that price?

A horse and rider appeared on the horizon and she knew a special relief. It was him! She knew by the way he sat a horse, by the way the horse moved beneath him, at one with his rider. She knew him too from something that had nothing to do with physical recognition. Safety, protection, was riding towards her. Her belly was warm with it. Here was a man she could trust, who was fine and strong and good, with the ability to make his promises a reality.

Her conscience whispered one last reminder before she let herself be swept away. *You've come to discuss your options, nothing more. Already, you know that one of those options is unacceptable even if he offers it. You cannot run away with him. Remember what he will cost you. It cannot be for ever. It can only be for now.*

But still, he might know a way out that didn't involve dishonouring her family.

Archer's eyes were merry as he pulled close alongside her mare. 'I thought you would never get here.' He leaned from the saddle, angling for a kiss.

'Me?' She laughed, the tension that had plagued her these past few days starting to lift. '*I've* been waiting on *you*.'

'But I'm the one who has been here three days already,' Archer argued pleasantly. She liked the way his eyes settled on her face, the smile on his lips. He cocked his head and studied her, seeing too much, she feared. His smile disappeared. 'What is it? What's wrong?'

'When you offered me protection, what did you mean?' She watched him carefully, knowing those words changed everything. They'd gone from being a casual *affaire* to expectations. He would know now that among her reasons for coming was her desire to claim his promise, one he might not want to have made.

But there was no hesitation from Archer. He was off his horse and at her side, swinging her down. The reins of both horses were in his free hand as he said, 'Let us walk and you will tell me everything. Hold nothing back, Elisabeta, it will do no one any favours.'

She told him all of it; the bedroom full of a harem's furniture, its restraints and potions, its drugs, all of it designed to strip away a participant's choice, none of it meant for mutual pleasure, but instead the pleasure of one man whose satisfaction came from the submission of another. 'He wanted to punish me for the fight at the ball.' She worried her lip as she made her admission. 'I hate that he succeeded. I haven't been able to forget about that room, about the images of what he intended.' They'd haunted her sleep. He'd had his revenge.

'The bastard should be castrated,' Archer ground out when she finished. 'I'm glad you came to me.' He was looking at her with his gaze intense, his mind whirring behind those dark eyes.

'I have to find a way out. I need you to help me think of options,' Elisabeta explained.

Archer gave her a rueful smile. 'Ah, then it's more of a case of running *from* Ridolfo than running *to* me. It's rather a blow to my ego.'

'No, not entirely,' she said quickly, realising her mistake.

Archer stopped walking, the horses halting behind them. 'I would help you regardless. Don't think for a moment my assistance is predicated on having you in my bed. I'm not that sort of a man.' Not a man like Ridolfo who thrived on submission. 'We will think of something. Perhaps there is information that can be leveraged against him, information that he would rather protect in exchange for giving up this marriage. If that fails, I can challenge him to a duel, and should *that* fail, I can always spirit you away.'

He would too, Elisabeta had no doubt. That was something she had to prevent. 'I don't want you ruined in the process, Archer.' She had to draw the line somewhere. This was her mess, not his. 'It is too much to ask of someone who hardly knows me.'

Archer grinned for the first time since she'd begun talking. 'We know each other better than you think.

Still, there is more to learn and we have a week.' He squeezed her hand in reassurance. 'Don't think about him and his lurid promises any more. How much time do we have?'

For ever. No, she couldn't think like that. Her hands played with the reins. 'Just the week. I need to be back in town before the *tratta*. My uncle has business and he expects Giuliano to watch the early horse trials. Giuliano will want my opinion, privately, of course.'

'Of course.' Archer grinned. 'Don't worry, Giuliano's secret is safe with me. How did you manage to get away?'

'I told my uncle I needed to come to terms with the changes in my life. I thought the quiet of the country would do me good, help me clear my mind.'

'And when our week is up? Do you mean to consent even after all Ridolfo has revealed?'

She lowered her eyes. 'I suppose that depends on the options we come up with. Don't ask me for any answers. I came, didn't I? All I know is that I can give you this week.' This week to explore one another along with the options.

'Elisabeta—' he began, but she cut him off, raising her eyes to his once more. Her voice was strict but soft. She wanted no more talk of running away. It was the one option she couldn't allow herself to think of.

'Archer, don't. Don't rail at me for answers I won't or can't give. You know any decision we make will cost dearly. We have a week. That is all that is certain.' Who knew, maybe in a week the bubble would be off their wine. Maybe she'd realise he was only a man with a man's faults, no better than any other. But there was also the risk that after a week, she'd realise something else altogether—that he was *the* one, the *only* one.

Archer smiled, his posture easing. He understood the dilemma even if he didn't want to accept it. 'If it's only a week, let's make it count.'

They did make it count, every hour, every day until the week became a blur of memories: luncheon picnics on hillsides surrounded by olive groves, dinner picnics amid vineyards popping with this season's grapes. Evenings spent in his arms, staring up at the stars. The carriage ride back to her uncle's villa. For all the days she had with him, there were no nights. If there was one blight on the week, that was it.

The servants at the villa expected her to be out visiting or walking to the village, or riding. It was nothing unusual for her to be gone during the day. With no one else to care for at the villa, it was a relief to them to have her taking dinner with one of their neighbours or enjoying a quiet evening entertainment. But it would be irregular indeed if a woman pledged to another did not come home at night. So each night, she left Archer with the promise to see him in the morning.

That didn't mean the days were bereft of passion. There was plenty of opportunity to make love in the outdoors, on picnic blankets during the lazy heat of the afternoon, or in the evenings with early stars overhead. Perhaps more than the picnics and the love-making, there was the talk. The week was a chance to learn about Archer and for him to learn about her.

She treasured each trinket of information; he had an older brother, Dare, who would be an earl some day. He had had a mother he'd loved. He talked of his Newmarket horses and of his home in England. He was like her in that regard. She loved her home in Siena, her life in her uncle's home with Giuliano and Contessina. She had missed it thoroughly when she'd married Lorenzo.

'How can you stand to leave it all?' she murmured one night as they lay together under the stars, their bodies relaxed after wine and love on a blanket, the warm summer breeze passing gently over them, their clothes open and rumpled. She traced a circle around the aureole of his breast with a fingernail. 'It sounds lovely. Don't you miss your family? Surely your father needs you.'

She felt him tense and wished she could take back the words. She'd inadvertently hit on a sore spot and yet some perverse sense of peeling away his layers urged her to go on.

'My father needs no one.' His tone was gruff. 'That's why I left. I'd had enough of jumping into the breach for him time and again, making excuses for him when he was absent. I couldn't live with someone who treated people so callously as if they had no particular worth.'

She knew he meant for her to hear resentment, but Elisabeta heard something else beneath the gruffness. 'You can't stop loving him anyway?' she ventured. She had a little experience with that. Her uncle wasn't perfect, but she knew in her bones that he was the best he could be for her and she loved him anyway.

'Maybe. I don't know if I'd call it love exactly.' Archer paused, his eyes riveted on the stars. 'The thing is, I feel guilty about caring for him. I should feel nothing for him after the last time. What he did was unforgivable.'

She was close to something now, something that defined him at his core. If she could just know it, she would know him. Elisabeta raised up on an arm, lifting her head from his chest. Her voice a mere whisper. 'Tell me, Archer, what did he do that was so bad?'

Archer's eyes glittered in the dark, full of raw emotion. 'He left my mother to die without him.'

The words tumbled out before Archer could stop them, eight words he'd never spoken out loud to another, not even Haviland. These eight words embodied the belief that had driven him from England. He could not stay where his hatred was rooted, could not stay with a man who had so callously disregarded his wife in her last hours, a woman who had given him her life, her love, for thirty years without question even though it had meant leaving her own family behind.

To her credit, Elisabeta said nothing. Another might have tried to soften the thought with useless phrases: you don't mean that, or, surely you're mistaken. But he did mean it, he believed it. He was there. He knew. Elisabeta only nodded her head solemnly and in expectation. There was no going back once the words were out. One could not utter such a sentence and declare the conversation over. The horrible statement deserved explication.

He turned on his side to face Elisabeta, copying her pose. She waited patiently for him to begin, her neutral silence giving him strength. If he could just hold her gaze, focus on her eyes, on the beautiful soul he could see in them, maybe he could get through the telling.

'My mother had consumption.' He began with the facts. Facts hurt less. 'The end was bad, it always is with consumption, and it lingers far past the patient's strength.' It was the first time he had talked of those days. Not even Haviland knew how beautiful, how terrible, those last days were. They were private and painful.

'I sat with her for hours, helpless to do anything more than that. I held her when she coughed and the pain racked her thin body. She had lost so much weight. I gave her water, and later laudanum when the pain was too bad for consciousness. I told her stories, telling back to her all the stories she'd told me in my childhood, taking her back to the home of her youth and the family she hadn't seen in thirty years. When I ran out of stories, I read all of Uncle Giacomo's letters. It was what she'd wanted that last day.' He had to stop and collect himself. Elisabeta reached for his hand and held tight. 'My brother, Dare, sat with us,' he said, able to go on. 'The two of us took turns reading to her.'

'And your father? Where was he?' Elisabeta encouraged softly.

'In Newmarket. His prize mare was in foal.' The bitterness in his tone was unmistakable. Even after all these months, it still rankled that he could have walked out on her for a horse. 'The mare gave birth to a fine filly. He named her Vittoria in my mother's honour.

'It was the last straw for me. All my life, he'd been absent when we, or others who claimed friendship with him, had needed him. Dare tried to stop me, but I wouldn't listen. When my father arrived home that night, I took a swing at him. I knocked him to the ground.' They had fought until Dare and some footmen had been able to separate them. He had some regrets over that choice—a son does not hit his father easily—but those regrets were not enough to stay. 'My father knew when he made his decision that morning that she would not be there when he returned,' Archer bit out. 'He said it was too hard to watch her die, so he left—' he scoffed here '—as if it was any easier for the rest of us to watch it, to participate in it.' He held Elisabeta's gaze.

'She was the beauty in our lives, the light. She kept the three of us united. Unity is not an easy thing to come by in a household of stubborn males who only got more stubborn as they got older. What we wouldn't do for each other, we'd do for her. *Capisce?*' Archer said softly. 'My uncle says she was always like that. She could get a man to do just about anything.'

'She sounds like a wonderful woman,' Elisabeta said softly, her tone urging him to go on, and he did. He couldn't seem to stop talking.

'Oh, she was. It's been almost a year since she passed. Part of me hopes missing her will get better. But part of me hopes it doesn't. If I am missing her, I am also remembering her.' Archer paused and gave her a considering look, his mind working behind his dark eyes. His voice was quiet, almost reverent when he spoke. 'Sometimes I feel that if I stop missing her,

I'll stop remembering how much she meant to me, how much she did for me and for my brother, how much she must have given up.' He shook his head. 'I had no true idea how much she must have sacrificed to come to England until I came here. She had a family, a good one, and she never saw them again.'

'She had a new family in you and your brother and your father. Perhaps that was enough, or perhaps it was all she wanted,' Elisabeta said. 'I often think if I had a family like that of my own, it would be enough.' It was her turn to hesitate. Archer watched her worry her lip, choosing her words carefully as if voicing them for the first time. 'You might find me selfish, but I think it would be wonderful to have a small family, just a husband and children, all to myself, to never have to worry about cousins and aunts and uncles and how everything I did affected every one of them. There would only be my nose in my own business.' She shuddered. 'It sounds so ungrateful when I say it out loud, forgive me.'

Elisabeta sat up and reached for the forgotten bottle of wine and their empty glasses. She sloshed the bottle. There was a little left. She split it between the glasses and handed him one, a smile on her face. 'Drink a toast with me, to her memory, and to her sons.'

They drank before Elisabeta set aside her glass and moved over him, straddling his thighs, her hand cupping him. He could feel himself rouse to the squeeze and caress of her fingers, of her nails, running along the inside of his thigh.

'What did I do to deserve this treat?' Archer put

his hands at her waist, his thumbs pressed low on her hips.

She bent over him, her hair brushing his nipples as she took his mouth in a generous kiss. 'You told me. Thank you.' She stroked him hard then, his arousal flaring to full life. She rose above him and came down on his cock, confident and sure of its entry. She moved on him, and Archer groaned. Had anything felt this good? Felt this full of life? Of hope? When she rode him, when they were together, anything was possible. He let his climax come hard and swift, his body bucking against hers, his head arched to the sky, the stars witnessing his pleasure even as they witnessed the silent realisation of his mind. He had only one night left and he had yet to convince her she had options.

Chapter Thirteen

It was to be their last night. Elisabeta's hands trembled as she fastened a necklace, a simple gold chain with a gold heart-shaped locket, about her neck. The week had flown. In the beginning it had seemed like an abundance of time, but now the hourglass that held the sands of her freedom was rapidly emptying. They'd not spoken again of her choices, opting instead to speak of themselves and getting to know one another in a fuller sense. She knew what it meant: there were no options that allowed her to deny Ridolfo without shaming her family.

She pushed the thought away and stepped back from the mirror, running her hands over the folds of her skirt. She would not sully the evening with thoughts of the future. Tonight, she couldn't think of what came tomorrow, only what came now. She'd dressed carefully with that in mind. Archer had said only that he had something planned, something special. Although that was true of everything they'd done this week. Every picnic, every walk had been special. Every day had been special, but this evening the night would have its moment. The arrangements had demanded a little subterfuge. She'd told the staff at the villa she was spending the night with friends. The entire week, she and Archer had been careful to plan their days away from the villas where no one would see them, where no one was likely to recognise them and pass that sighting on to family members.

Elisabeta stepped back from the mirror. She'd brought the dress on a whim, a bold red silk cut tight through the bodice and full through the skirts. It wasn't exactly the kind of dress one took to the country. It was better suited to a grand ball, or a seduction. Elisabeta smiled. That made it perfect for tonight. It was time to go.

Archer seemed to be of the same mind. When she arrived, he came out to meet her dressed in dark evening clothes, immaculately groomed. 'My lady.' He helped her down from the carriage. 'You have rendered me speechless with your beauty.'

'As you have rendered me with yours,' she replied, liking the way his gaze lingered on her in appreciation. That alone made hauling the dress out to the country worthwhile. She let her own gaze linger too. She had seen him in formal attire before. The night of the Pantera party he'd come dressed up, but there'd not been time to drink in the sight of him. She was not in the habit of thinking of him as the son of an English lord. It was easy to forget all that when she saw him working with the horses or tramping through the countryside in dusty boots and a loose shirt. On those occasions, he was only Archer Crawford, and this week she'd only thought of him as hers. Not as a lord's son, not as a member of a rival *contrada*, just hers. It was a dangerous way to think of him.

'I have set up our meal al fresco. Shall we?' He tucked her hand through his arm and led her to the olive grove where candles were lit on a white-clothed table. Wine stood uncorked, waiting to be poured, and covered dishes couldn't quite hide their delicious smells.

'Oh.' A little gasp of delight escaped her. 'Archer, it's wonderful.' She couldn't imagine a lovelier setting, the stars coming out overhead, the candles flickering in their protective glass.

He held out her chair and poured the wine, serving her before he raised his goblet in a toast. 'To one more night with the most beautiful woman in the world.'

She blushed. He had a way of making her believe it was true, of making the words sound like more than empty flattery. Perhaps that was part of his charm, part of the reason she'd found him irresistible from the start. He gave a woman his attention, and in doing so, he gave her his sincerity. The woman he loved would never feel like a possession. She would feel cherished.

Archer lifted the cover off a gorgeous green salad of arugula and pear sprinkled with slivers of pecorino.

'We are entirely alone. I've sent everyone home, so you'll have to suffer my poor attempts to serve.'

He gave her a wink and took her plate, filling it with the summer greens. They ate in the slow Italian style of courses, moving languorously through the dishes, savouring the tastes and the conversation. *Insalata* gave way to pasta with bits of mushroom and pancetta mixed with it, and more pasta, this one with a meat sauce. The loaf of bread disappeared slice by slice, one bottle of wine gave way to two. The candles burned down, the stars twinkled, the night deepened.

She could not recall a time when she'd laughed so much. He told her stories of his childhood, the things he'd done that he probably shouldn't have, such as the time he'd skipped out on lessons with his tutor to go swimming. 'I got out of the river to find my clothes missing.' Archer chuckled. 'My tutor was standing there, though, looking none too pleased. When I asked where my clothes were he said, "You took away my time, so I have taken away your clothes." He gave me a choice. I could either walk home naked or I could give him double time the next day on my Latin.' Archer made a face. 'I gave him double time on my Latin, of course, but it was the last time I skipped lessons. Four hours of Latin is a horrible punishment to inflict on a boy.'

Elisabeta smiled, imagining the boy in the man seated at the table. 'Were you always so rebellious?'

'Only when there's something I want badly enough. Rebellion is most useful when used sparingly, otherwise it loses its point.' Archer's hand closed over hers, his eyes holding hers, his meaning clear. He wanted her, was willing to fight for her if she would let him.

He let her hand go and reached for a small box tied with a ribbon. 'I have something for you, I almost forgot.'

A present. For her. She felt the sudden sting of

tears over the little wood box. It was silly and yet when had someone given her a gift for no particular reason? She couldn't remember. Elisabeta untied the ribbon, almost reluctant to ruin the idea of a present by opening it. Inside was a small, carved wooden horse, polished with a chestnut stain. She smiled, recognising it immediately. 'It's my mare.'

Elisabeta ran her hand over the smooth lines of the carving, a suspicion taking root. 'Did you make this? It's beautiful.' She could see that he had. The praise made him uncomfortable. The ever-confident Archer squirmed slightly in his seat.

'It's just a little thing, it's not fancy.'

'It's a *treasure*,' she corrected. Because it was from him. Because it might be the only thing she ever had of him after tonight. 'Every time I look at it, I'll remember our afternoon ride, and I'll remember this evening when you gave it to me.' She was nearly beside herself with the pleasures of the evening. Never had she been romanced so thoroughly, or so well: the food, the wine, the stories, the laughter, the gift. But it was his next words that had her melting.

Archer rose from the table and held out his hand to her, his eyes an amber smoulder. 'Elisabeta, come to bed with me.'

She met his gaze evenly and slid her hand into his with a single whisper of the word 'yes'. She knew even as she said it, as they climbed the stairs, tonight was a watershed. Tonight's intimacy would be different than any of the intimacy they had previously shared. Tonight would push them closer to resolution one way or another.

Everything that had transpired between them had

led to this. To this room lit by candles, and scented with sage and thyme, to this bed with its quilt drawn back revealing clean, simple white sheets. To this moment, with this man. Elisabeta swallowed. Tonight they would be naked together in a bed. This would be unlike anything they'd done so far. The thought came to her suddenly. It would be like a wedding night, a real wedding night, with a man who knew what he was about and who cared for her. It made her nervous and excited all at once. But Archer was all confidence, guiding her to a chair near the bed, stepping away from her to remove his coat and his shoes.

His hand worked his cravat free, drawing it from around his neck before his fingers deftly worked the cufflinks at his wrists, making his intentions plain. He meant to disrobe for her, meant for her to watch him. 'Look at me, Elisabeta.' His voice gave the low command. 'Tonight, I would come to you as Adam came to Eve.'

Her throat went dry, expectation replacing her nerves. He made an offering of himself then, stripping off his waistcoat and shirt to reveal the muscled planes of his torso, the broad shoulders, the tapered waist where his hands rested in provocative suggestion, his thumbs hooked at the waistband of his trousers, his hands spanning his hips, fingertips pointing towards that most manly part of him. She could not ignore it, nor did she want to. She was eager for it, to see with her eyes the unadulterated sight of the phallus that roused to her touch. She had felt it, massaged it, seen it in part, but always his clothes obscured it in some way. Tonight, it was to be completely on display for her, every glorious inch.

Archer pushed his trousers past lean hips, his eyes watching her watching him, his movements confident, but she caught a flash of caution in his eyes. He wanted to please her, wanted her *to be* pleased by the sight of him, she realised. It was rather novel to think of the competent, self-assured Archer as having doubts of his appeal. But he need not have worried. He did not disappoint. She inhaled sharply, a reverently breathed 'oh' escaping when she exhaled. 'Oh, Archer. *Che bello, molto bello.*' The words were entirely inadequate. This was no sickly adolescent boy who stood before her. Fully naked, he was Adam and Adonis, Prometheus and Apollo all in one, his phallus a gorgeous jutting obelisk, a pillar of masculine strength at the dark core of him.

He let her feast, her eyes devouring him. He had done this for her, to put her at ease. He would not undress her as if she were his to command, to do with as he pleased. He would meet her naked as an equal.

She rose. It was up to her now and she was eager for it. She wanted to be naked with him, wanted him to see her as he had not seen her in their earlier encounters. He too had only seen parts of her, but not the whole, not all at once. She would give it to him, her gift. 'Sit for me, Archer. It's your turn now to look at me.'

She managed the fastenings of her gown with hasty fingers, letting it slide from her body like a curtain falling away to reveal a piece of art. She let the candlelight play across her body, the light casting provocative shadows and highlights over her breasts, over the triangle between her thighs. Archer's eyes went dark and she revelled in his overt response.

She lifted a leg, balancing her foot on his knee and slowly rolled down a stocking, offering him a tantalising view of long, slim limb and feminine juncture. She shifted legs and watched his throat work.

Elisabeta stepped back and lifted the chemise of thin summer cotton over her head, knowing that when she did, she'd be fully exposed to him, every private inch open to his perusal. She wanted to tell him, wanted him to know. 'You're my first...' she began, the words coming awkwardly.

Archer rose from the chair and came to her, drawing her close, taking her mouth in a slow kiss before he spoke, his body bare and hot against her. 'Your first what?' His words feathered against her lips.

'I've never been naked with a man before.'

He smiled, his forehead pressed against hers, his words a sibilant seduction. 'There's nothing better than naked sex. Let me show you what I mean.'

Yes, show me, love me. This was what a wedding night was supposed to be, this reverent consummation of passion. She craved him body and mind. She went easily when he urged her backwards to the bed, his body following her down, covering her with his strength, with his length. This was straightforward lovemaking at its finest if not its most sophisticated. Archer's body was above her, his arms bracketing her head, muscles tensed to take his weight, her legs open to him, his phallus brushing against her curls as he levered himself into position.

He thrust, and she closed her eyes, letting go of everything, letting her senses wrap around the totality of this pleasure, the feel of him moving in her, of her own response to him. He was driving them towards union, towards climax. His command came hoarse and guttural. 'Look at me, Elisabeta, I want to be in your eyes when we shatter. I want you to see what you do to me.'

Her eyes flew open and the intimacy of their act ratcheted to another level. To see him, to see the intensity of his desire in those beautiful eyes, was like seeing to the depths of him. He was exposed intimately to her in those final thrusts, locked to her in gaze and in body in a connection that transcended pleasure. In these moments she was worshipped entirely by his body, by his mind, by his soul. She'd never known anything finer. This was perfection personified.

But perfection could not be sustained. It existed in moments only and it did not solve any of her problems. When she spiralled back to earth, drowsy in Archer's arms, she was still Elisabeta di Nofri, desired by one man who promised her personal protection, but betrothed to another who had no intention of loving her, only possessing her by whatever means possible. She was still a woman who had to make a dreadful choice: to trade her family's pride for her happiness or enter into an unholy alliance in order to preserve it. But she was different. No one could make love the way they had and not be changed by it. But for what purpose? And how?

She didn't need to know, not yet. The night had hours to go, and Archer had stamina to match. But all the slow, lingering lovemaking in the world could not hold back the night and eventually the dark realm of their passion slipped its leash, letting sunrise and reality intrude.

* * *

'I have to go,' she murmured as the sun filtered through the high window. She slid out of bed before Archer could protest, before she lost her resolve. Workers would be arriving. Horses would need to be fed. Her own villa would be expecting her to come and claim her trunks. She was supposed to set out for home today. She reached for her clothes, gathering them up from the floor. The sheets rustled as Archer shifted. She could feel his eyes on her as she pulled on her chemise.

'Go where? To him?' There was heat in his words as he levered up on an arm.

She gave an exasperated sigh as much for herself as for him. 'Archer, what choice do I have?' Why did he insist on this discussion? It always ended in an impasse. She turned to look at him, but that was a mistake. Archer by morning presented a different kind of sensuality, one that was no less potent or persuasive than his brand of midnight seduction. A sheet lay draped across his hips, his torso exposed, muscled and smooth and tanned from days in the sun—days he'd worked shirtless alongside the grooms. The image sent a bolt of uncontrolled lust through her. She was giving up all of this for a marriage with a man who saw her as nothing more than a slave to his pleasure? But she knew why.

'You have every choice,' Archer fired back. 'You want your freedom, well, take it. I am giving it to you.' He waved a hand in the air. 'How can you walk away from this, from me, from what we shared last night?'

That made her angry. Didn't he understand how

brave she had to be to do just that? He'd all but called her a coward. She jerked on her gown and shoved her feet into her slippers. 'My family's honour demands it. Honour is no small thing in this part of the world, in case you haven't noticed.'

Now it was his turn to hurt. Her sharp words had found their target as she'd known they would. He prided himself on being a man of honour. But Archer was not so easily felled.

'Nor is it in mine,' he replied. 'What of your personal honour? Is that a smaller consideration?'

'It is my personal honour to be of use to my family.' She came to sit at the edge of the bed. She didn't want to fight with him, she just wanted him to understand. This decision was not easy. 'When my parents were killed, my uncle took me in without hesitation or reluctance—another mouth to feed, another girl to bring up, another marriage to arrange. He spared no expense. I was older than Contessina and he begrudged me nothing, even knowing his own daughter would need all the same expensive trappings to make her bow to society a few years later.

'Now, he has found me another wealthy marriage to replace the one I lost. If I bow out, I will shame him. Worse than that, I could cause actual physical hurt. I do not want Giuliano or my uncle involved in any duel of honour over me. How would I ever face my aunt again, knowing I had killed her son or her husband? What I do reflects directly on them. Whether I agree with the system or not, my family is responsible for me. I will not have them dragged down because of my selfishness.'

Archer's eyes were hard. 'I understand your ar-

gument and in theory I respect your commitment
to your family, but I cannot agree to it in practice.'

Elisabeta rose from the bed. She'd failed to persuade him. '*You* don't have to.' She headed towards
the door—better to leave on this note than a more
dangerous one, a more tempting one.

His voice halted her. 'You're not thinking clearly
right now. Will you promise me one thing before you
go?' Archer stayed in bed. Smart man. He knew better than to try to force her acquiescence. 'Do nothing hasty. I will be in town soon. I have to bring the
horses for the *tratta*. Wait for me. I will think of
something. Trust me.'

'And will you promise me something? Stop making it harder than it is,' she shot back. He had to let
her go for his own sake. *Stop showing me what is
possible between a man and woman. You can stop
tempting me with a future that doesn't exist. You can
stop making me love you.* But it was too late for that.

She already did and that damning thought followed her home. She had fallen for Archer Crawford.
It wasn't supposed to happen like that. He was supposed to have been her tool only, a stranger passing
through who could appease her desire, her curiosity,
a safe harbour in which to satisfy both. She had not
expected any of this to happen when she'd tempted
him into the alley. He'd been part experimentation,
part discreet rebellion. He was never supposed to
part of her future.

Chapter Fourteen

The future was an uncertain thing indeed. If anyone had told him four months ago his uncle would hand him his dream on a platter, he would have been thrilled beyond words. Yet now, the dream seemed tarnished, not exactly the shining opportunity he'd once thought it was.

It was one of the many thoughts that occupied Archer's mind as he sat at the long table inside the villa with his uncle who had come out to see the horses one last time before the *tratta*. Needless to say, it was not one of the thoughts he should have had his mind on. None of the thoughts were. He should not be thinking of the forbidden Elisabeta or what he could do to dissuade her from her stubborn refusal.

'Life at the villa suits you.' His uncle poured them a glass of wine, cheerfully oblivious to his distraction.

'It does,' Archer answered truthfully. His time here had been all he'd hoped, further proof that he'd chosen well in coming to Siena. He was his own man here, as he hoped he would be, and he was connecting for the first time with a family he'd always known existed, but had never known in person.

'The two chestnuts are coming along.' His uncle picked up a cluster of grapes from the platter between them, settling in for a discussion of the horses and which ones Archer would bring back with him for the *tratta*.

Archer nodded in agreement. 'Their legs are strong. They are cornering well.' Archer had studied the maps of the Palio course, the circular track of the race. 'Either of them will be able to navigate San Martino's curve.' It was the most dangerous turn of the Palio course and the bane of many horses. Of course, the horse's skill wasn't the only factor, just the only factor that could be trained for. Successful cornering also depended on whether or not another rider was out to cause a wreck and that depended on what *partiti* had been struck between you and other *contradas*.

'Which other horses do you think we should bring to the *tratta*?' The *tratta* was the official selection of the horses, held three days before the Palio itself. The question was asked casually, but Archer did not miss the honour the question did him. Once more, his uncle had asked for his opinion, a sign that he was willing to be guided by Archer's choice.

'I think there will be two more plus the chestnuts ready to go.' Archer named them, watching his uncle nod.

'What about the grey?' his uncle asked when he finished.

Archer shook his head without hesitation. 'He's too green. The horse is fast, but he is skittish. I don't think he will respond well to the noise and activity on the day of the Palio. I've run some simulations out here with gunfire and they haven't gone well. But he is young. Next year, perhaps.'

His uncle's face broke into a grin, and he slapped his knee with a hearty chuckle. 'Spoken like a true Ricci! One would never guess this is your first Palio, *mio nipote*. There wasn't an ounce of prevarication to your answer either. You've got spine.' His eyes twinkled proudly. 'But we knew that the moment you got up to trouble in Pantera.'

Archer grinned but he was instantly on alert. The conversation was moving on from horses and he wasn't sure he wanted it to. He'd hoped 'out of sight, out of mind' had been good not only for the *contrada* tensions. 'I trust the situation in town has cooled in my absence,' he said neutrally.

His uncle shrugged and waved a hand in dismissal. 'It has. The lady's uncle did his part as well. He announced the engagement, and the wedding will take place the end of August. Oca is satisfied now that it is official. I heard Ranieri gave her a tour of his home and then the bride-to-be took herself off to the country to "reflect". A nice house and full coffers can do much to change a woman's head. Women are eminently practical creatures when it comes down to it.'

So that was how her uncle was playing it. His own uncle was watching him carefully for a reaction. Archer was equally careful not to give one. He knew a different interpretation of the reason for her visit to the country and had a far different understanding of the visit to Ridolfo Ranieri's home. He could not tolerate the thought of all her beauty and passion sacrificed to a man she didn't love, a man who didn't respect her. But she would do it for the sake of her family. Only he stood between her and that decision.

'It is for the best, don't you agree?' His uncle's probe was not so subtle. 'A beautiful, fiery woman left unwed can be dangerous for a family, especially if she's widowed and thinks she might act on her own.'

'In England a widow has certain social privileges,' Archer offered a veiled defence.

'A discreet widow here might manage the same,' his uncle acquiesced but the implication was obvious. Elisabeta di Norfi hadn't been discreet and in her indiscretion had sacrificed that privilege. 'In any case, such a woman isn't for you. You've mentioned you are not intending to marry in the near future. Is that still true?' More not-so-subtle probing on his uncle's part.

'How do you like it out here at the villa with the horses? I'm told constantly about what a fine job you're doing here. The men say they've never seen someone who knows so much about horses and that you're a bruising rider.'

It was the praise, the recognition Archer had once hoped to acquire. Now that it had come, Archer was wary of it, linked as it was to his marital prospects and the direction in which those prospects should be aimed.

'I like it out here very much. It has proven to me that I made the right choice in coming.' Archer could see his uncle's approval in the nod of his head. He ventured the next part. 'I would like to purchase a property of my own. I want to make my home here.

I am done with England.' The words should have excited him. It had been a plan of his for many months as this tour had come together. Today, those words left him empty. Staying meant he couldn't run off with Elisabeta, couldn't take her away from Ridolfo, although it was unclear that was something she'd even allow.

'And done with your father, no doubt?' Uncle Giacomo said shrewdly. 'But I would warn you, distance alone won't solve your problems.' He pointed to his chest. 'Your father is your father, your flesh and blood, your family. He will always be with you.'

His uncle leaned forward. 'You need to work out for yourself if you're running *from* your father or *to* your mother's family.' Hadn't he said something similar to Elisabeta? There wasn't time to think about it. His uncle continued, 'Rest assured, we're glad to have you and to that end, I have a proposition I want to discuss with you. I want you to take over the villa and the horses.' He could live here year-round. It was a generous offer, one that spoke to his uncle's wealth that he could simply give over a villa without a moment's hesitation and one that spoke to the family's generous acceptance of him.

In the Italian view, Archer didn't have a choice. Family was family. Still, not everyone had uncles giving them villas. The offer touched him. The offer changed everything. He had something now beyond himself to offer Elisabeta, a respectable life. What would she make of this offer and what it might afford her? 'You are too good, Uncle…' Archer began delicately, wondering what his uncle wanted in exchange for this generosity. He felt guilty too. Perhaps this was a reward for having given up Elisabeta?

His uncle shrugged and made a small gesture. 'I would be honoured to have your family in this house in the future.'

In those moments, Uncle Giacomo seemed to live his years. Usually energetic, shrewd and sharp, Uncle Giacomo appeared ageless, certainly younger than his fifty-two years. In the letters written to his mother, Uncle Giacomo had taken on an immortal image to a young, impressionable Archer; the older brother who never made mistakes, who was the main-stay of the family through the decades, a fortress of stability, an enduring rock.

Not so now. It struck Archer how much loss his uncle had endured over the years: his younger brother, Pietro, dead on a dare at thirty in an accident that occurred when racing a horse through the cob-blestone streets; his sought-after sister married to an Englishman and carried away, never to be seen again except in letters; his own wife childless. For a man who valued family, Uncle Giacomo's had dwindled.

His uncle leaned across the table and gripped Ar-cher's wrist. 'It means everything to your aunt and me to have you here. You must never think of your-self as a burden. Family is never a burden. You're very like her, you know.' His uncle's eyes were sad. 'I wish I could have seen her again. Was she happy?'

'For the most part.' Archer would not lie to this man. 'My father is sometimes a difficult man to live with. He wants his way in all things.'

'Vittoria knew that before she married him. But he was a handsome man and wealthy. He rode like a master and cut a romantic figure. All the ladies in the *contrada* were taken with him.' Giacomo sighed. 'They all found his occasional aloofness romantic. Women, who understands them? All that brooding was attractive to them. I found it tiresome. I always thought the match an odd one. The Riccis are not poor people, but we have no title, we are not a noble family, just a rich one with horses and property. I would have thought your father would prefer a wife with a different sort of background. But in the end, love overrode all those considerations.' He held up a hand when Archer would have protested. 'He did love her, Archer, no matter what you think. Some people just have difficulty expressing it.'

His uncle rose from the table, his composure restored. Archer rose with him. His uncle placed a kiss on each cheek. 'Bring the horses up to town in a couple of days. The Palio track is being laid and there will be unofficial night trials before the *tratta*. Bring a few riders with you—you can't ride possibly ride all four horses at once.'

'Ride?' Archer queried, unable to believe the good luck that had just landed in his lap, and then he questioned it. Perhaps this too was a reward for good behaviour—good behaviour that hadn't happened.

His uncle laughed. 'Just for the night trials. Don't go getting any ideas.' His uncle waggled a finger at him playfully. 'You've done well, Archer. I am proud and your mother would be proud too.' He lowered his voice. 'Did she ever tell you that she rode in the night trials once? No? She did. The riders are all amateurs, the real jockeys don't usually risk it. She was in disguise, of course. No one recognised her except

Pietro and me. We were furious with her for taking such a chance, but who could deny her when she rode so well? Eh?' He clapped Archer on the shoulder.

His uncle felt in his pocket. 'I nearly forgot this. A letter came for you yesterday.'

Archer studied the outside, recognising the firm hand immediately. It was from Haviland, and Archer scanned the contents with a smile. It would be good to see him. 'My friends will be in town for the race.'

'They will stay with us,' his uncle volunteered. 'It will be good to have a house full of young men. We'll see you in town soon.'

Town. A chance to prove himself once more, a chance to move one step closer to his dream if he still wanted it, a chance to make good on his promise to Elisabeta. But it came at a price. He would have to act soon. It looked like Haviland and company was just in time. He could use a friend or two or three.

Archer stayed at the table long after his uncle left. He fingered the letter, his thoughts coming fast. He was excited to see his friends. He'd missed them and he needed them. But when he and Haviland had decided to rejoin forces in Siena plans had been different. He'd thought he'd be riding in the race. He'd also not thought he might be potentially fleeing the city with a woman in tow.

Admittedly, the last was putting the cart before the horse. Elisabeta had not agreed to anything. But the bottom line was still the same: he'd thought things would be different, more settled, when he'd made the suggestion to Haviland.

He wasn't sure how his friends would feel to arrive and then potentially be separated again, especially Haviland, who was arriving with a wife in tow. He wasn't sure at all how Haviland would feel about dragging her into this mess. In fact, he wasn't sure how forgiving Brennan and Nolan would feel. He'd left without telling them, leaving Haviland to explain. And now, he might potentially be doing the same thing all over again when they arrived. He'd invited them to travel across Europe at the expense of cutting down their time in the Alps only to run out on them again.

Archer played with a corner of the letter. These were answers he didn't have—yet. But he would, soon. The Palio had become a dream and a deadline.

Chapter Fifteen

The night trials; a chance to be free, a chance to be wild, a chance to prove to herself, if no one else, that her life wasn't over, a chance to escape reality for just a few giddy moments. Elisabeta twisted her long hair up under a cap and checked her reflection in the mirror, making sure her disguise was intact. Women didn't ride in the unofficial night trials. She laughed a little at the syllogism the idea created: women didn't ride in the night trials; Elisabeta di Nofri was riding in the trials, therefore, Elisabeta di Nofri couldn't be a woman.

Sometimes she wished she wasn't. If she were a man, she wouldn't be facing an unwanted marriage, or a lifetime of men making life-changing decisions for her. She would be free to live in the country, surrounded by her horses, to marry where she would and when she wanted. Her life would be her own. She gave a wry smile. But then there were other things she would have missed, like Archer.

She couldn't change the past or what she was. All she could do was take refuge in the idea that the syllogism would protect her tonight as much as the disguise. People didn't expect to see a woman ride so they simply wouldn't scrutinise her too much. It would be dark as well and that would be additional camouflage.

Who else would be there? Would Archer come to watch the trials? Maybe he would be there to ride. The riders tonight would all be amateurs. The night trials were for the horses, a chance to practise on the Palio track. A thrill of excitement went through her at the prospect of seeing him. She had been patient as he'd asked. Would he bring answers that she could live with? It had taken all her fortitude to leave him in the country. She didn't relish the idea of having to walk away from him again. If she did, this time would be the last time.

There was a low whistle outside her window, Giuliano's signal that all was clear. It was time to go. Tonight, she would ride and ride, and for a little while, no man would stand in her way.

La terra in piazza were the first words to run through Elisabeta's mind when she saw the track. It was well after midnight but even in the dark, she could sense the transformation of the town's central piazza into a race track. The excitement she'd grown up with as a child swept through her anew. The expression *there was dirt in the piazza* also translated into an expression of hope. *La terra in piazza*—there is dirt in the piazza—was one of the first expressions any Sienese learned. It meant not only that the Palio was coming, but that good times were coming again. Everything would be better soon. This year, more than ever, she wanted that to be true. But what good times awaited her?

Giuliano led out one of her uncle's three hopeful contenders, and she grinned when she saw the bay—the gelding was one of her favourites. Giuliano tossed her up with a wink. 'Have fun.'

'Thank you for this.' She squeezed his hand as she gathered the reins and settled on the horse's bare back. All the horses were ridden without saddles or stirrups for the race. She and Giuliano had negotiated something more than a truce for the debacle at the party, each them understanding they bore part of the blame. She was cognizant of his attempts to make up to her for his part in the trouble. She'd done her part too. She'd been the model dutiful niece since her return from the country, going everywhere with an appropriate cortège of women from the household, or with her uncle and Giuliano as escorts. No one could say she'd been indiscreet, giving credence to Giuliano's report that she'd had nothing to do with the Englishman at the party. No one would suspect she was anything but the dutiful bride-to-be.

She wondered if she'd managed to fool Ridolfo, or if he saw through her charade of compliance. The cruel visit to his home still haunted her. He had not said anything to her uncle about the outcome of the visit. He knew very well he couldn't without exposing his part in provoking her. He knew too that her uncle would not tolerate such threats aimed at his niece.

Secrecy worked in his favour. By not telling, Ridolfo had taken away a piece of her leverage. She could not use his threats to break the betrothal. He was a shrewd opponent who understood human nature far too well. He knew how to use her very nature against her.

She would not think about him tonight, not when there were horses to think about. Elisabeta turned her horse towards the track, joining the other riders. That was when she saw *him*, tall and proud on the back of a strong chestnut horse. Archer was here.

Her pulse leapt in recognition, but she could do nothing more to acknowledge his presence at the moment without giving herself away. That would have to wait until later. Until then, she would have a little fun of her own.

Elisabeta lined up in a group that contained Archer and his horse. For these amateur trials, horses usually raced in smaller groups of five or six so the track wasn't as crowded. Someone acted as the starter and there was a rope stretched across the starting line to simulate the race conditions. Around the track, spectators had gathered to take notes on the contenders, most of them were *capitani* who would vote on the ten horses in a few days at the *tratta*.

The signal came to start, the rope dropped and they were off, flying through the straight away and then into the San Martino curve. It was sharp, a few degrees over a right angle, but her horse managed beautifully, not losing pace as he exited the turn and headed into another straight-away zone. Archer was in front of her, riding well, but she knew this track better. She would make her move after the Casato turn.

She did, urging her bay to slowly eliminate the gap between them. Predictably, Archer slowed for the curve, wanting to learn its nuances and degrees. It was a sound strategy. While the San Martino curve posed a continual danger throughout the race, most accidents that happened on the Casato, happened during the first lap. But she had the edge of experience here and she used it to push her mount through the backside of the turn and surge to full speed in the last straight away of the first lap. She knew her own surge of satisfaction as she passed Archer, her horse stretching its legs into the second lap of the race.

The second lap was more difficult. She'd not been in the lead for the first and that made her job more defined. She knew she had to move the horse through the group, had to make up ground. But now, she was in the lead and the ride was different. She had to defend that lead. That meant racing the track with all its inclines, declines and curves, but also racing to prevent others from passing her. She was particularly conscious of Archer behind her, his chestnut yearning to pass.

She took the second lap and moved into the third and final, paying attention to her horse's physical response to the exercise. How was his breathing? How was his pacing? These were the items a rider paid attention to in the trials. They were far more important than winning an unofficial trial. Giuliano would want a full report from her and from the other two riders of the condition of the track, their horses and the horses they had ridden against. He would use her report for planning the *partiti*.

Elisabeta cursed as Archer sped past her in the straight away after the San Martino turn. She'd been overly cautious in the turn, not wanting to tax a tiring mount further and he'd taken advantage of it. Tonight, she wouldn't stand for it. Elisabeta pulled even with him at the Casato turn and surged, forcing him to let her cut ahead unless he wanted to risk being pushed into the wall.

Merda! For the second time the same horse and rider had passed him. That alone was enough to make them interesting to Archer. The derrière on the rider made them even more so. Even in the dark, even with his body and mind filled with the adrenaline of the race, he wasn't so far gone he couldn't tell a woman's backside from a man's. Archer made a final push to catch the pair before the finish line, but there simply wasn't enough ground to make up the distance.

Giacomo and some other men from the *contrada* came out to congratulate him, exclaiming over the horse. Giacomo was already asking questions about the ride: what was the corner like? How did the horse handle at the Casato curve? Archer answered, but his eyes were drawn to the horse and rider to his left. 'Who brought that horse? The one that beat me?'

'Rafaele di Bruno's, I think,' Giacomo replied, eager to get back to the subject of their horses. That information confirmed his growing suspicion. Rafaele di Bruno was Elisabeta's uncle. Since these trials weren't about the *contrada*, but about the horses, it wasn't inconceivable that she had managed to wrangle a chance to ride disguised. After all, he had been given the same opportunity sans disguise. Suddenly, he wanted nothing more than to be done with his uncle's questions. He wanted to be free to go after her.

'I'll write up a report if you like,' he offered to

Giacomo. 'We can go over it in the morning.' He clapped his uncle on the shoulder and disappeared into the crowd of horses and men before Giacomo could protest.

It was no easy feat to find Elisabeta. The area was full of horses moving on and off the track with their riders as the second group came on. There were spectators too, even though it was well after midnight. The *capitani* had brought their *mangini*, which made for at least three people from each of the seventeen *contrada* present, plus grooms and riders. Unofficial these races might be, but they were full-fledged events none the less.

Luck was with him. He caught sight of her finally on the edge of the busyness and alone. He approached, not daring to use her name. He hailed her with a compliment instead, letting his smile and his eyes say the rest of it. 'That was an excellent piece of riding out there.'

She looked at him, letting her face do the same, and he felt his body stir to life as if it had been dead since she'd left.

'How are you?' Archer pitched his voice low, watching her face.

'I am well. How are you?' But it was a lie. Up close, he could make out the tightness of her jaw, the faint show of shadows beneath her eyes.

'It's no good, Elisabeta. I can see that you are not entirely all right. We must talk, we must plan in earnest now if you are to escape this marriage. I have ideas.' He did, just not ideas that she would approve of. She wanted it all. To lose the family was to lose everything. In light of that, no price was too great to pay. It was what he admired about her. But he would have to persuade her otherwise.

She stiffened suddenly, her eyes going to a spot over his shoulder. 'I have to go. Giuliano is looking for me.' She hesitated, her voice so low he nearly missed it. Her body brushed against his ever so slightly, the feel of it erotic for its brevity. 'Archer, light a candle.'

'Yes,' came his hoarse agreement. What would it have been like to have known her earlier? Would he have had a chance to win her? Perhaps being from Torre would not have mattered if his timing had been better.

Archer lit the candle, knowing full well she meant to come to him. He would have liked to have argued with her. He'd gladly have risked going to her, would have gladly risked the consequence of him being caught, but there'd been no time to plead his case. So here he was, at nearly three o'clock in the morning, lying abed alert, and hard, waiting. Hoping. Admittedly a position he was not used to. He was a man of action and this delicate dance of subterfuge was testing him sorely.

Had this been how Haviland had felt in Paris with Alyssandra: this desperation in wanting to seize every moment because it was going to end? Haviland had known the date of that end too, it had loomed on their travel calendar as a day in early June, just as the end for him and Elisabeta loomed as the day of her wedding approached in late August. Haviland had dealt with his desperation by changing the date to for ever and then by changing his circumstances. He'd decided to no longer be a traveller, to no longer be a man seeking a temporary escape from his burdens. He simply gave the burdens up and by doing so those burdens lost the ability to define his life.

Archer couldn't do that. For one, he wasn't temporarily escaping. He'd decided from the outset that this was permanent for him. He wasn't going back. His burdens had been given up. His situation, unfortunately, didn't mirror Haviland's. The fact that he was staying permanently in Siena meant he had to think about the consequences his choices had on others. He wished Haviland were here. Perhaps between the two of them, they would know what he could do in regards to Elisabeta.

A rattle sounded at the doors of his balcony and the doors swung in before Archer could rise and open them. Elisabeta stepped through the gauzy curtains and shut the doors behind her. She looked utterly enticing in her breeches and boots. How anyone could remotely think her a man with all those curves on display beneath those riding breeches was beyond him. He might have been immediately aroused, but he'd certainly not been immediately fooled.

She took off her cap in a flourish that brought her hair down in a cascade of dark waves. 'Your balcony is a little higher up than it looks.' She was flushed and still catching her breath. 'I haven't climbed like that in ages.'

'You took an enormous risk coming here.' Physically, socially, the risks had come in more than one form. The risks had been enormous. Archer launched the pro forma protest as he crossed the room to her. He was far more interested in doing other things besides scolding her. He drew her close for a kiss, forcing himself to linger over it, to savour it, when what he really wanted to do was devour her. He could smell the sweat of her, the scent of horse, and beneath that the remnants of her rosemary-lavender soap. The scent of her spoke her story: animal lover, enticing woman, risk taker, passionate lover of life's adventure. All of it was there and he hungered for it, for her.

Her arms were about his neck, her body pressing against his. She kissed with her entire being, not just her mouth. 'I didn't want to let those breeches go to waste,' she murmured beneath his lips. 'All the same, I think I've had enough of playing the boy tonight.' She stepped back, disengaging their bodies. 'Watch me, Archer. Watch me become a woman before your very eyes.'

She gave him a gentle push, and he sat back on the bed, watching, waiting, the room around him a reminder of the intimacy they were about to share. So many of his encounters took place outside of a bedroom, and certainly all of them took place outside his bedroom. *This*, what was happening here in front of him right now, existed on an entirely different plane.

Elisabeta pulled off her boots and went to work. She drew the shirt over her head and undid the binding around her breasts, unwinding the length of cloth with a slowness that tantalised. But nothing compared to the pleasurable torture of only being able to look at the body revealed to him in pieces and not touch.

His hands ached to take those breasts in his hands, to run his thumbs over the dusky nipples, to trace the rosy-brown aureoles surrounding them, to take his mouth and blow gentle breaths into that navel while his hands traced the sleek lines of her torso.

But his eyes, oh, how they feasted. She drew her breeches down over slim hips, entirely naked beneath as she kicked out of them, and he was breathless—he had seen her like this before, seen plenty of women naked and yet for all of his experience, for all of the women he'd pleasured, he was breathless.

She gave a satisfied smile, luring him with the dancing light in her eyes. 'You've seen me nude, Archer.'

His voice was a desire-laden growl of want. 'But not as often I'd like.' Every last word was true. He wanted to taste, touch, lick and lave, explore and worship each inch of her. His body was tight with the wanting of it, the needing of it as she stood there, brazenly naked for *him*.

'I could say the same of you. So...' her eyes ran over him in a show of anticipated appreciation '...if you wouldn't mind obliging? It's your turn.'

Chapter Sixteen

He was more than happy to oblige. He'd heard the boldness in her voice, but he'd seen the flicker of sad regret in her eyes as she'd made her demand. Not regret over anything they had done, but regret for what was to come—marriage to a man for whom she felt not the slightest bit of physical interest. He understood now why she'd risked coming. This might be the last time. He would make this good for her, for them.

Archer rose from the bed with deliberate slowness, letting the profundity of that thought strike him in full. *Would* this be the last time? Surely with the upcoming Palio festivities, there would be a chance, but a chance only, and certainly nothing that would guarantee a bed being present. He let his hands linger at the waist of his trousers, let her anticipate what lay beneath the fabric.

It was a rather erotic sensation to undress in front of a naked woman, the two of them an antithesis of the other, he in his clothes and she without them. If he were an artist, he would paint her as she was in this moment; sitting nude in a chair, legs crossed, hair falling over her shoulders, looking entirely composed, as if she sat this way every day. That was, until one looked in her eyes and saw the wildness, the want, the hunger that lurked brazenly.

Archer crossed his arms and lifted his shirt up and over his head in a fluid motion that left his chest bare and exposed. He felt her eyes run over him, saw the appreciation grow in them as she took in the tanned, defined musculature of his torso. 'I've always thought Adam would look this way.' Her words came with a breathless hitch to them and he knew a moment's pride in her appreciation. When had a woman ever taken time to savour him thusly? To enjoy simply looking upon him? Yet she did, each time as if it were the first.

He gave her a slow, sensual smile and watched her come alive with it. He opened the fall of his trousers and pushed them from his hips. She came to him, running her hands down his chest, skimming the surface of his skin with her fingertips, nails brushing nipples. He could feel them harden as she passed over, could feel the temperature of his body rise with each touch until her hand dropped low and closed over the core of him.

She held his gaze as she held him, let him see that her quicksilver eyes had become nearly black with desire. 'I've decided it is so much better to see you,' she whispered, running her hand the length of him. Already hard, he felt himself jump in her grasp, his cock taking on a life of its own, twitching its pleasure.

She gave a husky laugh. 'It's like a frisky stallion.'

She gave him a gentle push backwards, urging him to sit on the edge of the bed, a seductive smile on her lips. 'Let's see if we can't tame him a bit.' She knelt before him with a wicked look. 'Open your legs for me, Archer.'

She spread his thighs apart, hands firm on either side of his groin, perhaps to steady herself, he thought. Then, she took him in her mouth, and he knew it wasn't to steady herself, but to steady him. He could scarcely breathe from the exquisite contact of her mouth with his tender head. When he did breathe, all he could manage was a series of trembling pants, his hands gripping the edge of the bed. There wasn't enough stability in the world to anchor him against this.

Elisabeta licked his tip, giving a small moan of delight as she moved on to tongue the rest of him, to nip at his length with gentle teeth. She returned once more to his tip, upping the intensity of their play, sucking hard, turning the tantalising tease of her mouth to an insistent pressure of pleasure. Archer felt his body gathering for its climax, his balls tightening in anticipation of release. He arched back and let it come, let it fill her hand, pleased that the act held her in thrall. She did not shy away from his completion, but instead seemed to share in the awe of it with him. They had done this *together*. It added credence to his wildest of options—marry Elisabeta—and his hope that she might agree. What woman would walk away from this?

Amazing. Positively amazing. But how to tell him? How to convey the emotion rocketing through

her at what had transpired? Her eyes held his, unable
to look away. All she wanted to do was look at him,
to memorise every line and plane of him, the feel of
him, the taste of him. Her hand was still warm about
him where he pulsed with half life, the tension starting to leave his body.

'I've not...' she began, faltering for words.

*I've never done that to another man with my
mouth before, never thought I would want to, never
thought a man would compel me to madness, but you
do. You have me climbing into bedrooms in the dead
of night, risking everything for one more moment of
pleasure, one more night of impossible hope.*

Archer put a gentle finger over her lips, his voice
quiet. 'No words, Elisabeta. They would be inadequate anyway.' He drew her up then to his lap and
she straddled him so that they were bare skin to bare
skin. It was simple, beautiful contact. He kissed her
long and slow, letting their mouths play. 'I can taste
myself on your lips, Elisabeta,' he whispered. 'That
is a heady reminder of the pleasure you've brought
me and the pleasure I owe you in return.'

'Owe?' she murmured, biting at his lower lip.
'Lovers give, Archer, they don't owe,' she reprimanded gently.

He grinned, and she could feel his mouth widen
in a smile beneath her own. 'Give, then. It is a pre-
lude to the pleasure I will *give* you.'

'When?' Elisabeta teased, moving her hips against
him and feeling the first flares of new life in his
groin.

'Soon, very soon.' Archer gave a low rumble of
laughter. He leaned back, taking her with him so

that they lay against the pillows, side by side, able to look each other in the eye. This was comfortable intimacy, with him propped up on an arm, looking down at her as if they had all the time in the world, as if the night weren't fleeing.

'Tell me about your uncle's villa and the horses,' she prompted. She wanted to use every minute of their short night to her benefit. She wanted to touch him, to make love to him, and when that wasn't possible, she wanted to know him as she'd come to know him in the country. She wanted the closeness that came with knowledge, even if it made it harder to let him go.

'He has offered the villa and the farm to me. My uncle has been all that is generous and gracious. He has welcomed me as a son. I have only to breathe a wish and he sees it granted. Do you want a horse farm? Here, have the villa. Do you want to ride in the Palio? Here, take my horses and ride them in the unofficial trials. Do you want a bride? We will find one for you.' Archer shook his head with a chuckle. 'I think all I would have to say is "I want to marry on September fifteenth" and I would only need to show up. It would all be there for me.' He grinned.

Elisabeta's hand stalled on the muscled ridge of his biceps. What did she say to that? Everything changed. Taking on the villa implied a permanence she hadn't anticipated. Always she'd thought there'd come a day when Archer would leave, later if not sooner. It was what made him safe. He would leave and take this secret affair with him along with her heart. But now? Now there would be no more talk of running away, no more sense in even contemplating that fantasy. He meant to stay. He'd been given a farm. He'd been given his dream. She was all that stood in his way.

Stay. The word had riveted all of her attention. She'd barely heard the rest. He was staying. She'd not bargained on that.

How perfect.

How awful.

How perfectly awful.

'What?' Archer studied her in the silence. 'Have I rendered you speechless with my insensitivity for the Italian way?'

'No, not at all.' She gathered enough control over her voice to turn the conversation coy. 'I was just wondering, *do* you want to marry on September fifteenth?' Perhaps he did. It had struck her anew that if he stayed, he would eventually marry here. It would be quite the torture for them both: he watching her marry Ridolfo and she having to tolerate whomever he chose. Of course, all that assumed current feelings remained constant and perhaps that was a large assumption to make indeed.

Archer came up over her, his mouth teasing hers, his renewed erection flirting with her core as his hips pressed. 'I could go sooner or later on the date, depending on the girl. Do you know anyone who's available?'

'Archer, don't,' she warned. These were things they could not say to one another even in jest. 'This changes nothing.'

'It changes everything,' Archer was quick to respond. 'I have something to offer you, here. You needn't marry him. You can marry *me*, we can have our life in the country. Choosing me no longer means choosing to flee in shame.'

Marry Archer? It was a stunning idea, one that went far beyond his original offer of protection. But it wasn't enough. 'Marriage won't be rid of the scandal. The scandal will still be there. His offer is on the table before yours. The engagement is official.'

'I will find a way around it if you would have me. It is merely the last obstacle. Will you? Have me?' Archer queried. He wound a curl around one long finger.

If he stayed, he would be here, but out of reach. She didn't dare seek him after her marriage, not after the horrors Ridolfo had promised to inflict. He would not tolerate it. No one respected a man whose wife was unfaithful. An affair would disgrace her family, her *contrada* and herself. Yet to encounter him, to know Archer was nearby, would be torture to consider. To know that pleasure was at hand and she could not take it. It would be a Sisyphean task. He was offering her everything and yet it was nothing without the one thing she wanted as much as her own freedom to choose. 'I won't be a pity project, Archer. I don't want you to marry me just to save me. You would come to resent me.' And yet, she wanted to say yes. He'd very nearly found a way for them to have it all—her freedom, his dream of a horse farm in Italy near his mother's family. But it was a plan born of desperation, born of spontaneity. He'd never once spoken of love and she would not trap him. He would come to hate her for it. She'd never meant to embroil him.

Archer gave a rueful smile, his eyes amber coals

come to life, his dark hair falling forward over his face, skimming his shoulders. 'I would not have offered if I didn't mean it, if I didn't want it. Let me show you how much.' Then he silenced her with a kiss that was long and slow and obliterating.

'You're playing with fire now, Archer,' she warned between hot kisses.

He turned serious, There was no joking now. 'Then come for me, Elisabeta, and let us burn together.'

He was ready for her again, evidence of his arousal pressing against her stomach, and she was ready for him, ready for the pleasure, a different sort of pleasure than what they had shared earlier. His hand cupped her breast, running the flat of his palm over her nipple until she felt it peak for him, and he took the straining peak in his mouth, laving it with his tongue as she'd done for him. She arched for him, pressing her body against his, wanting this foreplay and yet wanting more than this. She wanted it all. 'Take me, Archer,' she urged, her legs widening for him so that he was cradled between her thighs and there was no question of his welcome.

He did not deny her. He slid home in one powerful thrust, a guttural cry escaping him at his reception. She could feel her own slickness as he entered, could smell the scent of her arousal mingling with his, could feel her body live the words of her mind, *Yes, this is and more...* And there *was* more.

His body set the rhythm and hers followed, hips rising to join his, legs wrapping about his waist, holding him tight as they sought release together. She revelled in the feel of his body pumping into hers, primal and alive in these exquisite moments. She revelled, too, in her own body's response; the rising of the pleasurable ache she now knew signalled the approach of climax, the racing of her pulse. They were near, so very near, she felt the signals in her body and in his. Archer gave a final thrust and they reached out to grab it together, soaring, falling into pleasure, into the impossibility of perfection,

She must have slept. When she awoke, it was with a languorous sense of satisfaction permeating her bones; her body was exquisitely sore with loving, her lover's body lay against her, his arm draped across her in wondrous possession. The sun fell warm across the sheets. *The sun was up!* Panic set in. She had not meant to stay so long. She'd meant to leave before sunrise.

'Archer!' she gave a frantic whisper. 'I've got to go!' In the distance she heard the church bells sound the hour and her panic eased slightly. It was only six, but it was still far later than she'd meant it to be.

Archer stirred and opened sleepy eyes that made her heart flip. What she wouldn't give to lie abed in the mornings with this man and rekindle the passions of the night. 'There is still time. It will be all right. People will be sleeping late because of the trials. I'll walk you back.' He rolled out of bed and reached for his discarded breeches.

'No, that's far too incriminating.' Elisabeta shook her head, hurrying into her clothes. She twisted her hair up in a hasty bun—it would fool no one on closer inspection and there was no time to bind her breasts. 'If anyone questions me, I'll tell them I was out on business with the horses. But if I'm seen with you, there will be no good explanation.' She could see Archer didn't like the plan. It was not in his nature to let another take risks on his behalf. *He* was the rescuer.

'Are you sure? Perhaps I could go part of the way with you?' Archer insisted. He was all protective warrior, ready to leap to her defence as he had been at the ball, her safety his first concern and the primal woman in her thrilled to the knowledge that this bare-chested warrior had been hers.

She went to him and put a hand on his chest. 'I'm sure, Archer. It is better this way.' Better in case she was seen, better because a swift goodbye was better than a prolonged one that left time for regrets. Now, it was all a rush, all of their efforts focused on the getaway and not the import of what her leaving meant. But their eyes caught at the last moment. She wasn't going to get away that easily. His unresolved proposal passed between them. His hand covered hers where it rested against his chest.

'I will come to you, tonight. You are to take no more risks. Let the risks be mine from here on out.' He kissed her hand and then her lips. He tugged at that hand and led her towards the bedroom door with a wink. 'I know a better way out. It's called the stairs.'

He would come for her. A thrill of excitement surged through her at the idea of an illicit assignation in her room. But he was coming for more than her, he was coming for an answer.

* * *

The *troia*! She had dared to go to him, that English *figlio di puttana*. Ridolfo Ranieri spat into the gutter and pressed himself against the brick of the building. It would not do to be seen now. His man had woken him with the news and he hurried out to watch and wait so he could see it with his own eyes. Elisabeta di Nofri had climbed into the Englishman's bed the moment he returned to town and now she swaggered down the empty street as if she hadn't a care in the world.

Ridolfo passed a hand over his eyes, his anger growing. He'd not accepted his cousin's explanations, or Rafaele di Bruno's or that son of his Giuliano's the night of the party. He'd suspected something more was up. A woman that beautiful couldn't be entirely innocent of attracting the wrong sort of attention. Those sort of women encouraged it. He'd set his own spies on the di Bruno household to watch her every move. He'd just about been willing to give up. The past weeks had passed without incident; she had seemed reformed enough from her reflective retreat in the country, but then the report had come that his man suspected she'd gone to the trials in disguise and it had all unfolded from there.

Rafaele di Bruno and Pantera would have to pay for this treachery against Oca and his cousin. He was a wealthy man, respected for his business acumen in the community, but she was making him look like a fool. Only a weak man tolerated such behaviour. But most of all, Elisabeta would have to pay and so would the Englishman for their treachery against him. Anyone who crossed Ridolfo Ranieri would live to regret it. Timing was everything and the time was not yet, but soon. Very soon, the Englishman would receive a most unpleasant surprise.

Chapter Seventeen

'This is a grand surprise indeed!' Archer thumped Haviland and the others on the back in genuine delight as he stepped into the *loggia* to find Uncle Giacomo holding court with his friends. 'You've arrived early. I wasn't expecting you until tomorrow,' Archer exclaimed. 'This is even better, you are here in time for the *tratta*. Today, the horses are selected for the Palio.' He stepped back to survey the group with a smile. 'I am glad you are here. Please, eat. There's prosciutto and melon, bread and coffee, always coffee in the morning.' By Jove, it felt good to see them! Nolan and Brennan were obscenely tan from days spent outdoors on the mountains and Haviland looked…happy. His earlier worries seemed foolish.

Haviland laughed as everyone took their seats. 'You sound like your uncle. He's been feeding us since we walked in.'

Giacomo grinned and shrugged. 'It's what we do.' He rose from his chair. 'I will leave you gentlemen to catch up. I have errands to run before the *tratta*.' He wagged a finger in Archer's direction. 'Don't forget to come to the *tratta*, though.'

'He is fond of you,' Nolan commented as the older man left the room.

Archer smiled. 'I am fond of him too. It has been good beyond words to meet him and my mother's family at last.' He looked around the table. 'Where's Alyssandra, Haviland?'

'Still in bed,' Haviland replied slyly. 'Perhaps where you'd like to be? Tell us, who is she?'

Archer feigned ignorance. How did Haviland know? His friends had only been here for a few minutes. 'What makes you think there's a she at all?'

Nolan tutted and shook his head. 'It's no good pretending, old man, all the signs are there: sleeping late, the dark circles. You've been up all night, several nights in a row. I've been around Brennan enough to know what that looks like.'

Archer pushed a hand through his hair, prevaricating. Did he tell them? He tried to sidestep it once more. 'It's a busy time with the race. I just got back from the countryside.'

Brennan gave a hoot of laughter. 'This is *not* about a horse, Archer. How stupid do we look?'

Nolan shot Brennan a glance. 'Perhaps he thought we were so stupid we wouldn't notice he was gone.' Nolan's quicksilver eyes turned on Archer. 'Why didn't you tell us you meant to leave us in Paris?'

There it was. The reckoning he'd feared. They would be angry they hadn't been told, as if not being told reflected in some way on the quality of their friendship being less than the quality of friendship he held with Haviland. That wasn't the case at all.

The decision wasn't about them. It was about him. 'I apologise...' Archer began. 'The decision wasn't meant to offend anyone.'

'We would have come with you,' Nolan insisted. 'Old Haviland could have got married by himself or we could have caught up.'

Archer shook his head. Nolan wasn't going to be put off. It was time for the truth, the real reason he hadn't told them. 'No, you had plans for the Alps. I didn't want to get in the way of that when I wasn't sure how things would turn out here.' The words seemed inadequate to convey all he felt, but that was it in a nutshell. He hadn't wanted to fail in front of his friends. What if his uncle hadn't been welcoming? What if he hadn't liked Siena? He would have brought them along for nothing. This was simply something he had to do on his own.

Silence descended on the table. They understood. Each of them had their own demons, their own dreams, their own risks that had to be faced alone. Brennan smiled, breaking the solemnity. 'Well, that answers part one of the stupid question. Let's get back to the other part. Who is she?'

Now it would be Archer's turn to be the idiot. What would they think once he told them about Elisabeta and his mad scheme? Archer stalled for time and helped himself to more melon. 'It's complicated.'

Nolan leaned forward. 'It always is with a woman. Do tell.'

Archer looked at them. They were his best friends, no matter how wild they were. He could trust them with this as perhaps he should have trusted them with his decision to leave Paris early. He lowered his voice.

'It's private. My uncle feels that I shouldn't see her. She's from another *contrada* and she's betrothed to a loathsome man.'

Nolan grinned. 'She's forbidden, the daughter of a rival and pledged to another? Lucifer's balls, Archer, Shakespeare would be drooling on himself, "two households both alike in dignity" and all that. The only thing missing is a hero's proposal of marriage to whisk her away to a happy ever after.' Nolan paused, Archer feeling the weight of his gaze. Nolan always saw too much in others.

'Oh, hell, Archer, you didn't?' Nolan gaped at him.

The others were looking at him too in stunned surprise.

Haviland was the first to recover. 'When?'

'Just this morning.'

'At a most opportune time, no doubt, when she was thoroughly ploughed—' Brennan winked '—and refusing you was the furthest thing from her mind.'

'I didn't "plough" her,' Archer corrected.

'Of course not, you *made love* to her.' Nolan chuckled. 'Good Lord, you're besotted with her.'

'He's not besotted, he wants to rescue her,' Haviland said shrewdly, sounding far too like Elisabeta. Haviland, always the voice of reason, steepled his hands. 'Marriage is a big step. Are you sure it's for the right reasons? If you want to rescue her, perhaps we can find another way.'

Archer blew out a breath. 'This is why I didn't want to tell you. I knew you'd try to talk me out of it.' Marrying Elisabeta was admittedly a mad idea, but one that had slowly taken hold since the countryside. Still, Haviland's comment had hit its mark.

Was that what he wanted? Or had his subconscious prompted it because he knew their *affaire* couldn't go on this way without resolution? 'If you knew her like I do, you'd understand.' They had not watched her with the horses in the country, hadn't seen her heart etched on her face when she spoke of her family. This was a woman who loved deeply and without reservation even at the expense of great personal sacrifice. To have the love of such a woman turned his way, to share a life with her, would be a treasure beyond imagining, beyond deserving.

'Well,' Archer said, filling in the silence, 'it hardly matters yet. She hasn't accepted.'

'Why ever not? You really should have asked her after you ploughed her,' Brennan put in. 'Women will say yes to anything after great sex.'

'Even you, apparently,' Nolan ribbed him.

'For the second time, I didn't plough her. That's so crass, Brennan,' Archer protested.

'Will we get to meet this paragon?' Haviland asked before Nolan and Brennan could degenerate the discussion further.

'You will likely see her at the *tratta*.' Archer stood up. It was as good of an opening as any to change the subject. 'In fact, we should get going if we want a good spot.' He smiled at his friends. 'I *am* glad you're here.' And he was even if they were shocked by his news. They would stand beside him come what may.

The *campo* in front of the Palazzo Pubblico was full, everyone gathering for the *tratta* late that morning. The excitement of anticipation filled the air as Archer and his friends joined the Torre *contrada*.

The unofficial late-night trials were over and now the horses for the race would be chosen. Then, that afternoon, the chosen horses would be assigned to the neighbourhoods. They would waste no time after that. The first official trial would be held that night. There would only be three days remaining before the great race. He would have responsibilities for his uncle as one of his *mangini*. It would be harder to slip away, nigh on impossible if Giacomo was to be believed. The nights before the race were manic, with *capitani* and *mangini* arranging secret *partiti*.

A certain anxiety underlay Archer's excitement. With all the activity of the next three days, what would become of him and Elisabeta? Had last night literally been that, their *last* night? Would the affair merely fade into the background as the Palio took centre stage? It would be a convenient out for her if she meant to reject his offer. With her wedding to Ridolfo lurking on the calendar in two weeks, they would simply run out of time.

She had not rejected the idea of marrying him, but she had not affirmed it either. Had it crossed her mind too that he might be her salvation, her way out? Or was she too noble to impose on him? Perhaps she feared his affections only stemmed from the desire to rescue her. How did he convince her otherwise? How did he convince anyone otherwise? Those who knew him knew he'd not come here to marry. He'd said it out loud often enough. His plan to wait had made sense in the beginning. He was starting a new phase of his life away from England, away from the grief of his mother's passing. It was hardly a 'good time' to start a new intimate relationship, but Elisabeta offered him a relationship of mind and body and soul, something he'd never had before. He was too smart to throw it away.

If his parents' marriage had shown him the risks of love, Siena was showing him the beauties of it. If he could have that, what wouldn't he risk for it? Was it possible? Elisabeta thought it was. It was why she resisted being bartered away in marriage to Ridolfo. If it was possible for her, was it possible for him? For them together? He'd based his proposal on the hopes that it was. These were the thoughts that kept him well occupied through the early stages of the *tratta*.

'Seriously, Archer...' Nolan leaned close amid the crowd, sensing his distraction '... I ache for you. You have fixed your attentions on a woman you cannot have. But have you thought it through? What can come of this infatuation but trouble? If your rivals, or her rivals, learn this affair has continued...' He let his words trail off, his eyes sad as they communicated his meaning.

Archer winced. He hated how astute Nolan could be. Even after only one day, Nolan seemed to grasp the intricacies of Sienese life. If Oca learned of this, it would mean they had grounds for revenge. They would believe that not just Archer, but Torre had violated the truce after the Pantera party. Archer's proposal would bring a feud to Torre.

'The Palio is dangerous enough,' Nolan said lightly. 'We don't need to invite more trouble.'

'Her fiancé's *contrada* isn't even racing in this one,' Archer said defensively. The remaining three slots for the Palio had been drawn while he was in the countryside. Oca would not be among the ten *contradas* in the contest. But that wouldn't stop Oca from trying to negotiate contracts that would prevent their rivals from winning. It was horrible for a non-racing *contrada* to have its enemy *contrada* win. It was almost as bad as losing it yourself.

Brennan nudged him. 'Look, here they come!' A cry went up from the crowd as the first horses were sighted, being led through the crowd to the courtyard of the Palazzo Pubblico where their health would be determined. Conversations began immediately as the horses passed by. All about him, Archer could hear snatches of conversation: would Jacopi's Morello be selected again after winning in July? Would this horse? Would that horse? See how this one holds his foot, perhaps it is a strained ligament? Didn't that one suffer a fall in one of the night trials? The energy in the piazza swelled, contagious and rambunctious. It was hard not to get caught up in the excitement.

'There's my uncle's horses!' Archer pointed a little farther down the line of animals being brought in. Not only would they know today which horse Torre would get to race, but they'd know if any of his uncle's horses, *his* horses, would be racing too. He'd worked hard with them for this moment.

If an owner's horse was chosen for the Palio, the owner was paid a handsome stipend for the honour although there was no guarantee that horse would race for the owner's *contrada*. One of Uncle Giacomo's horses might race for one of the other neighbourhoods. There was another bonus as well for the owner if his horse went on to win. As Giacomo had been fond of telling him, there were a lot of ways to win or lose on the Palio—it was more than simply crossing the finish first.

The crowd quieted a bit as the last of the horses, twenty in all, disappeared into the palazzo's courtyard. Now they would wait for the doctors to ascertain the health of the horses. This was paramount. A sick horse would not be replaced. If a *contrada*'s assigned horse became ill or injured, they would not be given a replacement, which was why Archer's job of guarding the stable was so critical. *Contradas* were not above trying to render another's horse unable to race.

The crowd grew restless waiting for news. Archer searched the gathering for signs of Elisabeta. There were plenty of women here—perhaps she'd come. But if she was here, he couldn't find her. At last the announcement was made. All the horses had been declared sound. Archer let out a breath he hadn't realised he'd been holding. His uncle's horses had passed. Archer knew a moment's relief. They'd been horses he'd personally recommended. He would have had some answering to do if those horses had not been found sound.

The energy of the crowd started escalating again. People got out little scorecards to take notes as the *capitani* separated the horses into groups of four or five to run mock races, but the races held little appeal for Archer. He knew these horses. He'd raced alongside them for three breathless nights and he'd already passed on his recommendations to his uncle. The crowd held all of his attention now. Was Elisabeta here? Archer's gaze scanned up to the balconies lining the perimeter of the square, a smile spreading in slow satisfaction across his face. There!

He spied her sitting at one of the balconies, and his breath hitched for a moment as he let the beauty of her wash over him. 'She's there, on the balcony.' He pointed her out to Nolan and the others. She was stunning, dressed in white, holding a parasol to match. The white was an ideal foil for her dark hair. Even at this distance with a crowd and half a piazza between them, one could sense the vibrancy of her, the life that radiated from her. She leaned forward to hear one of her companions and then she laughed. He knew the sound of that laugh. He could hear that laugh in his mind despite the noise of the crowd. He knew how her eyes would be dancing at this moment as she made her response—something witty and funny.

Nolan let out a low whistle. 'She's gorgeous. No wonder you've proposed.' Archer barely heard him. He was too busy letting his imagination conjure up another fantasy, one from the near future; one of Elisabeta sitting at a balcony with a small dark-haired child on her lap, his child, *their* child, anxiously awaiting the outcome of the *tratta* to see whether the horses from their stables in the country would be selected to run. Aunt Bettina and Uncle Giacomo would be with them, the women laughing together. Then, Elisabeta would spy him in the crowd and give him a wave and the world would vanish as it did now. Maybe later that night they would lie in bed celebrating their success and he would tell her the story of his first *tratta*, of how he'd looked up to see her all in white and perhaps that was the first time he knew, really knew, that she was meant to be his.

A heavyset man lumbered out on to the balcony and exchanged words with Elisabeta as he took up a seat behind her. Immediate, primal dislike surged through Archer. Beside him, Nolan murmured, 'Is that the bastard she's to marry?'

Ridolfo was turned out in splendour today. He wore his wealth in his clothes and his paunch. His money had no doubt secured the luxury of a balcony as well. Only a rich man could afford such indulgences. Ridolfo leaned close and the life seemed to go out of Elisabeta. Her gaze no longer looked out over the piazza, but down at her hands, her mouth no longer moving in sparkling conversation.

The mayor had begun drawing the horses and the crowd boisterously awaited the announcement of each result. After the first five drawings, both of his uncle's chestnuts had been assigned to other *contradas*, which was both good and bad news. Archer wouldn't have minded Torre drawing one of its own mounts. One of them had gone to Pantera. He did not remember who had drawn the other. Aside from Jacopi's Morello, the Torre horses were very promising competitors. Jacopi's Morello, the bay that won the last Palio, was still available, though.

Perhaps later, he'd reflect on the irony of it all: here he was, in the piazza on the most important day before the race he'd waited his whole life to be part of. He should be drinking in each moment, seeing each moment as part of the fulfilment of a dream, and yet all he wanted was for it to be over. He wanted to escape, to go to Elisabeta.

Around him, the Torre men were getting nervous about him. Seven *contrada* had already been drawn. The mayor drew again. 'The next horse is Jacopi's Morello!' Torre held its collective breath. There were only three *contrada* left in the other urn. The slip of paper came out, the name was read. 'Torre! Jacopi's Morello goes to Torre!'

'We got the bay, we got the bay!' Someone next to him grabbed Archer and kissed both his cheeks. Men went crazy with excitement, pumping fists and hitting each other rather heartily on the back in congratulations as if they had anything to do with the luck of the draw.

His uncle came out of the building and spied him, throwing an arm around him as they were pushed along in the wave of Torre men going to claim their horse. 'You know what this means, right?' Giacomo yelled over the cheers as Archer's hand closed in possession over Morello's bridle. 'It means we're going to have to work our butts off! I'll be out negotiating *partiti* all night, and you, *mio nipote*, for the next three nights, will be guarding this horse with your life!'

The prospect, the acceptance, should have thrilled him. The day had been a success beyond words. His uncle had two favoured horses in the Palio, horses that had been brought to town on his recommendation. He'd proven his worth to his uncle on those grounds, and his uncle's *contrada* had won the prime horse for the race. It would be his honour to watch over that horse and he was cognizant of what that opportunity meant. He'd be able to prove his worth to the *contrada* now that he'd proven it to his uncle.

But all he could think of as someone started a loud rendition of the Torre neighbourhood song was that it left damn little time for Elisabeta.

Chapter Eighteen

Damn her! She had been watching *him*, that blasted Englishman. How she could find him in that sea of people down there was beyond Ridolfo, but somehow she had and her face had lit with a soft smile, her eyes had danced. He'd watched her come alive and he hated it. She never looked at him that way. She should. He was Ridolfo Ranieri, the richest man in Siena. Any woman in town would understand the honour it was to be his wife.

But not Elisabeta di Nofri. No, she had not only flirted openly with the Englishman, she'd gone to him, sneaking out in the middle of the night dressed as a boy. How dare she sit there, pretending she was innocent? 'Your gaze is too bold,' he snapped. 'A modest woman would keep her eyes downcast.' The wedding was only two weeks off. He would teach her manners by then. No woman would make a fool of him by openly hungering after a foreigner. He watched the life seep out of her, her eyes going to her lap, and felt a sense of satisfaction. A man who couldn't master a wife was no man at all in his opinion.

His satisfaction was short-lived. Torre had drawn Jacopi's Morello. Did he imagine it or did his bride's shoulders straighten infinitesimally in defiance at the announcement as if to say 'hah, it serves you right for making me look away'?

Down in the piazza, he could see the Englishman and his *contrada* celebrating. Fate had shown undue favour to the Englishman since his arrival. Ridolfo stood to go back inside, an idea forming that would separate his bride from the Englishman for good. There were plans to be laid. He would have vindication and she would unwittingly be part of it.

When he was done, the Englishman would be sorry he had ever met Elisabeta di Nofri, and Elisabeta would be grateful for the protection of her fiancé. He was already imagining the ways in which she might show that gratitude. He would speak to her uncle tonight. The time had come to set his plan in motion. There would be partying and celebrating in the *contradas* like Pantera and Torre who had drawn good horses. But tomorrow, Elisabeta would be the agent of her own downfall.

Elisabeta tried not to stare. She tried to be involved in the conversations going on around her as the *contrada* dined at long tables set up in the street. But her gaze kept going back to the table where Ridolfo sat with her uncle. They were deep in animated conversation. Giuliano was already out performing his duties as a *mangini*. With her cousin gone, she had no way of knowing what Ridolfo discussed with her uncle.

A nervous ball formed in her stomach, and she pushed away her plate. Ridolfo had been positively possessive at the *tratta* today, his words and his touch all designed to remind her of her submissive place beside him as his wife. They also reminded her of another proposal she had yet to answer.

Archer had been serious. He would brave the consequences of his proposal for her. Could she be brave too? If she loved him, was it fair to reach for the happiness he offered or was it perhaps more fair that she cut him loose from this entanglement? If she loved him, should she set him free? Or should she embrace that love with all its risks? But love for Archer wasn't the only consideration. There was her family too. Loving Archer would hurt them. Perhaps it was better that she couldn't see him tonight after all. He'd be busy with the horse and she was no closer to an answer to their dilemma.

From the table, her uncle motioned for her to approach, and she rose with dread. What would Ridolfo want with her now? Would he seek further atonement for having caught her watching Archer this afternoon? Had he told her uncle?

'Niece,' her uncle began in casual tones, 'I want to know more about this chestnut we've been assigned. I think Torre will talk to you. Tomorrow, I need you to go to Torre's stables and ask the Englishman about the horses.'

'Of course, *Zio*, I would be glad to go.' She *was* glad to go too—it would give her an excuse to see Archer.

* * *

Elisabeta had been so glad, in fact, that it didn't occur to her until the next day when she set out for Torre that she should be suspicious. Why her? Why not Giuliano? Why ask at all when her uncle was an excellent judge of horseflesh himself? Surely there was nothing about the chestnut that her uncle couldn't divine already. Something was afoot. It was a good thing she was going to see Archer; she could at least warn him so he could take measures to protect himself from whatever came next.

Protecting Morello was no small matter. Archer yawned. He'd been awake the previous night and nearly all day. The only break he'd had was when the grooms had come to get Morello ready for the first official evening trial and then again in the morning for the next trial. There would be six official trials in all. He'd gone with the grooms to watch Morello run this morning at the second trial. Now, Morello was being brushed and settled for the afternoon before going out for the evening trial.

Archer wished he could do the same. He was bone tired in part from having been up for days and in part because there wasn't much to do in the *contrada* stable except play cards and keep Nolan's card-playing tendencies on a leash. He didn't need Nolan fleecing his relatives.

It might be a prestigious job to guard the horse, especially when the horse was a favourite to win, but it was an unexciting one. So far, there'd been no trouble at the stable, at the track or on the streets. He'd been warned that often unhappy *contradas* didn't hesitate to start a scrap in the streets if they thought their horse or rider had been treated unfairly during a trial.

The most he'd had to guard against were too many neighbours stopping by to pet the horse, or too many of the *contrada*'s marriageable girls stopping by to smile at him—probably encouraged to do so by his uncle. While it had taken no small amount of diplomatic skill to keep the neighbours and girls away without hurting feelings, it was hardly the stuff of which excitement was made. And still, the issue of Elisabeta plagued him. Being unable to see her meant being unable to have his answer. He was restless, eager to do something about it and frustrated because he could do nothing while the Palio loomed.

Archer pushed a hand through his hair and squinted at the far end of the stable. Someone was there, leaning against the wall. He blinked. Not someone, but a woman.

Surely it wasn't her? That would be almost too good to be true. But it was. His blood began to thrum, his pulse began to race. Elisabeta was here, as if his very thoughts had called her to him.

He strode forward, his weariness falling away with each step. 'Signora di Nofri, what a pleasant surprise!' He took her hands, letting his smile say for him what he could not say out loud in front of the others milling about the stables.

'Signor Crawford, it is good to see you.' Her greeting was formal, polite, but her eyes danced. She was not indifferent to him. Her thumbs moved over his, secretly, hidden within his grasp. 'I came to congratulate you on your good luck in drawing Morello. My uncle says that horse will not disappoint you.'

'And Pantera's horse will not disappoint either.' Archer smiled to confirm they weren't entirely talking about horses.

She blushed and looked away demurely at the veiled compliment. 'Thank you.' Something was on her mind. Now that the pleasantries were disposed of, she was distracted. Archer waited for her to decide her approach.

'I have a question to ask about the chestnut. My uncle thought you might have some knowledge.' The question was odd. The *contradas* didn't seek out one another's advice on horses. Instantly suspicious, Archer took her arm.

'Come walk with me. There is a more private place where we can speak.' Perhaps it was the crowd she wanted to avoid, although in truth there were only two grooms remaining. It might be that there was no question at all, but an excuse to speak with him. Perhaps she'd not come with a question, but an answer. His pulse sped up in anticipation.

He led her to a quiet place in the stables, an empty stall where they wouldn't be disturbed. 'Now, tell me what's on your mind. Have you come with an answer to my proposal?' It didn't matter to him what it was. It was enough right now to hold her, to run his hands down her arms, to simply see her.

She held his gaze. She was trying to tell him something beyond words, but he could not puzzle it out. 'Ridolfo and my uncle wanted your opinion on his weight. They were worried about him being too thin.'

He was disappointed. She'd not come of her own accord, but that was telling too. She was the messen-

ger. Ridolfo had sent her. Her uncle had sent her. That
they had let her come or perhaps *insisted* she come
had made her nervous. She too suspected something.

Archer bent his lips to hers in a soft kiss meant
to reassure. 'Did they send you to spy on Torre?' he
asked between kisses.

'I don't know.' Her arms slipped about his neck,
and he drew her close, his body hungry for the feel
of hers.

'I saw you at the *tratta*.' His mouth pressed a kiss
over the pulse beating at the base of her neck, his
hands moving in slow motions up and down her back.
'You were beautiful dressed all in white.'

She gave a little gasp as his teeth nipped at her
throat. 'I saw you too.'

'Is that why you looked away? Ridolfo caught
you?' Their private glances had been marked even
in a crowd. Had she been sent as a warning? Was
she being forced to act as a pawn in some act of *contrada* revenge? Primal protectiveness surged in Archer. She was his no matter what arrangements had
been made by other men, and he would not have her
subjugated thus.

'I came so I could warn you, but I don't know
about what, only that I think they're plotting something.'

She was beautiful in her concern. All the feeling she didn't dare admit to him with words shone
in her eyes. His body pulsed with life, with arousal.
He had her backed against the stall wall with no one
around and her own body was willing. He could have
her and in moments it would be over. This would not

take long, so great was his need, and hers too. He just needed a sign from her.

'Archer.' His name came from her lips, a gasping moan of a word as her hand sought him through his trousers. 'Archer, I want you, here.' She drew the length of him against her hips and pressed herself to it. 'Please, Archer.'

They had done this before—they were good at walls. He lifted her and her legs wrapped about him, their bodies coming together effortlessly, his phallus thrusting deep and hard, hitting the core of her the first time. He delighted in her moan of satisfaction, recklessly not caring how loud it was or who might hear. Maybe some small selfish part of him wanted her to be heard, wanted them to be discovered, wanted to spill deep inside her and find purchase. If so, the betrothal to Ridolfo could be broken. She would have no choice then. She would have to choose him. But his conscience was greater. He could not trap her by taking from her the one thing she'd come to him to save.

Her head went back against the wall, her body arched as he thrust again. He felt her hands brace against his shoulders. Oh, this was heaven what they could do together, knowing he could render her senseless, push her to a point where all things seemed possible, a point where she could walk away from her obligations and walk to him. She moaned. He felt her body clench around him, feeling his own body approach its point of no return, its final hill. Ecstasy awaited at the top of this thrusting climb. He wished they were naked, wished he could feel his bare skin against her. But it was enough to move against her, his mouth at her shoulder muffling his cries, enough to climax with her into satisfied bliss, each of them heaving hard against the other.

'I wish it would get old.' She sighed, her neck arched against the wall, her breaths coming in pants.

Archer laughed softly. 'Why would you ever wish that for something so wonderful?'

She opened her eyes and held his amber gaze. 'Because then it would be easier to let you go.'

'Don't.' After all that, she was still insistent on avoiding his solution out of some misguided idea that she could save him from a mistake. His hands were still wrapped about the round globes of her bottom, his phallus still lingered in her, her legs still wrapped about him. 'Don't let go, Elisabeta.' He gave her a sensual, confident smile that betrayed none of his frustration.

'Why let it end, Elisabeta, when it doesn't have to?' He kissed her when she would have protested the obvious: she was pledged to another. 'The solution is simple. Marry me instead.' He spoke the words so softly, she thought she might have imagined them, heard them because she wanted to hear them, her desperate dreams come to life. But the offer didn't make accepting it right.

'Do not sacrifice your hopes for me. You can have it all. I can bring you only scandal if you stay and only heartache if you go,' she whispered back, taking his mouth in a kiss of her own, feeling him stir inside her again. 'You didn't come to Siena for me.' He would come to resent her eventually if she let him give up his hopes. Had he realised yet that there would be a price for marrying her? 'I am not your dream, Archer.'

'True enough, Elisabeta,' he argued. 'You were not my dream, marriage was not my dream then, but it is now where you are concerned.'

'No, you want to rescue me, Archer,' she murmured at his ear, her fingers playing through the ends of his hair. 'It's what you do.'

'I would want *this*, I would want *you* even if you were not in this predicament.' Archer was determined and her arguments were tired ones. They had lost their power. She had nothing new to throw at him. He sensed that he had her close to breaking. It meant she was open to his proposal, wanted it in fact.

'Archer, it isn't only about us.'

'Maybe it should be,' he said fiercely. 'Maybe that's what has been complicating this from the start. Let this be about us and only us.' He heard the possession in his words, felt her body rouse to it, the way a woman's body has always roused to a warrior's desire knowing that he would fight for her.

There was the pounding of boots in the aisle outside the stall, a shout. 'Signor Crawford! Morello needs you!'

Archer dropped her with haste, moving his body in front of hers. 'What is it, boy?' he barked, striding out of the stall and taking command while she used the time to assemble herself.

'It's Morello, he won't eat his hay.'

Archer flashed her a brief look: *Is this what you feared? Did you know?* He questioned the boy. 'Was anyone near the horse or his feed?' He could only be in so many places at once. He was supposed to watch the horse, there were horse boys to watch over the feed.

The boy was pale when he answered. 'No, *signor*, not around the horse.' Archer started down the aisle to Morello's stall, the boy in front of him. Beside him, Elisabeta was trembling, her quick mind assembling pieces and assigning blame.

'This is all my fault, Archer. I should not have come. This is Ridolfo's revenge. He has gone after the horse because of me.' If Ridolfo had done something to the horse, the man would have to answer to him. The horse was innocent in all of this. She was struggling to match her step to his long strides. 'This is my fault for reaching for what wasn't mine, for not playing by the rules and being a dutiful niece.'

Archer shook his head. 'We'll talk about it later.' He would sort motives out once his temper had cooled. Right now, taking care of Morello mattered more.

At Morello's stall, Archer bent down to grab a handful of hay. He smelled it, cracked it open and examined it with a careful eye while the stable hands looked on. He passed some to the others with an explanation. 'Morello won't eat it because it's been tampered with. It's got angelica on it. Horses don't like bitter tastes. It wouldn't have hurt the horse necessarily.' He turned to Elisabeta, hoping to give her relief. 'But it would have starved him if we had let it go on for a day or so.' Just long enough to keep him from running in the Palio.

It wouldn't have hurt the horse *this* time. But this was, Archer feared, the opening salvo designed to act as a calling card and to put Torre on guard. Perhaps even to provoke Torre to violence. Everyone knew Torre and Oca were not above brawling in the streets.

Archer began querying the other boys now—was there any time in which the food was unguarded? He was patient with them, not wanting to pass blame. One of the boys pointed a finger at her. 'The food was unguarded when she came. She needed to know where to find you so we brought her inside. You can't trust anyone, especially not a woman.' The boy flashed accusing eyes at Elisabeta, and Archer felt his world crumble.

What she had done would be all over the *contrada* by evening. His uncle would know she'd been here and that disaster had nearly followed in her wake. Already, the other boys were shooting daggers at her with their dark eyes.

'It's not like that, Archer. I came to warn you.' Elisabeta wasn't afraid to argue but he was afraid to listen, afraid to admit that he had been duped. All of her talk about loyalty to family first, all of her reticence to respond to his proposal made sense. She had made no secret in the beginning that she'd only wanted sex, only wanted pleasure. She might not want to marry Ridolfo, but in the end family and tradition were too difficult to overthrow. And who knew, perhaps she had cut a deal more to her liking if she performed this one service.

And yet, she'd run to him. She'd been afraid in the countryside, afraid of life with Ridolfo. That sort of terror could not be feigned. 'I think you should go.' He would decide later if his words were a dismissal or protection. Whatever safe haven he'd created for them was gone now.

Chapter Nineteen

Her uncle feted her as a hero when she returned. Never mind the tear-splotched face, never mind the anger that roiled inside her. Ridolfo made sure everyone knew what a grand service she'd done for Pantera and for Oca. Her desire to warn Archer, to protect him, had been used against her. She never should have gone, thinking she could warn him. There'd been nothing to warn him about, *she'd* been the threat, the distraction that led to tampering with the hay.

She could not forget the way Archer had looked at her, his sharp mind tallying up the strikes against her. She knew what he'd been thinking in those moments; she'd used him and then betrayed him. Nothing could be further from the truth. Today, she'd been so close to saying yes. Now, he would never ask again. Unless, when he had time to cool his thoughts, he would come to see it differently, come to see her words as truth. She had come to warn him, nothing more. Ridolfo had set her up. He was still setting her up.

The story was told over and over at dinner, embellished until it reached epic proportion; how the Pantera beauty had distracted the Torre stable long enough for the *mangini* of Pantera to leave heavy traces of angelica on the hay and leaves of angelica buried deep inside the haystack.

The only quirk to the story was that the Torre *mangini* had figured out what had happened far more quickly than they would have liked. They would have preferred Morello off his feed for a day, too weak to make a good show at the races, but essentially none the worse for the prank.

She hated the story. Hated that everyone, even those beyond the *contrada*, would hear her part in it and assume she'd done it willingly when in fact she'd done it accidentally. She'd not had any intention of setting up the prank. She thought she'd known the reason Ridolfo had sent her: nothing more than a cruel snub to Archer and perhaps a strong reminder to her of what she couldn't have. Perhaps even as a reminder to her that he was powerful and she was not. But she'd been wrong.

Once this story made the rounds, Archer would want nothing to do with her. It would confirm for him that his *contrada*'s accusations were right. She'd spoken to him so many times of the importance of family loyalty. Archer would think that was where she sided and why she'd resisted his proposal. He would feel used and betrayed. He would think there had only been sex between them, a sex that meant nothing beyond its physical pleasures, that she'd strung him along.

Beside her at dinner, Contessina squeezed her hand, caught up in the excitement of the story and entirely oblivious to her own distress. 'You're so brave, Cousin! I envy you.'

'So brave, that I fear Torre might seek retribution,' Uncle Rafaele called down the table in good humour. 'Contessina, you might do us a service and stay the night in your cousin's room in case they try to steal her away. They've already crashed one party, I wouldn't put it past them.'

Ridolfo nodded his approval, and Elisabeta knew the matter was settled. Ridolfo was fat, not stupid. He suspected she would run, that she would try to reach Archer one last time, all of which assumed Archer would still have her after the debacle of today. Now the chances of running were slim indeed with Contessina in her room. She might as well suggest they put a lock on her door too. Which they probably would now that everyone would view it as protection and not imprisonment. Only she and Ridolfo would know the difference.

He knew, though, there was no question of it. His narrow eyes had studied her throughout the meal in a most uncomfortable manner. He was watching her, assessing her. His gaze was part that of a butcher or horse trader assessing his newly acquired product and part shrewd businessman calculating his next move and hers. He was drinking heavily. She had lost track of how many times his glass had been filled during the long meal.

This would be a night to avoid him, something she'd been successful in doing thus far. Ridolfo seldom came to the house, but the days before the Palio made for new alliances. With Oca not running, Pantera's involvement with the race was critical to him, his one personal connection. Of course, Oca had their other alliances, but they were not Ridolfo's personally. He knew his leverage rested with Pantera and with her.

Elisabeta rose from the table to go with Contessina and her aunt and the other women of the house, but Ridolfo's voice stopped them all. 'Rafaele, I would speak with our lovely heroine for a moment if you will permit it?'

Her uncle could not refuse, nor would he see any reason for it. With the wedding two weeks away, it was a perfectly natural request. 'Please, Ridolfo, use the garden,' her uncle offered. She shot a covert plea for help in Giuliano's direction just in case she still had an ally in the room. She wondered if he knew of Archer's nocturnal visits? If he did, he'd said nothing, his time consumed with the Palio.

At least the garden was somewhat public given that it had no doors or windows and was out in the open. She wouldn't be in a confined space with him and she supposed there was plenty of statuary and dirt to throw at him if it came to that. Surely it wouldn't. If the garden was public for her it was public for him too.

Ridolfo insisted on touching her, taking her arm on the short walk to the garden, his hand dropping to the small of her back as they strolled among the shrubs and artwork. She tried not to flinch. His touch was nothing like Archer's. Where Archer's touch caressed and teased, inspiring visions of glorious pleasure to come, Ridolfo's touch was heavy and possessive. His touch claimed, marked and invited no images of pleasure. Quite the opposite, in fact: images of servitude and punishment for disobedience. He was a man who would have his justice.

'The *contrada* thinks you a heroine...' Ridolfo began, harmlessly enough. He smiled in the lantern-lit light, revealing yellowing teeth behind his lips. It was something one could ignore at a distance, but up close it was impossible to dismiss. Archer's mouth on the other hand was clean, full of straight, white teeth.

She had to stop. She was only making this worse on herself if she let every thought lead back to Archer. Archer had all but repudiated her today. No, that wasn't quite true, he'd also offered for her, offered to declare his intentions publicly. But that was before Oca's treachery was discovered, before she'd been implicated. Did his offer still stand? A small kernel of hope had stubbornly kept flaring throughout the evening that Archer would understand she had been used, that he would come for her. But then she'd remember the flat look in his eyes and the kernel would retreat only to resurface a few hours later.

'I did not ask to be a heroine,' Elisabeta replied modestly. Ridolfo liked humility in women. Perhaps, like a fire that could not burn without oxygen, his wrath could be deprived of fuel as well. If she was humble, there would be nothing for him to take issue with. She had to keep her temper.

'Heroine or whore is the real question.' Ridolfo's tone became harsh. 'Your uncle can spin the tale however he likes. It's good for me if you're painted with a kind brush. But you and I know the difference, don't we?' His hand moved to grip her arm in a tight vice. His beefy sausage fingers were digging in hard. 'You went to his bed at least once. I saw you leave him early in the morning after the first night of the unofficial trials.'

'You saw me? Or your spies saw me?' Elisabeta spat. So much for keeping her temper. At the first provocation her temper soared, but anger was better than fear. It was fair to say that she was more than a little frightened. Her strength was no match for Ridolfo. Her arm hurt where he gripped it, and she'd been caught. He or his minions had seen her. But she would not give Ridolfo the satisfaction of her fear. She would, however, not hesitate in letting him see her anger. She would give him a fight.

'I was alerted immediately and I came to see it with my own eyes.' He shook her arm. 'How convenient it was for you. Your uncle was out of town that first night and you took every advantage of his absence to blacken his name; riding on the track, dressing as a boy, sneaking off with the Englishman, going to his bed.'

His face was close to hers now, his breath a lingering menu of the evening meal. 'I came down to the street and saw you myself. It is a hard thing to see your fiancée's betrayal with your own eyes, but I would not believe it of you any other way.'

'Of course you believed it of me. You wouldn't have spied on me otherwise,' Elisabeta dared to contradict him.

'Not spies, guards. They were for your protection,' he sneered. 'After the incident at the party, I didn't dare leave you unguarded. Such a jewel like yourself should never be left unprotected. *Never*, Elisabeta.'

His message was clear. This was a mere precursor to what her married life would be like. There would be guards, escorts, everywhere for her. The town would look at such gestures with approval. A man should protect what he loves, what he treasures. No one would see anything wrong with the wealthy Ridolfo employing men to watch his beloved. But she would know otherwise. Every day was to be imprisonment with gaolers everywhere. She yanked at her arm, struggling to free it, but Ridolfo was too strong.

'We are not done yet. There is the issue of consequences for your infidelity.' They'd reached the edge of the garden where a wall separated the private home of Rafaele di Bruno from the city streets. Elisabeta would have preferred to be closer to the interior of the house, closer to the chance of family or servants walking by. Being out here beyond the lanterns, beyond family, was unnerving, especially when she sensed Ridolfo had orchestrated it this way on purpose. This was not an accidental destination.

'I am not your wife yet,' Elisabeta reminded him. 'Until then, your official jurisdiction over me is in question. My uncle is my guardian at present and even that is somewhat nebulous given that I'm a widow and of age.' Her case sounded stronger when she voiced it out loud. Her confidence urged her on. 'You have control over your consent to the betrothal and that is all. You may end this arrangement at any point.'

She had pushed him too far. She saw it in the narrow beads of his eyes a fraction of a second before she felt it in his grip, in the pressure of his body pushing her back to the wall until she was pinned between the rough brick and the fat of his stomach. 'You would like that. Perhaps that's what you've been after all along. Did you want me to catch you with the Englishman? Did you think that would be enough?' He was breathing hard now, angry and excited all at once. His cock stirred against her leg in frightening arousal.

'I have wanted you in my bed for quite some time and I will have you. I have built a trade empire by negotiating for anything I ever wanted and I've got it. You are no different, Elisabeta. I wanted you and I shall have you. Used goods or not.' He was rough with her now, his hands tearing at the laces of her bodice, her attempts to push them away only encouraging him to press her harder into the wall where breathing became difficult.

'I had no illusions about being your first, although I doubt that boy husband of yours made much use of you. But I will be your last and I will be your only from here on out. You will not put another man before me, ever again.'

'Ridolfo, please.' Elisabeta pushed at him with both hands, starting to fight him in earnest as his weight crushed her and his intentions became brutally obvious. She forced her gaze to stay on him, like a wolf in the wild faced with a foe. To look away would be to admit defeat and that would be a grievous mistake at this critical moment. 'You are not thinking straight. You will regret this in the morning. You don't want us to come together like this.' She tried not to cringe as she said the words, tried not to imagine other times, other walls, with far more pleasant outcomes.

'What I don't want,' he snarled, his free hand working open his trousers, 'is to go to the altar with you with no assurance there isn't an English bastard already in your belly. At least I can muddy those waters and why shouldn't I? You've already played the *troia* so you shouldn't mind doing it one more time. You might even like what I have to offer you if you give it a chance.'

Elisabeta kicked at him, but the close proximity of their bodies rendered the kicks impotent. If only she could render the same for him. She struggled, but that seemed to incite him further. She bit at him and earned the back of his hand and a string of cursing. That was when she screamed, not caring who it brought as long as it brought someone. He had brought her out here solely for this purpose.

Noise was not what Ridolfo wanted. He wanted absolute privacy for this reckoning. She'd taken that from him and she was going to pay. She was falling before it registered that he'd thrown her. She was on the ground, on all fours, scrambling for distance and freedom, her knees struggling in the folds of her skirts, when the kick came, his foot finding her midsection between belly and ribs. It took all the wind from her. She had nothing left to struggle with, she could barely breathe. That was struggle enough. Panic welled. She had to fight that at least. Panic would only make it worse. The one thought passing through her mind was that she was going to suffocate right here at Ridolfo's feet. Although she should have been more concerned about Ridolfo would do next.

Ridolfo was cursing, his rage out of control. If he kicked her again, she would be finished. He might have done it if there hadn't been the rush of running feet on the gravel. The footsteps sounded overloud to her. Perhaps they were meant to be. The sooner Ridolfo heard them, the better.

'What has happened?' It was Giuliano and he was on his knees beside her instantly, his arm about her as he helped her to stand.

'It is none of your concern what happens between a man and his intended,' Ridolfo reprimanded.

She could feel tension rippling through Giuliano's body. He would not accept that explanation. 'She is my cousin before she is your wife and she's not even that yet,' Giuliano replied, his body ready for a fight. That was not what she wanted. She wanted no more men fighting over her or because of her. A horse had been risked today on her behalf. Archer was targeted for violence because of her. She would not have Giuliano suffer too.

'Please, Giuliano, let it be.' Elisabeta spoke each word haltingly, her breath still in the process of returning. She put a hand on Giuliano's arm and turned him towards the house. 'Just take me inside. I am sure Contessina is waiting for me.' She hated speaking the words, hated giving any sign of outward complicity with Ridolfo, but she hated more the idea of Giuliano hurt because of her. She could sacrifice a little pride for his safety.

'You're protecting him,' Giuliano growled ungraciously as he helped her back to the house. 'Did he hurt you? What a stupid question, of course he did. You were on the ground and in pain. What did he do? Did he hit you? Kick you?' Her face was too transparent.

'He kicked you, didn't he?' Giuliano pushed a hand through his hair. 'I should challenge him, that *porca miseria.* I should call him out. The fat bastard probably can't fire a pistol or wield a sword with any dexterity. I will skewer him like the pig is he.'

She felt some her temper returning. 'Do you think that's what I want?' She tugged at Giuliano's arm. 'Why do you suppose I covered for him? Not to protect him, but to protect you.'

'I could beat him,' Giuliano protested indignantly.

'That's not the point. I would not have you do murder for me. You would live with that the rest of your life.'

'So, better you live with him the rest of yours?' The colour had risen in Giuliano's face. 'He will hit you again. You are too stubborn,' Giuliano said quietly, helping her up the stairs.

They paused at the landing for her to gather her breath. She gathered her thoughts and her courage too. If she meant to do it, she needed to do it now or it would be too late. 'I need you to do something for me, Giuliano.'

'Anything, Cousin.'

'Go to Torre and see if you can learn what Archer thinks of me. If there's a chance…'

She didn't finish the sentence, her words choked off with emotion, but Giuliano knew. He squeezed her hand. 'I will find Archer and he will come for you.'

Elisabeta cut in swiftly, alarmed by the potential behind those words. 'Not by force, Giuliano. Promise me. Archer has to come of his own free will. I won't have him any other way.' It was quite a gamble to take. Who knew what Archer thought of her now?

Chapter Twenty

'What do you think of your lovely widow now? Maybe it's a good thing she delayed on answering your proposal,' Nolan asked as they sat around the long table in the *loggia*, drinking wine and talking late into the night, or maybe it just seemed that way to Archer. He'd been up for days, literally.

By rights, this should have been a joyous occasion, the kind of evening young, single men lived for. There was good food, good wine and excellent company. They sat around the table catching each other up on their adventures since Archer had left Paris. Alyssandra, Haviland's new bride, had discreetly excused herself an hour ago, sensing the need, no doubt, for male bonding. Archer wished he could go too. Sleep sounded good. Forgetting sounded even better. For obvious reasons, it was hard to fully celebrate when the issue of Elisabeta weighed on his mind and now Nolan had brought it to the fore with his question.

'They are calling her the Hero of Pantera,' Nolan

went on. 'I heard it in the streets on my way home. Pantera is saying she ruined Torre's hay.'

Whether *she* did was debatable, but the hay *was* ruined. They'd had to put in a special order.

'I envy everyone's quick pigeonholing of Signora di Nofri, when I am still sifting through the afternoon's events and trying to figure out what they mean,' Archer replied drily. *She's mine after all, why shouldn't I be the one who decides her story?* But was she really his?

'It is because you love her.' Nolan leaned forward across the table. 'There's nothing to sort through. It's very simple. They used her to gain access to our stables in order to conduct sabotage. Fortunately, you were too smart for them and it backfired. Our stable boys understood right away the part she'd played and were more than happy to expose her. Pantera and Oca won't be able to play the di Nofri card again.'

'Our stables?' Archer raised an eyebrow at Nolan. 'How quickly you've become Italian.'

'You're just prickly,' Nolan replied, pouring some more wine.

Archer smiled neutrally at his friend, unwilling to argue the facts. He was prickly on Elisabeta's behalf. He knew what no one else did. He'd seen what no one else had; the wariness in her eyes. He'd heard the carefully worded sentences and he believed he'd accurately translated their code. She'd known she was being sent as part of some nefarious purpose, but she hadn't known what that purpose was. Neither had she been in a position to refuse to come. If he was right, walking into the stables must have been akin to digging one's own grave. She knew eventually she would be exposed and she could do nothing to save herself. But she could save him, so she'd come to put him on guard, to see him one more time.

That was the theory he liked, at least. And if he was wrong? If she had used him, he was a fool who put the *contrada* at risk. So he sat and endured his friends' well-intended ribs. Elisabeta was right. There was something to be said for keeping one's business one's own. He'd never had his life as exposed as it was now.

'It's quite the Romeo-and-Juliet story, sans poison though,' Nolan said rather cheerily. 'A story of two people torn apart by forbidden love.' He gave an exaggeratedly dramatic sigh. Archer caught a sly look from Haviland that said they'd talk about this later.

A footman interrupted the party. 'Signor Crawford, there's a man outside. He wants to speak with you.'

Archer didn't show the slightest hesitation. He was out of his chair, almost in enough time to avoid Haviland's warning hand on his arm. 'Perhaps I should come with you? It might be a trap. The messenger may not bring a verbal message, but a more physical one,' Haviland warned.

Down the table, Nolan reached for the wine bottle. 'Oh, I *do* love Italy. There's adventure around every corner, even at the dinner table.'

Archer shot him a censorious look. Haviland had a point. 'All right, I appreciate it.'

'We'll come too.' Nolan and Brennan set aside their napkins and stood, not waiting for any argument. Archer smiled. He'd missed them, all of them, sorely since Paris. It felt good to know they had his back once more.

Haviland clapped a hand on Archer's shoulder as they made their way to the street. 'My goodness, I leave you alone for six weeks and look at the trouble you've got into.' He winked. 'Perhaps I should have left you alone a lot sooner.'

'I know, just look what happened to you,' Archer jested. 'You break free of the old home front and the first thing you do is run off and get married.'

'Isn't rebellion fabulous?' Haviland laughed.

'I hate to break up the bonhomie,' Nolan put in impatiently, 'but do either of you have a blade? A knife?'

'I do, in my boot,' Archer replied, earning a classic raised eyebrow of enquiry from Haviland. Archer shrugged. 'It's Palio season, you always go armed if you're *mangini*.'

'I've a knife too in my boot, but that's because I was travelling, *not* because I was wandering around your quaint little town here,' Haviland said with dry humour, shooting another look at Archer.

'Draw them, I see the man over there.' Nolan nodded towards a quiet, dark part of the street, perfect for an ambush or for staying discreetly hidden if one didn't want other late-night strollers to notice.

But Archer noticed who it was immediately. It was Giuliano, and Archer thought Haviland's recommendation to come with friends might not be amiss. Giuliano wasn't simply a messenger. He was one of Rafaele di Bruno's *mangini*, his son and Elisabeta's cousin. Just his being here suggested something was afoot.

Giuliano shook his head and held up his hands at

the sight of the blades. He let them approach before he quietly stated his purpose. '*Signori*, I come peaceably and secretly on an errand from Elisabeta. May we speak somewhere less public?'

'Come inside and take some wine with us,' Archer offered before Nolan could suggest the *loggia*. The *loggia* was open to the street and Giuliano would not want to be seen lounging with them after the events of today.

Wine was brought to a small room that opened on to the fountain and the internal courtyard. Giuliano made the requisite small talk as wine was poured; complimenting the vintage and asking about Morello.

Archer shifted in his seat, anxiously wanting to get on to the real business. He decided to help that business along with a direct question, his tone terse. 'Morello is fine. How is Elisabeta?'

Giuliano's dark eyes settled on him. 'I think that will depend on you, Signor Crawford. She risked much to come to you today and she was sorely used by Ridolfo. In turn, she was accused of treachery by your *contrada*.'

Archer turned the glass in his hand, wanting to appear unaffected. This was not new. He had suspected as much, but did that make it true? 'She has come through it well. I hear tell they are calling her the Hero of Pantera even though the mission was unsuccessful in achieving its ends.'

Giuliano gave a dismissive shrug. 'All is not always what it appears, *signor*. She has been crafted a hero and pitting the two of you against one another has made for a delicious Palio tale, sure to become legend: the beautiful Pantera woman attempting to lure the skilled Torre horseman; the Torre horseman outwitting the lady at each turn. It is the stuff of romances.'

Giuliano paused and said grimly, 'If all of this is done in the name of the Palio and the *contrada* we can preserve her reputation. Otherwise, she is nothing more than a common *troia*, a traitor to her *contrada* and a cuckolder of her fiancé.' There was no small amount of concern behind Giuliano's words.

'You said you came with a message and yet you sit here and slander my friend!' Nolan would have leapt for Giuliano if Archer had not stayed him with an out-thrust hand. His own temper was rising, but not for the same reason.

'Sit, Nolan. We will not draw blood in my uncle's house.' Archer thought he caught Haviland mutter under his breath something to the extent of 'I never thought to hear those words spoken together in a sentence'.

'You said her well-being depended on me. What would you have me do?' Archer asked calmly.

'You are the only one who can decide how the grand epic will end,' Giuliano replied. He'd given up any pretence of nonchalance. He leaned forward in earnest, hands braced on his thighs. 'Will you allow this story to have a happy ending?'

Archer studied him. Giuliano was tense, his jaw tight. There was something more at work here. He had not come as an ambassador of Pantera, which suggested the 'happy ending' he sought was not one where she married the wealthy merchant and lived for ever as the Hero of Pantera. Hope stirred. 'I think it depends on which happy ending you have in mind, Signor di Bruno,' Archer replied.

Giuliano's shoulders relaxed fractionally and he smiled. 'You understand my predicament, *signor*. I am grateful. Will you walk with me? I would speak with you alone.'

'I prefer you speak in front of my friends. Their advice maybe useful and we have no secrets among us.'

'All right,' Giuliano agreed. 'But what I am telling you must be kept in strictest confidence. I would not have anyone know what has happened. Elisabeta has asked me to come and ascertain her standing with you. You repudiated her this afternoon, most convincingly.'

'I had no choice,' Archer replied. 'I am not afraid to fight, but the fight must be prudent. At that moment, it was not. There was always the chance that my *contrada* was right and that she had used me. I would not be the first man to be blinded by love. I needed time to sort through it all and to think what would be best for us. To contradict my *contrada* too soon would not have served her well.' Archer slid a glance at Giuliano. 'You are right when you say she is either the hero or the whore. To have fought for her today would have branded her the whore you and I are so intent on avoiding.'

'You say you will fight for her? That you love her?' Giuliano pressed.

Why was it so hard to say the simple word? Was it that he didn't trust Giuliano not to make a fool of him, not to turn this into a deadly game? Or was it because there would be no turning back? Italian or English, a man's word was his bond. He gave Giuliano a hard look. 'I cannot play games over this. If I tell you the truth, may I have your word you will not use it against me?'

It was Giuliano's turn to waver. He drew a breath. 'Yes, let us have plain speech between us.'

Archer gathered his courage, thinking it was far easier to ride an unbroken horse than to confess his feelings. 'I love her. I would marry her and make a life with her either here or in England. My father is an earl. I am a second son, I will not inherit, but I have my own resources. I have the family string and my uncle has offered me his villa—'

Giuliano cut him off. 'I don't need any other qualifications.' But Archer could see that the brief recitation had pleased him. 'She cannot marry Ridolfo.' There was urgency in his tone overlaid with worry and genuine concern. 'I know she resists your offer because she is concerned about the family and the scandal, but I cannot allow those things to stand in her way any longer. Something happened tonight that has changed all that.'

Archer listened in appalled silence as Giuliano recounted the scene from the di Bruno garden. His fists clenched at his sides. 'Ridolfo knows, then,' he said grimly when Giuliano concluded. What else could have provoked such an act of violence? This was his fault. He'd left her open to harm. He should have fought for her today in the stable. He should have defended her with words at least. But that would not have stopped Ridolfo from knowing.

His blood was humming with the need for revenge, the need to see her and know for himself Elisabeta was all right. Dear God, Ridolfo had kicked her, had thrown her to the ground. What sort of man treated a woman that way? But he knew. One who threatened to tie her up, to compel her into sexual congress against her will, with drugs if needed.

'What do I do next? I have offered,' Archer repeated. He had done all he could do up to a point. She had to make the choice. 'I will not force her to exchange one unwanted wedding for another.'

'Your offers have been private ones,' Nolan put in, twirling his knife absently. He grabbed the knife hilt and leaned forward in earnest. 'What makes Ridolfo's offer so damning is that it's public. That's where the scandal lies. Face is at stake. Your offers, my friend, are private ones likely made at the most private of times. No one knows of them but the two of you.'

'Go on.' Archer's interest was piqued. Nolan was onto something. He needed to make an ally of her uncle, of her family.

'You need to declare your intentions. You need to go to her uncle and show yourself,' Nolan explained.

'I will go tonight.' Archer was halfway out of his seat.

Giuliano shook his head. 'You will get only one chance. This is a more delicate negotiation than you realise. Listen carefully, you are to come to my father's house tomorrow in the morning after the fourth trial and then you will make your best offer,' Giuliano said solemnly. 'Your uncle will know what you need. I will tell Elisabeta.'

His uncle Giacomo would be disappointed. He might lose the villa, might lose the dream, might even lose the family he'd just discovered. 'If my uncle does not approve, we will have no choice but to leave,' Archer said slowly.

'Can you live with that?' Haviland interjected. 'Think about yourself. Your dreams are here. Once sacrificed, they won't be regained.'

Then came Nolan's persistent question, quietly voiced and in all seriousness. 'Archer, is she worth it?'

'Yes,' Archer said solemnly, holding Giuliano's gaze. A horse farm could be made anywhere. He could go back to England and mend fences with his father. Perhaps this trip had been about coming to grips with that—his father had loved his mother and been unable to cope with her illness and her loss. His inability to do so had driven him to make poor decisions. Perhaps it was time to forgive him for that and get on with life.

Archer rose. He offered his hand to Giuliano. 'Tell her I will come to her tomorrow. I will not fail her. I must speak to my uncle.'

'About what?' Giacomo strode into the room. 'I heard we had a visitor.' He eyed Giuliano.

Archer drew a deep breath. The words were hard to find. He did not want to hurt this man, this brother of his mother. 'About Elisabeta di Nofri, *Zio*. I wish to offer for her.'

His uncle's eyes were shrewd. 'She is pledged to another.'

'A man who is unworthy of her,' Archer replied evenly.

'I know. I heard.' His uncle nodded to the corner by the door—he'd been eavesdropping. 'Still, there will be vengeance over this,' his uncle warned. 'Torre will be embroiled. It is not enough to merely offer for her.'

'He's right.' Nolan stepped forward, and Archer glared at him. Whose side was his friend on anyway? 'We have to disgrace Ridolfo, cause him to lose face so that Pantera can walk away from the match, so that the other *contradas* will be sympathetic to Pantera's choice.' Then Nolan added cunningly, 'And so you can stay. If Ridolfo loses face, you won't have to leave.'

Archer's eyes flitted between his uncle and Nolan. 'If that is acceptable to my uncle?'

His uncle did not hesitate. 'Of course it is. Did you think I would withdraw my offer of the villa and the horses over this? You are family. What did I tell you? Family is never a burden.'

Archer felt an enormous weight lift. One hurdle down. 'I will go tomorrow.' He smiled for the first time since that afternoon. Either way, the end would be the same. Elisabeta would be his. It was amazing what making a decision could do for a man. He felt good, he felt awake when he should have been dead on his feet.

Giacomo gave him a sly look. 'No, you don't. There is no "I" in Siena, just "we". *We* will go to di Bruno's.'

Archer nodded his assent. 'Of course I meant "we".'

'I hope that "we" includes us this time?' Nolan interjected, gesturing to the group.

'You needn't be involved—' Archer began, his guilt rising over having them here with so much unsettled. Guilt too over wanting them here in spite of it.

'Needn't be involved?' Nolan protested. 'We didn't come all this way to miss out on the fun. Of course we're in.'

There would be no gainsaying Nolan once he'd made up his mind, especially when that mind was apparently backed by the others. Archer raised his glass, more than happy to acquiesce. 'Well, then, I guess that's decided. *A domani*—here's to tomorrow!'

Chapter Twenty-One

'*A domani*? There will be no blood spilt in the house? Are you sure this is what you want? This place is just this side of crazy, Archer, and now you're attempting to marry a woman you've known for only a month. A woman who, I might add, is promised to another.' Haviland paced the bedroom while Archer finished dressing. The morning trials were over and they were free to make their way to di Bruno's.

'Not attempting. I *will* succeed. Attempt implies there is a margin for failure.' Archer inserted cufflinks into their holes at his wrists. 'Are you trying to talk me out of this?' He fixed Haviland with a stare that was part-scolding and part-stubbornness. Haviland's efforts would be futile. His mind was made up.

'It's just happening so fast,' Haviland protested.

Archer grinned. 'Says the man who married a woman he'd known for barely six weeks.' He was too happy this morning to take Haviland's concerns seriously. Haviland was merely trying to be a good friend, much as he had done for Haviland when their positions had been reversed in Paris.

'You're completely transformed,' Haviland ventured. 'You speak Italian flawlessly, you carry a knife in your boot all of the time, you've been climbing balconies.'

Archer laughed. 'First, I've always spoken Italian. You know that. I was raised on it. I just didn't have a chance to use it in England. Second, Siena is no different than London where you and I carry swordsticks and I've never been a monk.'

'We carry swordsticks to fight off the occasional ruffian, not to cross the street and talk to our neighbours.' Haviland warmed to the debate.

'It's Palio season,' Archer said, as if the Palio explained everything. To most Sienese, it did. Perhaps he really was starting to fit in. Archer wondered if this was how his father had felt when he'd first come to Siena? Had he too felt transformed by the energy and pace of Siena, the different customs and lifestyles? Archer tried not to think about his father too much, tried not to think about history repeating itself. His father had come to Siena not seeking a bride and had found one, just like him. His father had fallen head over heels in love, just like him. Like father, like son, seemed aptly applied for the occasion. But he hoped that was where the similarity ended. Were the Crawford men destined to love intensely but tragically? He was his father's son, but he hoped he was his mother's too. There was a knock on the door and Archer grabbed up his coat. It was time to go.

Downstairs was organised chaos. His uncle had indeed taken care of all the details. His uncle and his friends were turned out in their best. The *contrada* page was there dressed in full costume and out in the street along with a whole *comparsa*, or delegation, complete with flag throwers and a drummer waiting to accompany him. 'The only thing missing is the *duce*,' Archer joked with his uncle.

Giacomo slapped him on the back. 'You are the *duce*, Archer. It's the perfect role for you to play today.'

'The *duce*?' Nolan queried with a laugh. 'That's sounds rather dubious in English or French.'

'Get your mind out of the gutter,' Archer scolded good-naturedly. 'In the Palio parades, every *contrada* has a *duce*. He's to be the most handsome young man in the neighbourhood.' He fixed Nolan with a serious stare. 'You have to behave today. This is important, everything hinges on this embassy.'

Giacomo squeezed his shoulder reassuringly. 'Don't worry, we will do our best.'

They were coming! Elisabeta could hear the drums and the singing before she could see the *comparsa*. She flung open the doors to her little balcony and stared down the streets, her fingers gripping the railing. Archer was coming! Giuliano had told her as much last night. But to see it and to know it would not be a covert effort, but a public one with all of Torre behind him, was more than she hoped for.

The burgundy flag with Torre's pale blue-and-white decorations, bearing the Torre symbol of a crowned elephant and a tower, came into view. 'Contessina! Come help me dress,' she called to her cousin. She wasn't going to miss a minute of this. Elisabeta flung open her wardrobe and riffled through her gowns. Normally, she wore the standard fare of the white underdress with a dirndl-style overdress, but today she wanted something more sophisticated. 'There! This one, I think.' She pulled out a seldom-worn gown of pale sage and held it against her as she danced across the floor.

What a difference a day made, she thought as Contessina helped her into the gown. Everything had been so very bleak yesterday and last evening had been positively dire. But this morning, Archer was coming for her. She fastened a strand of demure pearls about her neck while Contessina worked on her hair. 'Nothing too fancy,' she suggested. 'It is just eleven o'clock in the morning.'

'A neat chignon, then.' Contessina smiled at her in the mirror. 'Isn't this exciting! Two suitors vying for your hand.'

Exciting didn't begin to describe it. Exciting, because Archer was coming, but also nerve-racking because Archer *was* coming and there was no guarantee his suit would be accepted. Her uncle had much to weigh in the balance when considering this about-face. That was precisely what it would be too—she was publicly promised to Ridolfo and now Archer would make his suit public as well. To change direction now would cause someone a loss of face, either her uncle or Ridolfo, not to mention Pantera and Oca as a whole.

Elisabeta slid her feet into matching slippers and made her way downstairs, her stomach full of butterflies. The impact of this on the *contradas* was no small matter. Her uncle was the *capitano*, no one but the *priore* had as much prestige in Pantera. Would he risk that status by neglecting his commitment to

Oca? Would he risk the face of Pantera? Oca would hate them and a *contrada* grudge was no small thing. People still talked about Pantera's interference with the Aquila rider in the 1752 Palio which led to Torre's victory. She had no doubt someone would bring that up again today.

Her uncle and his men were already assembled, her aunt and Giuliano were there and, to her dismay, Ridolfo was there too looking thunderous with his Oca contingent. Elisabeta took the seat between her uncle and aunt. 'What is he doing here?' she whispered to her uncle.

'You are publicly committed to marry him. He has every right to be here and defend his claim should he want to,' her uncle answered sternly, reminding her of the gravity of the situation. Then the doors opened and Archer stood framed in the doorway, surrounded by the splendour of Torre and all worry fled for the moment. Archer had outdone himself. She'd seen him in the clothes of a working horseman and in the guise of a weary, dusty traveller. Today, he came as a nobleman's son.

He wore polished black boots into which went fawn-coloured breeches tailored to perfection. Everything about him bore that same stamp of perfection from the tamed sheen of his hair to the impeccable knot of his cravat. He sported pristine white linen beneath a pale blue silk waistcoat and a coat of burgundy with a generous shawl collar that fell to his knees in neat, full folds. The colours, she was sure, were calculated to pay tribute to Torre and serve as a reminder that, for Pantera, an alliance with Torre would have benefits. Torre was one of the more powerful and prestigious neighbourhoods even if it was the most contentious. Torre was the only *contrada* with two enemies.

Archer bowed to her uncle, and she noticed for the first time the rapier that hung from his belt. For decorative reasons, she hoped. The other men in his cortège were similarly attired. They must be his English friends. His greeting might have been in the English style, but he spoke to her uncle in his flawless Italian, hardly even sparing her a glance, but that was by design. This was to be approached with the formality of a business transaction. Still, she hung on every word.

His case was well presented. He laid out his credentials: the son of an earl and a son of Torre. He was Sienese through his mother's family, proving he was more than an upstart Englishman. He was half-Italian too. He laid out his wealth: the horse farm, the string of racing thoroughbreds, the sport of kings, in Newmarket, his annual income, which sounded staggering to her. He outlined his position with his uncle at the villa, which he'd be given upon his marriage, and his obligations with his uncle's horses. He had no intentions of merely absconding with her to England. He meant to stay and become part of Sienese life. He was welcome in his *contrada* and had some standing in it already through his uncle, who had shown him great personal favour.

With each argument, Elisabeta's hopes rose. He was an eminently suitable gentleman. More than that, her hope rose that he wouldn't have to choose between his dreams and her. There was hope for her too; that she could have the life she'd always wanted;

a horse farm in the countryside, a loving husband by her side, eventually children, a *private* family. It was all so close, she could almost reach out and touch it. Her joy was nearly overwhelming. She wanted to run to Archer and throw her arms about him for making it possible.

Archer finished speaking. He took a respectful step backwards and gave her uncle a small bow to indicate he'd concluded. Those present in the receiving room were nodding their heads in approval. All her uncle had to do was say yes. Elisabeta very carefully kept her eyes downcast, not wanting to give away her excitement.

'These are indeed practical considerations when taking a wife…' her uncle began. 'Signor Crawford, you have comported yourself well today. You have much that recommends you and for that you are to be applauded. Your responsibility speaks well of you. However, there is still the issue of my niece's previous betrothal. You are aware, I believe, that she is currently promised to another?'

Beneath her lashes, Elisabeta watched Archer calmly accept the pronouncement. Her uncle would not make this easy for Archer no matter how impeccable his credentials. Her uncle simply couldn't. If he was going to concede his arrangement with Oca, he would have to make it look difficult. Perhaps Archer had anticipated as much as well.

Archer let his voice fill the receiving room for all to hear. 'I am aware of that, Signor di Bruno. I would not dare to intrude on another man's arrangement except for the fact that I am compelled by love. My feelings for Signora di Nofri are such that I cannot,

in good conscience, ignore them and know that I had
been true to myself or to her.'

'What of Signor Ranieri?' her uncle enquired patiently. 'Are his feelings of no consequence?'

'I cannot speak for his feelings, only my own. But
I was led to believe this match was made for purely
political reasons and that love had very little to do
with it. If you are looking for political gain, I assure
you Torre will prove most valuable in that regard.
There is nothing Oca can offer that Torre cannot
match or exceed.'

Bravo! Elisabeta thought. Her Englishman had
learned to think like a true Sienese. This was the
stuff of the classic Oca-Torre rivalry. Ridolfo was
halfway out of his seat, huffing with the exertion of
sudden movement and making his way towards her
uncle before Archer had drawn a breath.

'This is an outrage!' he cried. 'We had an agreement and you've let this Torre swine come to argue it.
He has no grounds. This agreement is not contestable.'

Elisabeta thought Ridolfo had made a rather poor
choice in vacating his seat and coming to stand side
by side with Archer. Ridolfo did not fare well in the
visual comparison. Where Archer was immaculate
in his attire and temper, Ridolfo's clothes fit poorly,
his trousers baggy to accommodate his paunch, his
linen wrinkled, his cravat drooping after a morning
in the sun at the trials. Never mind that most men in
the room looked the same. He looked unkempt next
to Archer and that was all that mattered.

Where Archer's delivery had been polite and well
paced, Ridolfo's angry outburst had been emotional
and not businesslike in the least. He looked like a

petulant child denied a treat. How could her uncle possibly prefer Ridolfo to Archer? How could anyone in the room blame him for entertaining Archer's offer? Yet, her uncle hesitated.

'She is to be my wife and everyone knows it,' Ridolfo protested. 'There is no reason to break the agreement.'

Elisabeta gripped the arms of her chair until her nails bit into the centuries-old wood. This was the sticking point. There was no reason. On her uncle's other side, Giuliano leaned over to speak into her uncle's ear. She thought she noticed her uncle's hand clench the arm of his chair, his face settling into stern features.

His eyes had narrowed to shrewd slits when he spoke again to Ridolfo. 'It seems there is reason after all. My son informs me you exhibited untoward behaviour involving violence towards my niece last night in my own home.'

Elisabeta sucked in her breath, daring a look at last directly at Archer. Giuliano had taken a huge risk, but it was masterfully done. The news had come from a credible source, not Archer himself, who would have appeared to have been biased. Ridolfo was not the only one who'd engaged in untoward behaviour in her uncle's home. If Ridolfo wanted to press the issue, she and Archer could be exposed. But that, too, would be risky on Ridolfo's part. If Ridolfo made it public knowledge she'd been sexually engaged with Archer, her uncle would feel compelled to allow Archer's suit and at the same time it would put Ridolfo in the role of the cuckold. No, she didn't think Ridolfo would take the chance.

Ridolfo made a short incline of his head. 'I am most regretful of my actions last night.'

'As well you should be,' her uncle continued. 'My niece is dear to me and I will not give her in marriage to a man who would mistreat her. You have nullified my need to honour the contract. Even if there was no counter-suit in the offing, I would still nullify it.' Elisabeta fought the urge to smile triumphantly as her uncle's words settled on the assembly.

'No!' Ridolfo fairly exploded. 'I was well within my rights, she...' He jabbed a finger her direction and Elisabeta froze. It was her worst fear. In his anger, he would risk exposing her. But his words never materialised. Archer's rapier was out in a flash and pressed to the soft skin of Ridolfo's throat.

'You will not slander her name within my hearing without paying the consequence.' Archer's voice was deadly cold, his hand steady.

Ridolfo's eyes bulged. He sent a silent plea towards her uncle. Her uncle nodded his head and Archer lowered his rapier. 'I demand recompense for this assault,' Ridolfo growled, one hand at his neck massaging the spot where Archer's blade had been.

'What would you have me do? Signor Crawford was only acting the gentleman,' her uncle cajoled, reminding Ridolfo that while Archer had played the gentleman, Ridolfo had not.

'I demand a chance to win her back.'

'What do you propose?'

'The Palio. Torre wins the Palio, Signor Crawford wins his bride.' Ridolfo spread his hands. 'Oca does not have a horse in the Palio so I can't simply wager my *contrada*'s horse against his. Besides...'

Ridolfo gave an innocent shrug '...Torre has the favoured horse. Chances seem fair to me. After all, I saw her first.'

Elisabeta held her breath. How could her uncle refuse without appearing to be the boor? But this was the last thing she wanted. It had almost been settled. She had the sensation again of having been so close. Only now instead of being within her reach, it was slipping away. To win, Torre would have to beat Pantera, who had already won the first Palio and who had a favoured horse as well, one of Archer's uncle's own excellent chestnuts. Would her uncle give up a Palio victory in order to secure her marriage to Archer? He could arrange to lose if it came down to it, but if anyone suspected such a thing, there would be hell to pay. No one with any honor willingly lost a Palio.

But it wasn't her uncle who answered the challenge. It was Archer's voice who filled the room. It was Archer's eyes that were on her, full of open affection as he spoke the two words that would feed the *contradas'* gossip for days: 'I accept.' A general upsurge of excitement spread through the room, everyone exclaiming at once. Elisabeta felt her uncle's hand cover hers where it lay on the arm of her chair, urging her towards restraint. She was not to undo Archer's efforts with any rash protests. But by the saints, had he any idea what he'd done? Oca might abide by the decision out of a sense of sportsmanship, but Ridolfo would not. She had to see Archer. She had to tell him. Archer had all but signed his death warrant.

Chapter Twenty-Two

'People have been killed in feuds for less!' Elisabeta blurted out the moment Archer strode into the dim interior of the parish church. The only light came from the candles on the votive rack. Her voice echoed off the stone walls. It sounded desperate and angry. She didn't care. Let him hear her concern. The church was empty and here he'd have sanctuary should Oca attempt anything. 'Do you have any idea what you've done?' He looked so alive, it was impossible to imagine anything could harm him. But she knew better. Vitality was an illusion. Lorenzo had died young. Youth did not protect one from mortality.

Archer's hands closed over hers, warm and pulsing with life. 'I know exactly what I have done. I have made it possible for you and me to be together.'

How could his voice be so steady, his hands so firm when he'd wagered so much on a single race? 'Our lives are staked on that race, Archer.'

He shook his head. 'With your permission, I have no intentions of abiding by any outcome of that race. If Torre should lose, will you come away with me?'

The pressure on her hands tightened infinitesimally, the only sign that perhaps he too shared some of her anxiety. 'It won't be a tidy getaway, but I'll have Amicus saddled and waiting. We can slip away during the celebrations right after the race.' He paused. 'It will mean, of course, that we won't be able to return. I don't think we'll exactly be welcome if I disregard the agreement.'

Elisabeta smiled. She understood the source of his anxiety now. It wasn't over the race. He'd already decided the race ultimately didn't matter. His anxiety stemmed from whether or not she would assent to living away from Siena now that the decision mattered. They'd spoken of it once before, but not with any definitive conclusion.

Her answer was more important than he realised. There was something he'd overlooked. 'Archer, whether Torre wins or loses, we can't stay here. If you are willing to forgo the agreement, you can assume Ridolfo Ranieri is too. If we stay, Ridolfo won't stop until you're dead. You have done more than offend him and he'll have the long-standing enmity between Oca and Torre to cover his motives.'

'I disagree. Torre will win and you will leave Ridolfo to me. But if it comes to leaving, will you?' Archer asked again, his eyes on her, solemn. She felt every ounce of the weight of that gaze. Elisabeta pulled her hands free and turned away from him, overwhelmed with guilt. Her foolishness had brought them to this.

'I've destroyed your dream.' She bowed her head and shut her eyes, trying to squeeze out the reality of what she'd done. His dream of becoming part of his Italian family had been shattered because of her. He couldn't stay no matter what happened on the race track. Even if she refused him right now and swore an oath to marry Ridolfo, Archer could not stay. He'd publicly declared himself. It was a touching but futile gesture.

She could feel him come up behind her before his hands even rested on her arms, warm and reassuring. His voice was private and intimate at her ear. 'You are my dream now. I think you have been since the moment I saw you in the piazza, from the moment I danced with you, from the moment you popped a forkful of *risotto alle fragole* in my mouth, I have loved you. You are like no other woman I've ever met. I mean to keep you, Elisabeta. I mean to love you for ever, whether you come with me or not. England, Austria, Siena, it doesn't matter where I am if you're with me.' He kissed her then, a sweet, lingering kiss just behind and below her ear and she was lost, but Archer wasn't done. 'If there's anything you're guilty of, it is having ruined me for other women. I'm not in the habit of begging, but I will beg for you. Please, Elisabeta, don't let me live my life without you.'

The words were quietly spoken and they meant all the more because of that. These were private words spoken from the very heart of a man. There would not be a prettier proposal ever and it was all hers just as this man was all hers. She turned towards him, her arms going about his neck. She pressed a kiss to his mouth, her voice a whisper against his lips. 'This means yes.'

Archer broke their kiss and stepped back, going

down on one knee. Her hand still clasped in his. 'Then let me make it official. Will you marry me? Right now? I do not want to wait until after the Palio.'

Tears threatened, and Archer rose to his feet, misunderstanding the reason for them. He'd pushed for too much. 'I'm sorry it is not a glamorous wedding. We'll wait if you want.'

She shook her head and swiped at the unwelcome tears. 'No, it's not that. It's just that I've never made such a monumental decision on my own before. This is all up to me.' She bit her lip, studying his face. 'I was never asked when I married Lorenzo. It was all arranged. Even the betrothal was done with a proxy. I never met Lorenzo until the wedding. No one has ever asked *me* before.'

'Then I am doubly glad I did.' Archer's thumb ran over her knuckles in a soothing caress. 'And you're wrong, you know. You have already made a monumental decision on your own, the night you crossed the piazza. *You* chose me first and today I choose you. Shall we? I have a priest and witnesses. It will be legal and it will stand up to scrutiny should it need to.'

Archer had thought of everything. On her periphery, a dark-robed figure entered the church from an interior side door followed by two distinct male figures: Giuliano and the man she recognised as Archer's friend Haviland. Her pulse quickened. This was going to happen! Archer had planned this for them, but also for her.

Archer smiled at her and the tears threatened again, but she managed. 'I will marry you, right here, Archer.' It was with foreboding that she said the words. She saw the practical wisdom of it, the victory of it and the sadness of it as well. A legally binding marriage would make her safe from Ridolfo regardless of what transpired. But she saw the romance of it too, and chose to embrace that instead of the grim reality: the next two days could see her a widow for the second time. She forcefully shoved the morbid thought away. She would not think of this good, handsome man lying dead.

Archer gripped her hand, reading her thoughts. 'I don't think Ridolfo will find me easy to kill. And there is still a chance Torre could always win.' She thought of the lightning speed with which Archer had drawn his rapier this morning and hoped he was right.

'Are we ready?' the priest enquired in gentle tones, asking them to stand before the altar, with Haviland and Giuliano on each side. Elisabeta nodded. She was ready. With Archer beside her she could face anything, a new life in a new place, a life away from all she knew if it came to that, and it most assuredly would.

The ceremony might have been impromptu, bereft of any of the traditional trimmings. There was no veil for the bride, no flowers, no music, no audience to fill the pews to brimming capacity, but Elisabeta had had all that before and it had not made that wedding any more special. Yet, this wedding was indeed the stuff of her dreams. She would remember every moment of it, every detail of it; the dress she wore, how the candlelight from the votives had flickered across the planes of Archer's face, how he had looked every inch the proud bridegroom as he repeated his vows to her, meaning each word.

It occurred to her vaguely that she was hearing his full name for the first time as he spoke it, 'I, Archer Michael Wolfe Crawford...' It was a beautiful name, a strong name. By the time it was her turn to say the vows, tears were streaming freely down her face. No wedding could be finer. He slid a simple gold ring on her finger, kissed her tenderly, sincerely, and it was done. She was his. More importantly, he was hers. If he thought the vows to love and protect were his alone to keep, he needed to think again.

Giuliano kissed her on the cheek and hugged her close. 'Be happy, Elisabeta. I'll wait until after the Palio to tell Father.' He winked. 'Maybe I won't have to.'

Haviland kissed her other cheek and offered felicitations. 'Make him happy.' She had no doubt she'd have Haviland to deal with if she didn't. But it was an irrelevant worry. She meant to make Archer happy, so very happy, and apparently she could start right away. There would be no wedding breakfast and she'd assumed the honeymoon would have to wait as well, but she was wrong. A small room in a quiet street away from the excitement of the Palio and the upcoming *prova generale* had been arranged for them.

'We've got to make it legal in all ways, of course.' Archer had winked at her as Giuliano and Haviland left them at the door.

It was the small room they'd met in once before, a lifetime ago when they'd merely been two people in a furious *affaire*. So much had changed. The room was furnished only with a bed, a bureau and a small table. But the room was well provisioned for them with a basket of food and water for washing in an ewer atop the bureau. If the ewer was chipped or the quilt on the bed plain, it seemed unimportant. 'I get the sense you had an idea of what you were doing when you got up this morning,' Elisabeta said slyly, sliding her hands up his shirtfront and working his studs free. Had it only been two days since they'd been together? It seemed much longer, an eternity.

His hands rested at her waist, letting her undress him, his mouth slanting to steal playful, errant kisses. 'How does it feel to be the Honourable Mrs Archer Crawford?'

Elisabeta wrinkled her nose. 'That sounds awful. No one will actually call me that, will they?'

Archer laughed. 'Only on invitations and only in England.' He paused. 'I mean to see Torre win that race, Elisabeta. Leaving isn't a foregone conclusion. I will fight for you and our life here.'

She didn't want to argue or point out that perhaps Ridolfo meant that as well and with the same intensity if only for different reasons. She gave him a coy glance, her hands finished with his shirt. They dropped lower, cupping him appreciatively. She loved the feel of him coming to life in her hand. 'I think the better question is how does it feel to be the *husband* of the Honourable Mrs Archer Crawford?'

He nipped at her ear. 'It feels quite good.' He worked the laces of her gown and slid it down her shoulders, while she worked his trousers and then his boots. It wasn't the most graceful of undressings, but it was fun. In the midst of the laughing and occasional collision of hands, they could forget the potential danger that waited outside in the streets. They could forget that Oca might be lurking to wreak their revenge, or that many obstacles lay in front of them before they could truly claim their lives together. In this tiny room, in this afternoon, being together was simply enough.

Clothes discarded, Archer scooped her up in his arms and carried her to the bed. He towered over her for a long moment, looking down at her with warm eyes, his arousal full and straining. His nakedness was glorious, but hers made her suddenly shy. She reached for a sheet, but Archer was faster.

'Don't. You're beautiful.'

'It's broad daylight,' Elisabeta stammered.

'All the better to see you, my dear.' Archer grinned. 'There's a reason my middle name is Wolfe.'

'*One* of your middle names,' she scolded as his weight came down on the mattress and he took up his place beside her, his head propped on one hand. 'That's a lot for a girl to remember.'

'Will you let me devour you?' His amber eyes glinted mischievously. 'There's something I've wanted to do, but I've been waiting for the right time. I think today is it.'

They'd already done so much, much more than she had ever experienced before: walls and hand-driven consummations, seductive undressings and multiple climaxes. Him on top, her on top. The variety had seemed endless to her. Only the wall had been repeated but that hardly counted, since it hadn't been the *same* wall. 'I can't imagine what else there would be.' But she gave him a challenging smile as she said it, daring him to prove her wrong.

'Oh, there's more, I promise.' He gave her one last infectious smile and went to work, or was it that he went to 'pleasure' instead? It started out relaxing at first, the soft caress of his mouth trailing kisses over her throat, down her neck to her breasts, where he stroked each of them in turn with his tongue, the relaxation starting to ebb as her body began to fire.

She gave a long shudder of delight, and he moved on, blowing a gentle breath into her navel, his hands lightly bracketing her hips with their grip. She ruffled his hair with her hands, liking the weight of his head against her stomach, but Archer wasn't done. He started to move down her again and this time there was nothing relaxing about it. Each touch of his mouth to her skin aroused. He kissed her hips, kissed the inner sides of her thighs, and her body tensed with anticipation, guessing his final destination. He meant to kiss her there, at the private juncture of those thighs! She was too aroused by the prospect to be embarrassed, to be anything but eager for his mouth on her.

Even so, this was more than a kiss. His breath feathered her curls, and she could feel her own dampness. The kiss didn't stop there. His tongue went to work on her furrow, his hands bracing her thighs while they parted her private folds so his tongue could lick the intimate length of her. 'Archer!' The sound of his name was nothing more than a mewl as he took her in a long, slow stroke.

He was enjoying this too, she could feel it in the pressure of his hands at her thighs as his desire rose, spurred on by hers. Then his tongue found the little pearl at the top of her cleft and she thought she'd go mad. His hand had done an admirable job there once before, but it was nothing compared to the exquisite pass of his tongue over its tiny, slick surface. Her mewls became full-bodied moans as she lost control.

He licked once, twice more, she gave a wanton scream and then he was mounting her, his own desire driving him to join her in the madness. She drew him to her with her arms, with her legs about him, and she met him with her hips, her mouth, tasting her own arousal on his lips. This was a frenzy of sensory pleasure. They crested quickly, their moans intermixed with incoherent love words, the sheets tangling about their legs as they seized their passion, plummeting into it head first. Most importantly, when they fell, they fell together.

Archer lay beside her, catching his breath, his head thrown back on his pillow, his hair a tousled mess, the faint sheen of sweat on his brow. Dear heavens, she'd married a sexual madman. A wicked smile played across her lips at the thought. Their lives would be full of adventure, in bed and out, at this rate. He rolled his head to the side and caught her gaze with a smile. 'What is going through that head of yours?'

'I was thinking you looked well used, not unlike a stallion put to stud.'

'Mmm.' He sighed, turning on his side to face her. 'I like that image. Perhaps it's an image we might improve on as the afternoon proceeds.' He gave a sensual laugh, drawing a finger down her breastbone in a gesture that raised delightful goose pimples on her arms, his voice low, his eyes wickedly mischievous. 'Every stallion needs a mare to cover. Roll over, my dear.'

They did improve on the image, in her estimation, that long afternoon. She found that she rather liked playing the mare to Archer's stallion. She revelled in the power of her lover-cum-husband, the strength of him as he held her by the hips and thrust confidently into her from behind, her body opening to take the entire length of him. Best of all, she loved the feel of his hot seed filling her deep in her womb. There was no longer any need for hasty withdrawals. Today was about beginnings of all types.

She was pleasantly exhausted as the heat of the afternoon gave way to evening's shadows. Even in their quiet street, the sounds of people preparing for the fifth trial, the *prova generale*, and arguably the most important trial of the six, drifted up to their little room. The hours of their honeymoon were fast coming to a close.

'We have some time yet,' Archer murmured, pulling her back down to him when she would have risen. 'We have until after the trial. No one will expect us until the *cena* tonight. Come, sleep with me and we'll see if I can't find the strength to pleasure you once more before we part.'

Elisabeta snuggled down next to him, a hand on the flat of his stomach. There would be parties tonight. Each *contrada* would host a large dinner in celebration of their Palio entry on the morrow. There would be food and brave speeches about their chances for winning the race. It was a grand night, but the thought of the evening's festivities dulled when she thought of spending them without Archer. She would have to pack tonight too. There would be much to do in case they had to flee. There were farewells to see to as well, notes perhaps to leave behind. Tonight would be a night of celebration, but also of sadness.

She must have dozed. When she woke, it was with a jolt of awareness that something was wrong. She sat up quickly, gathering her wits. Archer was already up, partially dressed and at the little balcony overlooking the street. There were people in the street and it was noisy. 'What has happened?' Archer called down to the crowd.

A voice filtered up from the throng, clearly not recognising him. 'The fighting has started between Oca and Torre. The Torre *fantino* is hurt. The rider from Onda drove the Torre horse into the wall at the San Martino turn! The jockey fell, crushed between the wall and the horse. Torre got even, though. In return, Torre took Oca at the Bocca del Casato afterwards. Torre got the better of it there, but it won't bring the *fantino* back.'

'And the horse?' Archer called back, but the man had moved on and no one else hollered back.

He was stricken when he turned from the window. 'We have no rider. Torre has no rider. Oca put Onda up to it.'

'Of course they did. Onda is your enemy and the only one of your two enemies to be riding in the race. Now that Oca can't trust Pantera, they have to use their other alliances.' Elisabeta reached for her clothes, dressing as Archer put on his boots.

'I have to go.' Archer raked a hand through his hair, worry plainly etched on his face. She could read his thoughts. It would certainly put a quirk in their plans if Torre couldn't race. How would they get away then? What if Ridolfo tried to come for her? She put her right hand over her left where her gold ring rested on her finger. He couldn't. He couldn't take her, she reminded herself. She was married to Archer now, quite irrevocably so. The church would have to support Archer's claim.

'What do you mean to do?' But she knew before she asked.

'Torre needs a rider. I mean for that rider to be me.'

'Archer, no! It's too dangerous. It would be the perfect opportunity to do you harm. You don't know how that race is, what people will do.' She couldn't lose him, not now.

'I do know the race, Elisabeta. I've been on the track.' Archer came to the bed and took her hands. 'Who better than me to race? My stakes are higher than anyone's. Tomorrow, I will race for us.'

'Your uncle may not approve…' Elisabeta began.

'He will. I can be quite persuasive.' Archer was all confidence. She wished she had half of his optimism. Archer was always so sure of himself, so sure he could make things happen. She loved that about him, it was more than part of his charm.

'I'll walk you back,' Archer offered, but she could see the need for haste on his face. He could hardly wait to get to his uncle's. She would not stop him.

Time was of the essence. His uncle would want to make a decision about a rider as soon as possible.

'I'll be fine. I know the back streets and I'll wait for the crowds to thin out,' she assured him. She knew how volatile the post-*prova* crowds could be. It was not uncommon for *contradas* to brawl as Torre and Onda had this afternoon because of a real or imagined slight to a horse or rider during the trials.

He kissed her once more and was gone, his footsteps fast on the stairs. Elisabeta pulled the sheet up to her chin. The honeymoon was over. What had she done? Her fear had driven her to this, her recklessness, her selfishness had all led to this. What had she been thinking to go through with the secret wedding? It had been entirely selfish.

The wedding gave her protection, but it did not give her or Archer a solution. A little sob welled up in her throat. She couldn't cry now. If she started, she might not stop. She'd married an innocent man, dragged him into the mire of her life, because she needed protection. But not just for that. Perhaps protection could be justified. She'd simply wanted him. Now he would pay for her actions.

Elisabeta rocked on the bed, keeping the tears at bay. This was what happened when one acted impulsively. She should never have crossed the piazza, should never have gone into the alley with him, should never have invited him to the masquerade and put him in Ridolfo's way. She should never have encouraged Archer by going to the country. Yet she had done all those things and they had led here; to a secret wedding, to a clandestine wedding 'night' in a rented room, to a man she loved, a man she had chosen.

The last thought gave her pause. It changed everything. A man she loved. She did not regret that. This worry, this pain, this was the price for love. Archer was no fool. He knew what it would cost him, what it would cost them. They would have to fight for this marriage and he had been willing to do that. She should be willing to do no less.

Torre might win tomorrow, a hopeful little voice whispered in her mind. She might be worried for nothing. Elisabeta smiled in the gathering dusk, the long shadows creeping across the floor of the room. The Palio was impossible to predict. There were so many variables one couldn't control even if one had a good horse and a good rider.

Did it really matter if Torre won? On the surface winning certainly solved several of their problems. But that no longer seemed to be the paramount issue. Their marriage was not about the race. It was about something more—about love, about freedom of choice, about two people who had found each other in this wide world. Archer had chosen her not just because he could protect her, but because he wanted her, just her.

Elisabeta rose from the bed and gathered up her clothes, a sense of calm settling over her. Wedding days were not for tears and doubts. They were for celebrations and hope. She had Archer now and nothing could change that. Just the thought of Archer was enough to make her smile. The race tomorrow might decide where they lived out their future, but it didn't decide their future. For weeks the Palio had been a deadline she was dreading, now she could hardly wait. The Palio signified her hope. The future was coming and Archer was in it. *La terra in piazza* indeed.

Chapter Twenty-Three

The *contrada* was in high spirits when Archer returned. Having comported themselves well in the brawl against Oca and Onda, the men of Torre were still celebrating. Drink flowed and there was much cheering and singing of the Torre song through the streets. The crowd was particularly thick as he neared his uncle's house. People had begun to gather for dinner. Archer wished he could share in their merriment. Perhaps they had not yet realised that while they'd won the street brawl they were without a rider.

Archer felt his throat tighten as he made his way towards his uncle's table, the words *be careful what you wish for* suddenly pounding in his head. He'd come to Siena for the chance to ride only to be disappointed early in that particular quest. Now the thing he had wanted so badly was available once more, but at a time when there was something greater at stake. How would he make a quick getaway, how would he disappear with Elisabeta if he was in the race? It was a trade-off he'd considered on the way over. They had planned to slip out of town unnoticed in the victory celebrations, if Torre didn't win. If he was on the track, it would be much harder to do and he would be so much more conspicuous. But that was what the marriage was for, he reminded himself. If they had to be conspicuous, so be it. The church stood behind him as of today.

Archer wound his way through the tables that had been set out in the streets for the *prova generale cena*, the supper that traditionally followed the fifth trial. At one table set up on a dais, his uncle was already seated with the Priore of Torre and other *contrada* officials. His uncle waved him over to take the remaining seat. Archer noticed that his friends were seated close by, and from the look of things they were in the thick of the impromptu celebrations. Nolan was sporting a bruise on his jaw and was busy apparently re-enacting a particular episode from the brawl with many gestures, having no Italian to speak of. His storytelling efforts were met with laughter from those around him, and Archer smiled to himself. Nolan had the ability to make himself at home wherever he went.

Up on the dais, Archer greeted the *priore* and the other officials with the traditional kisses before taking his seat. 'How is Morello? I heard there was difficulty at the trial,' he asked as soon as small talk had been dispensed. The sooner he got to the point the better. He wanted the issue of a rider settled immediately and he was prepared to fight for it.

His uncle shrugged, apparently not sharing his same sense of urgency. 'Morello is fine, thank the saints, because you only get one horse. The rules are clear. If your horse can't run, you can't race. There are no substitutes for an ill horse. Maybe after dinner you will take a look at his leg and wrap it for the night as a precaution.' But there was a twinkle in his uncle's eye and a secret message of congratulations passed between them. His uncle had helped him plan every aspect of his day. His uncle knew very well where he'd been.

Archer splayed his hands on the tablecloth and looked from him to the *priore* with grave seriousness. 'However, we cannot say the same for our *fantino*, our jockey. He is not able to ride. We need a rider, a good rider. We have the best horse according to the odds makers. It would be a shame to waste the horse on a rider who doesn't know his business.' He paused and looked meaningfully at his uncle. 'I think the rider should be me.'

His uncle sat still, his face inscrutable. Archer expected no less. His uncle could not risk being accused of undue favouritism, not yet. This had to be his fight alone. The *priore* shook his head. 'The offer is much appreciated, but it's not how things are done.' He smiled to soften the refusal, but Archer would have none of it. Archer leaned forward, his words rapid and earnest.

'Injuring a *fantino* the day before the race is also not how things are done. I would suggest that tradition has been exceeded. We no longer need to be bound by past practice. In fact, we do not ever need to be officially bound by the rules regarding the *fantini*. The idea that a *fantino* does not come from a *contrada* is a normative practice only. There is nothing in the rules that bans a rider from a *contrada*.'

The *priore* gave an exasperated sigh. 'It is not the preference.'

'Preference be damned,' Archer interjected swiftly. 'I am not going to see this *contrada* lose the Palio because you want to stand on preferences.' Nor was he going to lose Elisabeta because an incompetent *fantino* was aboard Morello. He wanted control of his destiny.

The *priore*'s eyes narrowed. '*Signor*, be careful you do not ask this solely for yourself. We all know of your wager with Pantera and with Ridolfo Ranieri.'

Archer would not be cowed by the implication of selfishness. 'Of course I ask it for myself. Who else has as much staked on the race as me? My bride of choice, my future happiness, my ability to stay in Siena with a clean reputation, all lie on the line tomorrow. Ridolfo is scared. We all know who precipitated the attack on our *fantino* today and why. Only a fool would ignore that reality. But it doesn't matter. Even without Elisabeta on the line, I would still be here asking for the honour to ride for this *contrada*, for my uncle who has worked so hard to ensure we have a victory.'

'And I would still be saying no,' the *priore* said firmly.

'I am the best rider. I've ridden in the night trials. I know the course, Morello knows me. Best of all, I am one of you, but still a newcomer,' Archer replied evenly. 'I will personally race anyone who says otherwise on my horse, Amicus, tonight to prove it.'

The *priore* shot a nervous glance at his uncle. Archer's gaze did not waver. He was getting to the *priore*. The man had nothing to stand on but tradition and while that was no small thing, Archer knew he had made compelling arguments.

His uncle leaned forward, joining the debate for the first time. He spoke directly to the *priore*. 'The way I see it, Archer is the best choice. I cannot negotiate a *partiti* for another *fantino* of any merit tonight. Ranieri has deep pockets and he's not left anyone open to a trade. Anyone I could find tonight who is not already riding tomorrow is not a rider who is prepared for the race. It would put us at a severe disadvantage. My nephew has put himself forward on his own. Remember, this recommendation did not come from me. But it is a good recommendation. He would not have offered if he could not do the job. I think he rides. I think he is our best hope.'

The *priore* sat back, hands clasped across his stomach, his jaw tight. He nodded his head. 'You are the *capitano*, Signor Ricci. If you say it is the best decision, then it is. Signor Crawford will ride.'

The sun had fallen, and the streets were lit with lanterns as the food was brought out, heaping plates of risotto and pasta, loaves of freshly baked bread, and bottle after bottle of wine. The atmosphere was merry. Toasts were drunk, songs were sung. The *priore* gave a speech, and his uncle gave a speech about the greatness of Torre, recounting their past victories and reminding everyone of the superiority of their horse and of their rider. Gobbo Saragialo might be injured, but Torre would rise on his nephew's shoulders.

This party would go on all night, but those at Archer's table had work to do. His uncle excused himself shortly after the speeches ended to take care of last-minute negotiations, sensing a need after today's altercation to take precautions against Onda who was riding tomorrow. Archer excused himself as well to take a look at Morello.

Morello was no worse for the trouble. Archer ran a hand down each of the gelding's legs to be sure, but he could find no telltale heat. He could have gone back to the party then. Since he was now the *fantino*, someone else had been given the duty to watch over the horse for the night. But Archer let the groom go get a plate of food. The truth was, Archer welcomed the quiet of the stable over the riotous atmosphere of the dinner. He had no desire to return to the party. If he couldn't be with Elisabeta, the stable was a good second choice. He leaned his head against Morello's and rubbed the horse's shoulder affectionately, muttering soothing words.

'Can you just imagine how crazy it will be when you win tomorrow?' a friendly voice drawled behind him. 'This place is insane! I mean that in the best of ways.'

'Hello, Nolan. How much have you had to drink?' Archer chuckled. He didn't need to turn around to know who it was. He could picture Nolan with a bottle in each hand.

'Not nearly enough, but plenty more than you, my friend. You of all people should be celebrating.' Nolan leaned beside him on the stall door. 'You're talking to horses again.'

'Always. They're good listeners.' Archer laughed and rubbed Morello's nose.

'Amicus looks good. I saw him today. He's filled

out. Everyone says he's a prime goer,' Nolan said casually.

'How would you know? You don't speak Italian.'

Nolan shrugged. 'It's not hard to guess what people are saying.' Nolan could read people better than a fortune teller. It was an enviable skill. 'Do you know what else I heard today? I heard you married Elisabeta di Nofri in secret.'

Archer tried not to look disturbed. 'If you heard it, it's not a secret, so I think there's a flaw to your logic.' If Nolan knew, who else knew? Was the entire *contrada* in on it? Would Torre keep his secret at least for a day? It was impossible to imagine an entire neighbourhood being very successful at it.

Nolan took a swig of rich Chianti straight from the bottle. 'That is fine, fine wine.' He passed the back of his hand over his mouth and winked at Archer. 'You'd never guess my father's a viscount.'

'No, one certainly wouldn't,' Archer replied drily.

'So, you are now a happily married man. Or perhaps unhappily married since you're here and she's not. Not much of a wedding night, I suppose. Still, a pretty ingenious plan, Arch. Win or lose tomorrow, the girl is yours.' Then Nolan sobered. He wasn't nearly as drunk as he pretended. 'I can't imagine Oca or Ridolfo will be appreciative of your efforts. Once they find out, it will make today's brawl look like a stroll in Hyde Park. Have you thought of that? There will be blood, primarily yours.'

'If I win, it won't matter. No one needs to know I stole a march on Ridolfo,' Archer answered quietly. 'If I win, he'll have to accept the terms of our arrangement.' He'd thought of little else since learning the news he was going to ride. There would be no discreet escape now. He would be the focus of public attention. The only way to contain Ridolfo and to avoid bloodshed was to win. Winning would protect his family and Elisabeta.

Nolan nodded in agreement with the wisdom of it. 'One victory solves much, but you're going to need a helluva a ride, Arch. This isn't like races in Newmarket. You've got Onda to worry about because they're Torre's sworn enemy. You've got Pantera to worry about because they've won once already and they've got a good enough horse to do it again. Who knows what Oca is up to? No doubt their allies have been paid well to make life miserable for Torre tomorrow. Besides that, you don't really know if you can trust any of the *contradas*.'

Archer gave Nolan a half grin. 'You've grasped the intricacies of the Palio quite nicely for a newcomer.'

'It's all about networks and who you know. That's what I do best.' Nolan shrugged, trying not to make too much of it. 'I like it here. This is my kind of place, I understand it.'

'Looks like you were pretty handy in that fight today.' Archer elbowed him in the ribs.

He nudged Archer in return. 'I am to be handier still. We all thought it was best if you didn't sleep alone tonight in case Oca tried anything or in case someone told them you were going to ride for Torre. So guess what?' His face split into a wide mischievous grin. 'You're spending your wedding night with me. I drew the lucky straw.'

* * *

Archer was still the recipient of drawing lucky straws or the unlucky ones depending on how you looked at it the next evening as the horses lined up for the Palio. He had indeed spent his wedding night in bed with Nolan who had promptly passed out and would have been absolutely no use if Oca had tried to break in. Now, with the hours-long Palio parade and the ride-the-horse-inside-the-church blessing behind him, his pants wetted down along the inside of his legs to allow for better traction against the horse's bare sides, the traditional *nerbo* for a whip in one hand, Archer had drawn the *rincorsa* position at the start.

It was not a position he would have chosen for himself. While nine of the ten racing horses lined up at the rope in an assigned order, the *rincorsa* horse, the tenth horse, stayed behind, waiting to be summoned onto the track when the official starter, the *mossiere*, had everyone situated to satisfaction. Then, and only then, would the tenth horse be allowed to enter the track. He would enter at a gallop behind the other horses when the starting rope dropped. While other horses would need a few strides to get up to speed, he would already be at speed. But there were disadvantages too.

Morello pranced beneath him, and Archer turned him in a circle, stroking the horse's shoulder with his free hand and keeping up a running patter of words to keep the big animal calm. Perhaps to keep himself calm too. He'd looked around the *campo* for Elisabeta. He thought he'd caught sight of her on the balcony she'd used for the *tratta*, but the light had been too dim for him to be sure. He hoped she was safe. He wasn't sure what would happen after the race.

There was no time to think about those things now. He could not afford to think about the future even if it was just a few minutes away nor could he afford to think about Elisabeta. All of his thoughts had to stay centred on Morello, the track, and everything he knew about the dangerous turns at the San Martino and Casato corners. The horses were nearly lined up now to the *mossiere's* satisfaction. It was nearly surreal to think that in a few minutes it would all be over.

Archer received the signal from the *mossiere*, getting permission to enter the track. He drew a breath and didn't rush his entrance. Archer had a little power of his own to control the race. The *mossiere* could not start the race until some part of his horse set foot on the track. A fair start usually assumed the *mossiere* dropped the rope once the *rincorsa* horse had started galloping, but not all of them followed that rule. His uncle had gone that morning to bargain a last-minute *partiti* with the *mossiere* just in case Torre drew the tenth spot.

Archer gathered his reins, looked once at the sky and thought of his mother. This would have been a proud moment for her. 'Are you ready, boy?' he asked Morello, edging him forward. Morello's ears flicked back. He was listening, he was ready. 'All right, let's go win this.' Archer circled Morello once more, signalling for a gallop, and the big horse leapt onto the track nearly at full speed. The rope dropped and the race was on.

Morello surged ahead of the pack still trying to

gather its speed. Archer took advantage and pushed Morello forward into the straight away. Even a slight lead would allow him the luxury of slowing to a safe pace through the San Martino curve. His uncle's statistics flashed through his head. This was the corner that posed the most likely risk of a fall on first and second laps. Safely through, he gave Morello his head. The bay wanted to run and Archer let him. A good rider knew when to respect his horse's wishes and Archer did all the way through the Casato curve when he reined Morello in.

The first lap was complete. The other horses had their rhythms now. A few moved to press him for the lead in the straight away as the second lap began. One of the riders leaned over to smack Morello with his *nerbo* as they went into the San Martino corner, causing the bay to take the corner faster than Archer would have liked. Archer could feel the horse's hooves slip coming out of the turn, could feel Morello lose his balance. Archer shifted his weight, helping Morello keep his feet. He would not go down! A horse screamed behind him, and Archer resisted the urge to look. Someone had crashed, a horse had gone down in the dangerously angled curve, but not him, not Morello.

The noise of the crowd was starting to rise to a fever pitch as Morello and two others raced neck and neck in the backside straight away. A challenger was on each side of Morello, and Archer saw the peril immediately. Between them, they could crush Morello. But it was either that or take his chances between them and the wall. Neither choice was an acceptable risk. Archer swatted Morello with his own *nerbo*, asking for more speed, the only option was to break free of these two and extend his lead.

Morello answered, the horse, too, wary of the challengers. Archer navigated the Casato curve at full speed. For whatever reason, most crashes at Casato occurred in the first lap only. Archer played the odds and took the chance. The crowd yelled its approval as Morello raced through without mishap. 'One more lap,' Archer yelled to the horse. He could feel the bay tiring. The horse had taken the race at full speed from the start. But other horses, other riders, were tiring too. Archer's own legs felt the effort of riding without a saddle.

The two challengers had fallen back. But a new one had risen. The bay representing the Giraffa Contrada gave chase after the San Martino turn and Archer urged Morello to run. Even exhausted, the horse was all heart. Morello ran. Giraffa's bay didn't give up. Through the second straight away they went, into the last turn and then a sprint for the finish, Archer laying on his *nerbo* in encouragement, his voice yelling hoarsely to Morello over the roar of the crowd. 'Go, go, go!' He could not lose—everything hinged on Morello crossing the finish line first.

Morello seemed to sense the urgency and found a last burst of speed, crossing the finish line half a length ahead of Giraffa's bay. The crowd noise was deafening. He saw his uncle surge down from the special stands constructed for the *capitani* and other elite guests, Ridolfo among them. Onda and Oca were on the move.

His uncle grabbed Morello's bridle, leading them quickly towards the exit from the track where they could be swallowed up by cheering Torre. Giacomo pumped his fist into air. 'We did it, *mio nipote*! We did it!' Archer let himself savour the victory, let himself savour the elation of having been part of it. This was a dream too. But the best dream was coming towards him. Elisabeta, dressed in a soft blue summer gown, pushed through the crowd with her uncle and Giuliano beside her.

Archer slid from Morello's back and made his way to her, his strong strides parting the crowd. Her uncle was beaming, and Archer's last reservations about Pantera not honouring the agreement slipped away. He had won her fairly. He would not need his secret marriage as leverage. He had eyes only for her, her eyes shining, her hair falling down, her mouth wide with a sensual smile. Perhaps if he'd had eyes for the crowd he would have seen the trouble before it was too late.

As it was, he only 'saw' it through Elisabeta, her shining eyes going wide, her mouth forming a warning scream. Behind him, Morello was skittish. There was motion behind him making the horse nervous. Someone was on the move and coming up fast. With no more than Elisabeta's silent scream to warn Archer of disaster, Ridolfo lunged from the crowd, knife in hand, sending Morello's hooves into the air.

Archer turned, not waiting for Elisabeta's scream to confirm the danger. The choice saved his life, but it was not enough to avoid the blade entirely. The blade took him along his arm instead of in the back, and Archer went to the ground. The older man had the advantage of surprise and it was working for him, that and his weight. The heavy bulk of him pinned Archer, but Archer was strong. He got his hands around the man's neck, his leg around Ridolfo's, seeking leverage to try to throw the man over. He squeezed with all his might, ignoring the fire in his arm. There would be time for pain later. He would not lose this fight…not with happiness so close.

Suddenly, arms grabbed Ridolfo, a knife flashing at Ridolfo's throat as he was hauled off Archer. Haviland was there, helping him scramble to his feet. Archer's first glance was for Elisabeta, to assure himself she was unharmed, his second was for the man with the blade.

Nolan held a knife to Ridolfo's throat, his eyes lit with unholy fire. 'Say the word, Archer, and I'll do him right here. There's no shame in it, he's turned backstabber.' Nolan would do it too, Archer realised, urged on by the crowd's adrenaline and his own brand of craziness.

The crowd had pressed about them, drawn by the spectacle. Now, they shouted their approval at Nolan's bloodthirsty suggestion. Archer reached out his good arm to Elisabeta and wrapped her in his embrace. He cast a glance at his uncle, who stood in a phalanx of the *capitani* from the *contradas*, all of them arrayed against Ridolfo. His uncle spoke. 'Ridolfo Ranieri broke his promise to abide by the agreement he struck with Pantera. He attempted to kill a man who did nothing more than fairly win a wager and claim his prize. His fate should be decided at the hands of the man he attempted to wrong.'

Archer took a deep breath. Ridolfo was sweating now, realising how close to death he was, how foolish his attempt had been. Archer wanted it ended quickly. He wanted nothing more than to be alone with Elisabeta, away from the crowd. He was starting to feel light-headed from the fight, the race, the lack of sleep. He had to keep his feet. There remained only this last thing to do, this last thing to settle before he could claim happiness. He felt Elisabeta's arm steady him about the waist and he found the strength for this final task.

'Nolan, drop your knife. I will not mark this celebration of Torre's victory with blood. Ridolfo Ranieri will live with his shame. However, he will do it elsewhere so that all of us may have a fresh start. He will leave Siena, never to return. He has until midnight tonight to make arrangements and take whatever he would like.'

The crowd roared its approval and he was hoisted onto Morello's back, Haviland's hand there to steady him. There was still the victory parade to manage, but sitting on Morello helped. 'I want Elisabeta,' he managed to tell Haviland, and she was there, swinging up behind him and wrapping her arms about him as much for herself as for him. He was glad for her presence.

'You've been strong for me for so long,' she whispered, her body pressed against his, warm and alive. Her hands slid over his where they rested on the reins. 'Let me be strong for you now. Better than that, let us be strong together.'

Archer grinned and waved to the crowd with his good arm. 'I like the sound of that.' He'd not come to Siena looking for trouble any more than he'd been looking for it when he'd stepped outside the Antwerp Hotel so many months ago, but he'd found it all the same, and more—he'd found a family, he'd found love. These two things were the true home-lands of the heart wherever they might exist on the maps of men.

Epilogue

The Ricci Villa in the Tuscan countryside

In Archer's opinion it was the best wedding break-fast ever, even if it did take place five days after the wedding and was 'lightly attended' by Italian standards. There was just the bride's family and the groom's family along with four of the groom's friends.

Archer looked about the long table set beneath the olive grove at his friends assembled and his new bride, his heart full of happiness, fuller than it had been for a long time. The grief he'd carried from England was put aside, no longer able to dominate his life. Grief might have driven him to Tuscany, but happiness would make him stay. The others would move on, but this was his home now and he had no regrets that his tour ended here. He'd hoped from the beginning that it would. He just hadn't counted on such a glorious ending.

They didn't have much longer. He could hear the commotion of horses and carriages in the courtyard.

Haviland and Alyssandra would continue their own honeymoon in Florence, studying at the Italian fencing schools for a few months before returning to Paris for Christmas with her brother. Nolan and Brennan had talked of slowly making their way to Venice for the winter revels of Carnevale. Archer chuckled at the thought of those two unleashed on Venice without him or Haviland to chaperon.

Archer raised his glass. He wanted to make these last moments count. For the occasion, they'd opened some of the champagne Haviland had brought from Paris and now it sparkled in long flutes. 'A toast, first of all to my lovely wife who is brave enough to embark with me on this journey called life wherever it may lead us. Second, to my friends, who stood beside me during great uncertainty. I could not ask for better companions. To Brennan, safe travels wherever the road takes you. I hope the women of Europe can survive you on the loose. To Nolan, whenever you find that special someone, I wish you a better wedding night than mine.'

'Hear, hear!' Haviland called out as they all clinked glasses and drank amid the laughter that followed.

When they had swallowed, Archer raised his glass once more, solemn this time, his injured arm wrapped carefully around Elisabeta's shoulder. 'One last drink, everyone, to the future, when we meet again.'

* * * * *

LET'S TALK
Romance

For exclusive extracts, competitions and special offers, find us online:

- **MillsandBoon**
- **@MillsandBoon**
- **@MillsandBoonUK**
- **@MillsandBoonUK**

Get in touch on 01413 063 232

MILLS & BOON

THE HEART OF ROMANCE

A ROMANCE FOR EVERY READER

MODERN

Prepare to be swept off your feet by sophisticated, sexy and seductive heroes, in some of the world's most glamourous and romantic locations, where power and passion collide.

HISTORICAL

Escape with historical heroes from time gone by. Whether your passion is for wicked Regency Rakes, muscled Vikings or rugged Highlanders, awaken the romance of the past.

MEDICAL

Set your pulse racing with dedicated, delectable doctors in the high-pressure world of medicine, where emotions run high and passion, comfort and love are the best medicine.

True Love

Celebrate true love with tender stories of heartfelt romance, from the rush of falling in love to the joy a new baby can bring, and a focus on the emotional heart of a relationship.

Desire

Indulge in secrets and scandal, intense drama and sizzling hot action with heroes who have it all: wealth, status, good looks…everything but the right woman.

HEROES

The excitement of a gripping thriller, with intense romance at its heart. Resourceful, true-to-life women and strong, fearless men face danger and desire - a killer combination!

To see which titles are coming soon, please visit

millsandboon.co.uk/nextmonth

MILLS & BOON

HEROES

At Your Service

Experience all the excitement of a
gripping thriller, with an intense romance
at its heart. Resourceful, true-to-life
women and strong, fearless men face
danger and desire – a killer combination!

Eight Heroes stories published every month, find them all at:

millsandboon.co.uk

MILLS & BOON

Desire

Indulge in secrets and scandal, intense drama and plenty of sizzling hot action with powerful and passionate heroes who have it all: wealth, status, good looks…everything but the right woman.

Six Desire stories published every month, find them all at:

millsandboon.co.uk

GET YOUR ROMANCE FIX!

Get the latest romance news, exclusive author interviews, story extracts and much more!